Barbara Cardy originally [...]
construction before moving t[...]
date, she has edited over 30 a[...]
lives in Kent with her two boys.

The Mammoth Book of Uniform Erotica

Barbara Cardy

ROBINSON

RUNNING PRESS
PHILADELPHIA · LONDON

ROBINSON

First published in Great Britain in 2015 by Robinson

A CIP catalogue record for this book
is available from the British Library.

ISBN 978-1-47211-884-4 (paperback)
ISBN 978-1-47211-885-1 (ebook)

Typeset in Plantin by Hewer Text UK Ltd, Edinburgh
Printed and bound in Great Britain by CPI Group (UK) Ltd, Croydon, CR0 4YY

Robinson
is an imprint of
Constable & Robinson Ltd
100 Victoria Embankment
London EC4Y 0DY

An Hachette UK Company
www.hachette.co.uk

www.constablerobinson.com

First published in the United States in 2015 by Running Press Book Publishers,
A Member of the Perseus Books Group

Books published by Running Press are available at special discounts for bulk purchases in the United States by corporations, institutions and other organizations. For more information, please contact the Special Markets Department at the Perseus Books Group, 2300 Chestnut Street, Suite 200, Philadelphia, PA 19103, or call (800) 810-4145, ext. 5000, or email special.markets@perseusbooks.com.

US ISBN: 978-0-7624-5619-2
US Library of Congress Control Number: 2014951235

9 8 7 6 5 4 3 2 1
Digit on the right indicates the number of this printing

Running Press Book Publishers
2300 Chestnut Street
Philadelphia, PA 19103-4371

Visit us on the web!
www.runningpress.com

Contents

Acknowledgements

THE CATERING TRADE © 2014 by Sarah Veitch. Printed by permission of the author.

TIPS © 2014 by Steve Gee. Printed by permission of the author.

REVENGE PRANK © 2014 by Annabeth Leong. Printed by permission of the author.

BLUES AND TWOS © 2014 by Zoe B. Printed by permission of the author.

SEX IN BLACK AND RED – WITH POCKETS © 2014 by Kay Jaybee. Printed by permission of the author.

AIRBORNE © 2014 by Tamsin Flowers. Printed by permission of the author.

SERVING THEM © 2014 by Elizabeth Coldwell. Printed by permission of the author.

MAMMY'S BOY © 2014 by Lynn Lake. Printed by permission of the author.

A LARGE BRANDY © 2014 by Jeff Cott. Printed by permission of the author.

CUM BUMPS © 2014 by Michael Bracken. Printed by permission of the author.

THE BAR CODE CHALLENGE © 2014 by Tabitha Kitten. Printed by permission of the author.

WHERE THERE'S SMOKE © 2014 by Courtney James. Printed by permission of the author.

LIFE ON THE NAUGHTY LIST © 2014 by Kannan Feng. Printed by permission of the author.

BIG TOP © 2014 by Lily Harlem. Printed by permission of the author.

BACKDOORMAN © 2014 by Michael Bracken. Printed by permission of the author.

A RIGHT ROYAL SPANKING © 2014 by Nicole Gestalt. Printed by permission of the author.

INCENTIVE TRAINING © 2014 by Theophilia St Claire. Printed by permission of the author.

SPEED TRAP © 2014 by Vivian Gwynn. Printed by permission of the author.

COMING CLEAN © 2014 by Angela Steele. Printed by permission of the author.

FENCED © 2014 by Sommer Marsden. Printed by permission of the author.

A COCK & BULL STORY © 2014 by Michael Bracken. Printed by permission of the author.

THE CLANDESTINE CARABINIERI © 2014 by Zorba Tocks. Printed by permission of the author.

NEW YEAR'S RESOLUTION © 2014 by Richard Hiscock. Printed by permission of the author.

THE COPS' WHORE © 2014 by Serena Akeroyd. Printed by permission of the author.

UNDERCOVER LOVER © 2014 by Landon Dixon. Printed by permission of the author.

THE FOREST RANGER © 2014 by Peter O. Savage. Printed by permission of the author.

NUMBER ONE © 2014 by Jacob Louder. Printed by permission of the author.

HOME DELIVERY © 2014 by Jean Roberta. Printed by permission of the author.

The Catering Trade

Sarah Veitch

Do something every day that scares you. Darren reread the mantra on his calendar and sighed: the problem was that almost everything scared him. Like Horace Wimp in the ELO song he had yet to find himself a life. A young-looking thirty-year-old, he spent his days walking along the coastline and his nights producing pizza and pasta at a large Italian restaurant. Now he arrived for his usual evening shift to find the manager shouting Anglo-Saxon into the phone.

"He's only gone and cancelled," Maximo said when he hung up.

"Who?" Darren asked.

"The buff butler – he's supposed to start tonight."

Darren was already a pale man but he blanched. This was a major disaster. The restaurant had put on a special 9 p.m. setting at fifty pounds a head with the draw being that drinks would be served by the buff butler. They'd had lots of bookings from hen parties and girls' nights out.

"Can't we find a replacement?" he asked.

"At such short notice? If I didn't have such a gut on me I'd do it myself."

Do something every day that scares you . . . The message he'd read that morning began to reverberate through Darren's underutilized mind. Didn't he owe Maximo this much? The man had taken him on straight from university, trained him thoroughly and always given him a generous Christmas bonus. Hell, they were practically family.

"Max, I'll do it tonight if you'll take over the kitchen."

There was a pregnant pause. "Really?" the manager asked weakly.

"Just get me the uniform," Darren said before he could change his mind.

Leaving the under-manager in charge, Maximo left and soon returned with a black posing pouch and a backless black apron: you could get anything in Brighton. Darren put them on and they were very small and tight. The pouch accentuated his bulge and the tiny scrap of material at the back showed off most of his small oval buttocks. He was glad that he'd never had a particularly hirsute crack.

"You've been like a son to me. Let me get you a drink," Maximo said mournfully and they shared half a bottle of an especially good red.

The first all-female party to arrive all winked and grinned when he brought them their drinks. (White wine served in medium-sized glasses.) The second girly group, who favoured Scotch on the rocks, wolf-whistled like construction workers on a building site. But the diners who had booked the trestle table for a dozen hospital staff were the ones who asked him to twirl around and show himself from every angle. They were on Jägerbombs. Enough said.

For the next three hours Darren brought seafood and liquid sustenance ("They see food and eat it!" Maximo quipped) to the assembled women then sadly announced that this was the last round, that it was closing time.

"My friends and I really like you. We're wondering if you'd like to organize a lock-in?" the thirty-something woman in charge of the Jägerbombs party said.

Darren hesitated until she lightly brushed his posing pouch with her palm. The touch sent sensations racing through his cock and it immediately stood to attention. She and the other hospital workers whooped approvingly and Darren hobbled, a menu shielding his growing manhood, into the kitchen before the other hens could see.

He hurried up to Maximo. "The hospital group wants a lock-in."

"And I want to get home to my bed at a decent hour," his boss said. This was standard practice as Max's wife did the late shift on the switchboard at the taxi rank and he had to get back so someone was there for their teenage sons.

"I know, Max, but they're offering me more than tips. It's been a couple of years since . . . you know . . . so I'd like to take them up on their offer."

"Only two years? Hell, you should try being in a long-term marriage," Maximo said, then grinned. "I'll leave you the keys. Go for it. If I were your age I'd do the same."

All of the other diners and the staff left. Darren and the girls from the hospital stayed. He locked the door, put on the closed sign and further dimmed the lights then, taking a deep breath, walked over to the dirty dozen to meet his fate.

"You're never going to remember all of our names but I'm Michelle," the leader of the pack said.

Michelle-and-Darren. In his head, Darren tried it out for size. He liked it. He liked her too: she had been funny and friendly throughout the evening without being loud.

"It's a pretty name."

"And that's a pretty pouch," Michelle said admiringly. "though I suppose you get told that all the time."

Darren hesitated. "I'm the chef here so I've never actually done this before, but when our buff butler let us down . . ."

"Why buff butler rather than buff waiter?" she queried.

"Because people like alliteration," Darren explained.

"So what made you step into the breach?"

"Oh, I just wanted to help out my boss."

"So you're kind as well as cute," Michelle murmured.

Darren took a deep breath, emboldened by the fact that she liked him. "We aim to please."

"And what exactly will you do to please me? To please all of us?" the thirty-something asked.

Darren took an even deeper breath and felt slightly dizzy. He quickly exhaled again. "I'll do whatever you ask of me. Your wish is my command."

The words so excited him that his manhood immediately sprang to attention for the second time that night and he moaned softly as Michelle began to caress it through the constraints of the tight black cloth.

"For starters, we'd like you to lie on the table on your stomach so that we can all have a feel of your arse."

Do something every day which scares you . . . The dishes had been cleared away but the tablecloth had smears of jelly, cream and raspberry sauce all over it. Nevertheless, Darren obediently clambered on-board and lay flat. Seconds later, he felt slim female fingers following the curve of his buttocks again and again before briefly delving into the crevice between them and rimming his oh-so-sensitive anus. He heard another voice say "My turn," before slightly longer fingers took over the task. For an untold length of time he writhed in ecstasy as the laughingly enthusiastic nurses took turns to explore his backside.

At last he heard Michelle telling him to turn over, so he flipped onto his back, proud of his thrusting hardness.

"Please," he whispered to no one in particular, "I need to come."

"Not until we tell you too," Michelle said, sounding thrillingly offhand.

His desire deepened and he put his hand on himself but she slapped it away.

"I'm going to tease you for a very long time but you must not orgasm without my permission. Do we understand each other?"

"Yes, Miss," he murmured, feeling as if he was in the midst of a beautiful wet dream.

He cried out as she dragged the posing pouch over his cock and threw it to one of her colleagues as if it was the bouquet at a wedding and cried out again as she took him in her mouth. Her lips were soft yet her tongue was probing, forceful. He stared down at her through half-closed eyes. The sensations brought on by being firmly lapped were almost overwhelming and his cock twitched and swelled.

"Do you want me to come?" he whispered, sensing that he was getting close.

"Not yet." The second after she uttered the command, she returned her mouth to his manhood. He could hear his increasingly harsh breathing echoing around the room.

"Now?" he asked a moment later.

"No." She teased her tongue around the hole in his shaft.

`I can't . . ." he eventually gasped.

She momentarily lifted her head. "Come immediately then or I may get bored and stop tonguing you."

She returned to licking and sucking and Darren felt the almost signal go off in his balls and his brain. Last night he'd gone home to his lonely bedsit and tonight he was being mouthed by an attractive and lively woman whilst eleven other young women watched and made encouraging sounds. He began to lift his hips more insistently, felt the pleasure rush through him and the spurting begin. He normally orgasmed silently (bedsit walls not being known for their robustness) but this time he let out an uninhibited groan.

"I'm getting strawberries and a hint of lime and furniture polish," Michelle said mischievously, licking her lips and doing a parody of a wine buff.

"And I'm getting dehydrated," Darren said, climbing shakily off the table and fetching himself a sparkling water and organic cordial drink.

Returning from the bar area, he brought over a spare seat and sat down next to Michelle, briefly kissing the top of her nearest arm.

"That was awesome."

"It's my thirtieth birthday so I promised myself I'd do something daring," she said.

He'd just had a pint of Guinness and a DVD for his. He looked around the table. "And the others are just here for backup?"

"Oh, most of them have hit the Big Three O as well in the past year or two and tonight they're living vicariously."

He loved a woman who used words like "vicariously". Being shut away in the kitchen, he rarely had the opportunity to talk to the female of the species and the few he'd met at clubs had been obsessed with big hair, small shoes and impossible-to-sustain-life low calorie diets. Some dieters had a salad in the restaurant for lunch (three hundred calories) every single day.

"Give me a few minutes to recover and I'll be happy to serve everyone," he said bashfully.

"Hear that, Carla? It's your lucky night," Michelle called out. She turned back to him. "Carla's decree nisi came through last week – she found the bastard was sleeping with her younger sister – so she really deserves a treat."

"Shall I use my tongue?" Darren murmured.

"She'd love that. All women do."

Darren filed that remark away in his brain for later contemplation. He'd always thought that women loved men with exciting jobs, classic cars and designer wardrobes but if what they really liked was being licked out . . .

"Are you all nurses?" he asked curiously.

"No, only half of us. I'm a clinical psychologist and Carla's my assistant. The others are in administrative roles."

Darren did a double take. "So, have you analysed me yet?"

"Hardly – it's my night off!"

"But you must have made some basic assumptions."

The wine that he'd enjoyed earlier made him less self-conscious, helped him to return Michelle's frank gaze.

"I think you're unusually well educated for this job."

"True – I have a degree in English literature."

"But you were too shy to teach."

"Right again."

"Cooking is a way for you to be creative yet still keep your distance from the world."

"Until tonight," Darren said softly.

"Tonight you've made contact with your submissive side."

She was right, he admitted to himself. The moment that these women had started to order him about he'd felt excited, and the more they had used him, the more aroused he had become.

"I'd love it if you'd help me keep in touch with that side of myself," he said, emboldened.

"That depends how much you please us for the next couple of hours," Michelle replied.

Brilliant – so the best night of his life wasn't over yet.

"I'll be the perfect sex slave," he promised.

"Then get on your knees before Carla," Michelle said.

After a moment's discussion with the group, everyone agreed that Carla should take off her panties and lie on the table on her back with her knees raised. Darren also clambered onto the table and crouched between her spread thighs. He was momentarily aware that everyone was leaning forward and staring at them both.

"Remember your only purpose is to please us," Michelle called and he turned his attention to the task at hand.

Well, the task at tongue to be precise. Carla had a nice set of pinkish-brown labial lips and a cute pink clit, which was already peaking from its hood in anticipation. He licked it and she shuddered and said, "Too much."

"Tell me exactly what you want," he murmured.

"Lick to one side and keep the pressure measured but constant until I come."

He could do that. He'd always wanted the opportunity to bring a woman to orgasm but his two long-term relationships, admittedly when he was younger, hadn't allowed him the opportunity as his equally young partners refused to tell him what turned them on. After being ditched for the second time, he'd lost confidence and had subsequently subsisted on the occasional one-night stand.

Now he licked away as if his life depended on it, enjoying the slightly sweet lubricant that Carla was producing. Her scent was equally pleasant and he had a first-class view of her neatly trimmed brunette bush. He preferred pubic hair to the waxed hairlessness that younger women favoured. He liked the natural look. He wondered what Michelle looked like in that department and hoped that he'd have the chance to find out.

Suddenly, Carla cried out and ground her pubis into his mouth. He kept lapping and lapping. His tongue felt bionic, as if it could go on all night. Just as suddenly, she moved away from him and rolled onto her side, drawing her knees up to her chest and cupping her pubis with both hands.

"Wow!" she said. "It's been a while!"

"For me too," he admitted, wriggling over to her and putting his arms around her waist so that they spooned.

They lay there for a moment then self-consciously sat up, only to receive a round of applause.

"Oh look, he's erect again," one of the nurses said happily.

"Me next," the woman seated next to her said.

Michelle held up her right hand. "Ladies, enthusiastic as Darren is, we can't expect him to make love to the remaining eleven of us in one session. I vote we choose one more person to benefit tonight then we make this a regular monthly event."

There was a general murmur of agreement then everyone wrote their name on a piece of paper and they stuffed them into Darren's posing pouch, which one of the women had reluctantly removed from her shoulder bag.

Let it be Michelle, let it be Michelle, let it be ... At the ladies' insistence, he pulled out one of the erotic lottery tickets and found it said "Jeanette". He called her name and found himself locking gazes with a small, elfin-faced girl.

`You can't be over thirty," he said, thinking out loud.

`No, I'm the baby of the group. I'm only twenty-two."

"Hopefully too young for a decree nisi?"

"Definitely. I've only had two boyfriends to date."

For the first time she looked slightly nervous – the Jägerbombs had run out – and Darren warmed to her.

"I'll do exactly what you want, Jeanette."

He belatedly – and foolishly – felt as if he was being unfaithful to Michelle, but cast a quick look at her and was reassured when she gave him the thumbs-up.

"Well." She was handed the carafe from further up the table and took several gulps of red wine. "I've only ever done it missionary style so I'd like to try something else." She looked around the room. "Any suggestions, girls?"

"A sixty-niner," someone shouted.

Darren blanched. His tongue felt numb after pleasuring Carla and if he used it again so soon he'd probably end up with lockjaw. He was pleased when someone else suggested woman-on-top.

"I've never wanted to go on top," Jeanette admitted. "I always think my breasts would look too small and I don't think I have a good enough sense of rhythm to bring a man to orgasm that way."

"I'll do whatever you want," Darren promised, looking deep into her eyes.

Jeanette hesitated. "I saw this film once where the man took her from behind . . . Not anal," she added hastily, taking another swig of her wine.

"Do you want to lie down on your tummy or get up on your hands and knees?" Michelle prompted.

Everyone immediately began calling "Hands and knees" and, blushing, Jeanette stood up and peeled off her dress, bra and pants.

Naked, she clambered awkwardly onto the table and embraced Darren who was also completely nude.

She was lovely, he thought, gazing down at her. Her breasts

were indeed small but suited the rest of her petite frame. He cupped them gently and they were gloriously silky. He kissed each nipple in turn and said, "I'm yours to command."

"Do it hard," Jeanette whispered directly into his ear.

"Shall I play with you first to get you wet?" he asked softly, wanting to give her as much pleasure as was humanly possible.

"No need. I got horny just watching you with the other girls."

"Less chat and more action. We've come here to see the show!" one of the other nurses whooped and, laughing, Jeanette got into position on her hands and knees. Darren gently touched her labia and she was indeed well oiled. Looking closer, he could see the arousal glistening on her flesh.

"Has anyone got a condom?" he asked sheepishly and one of the nurses obliged. She took the time to roll it sensuously over his shaft and they both stared down at the black-ribbed sheath of flesh.

Positioning his manhood – he was so hard that he hurt – at Jeanette's entrance, he stared over her back at Michelle, who nodded encouragingly at him.

"Don't come until we tell you to," she ordered for the second time that night.

The thought that he was merely their sexual plaything, a living dildo, filled him so full of sensation that he almost came on the spot.

He pushed all the way in and was gratified when Jeanette moaned. Doggy position, he knew, offered the deepest penetration.

"God, I can feel you right up at my cervix," she whispered excitedly.

"Fast thrusting or slow?" he asked

"Fast, like you have to have me."

Darren obediently increased his rhythm so that he was shafting her high-speed and hard. He gripped her waist to increase his purchase, aware that everyone was watching his small muscular arse move forward and back.

He looked down at himself as he entered her, pulled partway out, thrust forward. They fitted together perfectly. It looked and felt absolutely right. In, out, in, out . . . He felt as if he could go on indefinitely but all that changed as Jeanette's vagina closed in on his cock. She gripped him in rhythmic waves as she climaxed and he was even more aroused when she cried out.

He kept thrusting, thrusting.

"Don't come," Michelle reminded, staring at him intently.

The word *don't* echoed around amongst his scattered thoughts but, despite his best intentions, he came.

Moments later, his manhood shrank out of Jeanette and he carefully removed the sheath, tied a knot on the end and tossed it to one of the women.

"Has it been a while?" she asked, pretending to weigh the contents, and the other nurses cheered.

"Sadly, yes. I don't usually serve women of your calibre," he said and they cheered again.

"Ladies, don't encourage him – he disobeyed us," Michelle broke in, smiling broadly. "He has to be punished immediately if he's to learn how to behave."

"We should definitely give him a good spanking," Carla said.

The biggest woman of the group volunteered to go first. Darren gulped as she pushed back her chair, indicating that he should go over her knee. He obeyed and she was soon beating a tattoo on his muscular oval buttocks. He had small cheeks and she had surprisingly large hands. He wondered briefly if she could be a transsexual but didn't dare attempt to look up and check for an Adam's apple. Instead, he stared at the carpet and occasionally squealed as she slapped down at his vulnerable orbs.

The next woman had smaller palms, but she made up for that by using a wooden spoon which one of the nurses fetched from the kitchen.

"Complain too much and we'll use a spatula instead," she warned when he gasped and writhed.

By the time the fourth woman was spanking him, he was both loving and hating it as his backside felt as if it was on fire.

"Ladies, that's enough for tonight. We'll finish punishing him next month," Michelle said matter-of-factly.

"Might be busy," Darren muttered in a vain attempt to play hard to get.

"Busy over my lap having your backside pummelled until you realize who's in charge," Michelle replied.

Darren crawled wearily over to her and put his head in her lap and she caressed his hair.

"Book us all in for the same time a month today. That gives you ample time to launder your apron and posing pouch."

"Can I see you before that?"

"Only in your buff butler uniform. I love the power that it gives me, having you semi-naked and completely at my beck and call."

Darren took a deep breath, praying for an affirmative answer. "I could wear my uniform and serve you in the comfort of your own home whenever you desire."

Ten minutes later, he locked up and walked sleepily home. He was sorted. He'd cook for Michelle next Friday night and please her with his eager shaft, fingers and tongue. Then, at the end of every month, he'd service some of her colleagues in the restaurant while she watched – and potentially disapproved of – his every move. He was already guaranteed a prolonged spanking, Darren thought with a rush of pleasure, and would doubtless find many ways to ignite their collective wrath.

Tips

Steve Gee

"But I'm not a boy. I'm a girl," said Kaitlyn Saunders to the middle-aged woman in the job agency. The 22-year-old stared at the big woman sat opposite her and blinked in disbelief at what she had heard. "A female," the younger woman reiterated.

"Really?" The older woman raised her eyebrows and peered over her glasses at the slender thing before her. "You don't look much like a woman. Makes you perfect for the job as far as I can see."

Kaitlyn felt her cheeks redden. She was all too aware of how her slender frame appeared. Combined with her mop of pale straw hair and a freckled face, she looked more like a teenage boy. She was aware too that the older woman was staring at her chest. Without making it too obvious, Kaitlyn tried to push out her small bust as if to make her gender more plain.

"What size are you?" asked the older woman, frowning now as she stared at what little shape there was remained well hidden under the baggy pop-art T-shirt the girl was wearing. "Tell me, Miss Saunders, are you any bigger than, say, 30A?"

Kaitlyn felt more blood rise to her face. "I don't see what that has to do with anything," she snapped.

"Thirty AA then," said the woman, whose name badge announced she was Mrs Lloyd and she was here to help. The woman said it with an air of finality that would brook no argument. "You have the body of a boy and I don't suppose you'll get any bigger up there. Not now." With that Mrs Lloyd hefted her own rather large bust with a well-practised shrug as if to make a point.

"I don't want a job where I dress up as a boy," said Kaitlyn.

"But you'd like a job."

"Of course, or I wouldn't be here."

"Allow me to share with you my impression. You wear jeans, have hair like a boy would comb it and, as we have discussed, you have no bust. Therefore I am sure the Majestic would welcome you as a bellboy."

"Bell*boy*," the young woman repeated, the incredulity still in her voice, with the stress firmly on the last word.

"That was what I said. The hotel is looking for staff such as chambermaids, but especially they require a bellboy." Mrs Lloyd closed the folder in front of her and organized it with the time-honoured practice of banging the bottom edge several times on her desk. Several sharp raps to indicate the interview was over. "While you have no experience I am sure the manager, Miss Gordon, will consider your suitability as fairly as she can. The hotel's address is on the card in front of you and I would recommend you hurry along before . . ." Mrs Lloyd paused and regarded Kaitlyn again. "Before a better-looking boy comes along."

Kaitlyn didn't leave her seat. "You said they wanted chambermaids," she said, as sharply as she could. "Maids, as in girls."

"They do, but they require a certain, shall we say, shape to them." Once more Mrs Lloyd's eyes were on the non-existent breasts of the young woman.

Kaitlyn stood. "This is ridiculous. You are an employment agency and as such I would have thought—"

"We find people jobs," interrupted the middle-aged woman, her voice firm. "For people who do not have a job. Like you, Miss Saunders. We also try to find the best person for the right job. In my opinion based on twenty-five years' success in this, that is what I am doing. The job has a uniform with trousers. I would have thought for someone who wears boy clothes all the time it would be ideal. But—" the woman sighed as she gestured at the card on the desk "—it is up to you."

Kaitlyn hesitated. "The job . . . this bell thing." She didn't want to say the word "boy" if she could help it. "The wages don't sound great."

"Perhaps, but the tips are good. Or can be." Mrs Lloyd had

her head down, looking at some papers. She didn't need to look up to see how Kaitlyn might be reacting. "Very good at times. Depending on how well you do your job, of course, and providing the Majestic thinks you're good enough to even get to wear the uniform," she added. "Oh, and there will be a probation period as you might expect. Three months."

Kaitlyn felt her face burn even more and she was tempted to turn and stalk out of this so-called professional agency, but there was another woman who would get the brunt of her anger: this Miss Gordon, who had the temerity to ask the employment agency for something as old-fashioned and as inappropriate in today's world as a bellboy. "Trust me, I'll have a word with this woman," said Kaitlyn, as she snatched up the card from the woman's desk and left.

Two hours later, Kaitlyn stared as she stood on the edge of the pavement outside the red-brick and green-domed splendour that was the Hotel Majestic. The building looked solid enough, but clearly had seen better days, though it still retained an impressive facade and had an aura of fortitude. From what Kaitlyn could gather by poking around the internet on her mobile phone on the bus journey here, the hotel had been built in the same year as the *Titanic*. The story had it that the construction of that ill-fated ship had prompted the hotel's name, but, while the ship sank swiftly one fateful night, it took a lot longer for the Hotel Majestic to decline if not actually sink. Of course, no one would expect a hotel built on the white cliffs of Kent to fall into the Channel with any sort of rapidity, but the place had fallen on harder times. The imperious glories of the Edwardian era had long since gone, the appeal of a residential hotel overlooking the sea had almost certainly died out and, with cheaper holiday destinations available abroad, the hotel had been obliged to turn its attention to other attractions.

The sign outside the hotel announced in black letters on Day-Glo pink that the "Next Big Event" was an Agatha Christie Weekend, including a ball and murder-mystery fun. Kaitlyn snorted at the idea of women dressed in twenties flapper dressers and men in wide-lapel suits with polished white and black shoes wandering around the place, chattering in ways they imagined Hercule Poirot might, while looking for a length of lead pipe in the conservatory, while even she only had a vague idea what that might be.

But she herself wouldn't have to look, she figured. No one would expect a bellboy to speak to them. Just bow a little and carry a few bags and point the way around. She could be more or less part of the scenery, and if that old bag Lloyd was right, she would be given tips. That would make it worthwhile, she told herself, and no one really need know she was a girl under the uniform. In fact, there was a certain reassurance in anonymity. No one would know her name and probably not even give her a second glance.

Inside the place, the creaking floorboards under the Majestic's impressive but thinning carpet made silent entry impossible, and the once bright foyer with its polished walnut reception desk looked dowdy in the sparse light. It was a gloom, however, which happily did not penetrate far into the unlit corners to reveal the faded and peeling paint on old plaster, so some grand illusions were retained.

A young woman in a prim business suit at the reception desk looked up from writing in a ledger as Kaitlyn entered. "You must be here for the bellboy job," the woman said with a faint smile on her full red lips. "Mrs Lloyd called and said you might be coming. And yes, I think she's right. You *do* look like a boy."

Kaitlyn felt herself getting embarrassed again. It wasn't that she hadn't heard that jibe before, but perhaps she expected a little more from a hotel receptionist. Well, she told herself, I too could insult people from behind a desk if they paid me. For a moment she considered saying that but the woman in front of her had straightened up and her name badge was visible.

NORMA GORDON. MANAGER. MAJESTIC HOTEL.

"I . . . I think maybe I have come to the wrong place," said Kaitlyn, taking a half-step backwards.

"No, I don't think you have. In fact, I'd say Mrs Lloyd's done a very good job of getting you here. Yes, you look perfect." Norma Gordon nodded and smiled again.

"I'm a girl," said Kaitlyn, trying to head off the inevitable comment about her bust, or lack of.

"Which makes you absolutely ideal for what we need," said

the manager, putting down her pen and closing the ledger. "Kaitlyn Saunders, right? Or do you prefer Kay?"

"What? I mean, I don't mind ... Kay's fine," Kaitlyn acknowledged, as the manager came round the desk.

"Good. I like the look of you, Kay." Miss Gordon was alongside the girl. "Mrs Lloyd said you were right for the job and I trust her judgement." The woman smoothly caught Kaitlyn's arm and began to simultaneously turn her and steer her towards an office at the side of the foyer, a door marked: MANAGER. PRIVATE.

"Where are we going?"

"To see if the uniform fits of course. But I bet it does. Like a glove."

"Look ... I don't know I want to be a boy," protested Kaitlyn, but she didn't immediately fight being pulled towards the office door.

"You aren't, really. It's just dressing up. Pretending. Playing a part." The manager laughed easily. "We all do that nowadays, more or less. But you can do it in a free uniform." They were at the door and that was when Kaitlyn pulled her arm free from Norma's grip.

"Just a moment. I don't know why you aren't looking for a real boy." She couldn't help getting red in the face as she said it.

"Because," sighed the woman, "the business we get here would appreciate you being what you aren't. Weird, right? But trust me. Oh, and the tips are good if you do this right. Did Mrs Lloyd tell you that?"

"Yes," said Kaitlyn, and she allowed herself to be guided into the manager's office, which was where she saw the uniform, hanging up on the wall. Dark red, brass buttons at the front of the double-breasted jacket and a pair of matching trousers, with a yellow stripe down the outside of the leg. On a chair by the side of the jacket and trousers was a typical circular twenties bellboy round hat with no peak. It was nothing more than a shallow cylinder, but the yellow embroidery on the top displayed the name of the hotel in flowing script.

"Put those on. I'll wait outside." Norma smiled.

"There isn't a mirror," protested Kaitlyn.

"No, but you can trust my opinion on how good you look,"

said Norma and she departed, leaving the young girl alone with the uniform.

As it turned out the uniform fitted every bit as well as Norma said it would. The manager even whistled in a low, somewhat demeaning way as Kaitlyn emerged from the office in her bellboy outfit, which made the girl blush once more. "Very good, Kay. All it needs," said the woman, as she stepped up to the girl and reached for her head, "is the hat at a slightly more jaunty angle. There. Much better."

"It feels strange," said Kaitlyn, feeling the heat in her cheeks and catching a glimpse of herself in the glass of the main doors.

"But it looks fabulous." Norma grinned. "Everyone will love the look."

"Who's everyone?" Kaitlyn was startled by the idea.

"Everyone who books a weekend here. And the weekenders we find like to tip very well for personal services performed well."

Kaitlyn shivered. *Personal services?* Said that way, she wasn't sure what that involved. "Uh . . . I'll just be carrying bags right, and showing people to their rooms?"

"Of course," Norma said with a smile. "Being respectful. Even subservient. It's more than just showing the way. It's about opening up."

For a reason she couldn't understand, Kaitlyn felt her blush increase.

The first dozen or so guests who tipped Kaitlyn for carrying bags up to their rooms weren't particularly generous and the girl considered quitting. It wasn't that she didn't like the idea of what she did, or wearing the bellboy's uniform that bothered her. It was that the promise of decent tips clearly weren't going to materialize. I mean, she asked herself as she checked her reflection in the mirror in the staff quarters to make sure her little cap was at the best angle, what more can I do? I greet them nicely, smile, carry their bags and smile again. What else can I do?

Kaitlyn mentioned her disappointment to Norma, who merely raised an eyebrow. "Added value," was all she said. "Give that bit extra. The people who come here would really appreciate you opening up."

The pretend bellboy wanted to ask what more could she do but the manager was busy with bookings and clearly didn't want to talk about this.

For a while, Kaitlyn wanted take the uniform off and throw her cap down as a gesture of resignation. However, she had a job and that was something. Perhaps I've just been unlucky with the first guests, she told herself. The men after all do look at me a little oddly as if they expect me to do something, she continued her line of thought. The men, she reminded herself, and then she began to feel hot under her collar. The more she thought about it the more it began to dawn on her just who was coming to the Majestic and why they came.

They didn't come just for the theme nights and special events weekends, Kaitlyn understood in a moment of clarity. It was for personal services rendered, and she knew what she had to do.

The next guest she greeted was a middle-aged man. Plump and balding though smartly dressed, he stared at Kaitlyn as if he knew what he expected from whoever was inside the uniform. She carried his bags up to his room on the second floor, smiled sweetly, and licked her lips smoothly with her head inclined a little to one side.

"Will there be anything *else*, sir, I can help you with?" She dropped as elegantly as she could to her knees in front of the man. She bent forward and kissed the polished toes of his shoes lightly. "I am here to help, sir."

As she lifted her head, the man was grinning down at her. He unzipped his fly and an impressive, suitably fat cock came into view. "Yeah. Just one thing," the man said. "I'm sure you know what to do about this, boy."

"Yes, sir," said Kaitlyn. She took his hardening penis in her mouth. She sucked and rolled the cockhead in her mouth and brushed and teased it with her tongue as expertly as she could. Her flicking tongue concentrated on the tip of the man's swollen cock, and he was sighing appreciatively above her. It didn't take long to bring him off, and the man deposited his load with a satisfied groan.

Kaitlyn swallowed smoothly because, she thought, that was what a bellboy on his knees would do. Then when she had cleaned the man's wilting cock thoroughly, she withdrew her mouth. When she stood, the man asked his name. Not her name, as if he was convinced she was a boy.

"Kay, sir," said Kaitlyn. "I would be pleased to help you with anything else to make your stay at the Majestic even more satisfactory."

The man chuckled, produced his wallet and took out a twenty-pound note. "If you do that again tomorrow, boy, I am sure I will be well pleased."

"Yes, sir, all my pleasure." The Majestic's bellboy smiled as she took the offered tip.

The couple was, as couples always were who arrived for a weekend at a place like the Majestic, rather middle-aged, bordering on elderly. "I like to think of them as the YE's," Norma had explained one afternoon when she was going through the bookings list with Kaitlyn. "YE is Young Elderly. The advantage being, Kay, they still have a pulse and disposable income."

"As in tips," Kaitlyn had said.

"Tips and services, drinks and meals." Norma smiled. "After all, they don't earn us anything extra when they are asleep, do they?" With that, the bellboy understood what the hotel business was about.

Mr and Mrs Leyland were definitely of the YE class. They had a pulse and their matching suitcases were expensive. Kaitlyn had begun to grasp what the suitcases showed in people. Those visitors who dressed well but had cheap cases and bags were less likely to give a decent tip as they thought mostly of themselves. But matching luggage by a good manufacturer suggested these people could spend money anywhere. The only trouble was while Kaitlyn had serviced single men (going on her knees with her mouth open and an appealing look in her upturned eyes usually made the males get hard at once, with inevitable consequences) she had less luck with couples. Couples would tip moderately, but she couldn't offer her trademark welcoming service.

The Leylands turned out to be different. As Kaitlyn put the matching luggage in the bedroom, the man gestured to the bellboy. "I hear you offer a welcoming service," said the white-haired man with the sort of tone that suggested he was used to being in control of situations.

Kaitlyn shot a glance at the woman nearby, whose own dyed blonde hair gleamed in the light from the evening sun streaming through the windows. The woman, plumper than her husband, raised an eyebrow at the bellboy. "Get on with it," she said. "We are all adults here, aren't we?"

Kaitlyn gulped, blushed and dropped to her knees in front of the man, who promptly roared with laughter. "My, my, you really do pick the wrong horses, don't you?"

The girl scrambled to her feet, face more red than ever. "Um . . . I'm sorry, I thought maybe . . ." She had no idea what to say. She had a vision of this job coming to an abrupt end.

"Not me," The man snorted a laugh and waved his hand at his wife. "It's my good wife who needs your skills."

Kaitlyn stared at the woman. She impatiently gestured the bellboy to her. "It isn't always men who need good service," she said and began hoisting up her dogtooth-patterned skirt. She was wearing stockings, held up by suspenders descending from a white girdle. The dark bush around her sex was visible as she didn't have any panties on, though with a woman of her size and age the word "panties" would – Kaitlyn reflected later – seem inappropriate. The woman wasn't wearing any knickers. Mrs Leyland spread her legs slightly, holding up her skirt up to her waist. "Get on with it," she said, her voice husky with excitement.

Kaitlyn started to walk towards Mrs Leyland but stopped as the older woman glared at her and demanded she should approach on her knees. The girl in the uniform dropped to her knees as ordered and shuffled as fast she could across the carpet. The woman sighed, leaned back a fraction and at the same time pushed her wide hips forward. Kaitlyn wanted to gulp but she felt she shouldn't with both pairs of eyes on her. She had never had sex with a female before, apart from a brief groping experiment at school with her cousin who said everyone did things like that. But she had never had her mouth near any female's sex and now she could see the folds of the woman's slit through the dark hair in front of her face. She put her tongue out.

"Put that thing away," said Mrs Leyland. "You have a cute nose, boy, and that is what I want you to rub in my cunt. The tip of that cute nose. Up and down, understand?"

"Make sure you breathe in all the aromas while you do it,"

chuckled the old man to one side of the two females. Kaitlyn was aware he had his long thin cock out and was masturbating. OK, she thought, so he gets off that way, and she gets off this way. The tip had better be good, she told herself, as her nose nestled into the wiry pubic hair and into the wet folds of the woman's cunt. She could indeed smell all the aromas and, for a second, it seemed overpowering. But Kaitlyn was made of stern stuff and, pushing her revulsion away, she promptly began rubbing her nose up and down the slick, soft valley. She tried to look up at the woman to see if she was enjoying it, but all she could see was the swell of the woman's girdled belly. Then, to her surprise, Mrs Leyland dropped the thick tweed skirt over Kaitlyn's head, though she did give a small gasp of pleasure.

Under the skirt in the dark, Kaitlyn wondered how she was doing. When she had sucked men's cocks she had looked up to judge the pleasure on their face and, as most men would give a "tell" that they were about to climax, she had learned when to increase her motion or her sucking or nibbling. It was, she understood, the quality of the last moment that guaranteed the best tip. Now, she had no idea. She could hear the man saying something about punishing women and making them work hard to lick a mistress clean. Yes, he definitely used the word "mistress". Perhaps, Kaitlyn thought, it helped excite him as he wanked – after all, he couldn't see much but a bobbing shape under his wife's skirt. Or maybe it helped arouse the woman, but she wasn't replying, though her hips began to move faster on Kaitlyn's nose. Her small hat had been dislodged and Kaitlyn wondered, bizarrely, if it would matter. She worked her head harder and tried to push the tip of her nose against the woman's engorged clit, to be rewarded with a sudden gush of wetness, which, for an instant, made the bellboy think the old woman had let some pee slip out. But it wasn't urine. It was an orgasm, and, under the skirt, Kaitlyn could feel the woman shaking and her hands on the back of her head pulling her in and holding her there.

Kaitlyn wondered if she should use her tongue now, but that would mean moving her head away and Mrs Leyland definitely didn't want to let the girl's nose slip from her sopping wet cunt. The woman held the girl in position for a good five minutes until Kaitlyn began to panic, thinking she would run out of air. The thought occurred to the bellboy that she would suffocate in the most unimaginable way. Perhaps out of kindness or a sense that the kneeling girl was about to perish, Mrs Leyland let go and allowed the bellboy to scramble out from under her skirt. Kay saw her dislodged cap on the floor and went to pick it up, realizing that the man had – of all things – ejaculated into it. Nonetheless, she picked it up and, without a word, pulled it onto her short-haired head. "Will that be all, sir and madam?" she asked, though still on her knees.

"For now," said the woman, smoothing down her skirt as she turned briskly away, leaving her husband to tip the bellboy generously.

It was a uniform just like her present one. Same material, same colour and same style, but new. Even the cap was identical, though the embroidery of the hotel name was fresher and less faded. In every respect it was identical to the one Kaitlyn had worn for the past few weeks, apart from the Velcro that was. Velcro fastening, in a place she never expected to find it.

Kaitlyn blinked as she examined it before she managed to say, "Velcro. Right there? Why?"

"Right there" was at the back of the pants, running from the waistband at the back and down under the crotch. Almost invisible, she had to concede, but a Velcro fastening all the same. "Why?" asked the young woman again.

"Convenience," said Norma. "If you need to go to the loo, it will help. No taking your trousers off."

"But," began Kaitlyn with an air of bewilderment and then paused. "It isn't just that, is it?"

Norma shrugged a little. "Convenience, as I said. You want to keep your uniform looking smart, I presume. That's if you want to keep the job."

"Of course I do!"

"You may remember talk of a probation period. Well, it's three months since you joined. Consider this the final test of, shall we say, you proving you can do the job to, ah, satisfaction."

"You know I can."

"Then prove it."

"How?"

"Being open to new experiences."

Kaitlyn felt a surge of anger. "You're not telling me what I need to know."

"Fine, Kay. Then I will be direct. First of all, you enjoy all the tips you get, don't you?"

"Yes." Kaitlyn blushed a little at the memory of what she had to do to earn them. The tips were very good. Very good indeed. "But what's that got to do with anything?"

"Services rendered," said the manager. "And in an hour a guest will arrive who, shall we say, you owe a lot to. It will help repay that debt if you wore this new, improved uniform."

"I don't understand."

Norma sighed. "Your job as bellboy is to do what the guest wants. The more you do, the bigger the tip. The more satisfied the guest is, the more they will come back or tell others. I imagined that would be clear by now."

"I get that," snapped Kaitlyn.

"Then you will be grateful for what Mrs Lloyd has done for you. I mean she could have picked anyone for this job, but she chose you."

"So?"

"So she is coming here, and the new uniform helps enormously."

Kaitlyn opened her mouth to demand to know more and then gulped. "She wants . . . she wants to do something, doesn't she?"

"To the bellboy, yes," said the manager, quietly.

"Fuck," said Kaitlyn.

"Exactly." Norma smiled.

The new uniform fitted well and, as bellboy, Kaitlyn was ready an hour later to greet Mrs Lloyd. She hadn't changed much since they had last met, but there was a smirk about the older woman. Like she was about to enjoy something very special. "Let's see just how good you are," said the woman, looking Kaitlyn up and down. "Kay, I believe."

"Kay's fine, madam," said the girl in front of Mrs Lloyd.

"Of course it is. Then show me to my room, please."

Kaitlyn showed the way as requested. The woman had only a small overnight bag and, having set it down on the double bed, Kaitlyn retreated to the door. "Will that be all, madam?"

"No, Kay, it won't, as you well know. Come here and open my bag for me."

Kaitlyn did as she was told. Inside she could see a nightgown, a toothbrush, a tube of something unidentifiable and a strap-on. Long, ridged and a vivid shade of purple.

"I presume that is for me," gulped Kaitlyn.

"It's for both of us my dear, though I will be wearing it, not you. You will, shall we say, be the recipient. Now, undress me and buckle the cock on me. There's a good boy."

"I'm a girl, as you well know," retorted Kaitlyn.

"Your name's Kay. Bellboy. And as a boy, as far as I am concerned, you have only one hole down there. Am I not correct?" Mrs Lloyd grinned. "In which case you need to do what you are told, unfasten your uniform in the most convenient place and help me get some exercise."

"What exercise?"

"I find thrusting is excellent for the hips." The woman patted herself.

"You want me to undress you first?"

"I believe that was what I said." Mrs Lloyd gestured at herself, at her button-front dress. "Be a good boy and take my dress off. I believe young men can be excited by the sight of a mature lady in her smalls. Though perhaps not so small in my case." Mrs Lloyd gurgled a laugh. "Then you can fasten my friend on me and show me how the fastening on your trousers works."

Kaitlyn unbuttoned the woman's dress and helped her out of it. She looked formidable in her "smalls" and lifted both her arms this time. "Fasten the cock around my hips tightly, if you please."

With face burning at the humiliation, the bellboy complied. She couldn't help staring at the way the artificial cock jutted out from the woman's hips. In spite of all the turmoil in her it was mesmerizing. As the woman moved, the head of the purple plastic monster bobbed in rhythm. "Fascinating, isn't it, boy? Seeing a woman with one of these sticking out. Be that as it may, I need you to lubricate it for me – unless you want to take it dry."

"No, not dry," said Kaitlyn. She hesitated and gulped at what occurred to her. Make them come back for more, make the tip worthwhile. "You . . . You don't need lube," Kaitlyn said.

"Really?" Mrs Lloyd chuckled. "I wonder what I do need then?"

Without a word, Kaitlyn squatted in front of the woman, reaching back at the same time as her lips met the end of the purple plastic. As Kaitlyn's hands tore the Velcro at her rear apart with a satisfying ripping sound, she took the tip of the plastic between her lips and began to suck and lick. In a moment she was deep-throating the ridged plastic as if it was real. Above her, she heard the woman gasp in admiration.

"You're good, boy."

"Yes, madam," said Kaitlyn, as best she could with the plastic cock in her mouth.

"Hush, boy, you are making me very wet," chuckled Mrs Lloyd.

Kaitlyn slid her mouth off the glistening shaft, spun round and bent at the waist so her open rear was available to the woman. Thank goodness for Velcro, she thought as she put her hands on the bed to steady herself.

"Say please," purred Mrs Lloyd.

"Please," said Kaitlyn, and braced herself.

The strap-on cock was perfectly aimed and slid effortlessly into the bellboy's rear. Kaitlyn gave only a small grunt as the tip of the purple plastic cock pushed into her waiting backside. "Made to fit," breathed Mrs Lloyd.

"Yes, madam," said the bellboy as the middle-aged woman proceeded to fuck Kay's rear. "Very good, madam," she added.

"Very good indeed," grunted Mrs Lloyd, as she thrusted and sawed in and out of Kaitlyn. "You know, boy, I think you deserve a very good tip for this."

Revenge Prank

Annabeth Leong

Dolores Santi opened her locker and growled. The flash of pink inside told her all she needed to know. Her six months at Ladder 52 had been marked by prank after prank.

She yanked the object out of her locker and dropped it beside her. It rolled and unspooled – a bright pink replica of a fire hose, decorated with bands of glitter, complete with a watermelon-colored plastic nozzle that gave a hollow clatter when it hit the floor.

The guys in the locker room broke out into guffaws. She whirled. "This one's really funny, guys. I get it. The real fire hoses are way too heavy for a woman, so I need a special one. Might as well make it a girly one."

"Hey, hey now," said Jim Hernandez. He took a step toward her and her stomach flipped over despite her anger.

The things Dolores would have done to Hernandez if she'd had the chance . . . The man set records every year at the state firefighting games, and he had the body to match. Even in a station full of men in peak physical condition, he stood out. His bulky firefighter pants emphasized the size of his thighs and hugged his hips just so. His T-shirt, emblazoned with the station's logo, strained to contain his muscles as he moved. He quirked a cocky half-smile, his mouth apologetic but his eyes full of mischief.

"No harm intended, Santi. We're just trying to make you feel welcome. You should have seen the things we did to Tran when he joined up. We've barely gotten started compared to that."

"You guys have been going easy on me, then?" She hadn't appreciated the pranks – it had been hard enough to earn her position, and she didn't need constant reminders of how unusual it was. On the other hand, she loathed any sign that the guys were treating her differently than they would each other. It was a difficult balancing act to perform.

"Ask Tran," Hernandez said.

Dolores glanced at Gary Tran. The only Asian firefighter in the state, Tran lacked the beefy build Hernandez exemplified. He was plenty strong – she'd seen him in action – but his body was compact and wiry, capable of much more than initial appearances suggested. She didn't doubt the guys had put him through the wringer, too.

He shook his head, laughing. "They filled my entire locker with rice."

"Cooked or uncooked?" Dolores asked.

"Which time?"

She winced in sympathy. "You should have made Hernandez eat it all. Just a friendly revenge prank, you know?"

"That's the spirit," Hernandez said, breaking out into a full grin. "You've got to know how to give it back."

"Oh, don't talk that nonsense. You wouldn't have eaten all that rice."

"I would have if Tran had made me do it." Hernandez raised his eyebrows. Dolores blinked. He wasn't taunting or goading her, he was asking for something.

The atmosphere in the room had changed. No one was laughing now. They must have picked up on the charge between herself and Hernandez. It still contained a bit of anger, but, with a shiver down her inner thighs, Dolores realized that lustful tension had slipped in as well.

"You're saying you know how to take a revenge prank," she said slowly.

"If the other person knows how to deliver one," Hernandez said. The flirtatious challenge in his voice was unmistakable now.

Never taking her eyes off him, Dolores bent at the knees to retrieve the pink fire hose from the ground. She tested it surreptitiously, feeling along its length with one hand and tugging it. A real fire hose weighed much more, but this thing, braided from thick fibers, was no joke. She didn't know where the guys had gotten it, but it was at least thirty feet long, and it wasn't likely to fray easily. "So if I said we ought to find out what a girly fire hose can do?"

"I'd say, make me," Hernandez said, and lunged at her.

Dolores hadn't been expecting that, and she barely reacted in time to deflect him. Without pausing, he came at her again. He wasn't holding back or going easy, either. Only speed saved her from going down.

She didn't think she could win a wrestling match with Hernandez – the man was way too strong and too well trained – but she had to. This was yet another way she had to prove herself, and if she wanted to gain the acceptance Tran had among the guys, she needed to figure out a way to do the impossible.

The pink fire hose in her hands provided the answer. She had a weapon, and Hernandez was unarmed. The next time he came at her, she sidestepped but wrapped a loop of the fire hose around one of his wrists. From there, the balance between them began to shift. Dolores dodged each time he came after her, but gradually restrained him more and more. She tied him in random spots – the top of one thigh, his upper arm, back to the thigh.

Hernandez grunted in frustration, and the other guys started laughing again. Dolores took a risk and stepped in, working quickly to secure him completely before he could break free. Hernandez never stopped struggling, and the efforts caused him to tip over and fall on the floor at her feet. Dolores drove a knee into his chest and finished the job while the others whistled.

"Damn, Santi knows how to take a man down and keep him there," Sam Daniels said, nudging Fred Williams with his elbow. "She should have been a cop."

"I'm not enough of an asshole for that," she said, winking. All the guys at the station liked to rib the local police, and her jibe inspired a round of appreciative hoots. Dolores had never felt so much like one of the guys. In an odd way, she had Hernandez to thank for goading her into taking a stand.

She looked down at him. It was a thrill to have bested him, but she wasn't prepared for the way it affected her to have him at her mercy. Her pussy clenched and, instead of thinking of revenge, she began to think of satisfaction. The pink fire hose held him just fine, and she could see realization dawning on his handsome face.

"You know what I think a girly fire hose can do?" Dolores muttered.

"What?"

"Hold you still while I teach you a lesson you won't forget." The guys muttered speculation, but fell completely silent when she stood and kicked her way out of her pants.

"What the hell are you doing, Santi?" The Adam's apple worked up and down in Sam Daniels's dark throat. He was a good-looking man as well. Victory and lust intoxicated Dolores, and she envisioned a revenge prank that encompassed them all.

"You guys seem worried that I'll forget I'm a woman. That's what the pink fire hose is for, right? Same goes for the pink spray paint on my helmet? The sexy fire woman outfit you left in my locker?" She took a deep breath and shoved her panties down her hips. "But maybe the problem's not that I'll forget. Maybe the problem is that you guys aren't sure."

She stepped over Hernandez, one foot to either side of his head. Her labia parted. His eyes widened.

"What do you think?" Dolores said. "Does it look like I'm a woman?"

"Yeah. I, uh, think so."

She smiled at the way his voice cracked. "Think? That's not good enough. I'm going to make sure you know, and that you won't need any more reminders." Smoothly, she lowered herself to her knees, squatting over his face.

Hernandez stared up at her, frozen.

"Come on, Jim," Dolores said. "You know what to do with a pussy, don't you? Or have you never seen one before?"

The guys whistled again.

"I've seen plenty," Hernandez said. He struggled beneath her, thrusting his hips upward. "Crawl down a little lower, baby girl, and I'll show you a real good time."

"Oh, I don't think you deserve that. This is revenge, remember? You don't get to use your cock – I want your tongue." She indicated Tran with a jerk of her head. "Or should I see if Tran's got a better idea of how to treat a woman?"

Hernandez didn't like that suggestion. His tongue darted out right away, but she was too far away for him to reach. "Get down a little lower," he growled, "and I'll lick you until you cry."

"Lift your head and work for it," Dolores countered. "Or is your neck the only part of your body without a muscle?"

"You've got an attitude, woman."

"Ooh, we've gone from 'baby girl' to 'woman'. Maybe you're not as slow a learner as I thought."

Hernandez stuck out his tongue, and Dolores grinned.

"That's the idea," she said. "Now use that thing."

He lifted his head so his tongue could make contact with her clit. Despite her insults, the sensation was electric. Dolores grabbed the back of Hernandez's head and began to grind shamelessly against his mouth. She freely tugged his hair in one direction or another, guiding him to the spots where she needed to feel him. She let him lick all around her entrance, but when he tried to tongue fuck her like an actor in a porno, she laughed and pulled him back to her clit.

She had never felt so free to demand exactly what she wanted and no more and no less. Still riding Hernandez's face, she glanced up at the others. He paused in his licking. Dolores pulled his hair without looking down at him. "I didn't tell you to stop."

It gave her even more of a rush to force Hernandez to continue to pleasure her while she locked eyes with Sam Daniels. She felt a delicious orgasm starting deep in her pelvis, but she was in no mood to rush it. "Do I need to wrestle you, too, or do you believe I know how to handle a fire hose?"

"I believe you can handle anything you want to, *woman*." He emphasized the word "woman", letting it roll off his tongue.

"Good. Why don't you take out your cock? Why don't all of you take them out? I want to pick out a nice one. I'm probably going to have to handle them all to see which one I like the best."

The guys stared at her for a moment as if they couldn't believe what she'd just said. She clucked her tongue and gave Hernandez's hair a particularly vicious yank. "I thought you said you weren't going to make me wrestle the rest of you? Get those cocks out."

Zippers clicked. Moments later, Dolores found herself contemplating a varied exhibit of male desire. Daniels was uncut, the bright tip of his erection peeking out from his foreskin. Williams was long and iron-hard, and Tran had a lovely curve that Dolores thought might stroke her G-spot in just the right way.

Hernandez pulled away from her pussy. "Hey, what about *my* cock?"

"You keep forgetting the point of this."

"You don't even want to feel it?"

"Get back to work, and I'll do it as a favor." She bore down on him, pushing his head all the way to the floor, unafraid of drowning his face in her pussy. Dolores reached back, found his erection, and squeezed hard enough to make him tense beneath her. "It's nice, Jim, but you're tied up and I don't think you've earned more than that yet."

"I'm working harder than anyone." Her pussy muffled the words, but she could understand them well enough.

She smirked. "If I feel generous, I might ride you for a while, but I'm definitely not letting you come."

Dolores beckoned the other men closer. She made a show of examining their cocks, leaning in to peer at them, taking delicate licks to judge which tasted best, and measuring girth by wrapping them with her thumb and forefinger.

"Baby, I can make you feel good," Williams said. "The best."

"You're disqualified for calling me 'baby'," Dolores said. She loved having these four men at her disposal, desperate to please her. She smiled up at Williams. "When I'm ready, you can get on the floor next to Hernandez and suck my nipples. No teeth, or you'll be the next one trussed up in the pink fire hose."

She raised an eyebrow at Tran and Daniels. "Which of you can hold out the longest? I want to know about endurance. If I'm going to let one of you into my pussy, I need to be sure you can satisfy me."

"I can go as long as you need me to go, woman," Daniels said.

"Woman," Dolores said. "That's one right answer." Hernandez had begun swirling his tongue just the right way around her clit. He really was a fast learner. Dolores sighed and settled even more firmly on his face. She knew she could come anytime now, but she wanted to do it around a fat, perfect cock. Pleasure had begun to make her feel dizzy. She needed to decide soon, while she could still think straight.

She licked her palms, then held out her hands, one to either side of her. "Bring them here," she commanded. Hard cocks settled into each of her palms, hot, thick and heavy. She began to stroke them, grinning at the way Tran and Daniels gasped.

"Williams, you can start on my breasts now. Hernandez, don't slow down. I've seen you win too many competitions. I don't believe you're capable of getting tired. As for Tran and Daniels . . ." She gripped them firmly, speeding up the rate at which she worked their cocks. "You can come if you want, but it'll be the one who doesn't come who gets to fuck me. If you both come, maybe Hernandez will get his chance after all."

Tran and Daniels sucked in their breath. She loved the way they responded to her. She could feel their cocks twitching in her hand. They were both on the edge, both desperate to resist. Williams pushed her shirt above her breasts, pulled her bra cups down, and began tonguing her nipples in a way that made her squeeze her thighs around Hernandez's head.

Dolores didn't want to come before one of the men did, but the scene was almost too much for her. She applied her best technique, trying not to focus on the magic Hernandez was working between her legs.

Daniels pulsed in her hand, cursing as come pumped onto Dolores's skin. She grinned, but shook her head at him. "You're going to have to get on your knees and kiss me. You owe me thanks for giving you that orgasm, but because you came before anyone else did, that's all you get today."

Dolores released Tran's cock, but not before stroking that delicious curve with the very tip of one fingernail. She smiled up at him, meeting his knowing gaze. "Get a condom on."

He went to his locker, and Dolores abandoned herself to Hernandez's questing tongue between her labia, Williams's mouth on her nipples, and the soft heat of Daniels's lips. The muscles in her cunt were rippling by now. She was barely holding out, and she knew she'd come the moment Tran put his cock in her.

Tran knelt behind her, the head of his sheathed cock nudging her inner thigh. He put a hand on the small of her back. "Are you ready?"

Dolores didn't want to pull back from Daniels's kiss. "Mm-hmm," she muttered into his mouth.

Tran chuckled softly and slid his hand to her hip, supporting her. He adjusted the angle of her body, and Hernandez knew enough to follow. The licking never paused as Tran positioned himself and slid into her.

He made her feel every delicious inch, and that curved cock of his stroked her inner wall exactly the way she'd hoped. Dolores relaxed her entire body and abandoned herself to her orgasm, knowing the four strong men around her would have no trouble holding her up.

Tran fucked her through her spasms, each thrust filling her with a sharp, pleasant ache. This was revenge and satisfaction and ecstasy rolled into one. She closed her eyes to better savor every one of Tran's delicious strokes.

She could give them each a chance to make her come, and if she were feeling generous by the end of it, she'd finish up by riding Hernandez until he cried. She hadn't forgotten that earlier challenge of his – she knew she could endure his tongue just fine, as long as he could stand to administer it. She didn't think he was ready for what she could do with her pussy.

She clenched just thinking about that, and Tran groaned and thrust deep as he came. She would have been disappointed that it had happened so soon, but there were three other cocks in the room. Dolores thought she'd made great strides in teaching them to respect her, but she could only be sure if she took her time.

Blues and Twos

Zoe B.

If you'd have asked me six months ago if I had any sort of a thing for men in uniform the answer would have been an emphatic "No," and I would have considered any woman who did more than a bit odd.

But that was before my trip to the States at the end of summer last year. I'm still trying to get my head around what happened, but for the time being I know that there was at least one uniform that did something *very* special, for me.

My name's Zoe, I'm in my early thirties, degree educated and single by choice at the moment. I work as a senior buyer for a large, very well-known, American-owned supermarket chain. Last September, I had to fly to Atlanta to give a presentation at a major two-day sales conference.

I'd been able to postpone my flight home and take a few days' well-earned holiday.

The conference – and my speech – went well. I was power-dressed in an expensive business suit and fitted white blouse – with even more expensive lingerie underneath. I keep myself very fit, have a trim figure to prove it and I'm a natural blue-eyed blonde, a typical "English rose" in fact. I love the contrast of the ultra-professional, almost severe, clothing on top and secretly sexy underneath. It makes me feel powerful and good about myself . . . and I'm sure it rubs off, on my male colleagues at least. And, let's face it, in a cut-throat business world us girls need all the help we can get.

There was a bit of a party on the last night, with drinks on the company, and it was nice to catch up with colleagues from around the world and even meet some face to face for the first time, rather than via Skype or conference calls.

There was a lot of flirting going on, as there always is on these occasions. I guess my "single status" isn't a secret and I was "hit on" by a lot of the guys, but not by anyone I fancied enough to let him go any further and neither of those things worried me one bit.

I got back to my room around 11.30 just a little bit tipsy. I went straight to bed and discovered I was also a little bit randy and that was making sleep difficult.

I surfed the adult channels on the TV until I hit on some lesbian porn, or rather it hit on me. Don't get me wrong: I'm straight as a die, but that doesn't mean some "tasteful" girl-on-girl action doesn't get me going. I always pack a discreet, gold, lipstick vibrator in my handbag when I'm away on business and used this girl's best friend to bring me to a very satisfying orgasm while I watched the sisters scissoring and sixty-nine-ing around on screen. Then promptly fell asleep.

I checked out reasonably early the next morning and picked up the soft-top saloon the hotel had hired for me. My intention was to simply get away from it all, so I headed west and drove, top down, all day – stopping at one of America's great roadside diners for lunch – until I found myself leaving civilization behind and climbing up into the Smoky Mountains, part of the great Appalachian chain that runs all the way down the East Coast.

At some point I must have missed the Interstate, not that I had a real plan or even route in mind, because I found myself climbing higher and higher, with dense forest on either side, on a windy two-lane "blacktop".

Every so often I would round a bend and find myself gazing at a simply spectacular valley with the characteristic smoky-blue mist curling about the mountain tops. There was no other traffic about, I'd tuned into a local country-rock radio station and was having the time of my life singing along to classic tracks with the wind in my hair.

I'd actually found a straight long enough to put my foot down a bit when I glanced in the rear-view and saw the big Harley-Davison police motorcycle coming up fast behind me. The officer pulled up alongside me and motioned me to pull over.

As I'd been advised to do, I sat very still with my hands on the wheel while he dismounted and walked up to the car. Highway Patrolman Johnson – according to his badge – was a big man: well over six foot; wearing leathers, crash helmet and regulation mirrored sunglasses. He gazed at me for what seemed a disconcertingly long time before checking my papers, driving licence and then passport.

"English, ma'am?" he asked a little pointlessly.

"Yes, officer," I replied meekly, "from near London."

"Uh-huh. Been here long, ma'am?"

"Just a couple of days."

"Do you know what the speed limit is, ma'am?"

"Uh, seventy?" I guessed.

"No, ma'am, it's fifty in these parts and you were doing at least eighty when I picked you up. So I'm afraid I'm going to have to write you up a ticket. That'll be a hundred dolllars, ma'am," he said, reaching for his pocketbook.

Now, I certainly wasn't short of money, but I was pretty sure I didn't have that amount of dollars on me and absolutely sure he wasn't going to take "plastic". I really didn't fancy being arrested and hauled down to some godforsaken station for God knows how long.

To this day I don't know what made me say or do what I did, but I know that being in the middle of nowhere in a foreign country and alone was part of it.

"Isn't there some other way we can sort this out?" I pleaded.

"I'm not sure I know what you mean, ma'am."

"Well, perhaps I could do something for you and maybe what you can do for me is not write out the ticket."

"Get out of the car please, ma'am," he said, his voice hard, "and go round to the passenger seat."

I did as I was told and sat on the edge of the seat, like a naughty schoolgirl, with the door open and my feet on the edge of the tarmac. Officer Johnson came and stood in front of me, taking in my V-necked T-shirt, through which my braless nipples could clearly be seen, frayed denim miniskirt and wedge-heeled sandals: "Could you be a little more precise please, ma'am?"

Officer Johnson's leather-clad crotch was at eye level and only inches from my face and I thought, In for a penny, in for a pound, if he was going to arrest me then so be it. I reached forward and, with trembling hands, unzipped the stiff leathers. He was wearing snowy white boxers and I gently reached inside and drew out his tumescent member. He was either a very lucky boy or it was really was true about everything in America being bigger.

"Errm, excuse me, ma'am, what do you think—"

"Shhhhsh," I scolded and leaned forward until my lips were almost touching the end of his cock. He was uncut, which I believe is rare in the USA. I took hold of his shaft with my right hand and gently cupped his balls with my left: felt them writhe gratifyingly inside his sac and heard a soft moan escape his lips. I wanked him softly and gently until the first drop of pre-come beaded at the tip and I was able to fully retract his foreskin back over the swollen glans.

He was almost, but not quite, fully hard by now. I licked my lips appreciatively and then flicked out my tongue, swirling around the head until it was glistening, completely coated in my saliva, and I mopped up the pre-come.

"My, that tastes good, Officer Johnson," I breathed. "See, we can be nice to each other."

His cock was projecting upwards out of his pants and I opened my mouth as wide as I could before going down on him. I don't pretend to be some sort of professional fellatrix but that doesn't mean I don't enjoying sucking off a good hard cock and this certainly fitted the bill.

I glanced upwards to find him gazing, expressionlessly, back down at me, still wearing that crash helmet and those mirrored shades. I could see myself reflected in the lenses, sat with my head in his crotch, but, disconcertingly, nothing of his eyes at all.

I eased down his shaft, coating it my saliva as I went, then back up and down again, a little further each time. The first time I felt him hit the back of my throat it triggered my gag reflex and I withdrew, spluttering. But I kept trying until, eventually, I felt him penetrating me, his glans passing the point of no return and my throat constricting rhythmically around it.

My nose squashed up against his boxers and I realized I could smell leather, hot metal or oil, his sweat and some sort of soap.

They were all mixed together . . . and it was intoxicating. I withdrew again and just looked at him.

He moaned in frustration: "Please, ma'am." And, as I went back to work, his hands closed around the back of my head, fingers wound into my hair, and he began to set an increasingly faster pace.

I grabbed hold of the base of his shaft and began to pump it furiously, rolling his balls between finger and thumb of my left hand, and my lips and tongue whirling around his cockhead.

It only took a couple more minutes and I felt him stiffen, his cock seemed to swell even more and he pumped hot spunk into me as his orgasm swept over him. I tried to swallow it all but there was just too much. I felt some dribble out of my mouth and splatter onto my chest. I smiled around the shaft still lodged inside me as I thought of the ZZ Top track "Pearl Necklace".

I continued to suck contentedly at the cock until it deflated, then made sure I licked it clean before I tucked it back into Officer Johnson's pants for him and zipped up the leathers.

"Thank you, ma'am. I think that kind of completes our business here," he managed. "If you stay on the road for another forty to fifty miles, go through a couple of small towns, you'll find you're clear out of the State of Georgia altogether. I think that would be best for all concerned don't you, ma'am?"

He was walking back to his motorcycle when I called over to him: "Officer Johnson, does this happen to you a lot?"

"No, ma'am," he replied. "In fact you're the first."

He roared off with a wave and I sat for a while still slightly stunned. I cleaned myself up as best I could with some tissues then went back round to the driver's seat on slightly wobbly legs and set off myself.

I'd only been driving a few minutes when I became aware that I was feeling horny, incredibly horny in fact, and of a pooling wetness between my legs. I thought about what had happened: I had "earned" or "saved" $100 – whichever way you looked at it – for about five minutes' work, tops. I don't know quite what that made me, apart from randy, and I didn't really care. I was tempted to pull off again and finish myself off with my bullet, but decided to push on until I found a motel to check in for the night and some more X-rated movie fun.

About forty-five minutes and thirty or so miles later – and still in the middle of the endless mountain forest – I was almost relieved to finally see another vehicle heading toward me.

As we passed, I noticed it was a State Trooper Humvee and was horrified to watch in my rear-view mirror as it executed a handbrake turn and came roaring back towards me . . . with its blue lights flashing on.

Fuck me, not again, I thought and slowed until it came back past me. I followed the car for about half a mile until it indicated right and pulled off the road and a short way down a forest track. Within a hundred yards or so, the track opened out into a small clearing and the patrol circled until it was pointing back down the track . . . leaving me with no means of escape.

The patrolman got out and walked back towards me as, once again, I sat with my hands on the wheel. He was on the short side, probably no more than an inch or two taller than my five foot six, but incredibly stocky, with an almost palpable aura of power and strength, allied to the natural authority invested in him by his blue police uniform and the gun he was wearing.

"Do you know what the speed limit is around here?" he began angrily.

"Yes, officer. It's fifty miles per hour."

"And you were doing at least sixty."

"I was not!" I almost yelled. "I was going no more than forty-five."

"Are you calling me, Sergeant James T. Benson, a liar?" His expression turned to stone and his right hand dropped menacingly down to the holster at his hip. "Get out of the car, keep your hands where I can see them at all times. If I have to draw my pistol I will shoot. I'm arresting you for a State of Georgia traffic violation."

Feeling terrified, I obeyed instantly. The air in the clearing was hot and heavy and still. A cricket chirruped lethargically and deep, much deeper, in the forest a lonesome bird called, but there was a sense of oppression in the quiet and I knew with certainty that I was miles from anywhere. I could feel pinpricks of perspiration all over my body.

When I reached him, the policeman spun me round, pulled

my hands up my back so my forearms were one above the other and snapped on a pair of rigid handcuffs.

"Look, Sergeant Benson, I wasn't calling you a liar, I can explain," I pleaded. "I'm English, I'm a visitor here for a conference – my passport and documents are all in my handbag. I really didn't think I was speeding, honestly."

Sergeant Benson walked across to my car, found my bag and had a look at the documents, glancing up at me a couple of times as he was reading. He put them back but then pulled out my gold vibrator. He studied it intently, then, looking me straight in the eyes, put it up to his nose, inhaled deeply and slipped it into his trouser pocket.

I think it was a combination of terror and arousal, but I just burst into tears and got a serious case of the shakes.

"Please fuck me. Just fuck me now. I need to come so badly. I'll be good, I'll be a good girl. You can take me down to the station later, but just fuck me *nowww!*"

If my reaction was extreme Sergeant Benson's response was equally unexpected. He wrapped me up in a bear hug and I could feel the strength in him as he pulled me close: "There, there, little lady," he cooed sympathetically. "I ain't gonna hurt you none. These handcuffs can cause a body to become more . . ." He paused. "A-menable. I guess you must have one of those bodies. And I ain't fixin' to do nuthin' you don't want me to neither."

And I couldn't help smiling through the tears. "But, Sergeant Benson, I really, *really* do want you to fuck me. And I don't care if it does hurt, you know, just a little bit. So c'mon, cowboy, show me what you've got."

"Well if you're sure. It might just take ma mind off that traffic violation and you callin' me a liar an' all." He spun me round and pulled me back close into him until I could feel the growing bulge in his crotch against my buttocks.

His huge hands cupped my breasts through the flimsy T-shirt, massaging them surprisingly gently, but then pinching my stiff little nipples just hard enough to make me gasp. One hand dropped to my waist, unbuttoning my skirt, and I shimmied just enough to send it sliding down my legs and pooling at my feet. The same hand cupped my mound through my flimsy knickers – and we could both feel exactly how wet I was.

"My, my," he murmured, "it seems you ain't quite the little English lady I thought you was. We have words for women like you round here."

With that, he grabbed hold of my knickers and literally ripped them apart. He pulled my T-shirt backwards up over my head, leaving me naked except for my sandals. Grabbing hold of the bar of the handcuffs, he marched me round to the bonnet of my car and then roughly pushed me down over it. "Spread 'em," he commanded and roughly kicked my legs apart.

The metal of the bonnet was hot against my tits and I knew with humiliating certainty that bent over like this my pussy would be lewdly on display to him. I heard him unzip, then felt his cock, stiff and thick, slide deep inside me and heard him grunt as it did.

Sergeant Benson grabbed hold of the bar of the handcuffs with his left hand and lifted it slightly, but effortlessly, pushing my face and body down against the bonnet and forcing me to arch my back – giving him even easier access – then gave the cheeks of my arse a resounding slap with his right. I was completely helpless and we both knew it.

He fucked me with long strokes for a couple of minutes until he was embedded to the hilt, then leant into me, squashing me hard down against the bonnet until I felt its heat against my clit. I came like a train, uselessly yelling and thrashing about, and the fact that I could still feel his rock-hard cock lodge deep inside me just increased the intensity of my orgasm.

When the wave had passed, Sergeant Benson withdrew and stood me up. He unlocked the cuffs and let my T-shirt slip down onto the floor behind me, turned me around and locked them on again in front of me. Then he leaned me over the bonnet once again, but this time on my back.

Now I really was completely naked while he was still fully clothed and I felt more helpless, vulnerable and humiliated than ever.

Before I left for the States I'd been to the salon and had a fresh Brazilian so my pussy was smooth and bald save for a "runway" tuft of light-brown hair just above my slit.

Sergeant Benson studied it for a moment and then whistled appreciatively. "My ain't that purty. I swear I ain't seen a beaver pelt like that in all my years."

He slipped his cock back inside me and then growled: "Put your arms over my head and wrap your legs around my waist."

When I'd obeyed, he simply put his hands under the cheeks of my arse and stood up, lifting me off the car like I was a doll. I locked my ankles behind his back and settled down, impaling myself on his shaft. Fuck, that felt good and, as I started to buck up and down, I knew it wouldn't be long before I was coming for a second time.

It wasn't "passionate", it wasn't "lovemaking", shit it wasn't even comfortable. It was rutting, pure, animal fucking, and I was loving every second of it.

"Slow down, little lady. You've already had some fun and I ain't ready yet. You don't come without my say so. Y'all understand?"

He dug his fingers into my buttocks and squeezed so hard I could only squeal: "Uh-huh!"

Sergeant Benson straightened up, pulled back his shoulders and flexed his arms backwards. This effectively drew me up and towards him until our lips almost touched. He simply stood, stock-still, like this for a couple of minutes, breathing deeply through his nose as if he was trying to inhale my very essence.

Then, without saying another word, he turned and walked from the clearing, away from the road and into the forest. Out of the sunlight, the air was instantly cooler and I shivered as it caressed my sweat-sheened body. The forest was eerily quiet and oppressive, the only sounds – the scrunch of dry pine needles and small twigs under his boots – seemed muffled by the heavy air.

I don't suppose we went many yards but once I'd lost sight of the clearing I realized that, on my own, I would be well and truly lost. I think he must have somehow realized how I felt because he found some tree with a smooth, straight trunk and pushed my back up against it.

"That's right, little lady, out here there ain't no one to hear you scream so go ahead and yell 'n' holler all you like." And with that, he started jackhammering into me.

I could feel my orgasm welling up inside me and knew I'd soon be past the point of no return. "Please, sir, can I come? I'm s-o-o-o close. I need it. I need it now. Please let me, let me come," I begged, panting.

He stopped immediately, leaving me hanging on the edge. "No! You remember what I told you." He reached into his pocket and pulled out my vibrator. "Lick it!" he commanded.

I sucked it frantically and when it was fully coated in my saliva he reached underneath me and held it against my rosebud, pushing very gently against it.

Instinctively, I tried to struggle upwards, away from the intruder, but he just maintained the steady pressure until I was as high as I could get.

I held this position as long as I could, until the muscles in my legs started to shake with the effort. But resistance was obviously useless. As my strength gave out, I started to slip back down onto it . . . and felt the vibrator slide irresistibly into me and past my sphincter.

"Noooo! Ow-ooo!" I gasped

Then he turned it on. I could feel the vibrator and his cock rubbing together through the walls of my pussy and, combined with the gentle "buzz", it was nothing like anything I'd ever felt before . . . and I guess the same went for Sergeant Benson.

He leant forward and kissed me savagely, his tongue forcing itself into my mouth so, for one glorious instant and for the very first time, all three of my holes were filled simultaneously. Then his head dropped into my chest and he started biting my breasts, each sharp nip sending a bolt of pain straight down to my aching clit.

We came together within a few more seconds and a few more thrusts, both yelling our heads off . . . and hearing our echoes thrown back to us by the forest.

When we were finished – being the Southern gentleman he was – he walked me back to my car, still wrapped around him and with his deflating cock inside me, sat me in the passenger seat and removed his handcuffs. He "adjusted" his clothing and then went and collected mine, bringing it back to me in an untidy heap.

"I guess that'll be all, little lady," he said awkwardly and sounding just a little embarrassed.

"I guess so," was all I could think of by way of a reply.

He walked off towards his car, but, as he reached it, he turned back and called: "By the way, Zeke said to be sure to say hi if I ran into you."

I just stared like an open-mouthed loon.

"Zeke. Zeke Johnson. *Officer* Johnson. He's ma cousin."

Sex in Black and Red – with Pockets

Kay Jaybee

After slamming the front door behind him, Ryan stripped his favourite customer of her skirt and top the second he entered her home.

Beth hadn't bothered putting on any underwear; there was never any point. Ryan rarely had more than ten free minutes before he had to get back on his delivery rounds again, and she didn't want to waste a single second.

Running upstairs in front of him, Beth felt Ryan's sex hungry gaze on her backside. Once in her bedroom, he tugged his bright red polo shirt over his head, and threw it onto her bed. Beth followed the direction of his pointing finger and lay down on her double bed, wondering if today would be the day. Would she finally get to see her courier's cock? Would she get to run her hands over it, taste it, feel it ease inside her?

She buried her face into his top, inhaling the distinct aroma she associated with him: deodorant, hard work, cardboard and diesel. Beth gripped its sleeves tightly and listened hard for the noise she was desperate to hear. The noise she longed for. The sound that told her sex was coming.

At first all she could hear was the beat of blood pounding in her ears. Then it came, the telltale snag of Velcro, as her delivery man opened one of his black trouser pockets.

Beth's field of vision had barely registered her new courier's gorgeous brown eyes and suntanned face on his initial visit to her home. Her regular driver had coincided his retirement with the takeover of the delivery company she used to bring her weekly supply of outwork. Gone were Reg and his dull navy polyester uniform, and in came a handsome man wearing a very appealing, snug-fitting, red-and-black uniform.

As she'd opened the door to this new man, Beth's gaze had skipped past his undeniably firm crisp red-shirted chest and broad shoulders, delayed her eyes for only a millisecond on the slight, but under control, bulge of his groin, and settled upon his legs, and a myriad of pockets. There were just so many of them running up the outside of each leg of the combat-style trousers.

Admiring the curve of his lower limbs while trying to appear as if she wasn't looking at them at all, Beth's imagination had instantly filled each pocket with something far more interesting than what was probably really hidden inside.

Beth couldn't remember which of them had initially started the first conversation which went beyond "please sign here" on his third visit to her home, but she could clearly recall the gleam in Ryan's chestnut eyes as he'd asked her if she had a thing about legs.

Embarrassed that she'd clearly been less covert in her surveillance of his trousers than she'd believed, Beth's cheeks had coloured pink as the course of their flirty conversation led on, over a cup of coffee at her kitchen table, to her musings about the contents of his uniform trousers' many pockets.

That had been when Beth had stared into his eyes for the first time. The instant she had her body sent a hastily desperate plea directly to her crotch and then onto her brain to fuck this man as soon as possible. As if reading her mind, Ryan emptied the contents of his six trouser pockets onto the kitchen table as if he were a criminal about to enter a police cell.

Two pens (one black, one red), paperclips, a small roll of sticky tape, some loose coins, forms for missing parcels, a pad of Post-it notes and a packet of mints.

With each offering he made from the depths of his uniform, Ryan had kept his brown eyes fixed on Beth's blue ones. She could have sworn that she'd seen every sexual fantasy she'd ever had reflected back at her in his unwavering gaze. Her flesh had flushed as vivid a red as his shirt, as Ryan described precisely what each of the items was used for. Never had a group of such mundane objects sounded so erotically suggestive.

That was exactly seven weeks ago. A period of forty-two days, which had begun with a pair of paperclips being attached to her nipples, accompanied by a deliciously masculine tongue lapping at each of her breasts in turn. Methodical and relentless, his licks and laps had navigated every inch of her ample cream tits until Beth, half naked in her kitchen chair, found herself begging to be fucked.

Encouraged by her pleading, Ryan had sped up his movements until he'd triggered Beth into an orgasm that had shaken her to the core. Rather than then release his cock and sort out his own very obvious need as Beth had assumed he would, Ryan had apologized for the predictability of his use of the paperclips, told her how late he was and that he'd have to rush back to work.

Beth hadn't heard a word Ryan had said. All she'd been able to do was stare at her courier with a level of arousal she'd never previously experienced. The secretarial-type treasure from just one of his pockets had sent her into heaven without a single finger touching her pussy, or a kiss touching her lips. As Ryan had disappeared back to his van, the same two thoughts kept circling round and round her head: *What could he do with the contents of the other five pockets? What does his cock feel like?*

This was Ryan's seventh visit. Each week he had used a different item on her body, driving Beth to a swift body-wracking climax, but he'd never had time to fuck her. She badly wanted Ryan to stay longer, to visit her outside of work hours, *to see his cock, to feel its length within her, to give him a climax as good as the six he'd already given her …*

The sound of more Velcro being opened cancelled Beth's dick-filled thoughts and fantasies, and sent her heart thudding faster as she breathed through the fabric of Ryan's shirt. Then the rip of a third pocket being undone brought a sheen of perspiration prickling at the back of her neck. "Three pockets worth at once?"

"No, sweetheart, not three."

Ryan didn't say anything else as the fourth rip of Velcro echoed around the little bedroom, and Beth could feel her pussy becoming heavy with damp desire, while her breasts swelled against the pillowed caress of her bedlinen. *Oh my God, he's going to use four pockets worth at once! Which four? What is he going to do?*

Beth's mind fizzed with images of Ryan placing paperclips on her tits, tying her wrists with sticky tape, and sliding the packet of mints in and out of her sodden channel. Goose pimples dotted her bare arms as she waited for Ryan to act, her sex-laden thoughts tripping into overdrive.

"Are you ready, sweetheart?" Ryan whispered into Beth's ear, as he trailed his fingers through the loose brown hair that hung over her shoulders.

"What are you going to do?" Beth couldn't keep the trepidation from her voice, as his hand journeyed south and stroked her back, before heading to her buttocks and cradling each one in turn in his palm.

"Now then, sweetheart, you know the rules. You don't ask me that."

Beth squeezed her eyes closed. She knew she mustn't be fooled into relaxing by the gentleness of Ryan's touch. He had a way of taking her body to the very edge of pain – and she loved it. Not knowing how he was going to take her to that place at the boundary of her limits was part of the attraction, but that fact didn't stop her brain cartwheeling with possibilities. Gritting her teeth, Beth tried to breathe regularly as her courier's warm right palm continued to caress her flesh, but all she could think was *What is his left hand doing?*

Her question was soon answered. Something thin and pointed was being traced over the backs of her knees. The nerve-tingling sensation made her squirm against the bed, forcing a mew from Beth's lips as her nipples brushed the bedlinen.

As the slightly sharp edge continued to hop from leg to leg, Beth realized Ryan must be tracing the corner of a missed delivery card across her body.

"Nice, sweetheart?"

"Uh-huh." Beth tried and failed to pre-empt where he was going to run the card next, and her skin hummed in expectation of its touch. She could hear his other hand moving something on her bedside cabinet, and she had to wrap Ryan's T-shirt tighter in her fists to help resist the temptation to roll over so she could get an eyeful of his magnificent bare torso, and tight trouser-clad legs.

Ryan began to inch the calling card from her toes up towards her backside. Then, suddenly, Beth guessed what he was going to do before he did it, and she cursed her overactive imagination for sending her body into an increased state of arousal as he wedged the card firmly between her butt cheeks.

"Do not let that fall out. Yes?"

"Yes, Ryan." Beth licked her lips to stimulate some moisture back around her fast drying mouth as she clenched her arse.

She was picturing how bizarre she must look, when a sticky strip landed on her back. Beth heard the faint snap of Post-it note after Post-it note being peeled from the pad, and sighed as they were smoothed into neat lines down the length of her back.

Working at speed, Ryan soon covered her back. He then lay the yellow squares of notepaper over the curve of Beth's butt, running his thumb extra firmly over the line of sticky glue that adhered them to her flesh, making the missed delivery card tremble between her butt cheeks and her pussy juice flow faster so that it smeared across her duvet cover.

"Feel good, sweetheart?"

Beth, her eyes still shut, moaned softly, "Uh-uh."

"Good." Placing the last Post-it note into position, Ryan asked, "Out of all my pockets, which item did you enjoy the best?"

Beth didn't pause. "Paperclips."

Ryan laughed, his cock tightening at the memory of that day.

Beth was about to add that she desperately wanted to experience the only item in his trousers that she'd never seen – his cock – but the sound of a biro lid being popped off distracted her, sending an involuntary ripple through her pussy.

The first time Ryan had used the pens, he'd instructed Beth to grip both slim cylinders between her nether lips for what had felt like hours, but, in reality, could only have been five minutes. Meanwhile, he'd kissed every inch of her body as she'd fought not to let the insubstantial filling fall from her slippery opening. When she had inevitably failed in her task, Ryan had laid her over his knees and spanked her with beautifully hard strokes across her arse with one hand, while massaging her clit to climax with the other, before running back to work.

Beth wasn't sure if she was more surprised or more

disappointed when, rather than tease the butt of the pen around her pussy, Ryan pressed its nib over a yellow square, and began to run the ink from note to note in a maze of lines.

It was like having the weirdest massage ever, as the pen ink was applied against her skin through a veil of thin yellow paper. With nerve-tingling stealth, the pen travelled south, until finally Ryan hovered it over the cleft of her buttocks where the card was still wedged. Tapping the side of the pen against the top of the sticking-out rectangle, Ryan mumbled sounds of appreciation. Beth's buttocks quivered against her struggle to keep them clenched tight enough to stop the card from coming free.

"So pretty." Ryan flicked the card twice more. "Soon you are going to get onto all fours. You can rest on your elbows and your knees. As you move, I don't want to see *any* of the sticky notes fall from your back, or the card to shift from your arse." He gave a ragged sigh, which told Beth exactly how hard he was finding it not to screw her there and then. "Honestly, you look like a bitch with the strangest tail ever."

Beth listened carefully as Ryan added, "For each item that falls from you, you'll have to wait an extra minute for the paperclips; and for the fucking I know you want. You do want me to screw you, don't you, Beth?"

"Oh God yes." Beth felt a climax stir in the pit of her stomach, as the need for his dick between her legs grew alongside her yearning for him to exquisitely abuse her chest. Was he finally going to let her feel his shaft inside her?

Loosening her grip on his shirt, Beth started to plan how to get onto all fours with minimal fuss, but Ryan had picked up some of the contents of his next pocket.

"Can you feel these, sweetheart?" Taking three coins, he lined them up at regular intervals along Beth's spine.

"Yes."

"Now, as you get onto all fours, I want those coins to stay exactly where they are. Got that?"

"But that's impossible! The notes have made my back all slippery."

"True. However, if you want me to do what I know you long for me to do, then you'd better try really hard. If three items fall it will take longer to happen. Lose four, and it won't happen at all."

Even though she couldn't see his face, Beth could hear the excitement in his voice as Ryan added, "I don't think I have ever heard anything as sexy as the sound of you begging the first time I emptied my pockets for you. I can tell you, not screwing that hot little pussy of yours that day was the hardest thing I've ever done."

Abruptly, Ryan's voice changed. His patient but firm tone now gruff and urgent as if suddenly all his patience, all his self-control, had snapped. "Now Beth."

Ryan slapped her rump, causing a breeze of air to ruffle all the Post-it notes and the card shoved in her crack to waver, as her muscles automatically clenched harder.

Knowing there was no way she could do what Ryan asked without at least one of the coins falling off, Beth stiffened all the muscles in her back. She slowly crept forward one leg and arm, trying to keep the arching of her spine to a minimum.

She could feel the heat of Ryan's eyes radiating into her back, as her left knee edged into position and the coin nearest her neck slipped a fraction. Beth froze, remaining motionless until the money was still again.

Starting again, inching each limb along a fraction in turn, Beth was almost in position, when she allowed herself the luxury of exhaling a complete lungful of air. The moment she breathed out however, Beth realized her mistake, but there was nothing she could do to prevent the top coin from rolling off her back, and onto the bed with an orgasm-delaying thump.

Swallowing back her groan of defeat, Beth gripped the bedcovers between her fingers and toes as Ryan's pen came to her right calf.

"One error." Ryan slowly began to rummage through the things he'd placed on the bedside cabinet, counting down the seconds of the minute's wait for action under his breath.

Restless and anxious for more, at first Beth didn't feel the second pen as Ryan slid it up inside her. She was so wet that it sucked into her with frightening ease, and for an instant Beth was afraid it would completely disappear up inside. She didn't think she'd ever been so wet.

"Nice?"

"Yes."

"You know what you have to do, don't you?"

"I mustn't drop the pen."

"Good girl." Ryan came around to her head, knelt on the floor next to the bed, and lifted her chin, stroking her hair from her face.

Beth almost wanted to plead with him not to kiss her, not to touch her, to do nothing that would break her concentration and make her wobble, and therefore have to wait longer for the pen to be replaced by the magnificent cock she craved for, but she was powerless to stop him as he brought his mouth to hers.

Fighting her instinct to respond, knowing if she moved her head then another coin or the pen would drop, she closed her eyes against the piercing cavern of Ryan's gaze, as he began to speak, "I've been waiting for this for so long. I've made myself wait. I got off on the wait, but I can't wait any longer. Have you any idea how hard the thought of you, and the things you allow me to do to you, makes me? Do you know how hard I am right now? Can you guess how badly I want to sink my dick into your body?"

"I . . . " Beth got no further.

Ryan squeezed her chin. "Watch, bitch! See what you do to me. Have you any bloody idea how difficult it is to drive a van when I'm like this?"

With more speed than finesse, Ryan undid his belt and flies, shoved his trousers and boxers down to just below his butt, and waved his stiff slick-headed shaft in his hand. "Do you see, Beth? Do you see what condition you get me in whenever I come here, each time you let me do what the hell I like to you, when there is never time to do more than please that luscious body of yours?"

Her eyes wide, Beth rested her gaze on the most beautiful cock she had ever seen. It was all she'd dreamed: thick, long, but not too long, and rock solid for her.

Ryan, his shaft in his fist, clambered onto the bed and knelt in front of her, unbalancing his customer's carefully statuesque position, sending another coin to the duvet, as her pussy channel battled to keep the pen in place. Thrusting his hips forward,

Ryan teased the end of his dick around her dry lips while he carried on his frustrated monologue. "I drive around, knocking on doors, handing out boxes, and all I'm thinking about is how I can use the sticky tape in my pocket during my next visit. I spend my whole fucking day with a hard-on. It looks as though I've got a seventh pocket at the front of my trousers that is permanently full!"

Beth wanted to shout out in protest. She'd never asked him to only please her; and she'd wanted him inside her more than anything for weeks and weeks. There was no opportunity to voice her thoughts however, as Ryan sighed. "And now look what you've done! Another coin has fallen. Now we'll both have to wait longer!"

Beth didn't know if she was being accused or complimented; she felt oddly on the edge of bliss. Her butt was clenched, her breasts throbbed with neglect, and her channel was gripping the pen with all its might. Each wonderful sensation was serving as a reminder of how empty she felt and how frustrated she was every time Ryan delivered her quick, albeit inventive, but fuckless sex.

"It's a shame that coin fell off, because I was going to stuff your mouth with my cock, and let your tongue wrap itself around me, however I'll just resign myself to more waiting, and fill the space with these instead."

He ripped open his fifth pocket and took out an unopened tube of mints. Beth felt cheated as the paper-wrapped packet was eased between her teeth and his gorgeous shaft was taken away.

Ryan stood back on the floor. "I'm pleased to see you controlled yourself enough that time to keep the last coin, pen and card in place."

Beth tried to keep looking at his shaft, but her neck was beginning to ache from being held at such an awkward angle, so she only heard, rather than witnessed, him roll off his trousers, the unhooking of another pocket flap, and the unmistakable zip of a roll of sticky tape being opened.

"Oh God." She gulped as Ryan carried on talking. It was as if every frustration he'd imposed upon himself over the last seven weeks were exploding all at once in a verbal landslide.

"It's been so difficult not to be clichéd and predictable when it comes to using this lot on you, and sometimes I know I have been."

The noise of short strips of tape being torn off the roll stopped Ryan talking, and Beth felt her insides somersault as the gluey strips hit the tiny gaps between the Post-it notes and her flesh. She knew precisely how much it was going to sting when he tore it back off, taking the tiny invisible hairs from her skin with it.

Ryan didn't stop there, however. Beth heard the reel of tape being pulled again, and two more lengths were stuck to her, this time fixing the waving calling card firmly in place. "OK, so sticking everything in place is cheating, but I'm running out of time." Then he stuck two strips of tape either side of the mints, keeping her mouth open just enough for her to make noises, but not enough for her to be able to speak properly.

There was only one item left in his pockets now. Beth's pulse zipped from a racing pace to a full-out gallop as she tried not to think about Ryan's paperclips.

Climbing back onto the bed, Ryan lay so that his head was next to hers. Reaching between Beth's legs, he took hold of the end of the pen and rhythmically moved it in and out and from side to side. "Just hear that pussy honey squelching! Delicious!"

Beth puffed blasts of air out of the sides of her opened mouth. *Hurry up! Screw me! Don't run out of time!*

Ryan manoeuvred his head so he was directly beneath her right tit, making Beth jump as he blew hot air against her rock-solid nipple. "As I so subtly indicated just now, I spend my days dreaming about what we do, and I want more. More opportunities to do this, not just ten minutes snatched out of our working day. More time to fill your pussy, your mouth, your arse, and refill my pockets with new toys!"

A feeling of happiness dared to flutter in Beth's eyes as Ryan clasped his lips around her tit, then sucked and licked hard, until she felt the knot of her approaching orgasm build faster.

Panting out of the sides of her mouth, Beth gasped with ecstasy as Ryan wriggled further beneath her swinging chest and engulfed the left side in-between his teeth as he continued to manoeuvre the tiny makeshift dildo. She could no longer contain the shake that had been threatening to break out in her arms for the last five minutes.

Seeing how close she was to coming, Ryan stretched out an arm to the cabinet, picked up two paperclips, and flashed them before her eyes. "How bad do you want these, baby?"

Beth gurgled her response. "Very badly."

"And how badly do you want me to suck on your trapped teats afterwards?"

This time Beth's reply was even less coherent, but far louder and obviously positive.

"As badly as you want me to remove that pen and stuff you with my cock?"

"Oh God yes."

Moving quickly, Ryan snapped each clip in place, watching with fascination as each nipple flushed. Beth whimpered with pain as the piercing burn of the bite in her nipples took hold.

In the weeks that had passed since Ryan had first done this to her, she'd forgotten how much it hurt, but she'd also forgotten exactly much she loved it as Ryan's cool tongue lapped over and over each throbbing bud in turn.

With her mind bursting with images of how odd she must look, her jaw clicking from being held only partly open, her pussy being teased, and her clit rock hard and desperate to be touched, Beth's willpower deserted her.

The climax that had started in her belly, shot down to her toes, and then burst throughout her whole being, sending a paper-muffled scream from her mouth. Her knees buckled, and her legs sank down, causing the missed delivery card to brush against the duvet and send an extra shot of delightful pressure through her body.

Tearing the strips of adhesive from her butt and freeing the card, Ryan ignored the cries of pain that mingled with, and enhanced, Beth's orgasm. He freed the tube of mints, and yanked off the tape, stinging her skin around her mouth. He then scrambled for the only pocket in his red shirt, and rolled on the condom he'd hidden there.

With one hand landing on her neglected clit, and the other pinching her nipples tighter, at last, with an animalistic cry of relief and satisfaction, Ryan pushed himself inside his favourite customer's shuddering body, pumping out his seven weeks of pent-up lust with a grunt of gratification that Beth would never forget.

Watching him dress with his usual burst of speed, Beth beamed up at her courier from the tangle of her duvet. "You have to dash off?"

"I do. I'm already running late." He grinned down at her. "Was worth it though! Umm, look, how about I come back later? Is that OK? I mean it's been nearly two months, and I'd like to get to know you better. Anyway, I have a gift for you."

Beth glanced provocatively at her scarlet nipples and felt the ache between her legs that could only come from a thorough seeing-to. "Wasn't that my gift then?"

Ryan had only been gone a couple of hours before he was back, knocking on Beth's front door, a playful smile across his face. "Delivery for you, madam."

The parcel was wrapped in red-and-black paper. Beth couldn't stop beaming as she opened it. It was a courier's uniform – complete with red polo shirt, black combat trousers – and pockets.

"For me?" Beth automatically looked at the trousers' pockets, as she held them up, her eyes alight with pleasure. "Is there stuff in the pockets?"

Ryan winked. "Why don't you put them on, and we'll find out?"

Standing before him in a miniature version of the outfit she was so used to seeing him wear, Beth felt incredibly sexy.

"You look amazing. Sex in red and black."

"With pockets." Beth's eyes twinkled. Then, taking Ryan's hand, she turned towards the stairs, ripping open the first of her six Velcro pockets as they headed to her bedroom . . .

Airborne

Tamsin Flowers

Pushing open the door to the briefing room, Corporal Peppi Alvarez wondered for the thousandth time whether signing up for this particular mission had been such a good move. Sure, she might get her sergeant's stripes by the end of it – if it was successful – but she might also end up dead in a jungle in a tinpot South American dictatorship going through the motions of a struggle for freedom and democracy. Another little civil war which would drag on for years and simply replace one dictator with another under the guise of progress. And she'd volunteered to step right into the middle of it. Or jump, to be more accurate, with a parachute attached to her back and a partner she had yet to meet.

She looked around the room as the rest of the team filed in. There were the other four girls she'd been through Jump School with and a bunch of 507th Infantry soldiers all wearing their wings proudly on their sleeves. Inwardly, Peppi sighed. The airborne soldiers she'd met in training had all held a high opinion of themselves, jumping out of planes, on the battlefield and in the bedroom. She'd had enough of being hit on by testosterone-fuelled alphas who believed that throwing themselves out of planes like so many puppets on a string qualified them for hero status. And now she would be spending the next six weeks in close contact with one of them, no respite, no break from the ego.

The soldiers were noisy, joshing and showing off in front of the women as they settled into the back row of chairs. Peppi looked away. No point in speculating which one would be her partner. She'd find out soon enough.

"Operation Eldorado," barked the infuriated infantry major who was in charge of briefing the team. "Incursion behind enemy lines. Fact finding. Sabotage. Prisoner extraction. Each team pair will get an individual briefing on what's expected of them. First, the drop."

One of the guys near the back raised a hand immediately.

"Tell me your name, then your question," said the major.

The soldier stood up. Peppi looked round at him. What an ass, asking a question before the briefing began. Whatever he wanted to know was sure to be covered in the next couple of hours.

"Sir, yes, sir. Private Rawlings."

He was tall and bulky, the type of guy you know you want on your team, whether that's football or unarmed combat. A dark fringe flopped down over his eyes, long hair for going undercover and, holy hell, what eyes. The irises were as dark as the pupils, and the lashes – if she'd seen those on a girl she would have pegged them for false.

"What's your question, Private?"

"Sir, we don't accept women in the Airborne Division for a reason. So why the fuck do we have to play nanny to a bunch of chicks on this mission?"

Peppi felt her hackles rising.

"Private, these women are elite soldiers and they've all been through Jump School."

Peppi stood up. "Major, Corporal Alvarez. Might I address this soldier's concerns?"

The major looked at her, eyes wide with surprise. "Go ahead, Corporal Alvarez," he said.

"Private Rawlings," she said, through clenched teeth, "I passed out of Jump School with a maximum score. Did you do that?"

Rawlings looked her up and down, insolence in his dark eyes. "Yes, ma'am."

"Good. Then I won't mind having to jump with you. *Hablas español?*"

"Sorry, ma'am?"

"Do you speak Spanish? But don't bother answering that. My squad have been picked for this mission, soldier, not just because they can speak Spanish but for a whole host of other skills and attributes. And now I'm wondering why we have to jump with bunch of grunts we won't need tagging along once we've landed."

All hell broke loose till the major intervened.

"Shut up and listen!"

Peppi could never sleep when she was on-board a military transport plane. The loud drone of the engines was noisier than on commercial flights and the adrenalin pumping through her kept her wide-eyed and alert – even though she had no idea when she'd next have the chance to get her head down. She leaned forward to rest on the heavy pack that sat between her knees and studied her partner, sitting slumped and soundly asleep on the bench opposite her.

Private First Class James "Jimmy" Rawlings. Neanderthal. Sexist. A prime example of the type of soldier she despised. And she was about to embark on six weeks undercover with him. Travelling through hostile territory posing as husband and wife. Her life would be in his hands just as much as his life would be in hers. They had to be a team, tight as a real married couple and, already, she couldn't stand the sight of him. Perhaps that would make the relationship seem more realistic, she thought with a smirk.

"Enjoying the view, ma'am?"

Fuck. He wasn't even asleep and he'd caught her staring at him. She looked away and then back at him.

"What's that, soldier?"

His grin said she wasn't fooling him so she spent the remainder of the flight staring at the top of the pack between her knees. Minutes ticked to hours and then, just before dawn, the pilot announced they were approaching the drop zone. The teams made their final preparations and shuffled towards the back of the plane, lining up with their jump partners. Peppi checked Rawlings's chute was secure and he did the same for her. Seconds later, she was standing on the brink, spinning in the slipstream of the jet and then plunging through cold, screaming air, her stomach left somewhere behind her in the stratosphere.

As soon as rational thought returned, she pushed her body into a position that would slow her descent. It felt like lying on a bed of air, of nothing, but at this height it didn't even look as if the ground was rushing towards them and the features of the landscape were too small to make out. Far off, to the west, she could see the glint of moonlight on the sea and make out the rugged line of the coast. By the time she landed, she would be more than thirty miles inland.

It was difficult to move with the intense air pressure pushing up against her but she shifted her head to look up. Rawlings, in the same position, was approximately one hundred feet above her and behind, having exited the aircraft immediately after her. He gave her a thumbs-up with his gloved hand.

On leaving the plane, Peppi had been instructed to count to sixty before pulling the cord for her main shoot. As she reached fifty-five, she found the ring pull and put her index finger through the loop; on sixty she pulled it. It felt as if the air was being sucked from her lungs, the breaks being slammed on, yanked up hard on a harness that would any second slice right through her. But then a relaxation of the tension and – *silence* – so profound it was deafening.

Rawlings was a dark streak flashing past her, flailing in the air, tugging at his chest. And it only took Peppi a split second to realize that he was having problems with his chute. She watched in horror as he jettisoned the main chute and let it fall away, tossing and turning in his slipstream. But still nothing happened. No reserve chute. At terminal velocity he would hit the ground in less than two minutes.

"St Michael, Archangel, defend us in battle . . ."

She hadn't prayed since she was fourteen but now the words came unbidden as she jettisoned her main chute and streamlined her body for a vertical dive. If she didn't get this right they'd both be dead.

A thousand feet beneath her, Rawlings was spinning and out of control, his arms and legs outstretched as he tried to slow his descent. Peppi's descent was faster but there was no guarantee she would pass close enough to him. She scoured her memory for the techniques she'd just been taught to steer the course of her fall and angled her body to bring her closer to him.

At last, it seemed that Rawlings realized what she'd done and what she was aiming to do. He pushed against the rush of air to bring himself closer to the path of her fall. He was the experienced pro, not her, and Peppi wished she could take back her smart-ass words in the briefing. She hadn't a clue when she should pull her reserve shoot and she didn't have time for analysis . . .

Their bodies smashed together at more than one hundred miles an hour and even though they were moving in same direction it was like smashing into a brick wall. Immediately winded, Peppi grabbed at air, trying to make purchase, as her body tumbled away from Rawlings. And if he hadn't managed to grasp the leg of her pants, they would have lost each other to the winds. As Peppi struggled for breath, Rawlings pulled her in towards him, agonizingly slowly – and now the ground was racing towards them fast, every detail becoming clearer by the second.

As soon as he had one arm around her waist, Rawlings wrapped his legs round her hips, bending his knees to entwine his ankles round her legs.

"Hold tight!" he screamed into the rush of air.

Peppi hung on to him for dear life as he pulled the cord on her reserve chute. Then she was being ripped in two with the chute and the harness wrenching her upwards and the weight of Rawlings, clasped against her body like a limpet, dragging her down.

She screamed. And then they hit the ground.

Pain. Stars floating before her eyes. Her lungs were screaming for air. She was tangled and crushed under another body.

Rawlings groaned. "You alive, Alvarez?" he said.

Peppi couldn't speak but when she wriggled underneath him, he obligingly rolled off her. And there they lay for long minutes, just breathing and loving the feeling of the firm ground beneath their backs.

"We fucking made it," said Rawlings. "You saved my life."

Peppi grunted.

Rawlings sat up and looked down at her. "You fucking saved my life, Alvarez."

Dawn was creeping in and Peppi could just make out a look of wide-eyed wonder on his face.

"Your first field jump . . ." He shook his head and then before she realized what was happening, he'd swept her up in his arms.

Peppi moaned as the movement made her aware of an injury somewhere in the distant reaches of her left leg. But the brush of soft lips against her own quickly pushed the pain from her mind. She was sitting on Rawlings's lap and he ever so gently took her face in both his hands.

"You know what this means, Corporal?"

"No," she whispered, her voice cracked and hoarse. Surely there wasn't some Army regulation for situations like this.

Rawlings's face broke into a wide grin. "I'm yours. You saved my life, now I belong to you." Eyes, dark and mischievous, met her own.

"But you pulled the second cord," she said. "You saved my life."

"We're alive and we belong to each other. What could be better than that?"

Before she could answer his mouth was once more on hers, only this time it stayed there. She let her lips part under the pressure of his tongue and it snaked into her mouth, hot and sweet and insistent. Already awash with adrenalin, Peppi felt a surge of heat and a flood of endorphins. The pain that had wracked her body seconds before vaporized in the fires of his lengthening kiss and she wrapped her arms round the back of Rawlings's neck to kiss him in return.

Nothing reaffirms life more than the touch of one body against another, the brush of warm skin against warm skin, and without the need for words, they reached for each other's jumpsuit zips at the same moment. This was not about courtship and romance. No slow build-up of foreplay. No tender caresses and whispered nothings. Rawlings practically ripped the jumpsuit away from her body. She tugged his down, not caring when he winced in pain. She needed to feel his heat mingle with hers, she needed him inside her.

When they were both naked, Rawlings lowered her gently to the mossy ground and stretched himself onto her, anchoring her with the weight of his body. He brushed sweaty hair back from her forehead and sprinkled kisses down her jawline.

"I don't know what to say," he said.

"Nothing," she whispered. "Just . . ."

He needed no further encouragement. His hand ran down

her side and then swooped across her belly to the triangle of dark hair between her legs. She pushed up her hips in invitation and his fingers started to explore. She was wet and she spread her legs wide underneath him. At the same time, his mouth dropped to one of her breasts and she felt his tongue prod her nipple to life. Heat rushed to the spot, engorging the delicate bud, making Peppi moan as his tongue swirled round her areola. Her back arched, pushing her breast against his mouth, which he opened wider to suck more in. He pulled hard and then his teeth clamped down, making her yelp, causing her pussy to spasm.

A finger surged into her but she needed more. Her muscles were clenching and she knew what they wanted. She reached a hand down to where she could feel his erection, pressing hard against her stomach.

"Now," she said, using her hand to guide him into position.

With a deep groan, Rawlings pushed the tip of his cock up against her opening.

"God, you're so wet. It's beautiful."

He teased her for a moment, edging forward, inching back, until her fingers raking up his back finally spurred him in. Peppi gasped. Rawlings was a big man and his cock was fully in proportion, stretching her wide as he drove in hard. A flash of pleasure spiralled through her, a foretaste of what was to come, and her legs automatically went up around his waist as she opened herself to accommodate him.

Running her fingers through his hair, she pulled his face up to hers and locked her eyes with his. She'd known this man for less than twenty-four hours but in that time they'd been to hell and back. Together. Her mouth found his and she pushed her tongue against his lips, which immediately opened. Tongue pressing against tongue, chest against breast, hips grinding in unison. The friction of his pelvic bone against her clit stoked fires that were already raging and she was close to coming.

Rawlings bit her lip and ploughed into her as if he'd never fuck again. Peppi could taste blood, and the sweet pain combined with agonizing pleasure tipped her over the edge. Suddenly she was in free fall, spinning away from the here and now. But this time, Rawlings was with her and there was no fear, only waves of exhilaration rolling through her as they soared in unison through a rush of cold air.

Peppi clenched tight around him, her moans turning to a gasp as her orgasm intensified. Beneath her hands, Rawlings's back stiffened and his hips pushed hard against her. His climax shuddered through him and she felt his cock spasm deep inside her.

Gasping for breath, she let go of him and pushed her hands into the soft, cool moss she was lying on. Safe on the ground. Alive.

Later, they bathed in a river and buried the remains of the chute and their harnesses. Rawlings strapped up her hurt leg with infinite care and a gentle touch. He prepared food from their packs and started planning their next move. But, every few minutes, he would look up from what he was doing and stare at her with his deep, dark eyes.

"Hot damn, Corporal. You saved my life up there."

She grinned back at him – maybe this mission did have something going for it after all.

"And now, Private, you belong to me."

Serving Them

Elizabeth Coldwell

So there I was, with one cock in my mouth and another about to come over my tits, thinking this was all down to the dress. I'd taken up waitressing to help pay my way through university, not to get into situations where I might find myself having filthy sex, but for the first time I was beginning to realize that every job has its unexpected fringe benefits.

"Oh, God, yeah, just keep doing that," Rory muttered, as I slurped my tongue over the gloriously fat crown of his dick, and I fought to keep the smile from my face, hardly able to believe I found myself in such a satisfying position.

When Melanie from the temp agency had rung, asking if I was free to work at the weekend, I hadn't expected anything out of the ordinary. Most Saturday nights saw me at some function or other. Silver service waitressing had proved to be steady work – as long as you were courteous and managed not to spill gravy over any of the guests, you were pretty much guaranteed a job whenever you wanted one.

I hadn't had to invest in any fancy clothes, which was a blessing when most of my income was needed for rent, food and textbooks. Usually, a plain white blouse and black skirt would suffice. But not today. Melanie had been very insistent on that point.

"They'll provide a uniform for you, Jade," she'd told me. "Just make sure you're there at two o'clock."

"There" was a marquee that had been erected in the grounds of a local stately home, a short bus ride from my student accommodation – or it would have been, if not for the fact half the streets in the area had been blocked off for a charity fun run.

In the end, the diverted route the bus had to take meant I arrived fifteen minutes late. As I offered my apologies, I was ushered into a changing room and handed the outfit all the waitresses were expected to wear. A black satin shirtdress with silver piping around the collar, cuffs and hem, it looked chic and sophisticated on the hanger. When I squeezed into it, however, the results were anything but elegant. The dress looked great on all the slender girls already buzzing around the place, with their tight bottoms and neat little boobs. But the buttoned front strained across my big tits, the fabric gaping open just enough to offer glimpses of my scarlet and cream bra. And the satin fabric was so taut across my round, fleshy arse that I was sure the outline of my matching thong must be clear for all to see. I felt conspicuous and somehow slutty; a feeling that only increased when I walked out into the marquee with a tray containing half a dozen prawn and avocado cocktails and saw the particular guests I was expected to serve.

Gossiping with one of the other waitresses as we'd collected the food from the kitchen, I'd discovered the groom was a rugby player, while the bride's father had made his money in the City. As for the bride, she was by all accounts a spoiled, designer-clad nightmare. "We're dealing with a real Bridezilla here," she'd warned me. "Everything's got to be just the way she wants it or she'll pitch a tantrum. I'm so glad I'm not serving the top table."

I'd just shrugged. I'd worked at weddings like this before, and the one thing I had learned was the alcohol never stopped flowing from the moment the guests took their place at table till long after the happy couple had retired to the honeymoon suite. So I thought I knew what I was in for, but I hadn't reckoned on the occupants of Table Sixteen, one of my two allocated tables. These were the unattached members of the groom's rugby team: those without wives and girlfriends, the ones who hadn't bothered to scare up a date for the event. Six testosterone-filled young men in their fit, muscular prime, already knocking back the complimentary aperitifs. As I walked towards them, their expressions were those of a bunch of hungry wolves eyeing fresh meat. I'm in trouble here, I thought, wondering why their reactions had my pussy clenching with lust in response.

"So what's your name, darling?" one asked as I bent over to

place his starter before him. The movement caused the gaps in my dress front to widen a little more, and I could almost feel half a dozen hot, greedy gazes burning into my partially exposed chest.

"Jade," I replied, deciding the best policy was to be friendly. They seemed like nice enough guys, after all, even if they weren't so much mentally undressing me as mentally ripping off my uniform, splaying me across the table and sticking their cocks into every orifice.

"Suits you, love. You're a gem, you really are." As he spoke, he smoothed a hand over my arse, tracing the contours of my underwear through the thin material of my uniform. The professional thing to do would have been to slap his hand discreetly away, letting him know such behaviour wouldn't be tolerated. But I didn't; instead, I let his touch linger, a secret thrill shooting through me as he continued to feel me up.

Throughout the meal, that same erotic treatment continued. Most of the guys were content just to stare at my ripe curves as they threatened to burst free of the tight-fitting satin, but two were bolder. Rory, the heavyset blond who'd groped my arse, took every opportunity to slide a hand up my dress. At first, he was content to stroke the insides of my thighs; then, seeing that I offered no resistance, brushed a questing finger over the bulge of my pussy lips within my increasingly damp thong.

James, sitting to his left, had mastered the art of "accidentally" brushing my breast whenever I leant over to serve him food or collect his empty plate. I couldn't have told him off even if I'd wanted to. One look into those big blue eyes of his, and I was lost. Well-spoken guys who give off a bad-boy vibe are my secret weakness, and James had me at, "How are you?"

Between them, they were working me up to a state where nothing mattered but my growing need to come. If I looked increasingly flushed on my trips back to the kitchen, the satin dress beginning to stick to my overheated skin, no one commented. Maybe I was concealing my need better than I thought, or maybe everyone else was too concerned about doing their own job to notice what I was up to. Stuck in our distant corner of the marquee, well away from the top table, it seemed we could pretty much get away with anything.

By the time the speeches rolled round, James and Rory had clearly had enough of proceedings. I suspected they'd been conferring when I went to fetch the champagne to top up guests' glasses for the impending toasts, because they presented me with a proposal.

"Mike's speech is going to go on forever," Rory informed me, gesturing in the direction of the best man, who stood by the hastily erected microphone with a sheaf of notes in his hand. "Why don't we go somewhere a bit more private while he drones on, Jade, because you obviously want to get out of that dress as much as we want to get you out of it?"

"You can't be serious," I said, even though they so clearly were.

"Come on," James chipped in. "You won't be missed the next half an hour. Just leave the champers with the guys – if they need a refill they're old enough and ugly enough to pour it themselves."

Rory's hand was up my dress again, in a determined effort to worm a digit beneath the edge of my thong. When the pad of his index finger made contact with wet, swollen pussy flesh, I lost what little remained of my resolve.

"Where can we go?" I looked around me, seeing only the white, billowing walls of the marquee. Filled with stuffy air and stuffier guests, the scent of lilies almost overpowering, it didn't offer any secluded corners for a filthy liaison of the type James suggested. Perhaps they wanted to usher me beneath the starched tablecloth so we could fuck on the floor, in a forest of legs formed by the rest of the players. I pictured myself reaching out to stroke one straining, trouser-clad bulge after another, maybe even unzipping their friends' trousers and releasing their cocks while James and Rory took me in whatever way they fancied. It didn't matter that I'd never been with two men at once; the mood I was in, I felt like I could take all six of these guys, one after the other.

"You got changed into that outfit somewhere, right?" James cast another glance at my dress, no doubt imagining what I'd look like out of it. "Well, we'll go there. Rory and I will make out that we're off for a cigarette; give us a couple of minutes, then follow us."

I didn't want to know how they would get inside the room where all the waiting staff's belongings were stored, but I suspected James could pretty much sweet-talk his way anywhere. All it would take was one flash of his beguiling smile and doors would open. They made an interesting contrast, I thought, as he and Rory walked away from the table: one dark and lean, the other fair and built like the proverbial brick shithouse. If you didn't fancy one, you'd more than likely fancy the other. Me being me, I'd have happily settled for either. Now it seemed I was about to get both.

Waiting for a count of one hundred after they'd sauntered out of the marquee, I sidled out after them. When one of the other waitresses raised a querying eyebrow as I passed her, I mouthed that I needed the loo. She just nodded, and turned her attention back to filling glasses.

I paused for a moment on the threshold of the room where, hopefully, both men were waiting for me. If any doubts, any reservations about embarking on the naughtiest adventure of my life were to hit me, it would happen now. Nothing did; I wanted this, my first threesome, more than anything I could remember. Taking a deep breath, I tried the door handle, half expecting it to be locked. It turned easily, and I found myself being greeted by the marvellous sight of Rory and James, flies unzipped, lazily stroking their cocks in readiness for my arrival. I couldn't help wondering what they'd do if I didn't show up. What kind of games did two big, horny rugby players play when they were alone together? If I'd walked in a couple of minutes later, would I have found them with their hands on each other's dicks? Now, that would be something to behold . . .

I was interrupted in my musing as Rory grabbed my hand and pulled me to him. "Come here, you gorgeous strumpet. Let me do what I've wanted to do since I first saw you."

Before I could protest, he tugged at the buttons running down the front of my dress, undoing all but the bottom two. I feared that in his haste, he would rip them off, ruining the outfit – and how much trouble would I be in if that happened? But somehow, everything stayed intact.

"Very nice," he commented, casting an eye over my heaving, lace-covered chest. "But the view still needs improving." With that, he freed my breasts from the cups of my bra, one after the other, letting them flop over the underwired band. I felt my cheeks flush hot. What he'd done was so much ruder than if he'd stripped me entirely, making my tits the obvious focus of both men's attention.

So what happens next? I wondered. I looked from one to the other of them, barely able to tear my eyes from those hard, jutting cocks. Time almost seemed to stand still as I considered all the permutations, like a chess player thinking two moves ahead.

James took the decision out of my hands, moving round behind me to cup my tits. He strummed my nipples with his thumbs, making me purr with desire. I leaned back against him, rubbing my satin-clad bum against his straining erection. He pulled my hair from the clip that held it in place, letting the chestnut waves tumble around my shoulders.

"OK, down you go." He pushed me to my knees as Rory stepped up to me, so that I ended with my lips a fraction away from his friend's dick. I could smell the hot, ripe scent of aroused man; felt juice gushing into my thong in response.

No further instructions were needed. I opened my mouth and swiped my tongue over his smooth, silky tip. The groan that action wrenched from him told me he needed more, and I set about swallowing him down, inch by inch.

"Oh, fuck, yeah," Rory muttered, losing the ability to form coherent words as his cock found a welcoming berth in my gullet.

With James still standing behind me, I couldn't tell what he might be doing. Already, I missed those big hands of his cradling my tits like they were the rugby balls he played with every weekend. Wrapped up in wringing every drop of sensation from Rory, I only half noticed James walk over to a table and pick something up. I only realized what he'd fetched when he came back to me and raised his arms. At that, I felt something cold pattering down on to my exposed tits. I let Rory's cock slip from my mouth as I looked down to see what adorned them. There'd been a couple of small jugs of cream on every table, for pouring over the strawberry parfait dessert; James must have brought one with him when he'd left the marquee, and now he was using it to decorate my flesh.

"Smooth it into your skin," he ordered. "I want to see you play with those big, messy tits while you suck Rory off."

I did as he ordered, getting off on the thrill of having this nicely spoken man address me in such filthy language. With my mouth plugged full of Rory's cock and my nipples jutting out from between my fingers, hard and yearning to be sucked, I must have looked totally submissive. I didn't care; when the alternative was standing in that airless marquee, listening to the best man tell off-colour jokes about people I didn't even know, I'd have done anything James demanded of me.

When I glanced up again, James had his hand wrapped round his shaft once, tugging it with short, aggressive motions. His eyes were half closed; I didn't think he'd mind if I snaked one hand under the too-short hem of my dress and stroked my pussy through my soaking thong.

The door handle rattling brought us all back to the reality of our surroundings. "You in there, Maureen?" called a voice from out in the corridor.

We froze in an erotic tableau: Rory's dick still halfway down my throat, James paused in mid-wank. How would we explain what we'd been doing if we were discovered? For the two rugby boys, it would no doubt become the stuff of legend, a tale to be recalled and relived on boozy nights out, but I'd never be able to work for the agency again.

No one came in. Whoever stood on the other side of the door, having received no answer, had clearly gone in search of their colleague elsewhere.

"That was close," James observed.

"Not as close as I am," Rory replied. With that, he caught a hank of my hair in his big fist, holding my hand steady so he could really thrust hard into my mouth. Until that moment, I'd never thought that the fear of being caught in the act could be an aphrodisiac, but it seemed we were all more turned on than before. For James and me, our self-pleasuring became a race to the finish line, while Rory plunged ever deeper between my lips.

In the moment before James came, I looked up to see him aiming his cock towards my tits, unable to resist the temptation of shooting his load all over their contours. I had the thin strip of my thong pushed to one side now, and two fingers buried deep in my channel. The slightest friction on my clit and I would come, but I wanted to time the moment to coincide with James's climax.

Nothing mattered now – not the hideous uniform dress that had brought me to this point, not the possibility of the speeches ending with me still absent from my post. Rory bellowed, and almost before I had time to react, my mouth was filling with thick spunk. He came with the force of a champagne cork bursting from a bottle. Anything I couldn't swallow dripped from my lips to join the cream on my tits. In moments, James was adding to the mix, adorning my tits with pearly droplets of come. I rubbed it all in, not caring what kind of spectacle I presented as my cunt convulsed around my fingers and I reached my own peak.

Together, Rory and James helped me to my feet, holding me till I felt steady enough to stand unaided. "Thank you so much," James murmured in my ear. Thoughtfully, he used a handkerchief to wipe as much of the creamy goo from my tits as he could, though I knew I'd have traces of both men on my skin for the rest of the day.

When I finally made it back into the marquee, I knew I looked a mess, with my hair awry and my uniform buttoned up haphazardly, but I didn't care. I had the phone numbers of two hot men tucked in my handbag and an offer of waitressing work at a forthcoming rugby club function, which I'd accepted gratefully.

"Will I need to bring a uniform?" I asked.

"Oh, we'll sort something out for you," Rory replied. His wicked grin told me they'd have something rather naughty planned for me to wear. For these two, I'd be prepared to squeeze myself into anything, because I knew the real fun wouldn't lie in putting it on, but taking it off.

Mammy's Boy

Lynn Lake

Talk of civil war hung heavy in the soft, sweet Southern air in the early spring of 1861. But Cotter Longsmith was having none of it. The effeminate eighteen-year-old just couldn't cotton to his father's and his older brother's endless discussion of the grievances the South had against the North, and how the only solution to the problem had been secession, with possible war to fully establish an independent country, the Confederate States of America.

So, like on so many other evenings, he looked to his aunt at one end of the long dining room table and meekly said, "I'd like to be excused, ma'am."

His aunt, filling in for his long-dead mother all these twelve years, bowed her head and replied, "You are ex—"

"Are you going to sign up, then, Cotter?" his brother, Cleveton, interrupted. "Are you going to join the Confederate forces in the upcoming great struggle against Yankee domination?"

Cotter was already halfway to his feet, anxious to get away from the depressing talk of conflict. Now, he glanced at his brother across the laden table, his father at the other end, half standing, half sitting, undecided, irresolute; as usual. "I-I don't know," he responded honestly, if frustratingly. "Let's hope . . . it doesn't come to bloodshed."

"Bah!" Cleveton bellowed, throwing down his napkin. "There is no other way the situation can be decided." He pointed a long, accusatory finger at his younger brother. "And *you* will have to decide."

Cotter nodded and got fully to his feet. He started to walk away from the table. Until now his father stopped him.

"Just where are you off to, Cotter?" the old man enquired. "You always seem to bolt down your supper and venture forth somewhere."

Cotter looked at his father. How could he tell the old man that he wanted to flee the destructive talk of war, but, more importantly, that he wanted to visit his black mammy down in the slave cabins at the bottom of the plantation? He couldn't tell his father any such thing, of course. So, he said, "I want to check on the horses, Father. One of the mares is about to foal. And I want to see how the planting is going on the eastern acreage."

He did have a love for animals and the land. And his father couldn't begrudge him that. More than God's creatures and creation, however, Cotter had an abiding love for his mammy, Teulah, who had nursed and raised him as a baby and small child when his sickly mother was incapable of doing so.

"You may go then."

Cotter hurried out of the dining room, down the long hallway, out the massive front door of the colonnaded white house. It was just beginning to get dark, stars twinkling to life in the velvet sky. Cotter could smell the magnolias and hyacinths, as he hustled around to the back of the plantation mansion and then across the long, green lawn that led to the slave cabins down by the creek.

There were ten such shacks, some small, some larger, built of grey, second-hand plank-wood. They were well tended by the inhabitants, however, with gardens in back of most of them.

Cotter went directly to the small cabin at the end of the row, then listened anxiously at the weather-beaten, leather-hinged door. He could hear children's voices inside, laughter. His blood pounded in his veins, perspiration prickling his high forehead despite the relative cool of the approaching night. He glanced back at the mansion, up at the full moon, then knocked on the door.

The gaiety instantly ceased inside. "Who's there?" a young woman called out. The children giggled.

But the young woman and the children were immediately hushed by a stronger, deeper voice. "Come inside," this voice invited.

Cotter unhasped the door and pulled it open with a loud creak, stepped into the cabin.

Teulah was seated on a stool in the middle of the small room, six or seven young children gathered around her at her feet, sitting on the dirt floor. The young woman, Bellah, leaned against a wall. Everyone stared at the white man, as he entered the shack.

"I-I'd like to speak to Teulah – alone," Cotter said.

The children giggled again, clapping their hands to their mouths, their eyes bugging. Bellah pushed away from the wall and sauntered over to Cotter, her long arms swinging and broad hips swaying, her taut, young breasts jiggling in her tight-fitting blue cotton dress. "Maybe you want to 'talk' to me for a change, huh, young Mr Longsmith?" She licked her full lips with her bright-pink tongue, her dark eyes openly surveying Cotter's lean body.

"You hush now," Teulah scolded, getting heavily to her feet. "You come back here, Mr Longsmith, where we can talk proper." She gestured towards the rear of the cabin.

She was a large woman, heavy-breasted, with a round face and broad nose, thick lips and deep brown eyes. Her skin was the colour of molasses, as smooth and warm as the Southern air. She was wearing a white cotton dress that moulded to her voluptuous curves, and a white kerchief covered her dark, kinky hair.

Cotter eagerly followed after the woman's wide, shuddering buttocks, into the one other room in the cabin, in back. Where he had spent so much time with his mammy, as an adult.

There were two cots in the tiny backroom. A single candle flickered on a rickety table. Teulah sat down on the edge of one of the cots, making it sag badly. "You come closer to your mammy now," she said to Cotter, extending a large, dark hand. A warm smile broke across her gleaming face, her eyes shining, as Cotter stumbled forward, his white breeches with a bulging erection.

Teulah gripped his narrow waist with both hands and hugged the young man to her face. She could feel his beating cock against her cheek, swelling and throbbing. She drew her head back and expertly and firmly unbuttoned his breeches and pulled them down. Cotter's massive erection rose up into the air, surging with excitement, right in front of Teulah's beaming face.

"You *are* happy to see your mammy, aren't you? You've always been happy with me, haven't you?"

"Yes, Mammy!" Cotter gulped, feeling the woman's warm, spicy breath flood over his pulsating cock, her firm, warm hands on his bare hips.

Teulah brought her broad knees together and drew Cotter down over top of them, so that he was sitting on her knees, his pale-pink cock spearing out at her. Then she bounced the young man on her knees, setting his erection to bobbing.

Cotter grabbed onto Teulah's fleshy shoulders, tilting his blond head back with joy, his heavy balls bouncing off the woman's knees, his engorged cock bounding up and down to his mammy's motions. She could always make him feel so much better.

Teulah bounced him on her knees for a few minutes or so, until Cotter's cock started flinging pre-come from its gaping slit. Then she let go of his hips and pulled her dress down over her shoulders. Her enormous, dark breasts flopped out into the open, thick, purplish nipples jutting out as taut and upright as when she'd nursed Cotter all those years ago. He stared at his mammy's breasts and nipples, mesmerized as always, his mouth watering.

"Come to Mammy," Teulah encouraged him, taking Cotter's head in her hands and drawing his face down to her breasts. His plush, red lips instantly sought out a nipple, found it, engulfed it. Teulah sighed and shivered, as Cotter pulled urgently on her nipple with his mouth.

She cradled him in her arms like a baby, letting him nurse, letting his other hand find her other heavy breast and squeeze it, pinch her other engorged nipple. She had no milk to give him any more, but she still gave him all of her love – unconditionally. She had physical nourishment of another kind for "her boy" now. She stroked his fine hair, looking down into his pale blue eyes, feeling the hungry tug of his lips and heated knead of his hand on her sensitive breasts, all through her big body.

Cotter sucked eagerly on the rubbery black nipple filling his mouth, memories both wholesome and perverted flooding his mind and emblazoning his body. His cock jutted out almost straight into the air, his head and legs cradled by his mammy. He gasped and jumped in Teulah's arms with delight, when she reached around and firmly gripped his erection, stroked it.

Cotter worked his mammy's one abundant breast with his mouth, the other one with his hand, sucking nipple and part of tit, squeezing the overflowing flesh of the other tit. Flaming with passion unfit for a child, his mammy stroking his very adult erection with an unnatural mother's love. This was why he adored his mammy so, obtained from her the kind of twisted, true affection his own mother could never provide, and which he so desperately desired.

He exulted in Teulah's arms, getting his cock pulled. He gleefully bit into the woman's nipple.

She let out a cry and squeezed Cotter's cock, glaring down at the young man. "That's a bad boy," Teulah scolded. "Bite the teat that feeds you."

She indignantly humped her breasts out of his hand and mouth, then spilled Cotter out over her knees, so that he was lying face down across her legs, his bare buttocks showing. She looked at the twin, soft, pale mounds. Then she brought her beefy right arm up and smacked her wide palm down across Cotter's exposed buttocks.

He jerked across her knees, his cock pressed into her thick thighs spilling more pre-come; the erotic shock of his mammy's firm hand on his tender bottom thrilling him to the core. Teulah swatted his pampered behind gently but strictly, blushing the sweet young cheeks a vivid crimson. Cotter jumped each and every time her hand whacked his ass, little pain and much pleasure coursing through his body and leaking out of his cock. His mammy loved him enough to discipline him; something his own mother was too indifferent to ever do.

"You going to be a good boy now?" Teulah asked, dropping her wide, warm hand down on Cotter's heated, quivering butt cheeks and rubbing soothingly. "Give your mammy some pleasure?"

Cotter twisted his head up and looked at Teulah. He nodded eagerly, batting his long, fair eyelashes.

"Good boy."

Teulah lay back on the cot with a grunt, dragging Cotter over on top of her. He rode her vast body, cushioned by her enormous breasts, her ripened nipples poking his pink nipples, his hard cock pressing into her soft belly. He gathered her splayed breasts together and jumped his wet mouth from one nipple to the other, sucking, then washed his tongue over both glistening black protuberances at once. Teulah sighed and reached down and hiked up her dress, baring her furry pussy. Cotter yelped with joy as his cock sunk into the dense bush, submerging in the heated moistness beneath.

They stared at one another, love in their shining eyes. Cotter clasping his mammy's tits and shunting his pulsing cock along the dampened length of her pussy. Teulah gripping Cotter's reddened buttocks and kneading the sensitized flesh, pursing her wet, blue-black lips and kissing Cotter on his red lips.

Teulah spread her legs. Cotter thrust his cockhead through her thick pubic bush and wrinkled pussy lips. Teulah pushed down on his buttocks, embedding the young man's shaft inside her cunt.

They moaned, kissed, tangled their tongues together; mammy and her boy embracing as deeply as man and woman can. Cotter pumped his hips, stroking his cock back and forth in Teulah's pussy, revelling in the humid heat and satiny texture, awash in erotic emotion. Teulah dug her blunt fingernails into his thrusting butt cheeks and undulated up against him, making sure his long, hard cock plunged as deep as it could go into her shimmering pussy.

Cotter buried his face in between Teulah's breasts, pressing the pair up against his flaming cheeks, driving his cock faster and faster inside of his mammy. Teulah burrowed a pair of her fingers into Cotter's dilating pink asshole, locking her legs around the back of his knees and bucking in rhythm to his increasingly frantic motions.

The cot creaked and rocked, the pair groaning and gasping, the smacking of hot flesh resounding louder and louder in the small, sex-scented backroom. Not a sound came from the other room in the cabin. Not that Cotter or Teulah were hearing it, anyway. They were locked together, melded, bouncing as one in the throes of passion, the older woman and the young man, black and white, knowing no sexual boundaries.

Cotter jerked his head up out of Teulah's cleavage and hollered. Then he spasmed in his mammy's arms, against her massive body, his churning cock going off in her sucking pussy.

Ecstasy buffeted his body and burst out of his cock. Just as Teulah shuddered and screamed beneath him, her fingers biting into his ass and her pussy convulsing around his rupturing manhood. They joyfully came together as they always did as the climax to their coupling, lust and love and race intermingling in their hot, gushing bodily juices.

The war came as Cotter had feared – the war between the Southern and Northern states. His brother joined up immediately with the 1st Georgia brigade of the Confederate States Army. But Cotter had something else to attend to first – a final session with his beloved mammy, Teulah. The cabin rocked with their passionate cries and movements, more frenzied than ever.

Then Cotter stole a sum of money from his father's safe, and gave it to Teulah. Along with all of the knowledge he'd gathered about the underground railway which fleeing slaves used to travel to freedom. He couldn't stand his mammy being caught up in the turmoil of the war, the deprivation and devastation that was sure to follow.

He kissed her goodbye. She hugged him tight to her bosom.

Then he watched as Teulah and her entire family slipped out of the slave cabin and into the night, headed north, hopefully all the way to the Canadian border and true emancipation.

Only then did Cotter Longsmith don the grey uniform and gold braids of the Confederate Army, as an honourable Southern gentlemen. And a lovelorn mammy's boy. Like so many of his Dixie brethren.

A Large Brandy

Jeff Cott

On Secret Assignment Day, Brenda had a set routine. Her first task was to collect the parcel from the post office. This had to be on a day when Ted, her husband would be working late – so almost any day would qualify.

He was a self-employed printer and a full-time workaholic. On Ted's insistence, Brenda was a stay-at-home wife. She was also a secret plus size model, specializing in lingerie and club wear for the catalogues through an agency. She took her own pictures using Ted's top-of-the-range camera. On assignment days the spare bedroom became her studio.

The first-class holiday she was saving up for was just two more photo shoots away.

Once she'd reached her target, it would be time to confront Ted – he must take a month off work for the holiday or she would go alone.

In the spare room, Brenda opened the box carefully, enjoying this moment of anticipation. But the words "BABY DOLL DOMINATRIX UNIFORM" on the tissue paper protecting the outfit made her angry. Brenda replaced the lid.

She'd made it clear to her agent, Rupert, right from the start – nothing kinky.

Disappointment almost overwhelmed anger.

Rupert would have included a note with instructions. They'd never met, but he was sweet, his assignment notes were always encouraging and flattering.

Brenda fished the envelope out of the box and tore it open. He wouldn't be able to sweet-talk her this time.

But his first words made her smile: "Don't look like that,

Bren, just read on. This is a triple pay assignment. Now that I have your attention, you probably haven't even looked in the box yet. Do not be alarmed by what you find there, they're only props. Try on your costume, read the suggestions re the poses and give it some thought. By the way, I came up with the concept for this campaign and helped design your costume, which has been made to your exact size. Bren, trust me. I can't wait to see your pix."

She sat on the edge of the bed. It could do no harm to have a look. She removed the lid. The words on the tissue made her nervous but his words "triple pay assignment" plus reassurances helped to calm her.

She peeled aside the paper. In her mind's eye the outfit she'd expected had been all about zips and straps and tight leather. But the baby doll outfit was gorgeous and beautifully made. It was in stark black and white. The panties and the bra were in brilliant white, the sheer black nightie part had a touch-me shimmer to it and a sensual gossamer softness. Knee-high boots with ambitious heels, in soft candy twist black and white leather, completed the outfit.

Also in the box, her props – a gag, handcuffs, several skeins of coloured rope, a sea anemone like whip with the words "man flogger" emblazoned down the handle and an eye mask in soft leather matching the boots.

There was another envelope with a single word in Rupert's hand – "Scenario".

She opened it. The words "Baby Doll with Attitude" made her smile. "Think of a Frustrated Wife Empowered."

Rupert went on: "This costume combines the teasing femininity of the baby doll with the powerful sexuality of a dominatrix. Try it on. Get used to wearing it before you set up the photo shoot and adopt the Attitude. You will feel and look amazing. Don't make any changes to your make-up, (it's always perfect) and may I also suggest that you wear your hair up for this shoot?"

Ted wasn't keen on her hair being up so it didn't happen often even though she'd always thought it was her best style.

Brenda trusted Rupert's judgement.

She took a shower, thinking negative thoughts yet feeling positively excited.

In their bedroom, she dried her hair and pinned it up, enhancing it with a zebra-print scarf she'd had for years. It worked. She did her make-up with extra confidence thanks to Rupert's comment and finally put on a special perfume, not just Ted's favourite but hers too.

In the silent privacy of her own home, she walked naked and confident to the spare bedroom.

If the panties had seemed at first to be the most innocent item in the ensemble they were far from it. Brenda looked in the mirror and almost took them off there and then – white gossamer revealing her dark pubic hair. But she put the bra on anyway and although the push and thrust effect on her breasts was exactly as expected she felt . . . comfortable.

She put the eye mask on next. Not only did it make her look different, it made her feel different so now it wasn't Brenda she saw in the mirror.

The black gossamer of the nightie tumbled off her breasts perfectly but was cut at a wicked length – sometimes covering, sometimes not covering her panties, every movement no matter how small, flirtatious.

The heels were a little higher than she was used to but there was no doubt at all that she could walk in these boots.

As she made her way downstairs and walked around the house, confidence grew.

Rupert's words echoed. "Think . . . Frustrated Wife Empowered."

She wasn't frustrated with Ted. He was as lusty as ever although he was more strip than tease. She loved him more than ever but . . . despite plentiful sex only a random percentage of it satisfied her.

She made herself a four-in-the-morning coffee even though it was early afternoon and dusk was falling outside. Sitting at the breakfast bar, the challenge of the photo shoot loomed ahead and excited her . . . as did the thought of the distant holiday.

The tranquillity was spiked by the sound of Ted's car crunching up the drive. Heart racing, she was caught in the fight or flight moment. Flight would mean running up the stairs in high-heeled boots, getting out of costume and then back downstairs again dressed and normal. Fight would mean . . .

Too late, his shape filled the frosted glass of the front door as the key slid in the lock. She stood with her legs apart, hands on hips and her heart fight ready.

"Brenda?" He stood in the doorway amazed, taking in her outfit.

The question mark was good, giving her something to work with.

"Brenda is out. She won't be back until later, Ted, much later."

"Well who d'you think you are then?" His boyish smirk more often than not endearing now irritated her as he ogled her from boots to bra. When his eyes eventually found hers she said, cold and slow, "I think I'm the Baby Doll Dominatrix. My name is Brandy and from now on it's up to you, Ted. I can be from my heaven or I can be from your hell."

He blinked several times then turned away busying himself closing the door, hanging up his coat and keys as usual. "The computer's down at work," he said, seemingly surprised to find her still there.

"It might as well be down here, Ted, because you're going to be far too busy for any computer nonsense." The significant deep breath she took lit his eyes for a moment, but then he said, "Bren, if I could just . . ."

She shook her head slow and sure. "I thought I told you, Bren is out. I want you to strip to your underpants right there where you stand, Ted. Just to please Brandy. Brenda will never know."

His mouth gaped, an uncharacteristic indecision clearly visible.

She held firm. Those words of his, "If I could just . . ." had written off many an evening and weekend. "If I could just print this order"; 'If I could just deliver this order"; "If I could just finish these accounts . . ."

It was no wonder they'd never had a holiday.

Yet he began to undress, to obey. When eventually down to his pants, his erection pleased her. For once in their marriage she looked at his bulge without shy haste, with lingering expectation.

Encouraged by her look, he took half a step forward. Ted was more than capable of taking her right there on the hallway floor if she let him . . . *if she let him* . . . the words were exotic and delicious.

A single "tut" stopped him.

"Ted, first you're going to take a shower. When you think you are worthy of me you are going to report in the spare room wearing your blue swimming trunks."

They stared each other down but it was Ted who blinked first. He made for the stairs.

Brandy let him get halfway up. "If I hear so much as a beep out of that computer, Ted, I'm going to spank you. I will enjoy it. You won't."

He paused a moment before continuing.

Once Ted was safely upstairs with the shower running, she walked to the hall mirror and saw only Brandy; there was no reflection of the Brenda chaos going on inside her. And for all the provocative tease of the baby doll – it was the eye mask she loved most.

Ted's reaction to her outfit had been wonderful, but what was she going to do with him now?

Brandy knew the answer. The blue swimming trunks she'd ordered him to wear . . . *ordered him to wear* . . . the words were hypnotic, unreal . . . were more to punish him than to please her.

Upstairs, she fished the trunks out of the drawer and put them on the bed knowing he'd never find them on his own.

In the spare room, she cleared away the tissue paper and the box, but arranged all the accessories on the single bed. She knew nothing about tying someone up so the handcuffs would be useful. She didn't even know what position she wanted him in.

As if to contradict her, memory instantly supplied an image from childhood. It had been in an encyclopaedia. A mere mortal, having displeased the gods, had been tied to a tree with his hands above his head to await his fate. He was beautiful. His robes had been torn to shreds revealing a loincloth, which to her schoolgirl eye had a mysterious beauty tempting her to touch and discover.

The shower stopped. Brenda heard him padding off to their bedroom, sparking her nerves. Where to sit? Where to stand? She sat on the edge of the bed, crossed her legs, made sure the gorgeous bra was in full view and waited.

As thoughts of backing out threatened to form rain clouds across her fantasy sky she remembered that Ted had already accepted that "Brenda" had gone out and he was in the hands of another woman. His erection signed and sealed the deal. And she loved the fact that he had gone along with all this – so far.

He entered the spare bedroom tentative yet proud. The string of the trunks held his penis upright with its head held high above the cut. It had been a long while since he'd worn them, even in the bedroom.

She wanted to kiss him as normal, she wanted his kiss as normal, but even more she wanted to be able to say, "Brenda tells me you're quite the handy man."

He nodded.

"Now, Ted, if I wanted you against the door with your hands cuffed together and tied up above your head, how would I go about that?"

He looked thoughtful for a moment then left the room returning with a handful of his ties. Saying nothing he knotted one in the middle then flipped the knot over the top of the door making sure the knot was on the outside before he shut the door. The two halves of the tie dangled from the top of the closed door.

She nodded approval, smiling. "Come here."

As he walked towards her with his hands held out ready for the cuffs something told her this was all too easy and she knew those wonderful brown eyes so well . . .

She reached for the flogger not the handcuffs and, as he approached, flicked it at him. Although she had never used a whip before in her life, it lashed across his thighs with a satisfying swish-wish sound. It stopped him in his tracks, the mischief in his eyes replaced by surprise.

She stared him down. He would have overpowered her and she'd have been the one in handcuffs. "Naughty," she said, quietly putting the flogger between her legs provocatively so it stood upright and threatening. She cuffed his hands in front, refusing to meet his gaze, hoping that raw determination alone showed in hers. This gave her the rare opportunity to stare at his captive penis.

She locked the cuffs and hid the key deep in her cleavage in true Hollywood style. Not trusting herself to speak in case doubts and nerves leaked into her voice, she gestured him away towards the door. There were lash marks on his thighs. A little higher and she would have hit his penis. But then she found her voice or it found her. "Stop!" It chilled even her and stopped him instantly. She flicked the whip at his backside and although it twitched his buttock the range was wrong. "Take a half-step back, for me please, Ted."

He did it! He did it! A devil told her to give him six and from the first lash she knew the range was perfect, three on each side. The pink lines she'd inflicted were wonderful.

Her mind was racing – there was no going back from here. She had so many choices, so many things to achieve in this one afternoon.

"Thank you, Ted. Now go to the door and raise your arms above your head."

He obeyed standing with his back against the door. His eyes revealed a faint uncertainty, but he raised his hands submissively and didn't resist when she tied them up.

In the process, she made sure her breasts touched him at every opportunity, knowing that all he wanted, moment on building moment, was for her to touch his captive penis. This must be something new for him – wanting and not getting.

When she stepped back and took in her "prisoner", he wasn't the romanticized mortal in her girlhood picture, he was still Ted and as gorgeous as ever, but the sense of power she felt just by seeing him helpless and available made her feel hornier than she'd ever felt.

The man in her girlhood picture had his ankles and thighs tied and she relished the prospect of doing this, especially as the thigh rope had been positioned only a little below the loincloth.

Ted made no protest, not even when she pulled the rope tight. The only protest came when the back of her hand "accidentally" brushed the head of his penis. He squirmed and cried out loud a strange sounding mix of pain and pleasure, frustration and ecstasy.

"Don't come," she ordered.

Hands on hips, she admired her work then turned and walked slowly to the bed, loving the knowledge that his eyes were on her, wanting her. She bent unnecessarily to pick up the gag from the bed, the panties stretching tight over her butt.

He eyed the gag dubiously as she approached. It was a black ball on a bright red strap. "I think you're going to need this," she said quietly.

He shook his head, the first sign of dissent.

It made her nervous, uncertain what to do, unwilling to force it into his mouth and not wanting to start a battle she was likely to lose. She stood provocatively with the gag dangling from her fingertip. "Here's the deal. You give this a try and in return I will touch your dick."

He nodded. An idea came to her and she wished it hadn't. Unsure of herself but with slow and deliberate movements, she opened her mouth wide and put the gag in. It wasn't easy. The ball held her jaws apart so there was no possibility of conversation. It was a strange feeling.

With the gag in her mouth, she "kissed" him hard and urgent, the ball pressing against his lips and his teeth until he had to let it in.

Their lips, though stretched gaping wide and tight, met.

The smallest movement or micro pressure between them produced an erotic morsel, delicious but making her hunger for another and another. Ted responded with unexpected subtlety and exquisite tenderness as the kiss passed back and forth. His dick rubbed against her with delicious accuracy.

With a slow strong pressure, she transferred the ball all the way into his mouth and he cooperated. Brandy withdrew, buckling the straps behind his head. The surreal kiss was over and even though the gag looked ugly there was a kind of beauty in his willing vulnerability.

Breathless, she had to step away. Her lips, now free, felt sensitized and pleasure ripe.

Kneeling, she kissed the head of his dick. Ted writhed in pleasure, bucking against the restraints, but she had hold of his hips, keeping him under control, as she kissed him just as if she was kissing his lips, pressing his dick back against him until at last she pulled down the trunks a little and took him between her lips, starting to fuck him slowly. He seized, became motionless. At the last possible moment, she withdrew, left him hanging on the edge.

"Don't dare come until you're told." She pulled the trunks back up and his squirm was delightful.

She sat on the edge of the bed, gazing at him, aware that she was panting and of him watching the rise and fall of her breasts. She felt giddy.

His eyes were full of her and what she felt.

Having regained composure, she picked up the flogger and returned standing with hands on hips.

"There are five things you need to know." The whip swished across his chest. "One – Brenda is a highly successful Plus Size model." He looked horrified. The next stroke lashed over his nipples. "Two – she has earned enough money for a first-class holiday." The next raked over his belly. "Three – you are going to take a month off work and take her away." He watched in anticipation as she changed position slightly for the next stroke. Logically, his penis ought to be the next target, but the strands of the flogger flashed across his thighs and for the first time he flinched. "Four – in future, whenever you have sex with her, you are going to make sure she's ready to take her pleasure before you take yours." She paused, taking in the pink lines marking his body, and saw in his eyes a flinty respect. "Five." With no great force but a delightful swish-wish the whip kissed the top of his dick. "Ted, you are now about to come."

Brandy released his ankles and then the tie at the top of the door. He lowered his hands in short-lived relief. "Get on the bed," she shouted, whipping him randomly.

His thighs were still bound so with an awkward hobbled gait he made it to the bed, but not before she'd had a chance to decorate his backside further with the flogger. She was Brandy entirely.

He lay on his back.

"Hands above!"

He obeyed.

"Keep them there, else . . ." She whipped his thighs again, dangerously close to the bulge of the trunks. With quick urgent movements, she found scissors in the drawer by the bedside and hacked at the string until it gave. His dick broke free, mean and magnificent. It might not be the biggest in the world but it fitted her exactly and once inside he could make it tingle her brain and talk to her entire nervous system – when he wasn't in a hurry.

She stood at the foot of the bed stripping off the baby doll dominatrix uniform. Her only fear was that, out of uniform, she might revert to Brenda.

Taking no chances, she kept the boots and the mask on. With the key to the cuffs safely on the bedside table, she released him from the gag. A warning finger threatened him into silence. Ted coughed and spluttered. She wiped his mouth tenderly with a tissue.

"Open your legs." These were words she'd never expected to say to Ted and it was clear that Brandy had not left the building.

Brandy knelt between his legs. She took in the faint pulse-driven movement of his cock, the lash marks on his skin, his sit-up-and-beg nipples, the evidence of the gag on his face, the kiss-me-kiss-me fullness of his lips – but in the devilment of the moment Brandy thought, *No I'm not going to get on-board and fuck you, Mr Always-in-a-hurry*. Instead, she pretended to notice the clock and with great drama declared, "Look at the time! Brenda will be back any minute!" She grabbed hold of his dick and wanked him crudely fast and dry at first, but, within moments, her hand was hot, wet and silk smooth as spasms of pleasure knotted his body and his voice.

"Got to dash," she said brightly, as if just off to the shops.

She left him, slamming the door behind and fled to their bedroom.

This is crazy, Brenda thought. *It's never going to work.* "Fucking hell, Brandy, what've you landed me with?"

She washed her hands, dressed frantically in big black Brenda knickers, grey jogger pants and a baggy T-shirt she knew for sure would find her almost painfully aroused nipples with every innocent movement. And she let her hair down.

So now Brenda was ready.

The house was silent except for a zigzag bass thump, which she slowly came to realize was her heart.

As the beat settled, the silence intensified. This was taking too long.

After all the excitement – what if something had happened?

She opened the spare bedroom door and Ted was standing there – naked, still erect, the gag in his mouth and his hands cuffed in front.

As Brenda, she tried her best to sound shocked. "Ted, my

darling, who did this?" She rushed forward as if to rescue him but the cuffs weren't locked and the next thing she knew she was being kiss-gagged hard fast and strong, as he rammed it into her mouth and buckled it behind.

He hugged her viciously with one arm as the other hand bunched her knickers and pulled them up inside her. And then in a dizzy whirl he sat on the bed, forced her over his knee, the grip he had on her knickers controlling her whilst the other hand spanked her. The smacking sound filled the bedroom, as her cheeks went from warm to hot then stinging. Just as it seemed he would never stop, he yanked her up onto her feet, making her stand in front of him while he handcuffed her hands behind.

He forced her knickers and joggers down to her knees, grabbed her buttocks and pulled her to him, burying his face between her legs, mouth hungry for her, kissing her violently with overwhelming strength and unbridled passion.

He had one arm round her waist keeping her still whilst the other, in stark contrast, was stroking the heat of her buttocks with exquisite tenderness. When his tongue entered her, exploring and marauding, she began to tremble uncontrollably. Her legs lost all strength. When he found her clitoris, the real torture began and the sensation was so intense she tried instinctively to pull away, but he gripped her even harder as if there was no limit to his strength. He had his teeth pressed against her clit and relented only to make way for his tongue, which licked and flicked and wanked her without mercy. The gag couldn't stop an unfamiliar earthy groan from escaping.

The room spun as he stood, scooping her up in his arms, turned and – plus size or not – literally threw her onto the bed. She landed on her back, the metal of the cuffs hurting her wrists but it didn't matter, in the adrenalin moment, nothing mattered. He undid the gag and grabbed the scissors.

Spluttering, panting and helpless, she could only watch as he cut and ripped the T-shirt off her breasts. He got on the bed, without any sign that his violence was subsiding, and straddled her, hugging her legs together as he flopped on top. He buried his face in her breasts and squeezed them together. If he could have got both nipples in his mouth at the same time he would have, but one at a time was more than she could bear, as he kissed, sucked and teased them ruthlessly. Then he sat up on her, his eyes blazing. Now he too was panting and seemingly caught in a flash of indecision as if unlimited passion had suddenly found a limit. She wanted no limits and, in a whisper, said, "Don't stop. You can slap me, anything. Don't stop yet."

He slapped her breasts in turn. She could see in his eyes the pleasure from watching her breasts jiggle and bounce after each slap. His lust for her body was matched only by her anticipation of the fucking she craved. She closed her eyes in abandon, wanting everything, everything. This was another Ted, wild and untamed.

He got off the bed, but only to yank off her joggers and knickers, smiling on discovering that she was still wearing the boots.

She subtly opened her legs, but he pulled them apart. He got back on the bed and was inside her with one confident thrust. If anything his violence seemed to be growing, peppering specks of curried fear into her.

His kiss with its you-have-no-choice insistence was the dirtiest loveliest thing she'd ever experienced. She could taste the salt of herself from his mouth. The taste slashed a black line across her saffron erotic sky but only briefly. The taste was laced with him too, the taste was theirs alone, unique.

He had hold of her head and was kissing her so hard and fucking her so fast she felt guilty for thinking, *This is going to end too soon.* And the guilt was justified because it didn't end. In fact it began to seem as if it would never end. He was slowing, almost imperceptibly, and, as tenderness grew, she became aware of everything that had happened that afternoon – just an afternoon? It seemed like they'd had a month of love all together, experiences flashing like images ripped across an express train's window.

But he'd stopped now. His presence inside her was undeniable. All urgency had gone. She closed her eyes, everything mixing and merging, the discomfort of the handcuffs behind her, the warmth from the spanking, the pleasurable awareness of her breasts and the tickle-prickle of an itch between her legs – something demanding her attention but which she could do nothing about. She opened her eyes. He was waiting. Ted was waiting.

They were on a train together waiting in a station, birds

singing outside, a breeze whispering through the trees – at first. The whisper grew to a shout. On the opposite track an express train gorged its way through the peace.

It uprooted her out of the calm and she was on it, mind, body and soul clinging together in the rush. She realized, this was her body, it was all of her, all together . . .

A beautiful parcel arrived, wrapped onion tight but exquisitely unravelling. Slow motion pleasure dappled even the fastest clouds powering across her personal sky as the train hit warp speed.

Afterwards she thought of it as an explosion in a paint factory, every separate colour a feeling – every mix and merge a new feeling travelling from pastel to intense.

He withdrew and rolled her onto her side to release the handcuffs. Ted chucked them on the floor, coaxing her onto her back again.

The fire had gone. His eyes were now their usual burnt brown shade, but adoration stroked her.

Brenda could only guess what her eyes must be revealing – Viking raider? Greek god? Lord and master?

He was on top of her, hands either side. "Bren, there's no way I can take a month off work, the business would sink."

The everyday ordinariness of his voice sparked her anger.

"But for starters perhaps a long weekend?"

"Ted, you're not taking this seriously."

He kissed her quiet. "Longer term I can take on an apprentice, ease the load."

"But—"

He tried to kiss the "but" off her lips but she broke free, twisting and tumbling him off her.

"Ted, is this your best effort? A 'perhaps' long weekend?" She was pacing, anger in her belly, naked except for the boots, and without even knowing it was putting her hair up. He watched her intently.

"We've travelled all this way through years and years of no holiday at all to arrive at a 'perhaps'?"

"Bren, listen, if I could just explain . . ."

"You can just get your arse off that bed right now, Mr Workaholic. We've got a photo shoot to do. There are two incomes coming into this house from this day forward so get used to the idea of taking on extra staff. 'Perhaps'? 'Longer term'? Pah!"

Brenda stormed off into their bedroom intent on getting the baby doll back on. She needn't have worried – once the mask was on, Brandy knew everything was going to be OK.

Cum Bumps

Michael Bracken

Continuous shoulder rumble strips are intended to alert automobile drivers that they have drifted off the road and onto the shoulder, but my friends and I have another name for them: cum bumps. Letting the passenger side of your car drift onto the shoulder and letting your tires bounce over continuous shoulder rumble strips at just the right speed turns the entire vehicle into a giant vibrator that makes your lady parts tingle with delight.

I had just left my boyfriend's house late one Saturday night, frustrated once again by his inability to finish what he started, and was taking advantage of the rumble strips on a long stretch of rural highway, when I saw lights flashing in my rear-view mirror. By then, I was so close to orgasm that I wasn't about to stop. I couldn't pretend I didn't know a Texas Highway Patrol vehicle was tailing me, but I put another five miles on my car's odometer before the rhythmic shuddering of my vehicular vibrator finally sent me over the edge. My breath caught, my eyes closed for a moment, and my entire body shuddered as orgasm erupted within me.

I removed my foot from the accelerator, let my car drift completely onto the shoulder, and slowed to a stop. The highway patrol vehicle stopped behind me, and the trooper was out of his car before I had even shifted mine into park. I had left my boyfriend's place in such a rush that I had not put on my bra and it lay on the passenger seat with my purse. Though I had managed to fasten a few of the buttons, my white blouse was so thin I might as well have not been wearing it. Too late to alter my appearance, I leaned back against the headrest and pressed the button to lower the side window.

"Do you have any idea how far I—?" The trooper was all business until he flashed his light into my car, saw me flushed and having trouble catching my breath. "Ma'am," he asked, "are you OK?"

I'd just had an orgasm but I wasn't about to tell the trooper that. I did sputter, "I . . . I'm . . . fine."

All I could see was the tan, two-pocket uniform shirt stretched across his broad chest, the badge above his left breast pocket, and the nametag above the right pocket that read "Jones". He said, "I can call the EMTs for you."

Rushed to the hospital for an orgasm? Perish the thought. "I'll . . . be fine . . . in a . . . moment."

He pushed back his straw cowboy hat as he squatted next to my car. "Ma'am," he repeated as he rested his left hand on the open window. He wore a watch on his left wrist but no jewelry on his hand. "You don't look well. Let me call for help."

I took a deep breath and then another. "There's no need," I said. "I'm feeling better already."

He examined me closely and this time I think he noticed the thinness of my blouse and my lack of a bra. "You drove onto the shoulder several miles back," he said. "Didn't you feel the rumble strips?"

"That's what that was?" I asked as if I were completely clueless. "I thought I had a tire going flat. I thought I could make it home without stopping."

Trooper Jones finally asked for my driver's license and proof of insurance, and he carried them back to his car. By the time he returned, I had recovered from the post-orgasmic state I'd been in when he first approached my car.

"Ms Lynne," he said as he returned my paperwork. "I'm going to let you off with a warning. You need to keep your car in its lane at all times."

"Yes, sir," I said.

"I'm still worried about you, though. If you don't mind, I'm going to follow you to make sure you get home OK."

We had stopped near the edge of town, less than three miles from my house, and he followed me home. Once I had parked my car in the driveway, I grabbed my things and climbed out. Trooper Jones had stopped on the street at the end of the driveway and called through his open window, "Are you certain you'll be OK?"

"I'll be fine," I assured him. I'd had plenty of orgasms during my lifetime and had never had any negative consequences from them. I said, "This isn't the first time something like this has happened. I know what causes it and I know what to do about it."

"Would you mind if I checked on you later?"

I considered him for a moment, even though all I could see through his open car window were the epaulets on his uniform shirt shoulders and a ruggedly handsome face displaying real concern for my well-being.

"I wouldn't mind a bit."

"My shift ends in an hour," Trooper Jones said. "I could swing by shortly after that. That wouldn't be too late, would it?"

"I'll still be awake," I assured him.

Trooper Jones waited until I was inside my house before he pulled away, and he didn't return until almost two hours later. I had almost given up on him by then, ready to put him in the same category as my underperforming boyfriend.

I opened the front door as soon as the bell rang and found Trooper Jones standing on my porch. For the first time since he had pulled me over earlier that evening, I could see all of him at once and I took a moment to soak in the view, starting with the straw cowboy hat and traveling all the way down to the round-toed black cowboy boots and back up again. A lot of broad-shouldered, thick-chested, narrow-waisted, tight-assed Texan was packed into his uniform.

The tan two-pocket shirt was tucked into pants with a blue stripe and red piping on each outside seam. The epaulets on the short-sleeve shirt matched the pattern on the pants, and a primarily red shoulder patch on each sleeve featured the Texas Highway Patrol crest. A star-in-a-wheel badge over his left shirt pocket, nametag over his right shirt pocket, and a silver-buckled, black Clarino gun belt with Clarino holster and several pouches holding handcuffs and other gear completed the uniform.

I knew Trooper Jones was doing some examining in return because I could see the activity below his belt when his uniform trousers started to bulge. I still wore the blouse I'd had on when he pulled me over, but now it was completely unbuttoned, and I wore nothing else but black silk bikini panties.

"I just stopped by to check on you like I said I would, Ms Lynne," he said.

"Debbie," I said.

"I'm sorry I'm later than I thought I would be. I pulled over a drunk just before quitting time and knew I had to get him off the road before he hurt someone."

"You almost missed me," I said as I stretched, the motion causing my breasts to rise. "I was just about to turn in."

"Yes, ma'am," Trooper Jones said. Try as he might to maintain eye contact, he couldn't. He glanced at my chest and I was pretty sure I had him. He continued, "I can see that, ma'am. I'm sorry to bother you, but I've been worried, thinking maybe I should have called the EMTs."

"I'm fine," I said. I stepped back from the door and said, "Why don't you come in and let me explain everything."

Trooper Jones removed his straw cowboy hat and held it in one hand as he crossed the threshold into the foyer and stood next to the coat tree.

Once he was inside with the door closed behind him, I told Trooper Jones I didn't have a medical condition he needed to worry about, and I explained – without mentioning my inadequate boyfriend's failure to satisfy me earlier that evening – why I had been driving along the continuous shoulder rumble strips.

Trooper Jones laughed. "Apparently, it worked."

"It worked quite well," I said, "but that was more than two hours ago."

I shook my blouse off my shoulders, let it slide down my arms to my wrists and fall to the floor, giving him a good look at my stiff nipples and constricted areolae before I took the cowboy hat from his hand and hung it on the coat tree. Then I took hold of his wrists and guided his hands to my breasts. My breasts aren't small but his big hands completely engulfed them and my nipples pressed into his palms.

"Frisk me, officer," I said huskily. "You don't know what I might be hiding."

"You can't be hiding much," he replied. He slid his right hand around to my lower back and pulled me tight against him. I could feel the accessories on his belt press against me and I could feel the bulge in his pants doing the same. He moved his other hand around the back of my head, wrapped his thick fingers in my hair, and tilted my head back. Then he covered my mouth with his and kissed me long, deep and hard.

As his tongue slipped into my mouth, his right hand slipped under the waistband of my panties and his middle finger slid down the length of my ass crack. Before his finger could reach my tight little sphincter, I placed my palms flat against his chest and pushed him back.

"Don't you think you're a little overdressed to do a proper frisking?" I asked as I began unbuttoning his uniform shirt.

Trooper Jones needed no further encouragement and he quickly peeled off his uniform, revealing the throbbing thickness of his personal nightstick.

"Up against the wall," he commanded, as he spun me around and pushed me forward. I had to throw my hands up to catch myself and keep my face from smashing into the wall. He shoved one foot between my feet and kicked left and right, knocking my feet to either side as he spread my legs wide. "Feet back and spread 'em."

Then he frisked me. His thick fingers threaded through my hair. His large hands wrapped around me to cup my breasts and pinch my nipples. Then they worked their way past my waist, the curve of my hips, and the swell of my ass, down one leg and up the other, before he thrust a hand between my legs. Only the desire-dampened cotton panel of my silk panties separated his thumb from the tight bud of my sphincter and his fingers from the swollen lips of my pussy.

"I think I found something," Trooper Jones growled in my ear, as he pushed aside the crotch of my underwear and slipped his middle two fingers into my female opening.

I pushed back against his hand as he finger-fucked me, his thick fingers making a come-hither motion inside my pussy rather than the pistoning motion my boyfriend favored. I don't know how long he did that – a minute, maybe two – but it was driving me crazy and I told him so.

The Texas Highway Patrol trooper pulled his fingers from my

pussy and replaced them with his personal nightstick. His long, thick cock filled me in a way that my boyfriend's cock never had and I bit my bottom lip to keep from crying out with surprise and delight.

As he drew back and pushed forward, Trooper Jones reached around me. He slipped his hand inside my panties, cupped my pubic triangle in the palm of his hand, slipped the tip of his middle finger between my swollen labia, and stroked the tight bud of my clit in counter rhythm to the motion of his hips.

He fucked me hard and fast, and I knew I wouldn't need to drive for miles over continuous shoulder rumble strips to stimulate my lady parts when he finished with me.

I could barely support myself against the wall as his powerful thrusts slammed his cock into me again and again. My arms began to quiver as my orgasm drew near, and then I cried out when I came.

Though I continued to brace myself against the wall with one hand, I grabbed his wrist with the other and pulled his finger away from my overstimulated clit. My pussy spasmed around his cock as he continued fucking me and it wasn't long before he came, too, filling my spasming pussy with his ejaculate.

He collapsed against me and, because I wasn't able to support the weight of both of us with just one arm, I collapsed against the wall, sandwiched between the plasterboard and the police officer.

Trooper Jones's cock was still half erect when he pulled away and removed the pressure of his weight from me. I turned, leaned back against the wall, and looked up at him. "Do you treat all your suspects like this?"

"Only the ones who scam me out of a ticket."

"That was no scam," I assured him as I reached out and took his slick, semi-erect cock in my hand. "You're the one who thought I had a medical problem."

His cock, which had never gone completely flaccid, began to rise again as I stroked it, and I couldn't believe my luck. My boyfriend had always been "one and done" and was usually snoring within moments of finishing. Not Trooper Jones. He hooked his thumbs in the waistband of my panties and pulled them down to my knees. When he released them, they fell to the floor around my feet. Then he grabbed the cheeks of my ass and lifted me off the floor. As I wrapped my legs around his waist, I positioned the head of his cock against my slick slit. Then he lowered me until my pussy completely engulfed his erection.

I wrapped my hands around the back of his neck and rode him until we each came a second time, and I was surprised that the trooper could remain upright when all I wanted to do was melt after my second orgasm. My pussy clenched and unclenched, milking his rapidly softening cock until it finally slipped free.

I unwrapped my legs from his waist and Trooper Jones lowered me to the floor. As I leaned against his chest, I looked up and said, "I'm so glad you came to check on me."

"I'm glad I came, too," he replied, and we both knew what he meant.

Trooper Jones didn't stay long after that. We both dressed, though he had far more to put on than I did, and I walked him to the door. After he stepped onto the porch, he asked if he could check on me again another night.

I told him he could, but that next time I might resist arrest and he would be forced to use his handcuffs.

The Bar Code Challenge

Tabitha Kitten

This was my first Christmas working at Robinsons, a small supermarket located in the suburbs of town, which served the local community who didn't want to travel three miles to the nearest large superstore. I enjoyed working here and liked all of my colleagues, in particular my close friend Damon. There was always a lot of good-natured banter at work, and Stuart and Colin were unable to hold a conversation without it being laden with sexual innuendos. Since June they had been dropping hints about the Christmas party. Every Christmas Eve, once the supermarket closed for the festive holidays, there was a staff party. The doors were locked, food and alcohol consumed and then, once merry, they all played the Bar Code Challenge. I didn't know any of the game's details but it was obviously a good one because people were referring to it back in the summer.

The supermarket was going to close in a couple of hours for the Christmas holidays and I could detect a real frisson of excitement and not just because of the forthcoming festivities. Staff were smiling and singing and, in turn, I was glowing from anticipation although not sure why. I had no idea how the game was played or what would happen. I hoped it wasn't going to be a colossal anticlimax.

Ruby, the manageress, approached me and asked me to select items from the shop for the game. "There are nine of us here today so can you go and select two products from the confectionery aisle, two from the fruit and vegetable stands, two from household cleaning and three from dairy." She handed me a basket.

I could see some of my colleagues watching, with amusement

etched on their faces, as I stood looking at the supermarket's merchandise. I didn't actually know how the game was played and what products would be suitable so it was difficult to choose. Damon escorted me as I strolled around the aisles. I picked up a punnet of cherries and a bunch of bananas and saw his mouth twitch into a smile. He gave a low laugh when I selected a box of wooden clothes pegs and a large roll of cling film. At the next aisle he nodded approvingly when I chose a family-sized strawberry trifle, a carton of milk and a tub of raspberry yoghurt. Lastly, I picked up a packet of popping candy and carton of spreadable chocolate.

I returned the basket to Ruby. "What a brilliant choice," she said. "People will be pleased."

Impatiently, I waited until, finally, I heard Ruby shout, "Closing time." Colin and Stuart pulled down the shutters and locked the front doors. Now, it was time to party.

We all gathered in the large staff room. Food and alcohol were laid out on a table but I noticed people were drinking far more than they were eating, and that Damon kept passing me glasses of vodka.

"Are you looking forward to this?" Colin asked me.

"Yes, although I'm not sure what it's all about," I replied.

"You'll love it. Everybody does. But you'll need your phone though. It's always good to look back at the photos and videos when it's January and grey and cold outside. These pictures will warm the cockles of your heart," he laughed.

Ruby stood up. "Welcome, everybody, to this year's Bar Code Challenge." There was a loud cheer from everyone, including me. "We have a new member of staff this year, Grace," she said, as she smiled warmly at me, "so I will run through the rules of the game for Grace's benefit."

"There aren't any rules," said Colin.

Ruby laughed. "Well, not rules as such, I suppose. Anyway, Grace, welcome to the Bar Code Challenge."

"Thanks," I said, as expectant as the others.

"First of all, ladies and gentlemen, here are this year's products all selected by Grace." Ruby moved to a small table where the items I had chosen were displayed. "There will be four teams this year. Team one will be playing with household products and we have a roll of cling film and a pack of wooden clothes pegs."

"I don't want those," said the lady next to me, a tall, willowy brunette named Michelle. I felt a bit embarrassed, perhaps I hadn't chosen well and the cling film and clothes pegs weren't good enough.

Ruby pointed to more items on the table. "Team two will be our fruit and vegetable team and they will have bananas and a punnet of cherries." There was a loud cheer. "Now that's more like it," said Michelle. "I'd be happy with those." And, immediately, I felt relieved.

"Team three are playing with dairy items," said Ruby, "and we have a carton of milk, a rather large trifle and raspberry yoghurt."

"That will be so messy," said Colin. "I won't be clearing that lot up later."

"And, finally," continued Ruby, "team four will be representing confectionery with popping candy and chocolate."

"Now that would be fun," observed Michelle. "Fingers crossed I'm fruit and veg or confectionery."

Ruby produced two small boxes. "Now for the teams. As there are nine of us here today we will have three teams of two and one team of three. I have a box for gents and a box for ladies. Inside are the bar codes relating to this year's products. Select a bar code and attach it to your person."

I picked out a bar code and stuck it to my blouse. Ruby held up the scanner and zapped my bar code. There was the familiar bleeping and she declared, "Strawberry trifle." There was a cheer from everyone. We all had our bar codes scanned and found our team members. I discovered I was in the team of three along with Damon and Curtis, a large black guy employed as a shelf-stocker.

"Now we have our teams," said Ruby, "we can begin. Each team will take it in turns to make the most innovative use of their products and the best team will win. And, whilst they are 'in the act' as we like to say, an extra product will be added by the remaining players. Now, I think we will start with the fruit and veg team which is Connie and Stuart."

Everybody cheered as Connie and Stuart stepped into the

middle of the room. I still didn't fully understand what the game was about but, excitedly, I retrieved my phone from my handbag.

Connie sat on a chair. To my surprise, she rucked her skirt up to her hips to reveal pale pink panties and then began to unbutton her blouse.

I had always thought staff looked unattractive having to wear the supermarket's uniform of yellow shirt and brown trousers or brown skirt, but I had been mistaken. Connie looked really sexy with her skirt hitched up and her blouse unbuttoned. She smiled saucily as Stuart leaned over and lifted her breasts from the lacy cups of her bra. He massaged her pendulous orbs and tweaked the dark-brown nipples. I began to feel decidedly uncomfortable as I observed their sexual antics.

"Stuart, have you got one of the bananas in your pocket, or are you just pleased to see me?" she laughed.

"I'm always pleased to see you Connie. I'm rock hard," he replied.

Nervously, I looked around at everyone in the room, but they were all admiring Connie and Stuart. Nobody was embarrassed – clearly they had all done this before. Stuart reached down and, with a swift movement, removed Connie's panties so that they lay discarded on the floor. She opened her legs so that her pussy was on display, and I heard the clicking of cameras as numerous photographs were taken. I lifted my phone and noticed that my hand was shaking, but I also took a couple of snaps, transfixed by the way she casually revealed herself to her work colleagues.

Stuart knelt down between Connie's legs and began to rub her pussy vigorously, sliding two fingers into her depths. Shock reverberated through my body and I felt my cheeks redden as he worked his fingers quickly so that her juices began to pool around them. "And we have item number one," he said, as he picked up two cherries that were attached at the stems.

"They look like mini jiggle-balls," Connie giggled. "I could use them to tighten my pelvic floor."

"You're not to use the firm's produce for that sort of thing," Ruby chided with mock seriousness.

I watched amazed as Stuart pushed as many cherries as he could into Connie's wet hole. Moments later he sniggered. "Goddamn it, Connie, You've taken the whole punnet."

"They're only small and you don't get that many anyway," she pointed out.

Stuart bent over and placed his mouth at her entrance, and then, by using his finger and tongue, he started to pull the cherries back out. As he popped them out of her pussy he ate the fruit and spat the stone onto the floor. We cheered and counted as he devoured each one.

"I'm so glad they're cherries and not plums," Connie joked. "This size is more manageable."

"I'll just check I've got them all out," said Stuart. He inserted two fingers into Connie and slid his mouth over her clit. She raised her pelvis to allow him easier access and his fingers flashed in and out of her wet pussy. Secretly, I was urging her on, wanting to see what would happen. She started moaning and her breathing became ragged as Stuart finger-fucked her hard and kept his mouth clamped on her clit. With a scream, she shuddered and came. As we all gave a riotous round of applause, Stuart sat back and wiped his wet chin.

The atmosphere in the room was fun and light-hearted and I began to relax more, although it probably helped that Damon was still plying me with vodka. But, I had never indulged in any kind of sexual activity before where people just stood and watched me, or took photographs, and I felt a semblance of anxiety about being expected to perform for an audience.

"Where are those bananas going to go, Stuart?" Colin called out. "Are you going to make a fruit salad up there?"

"Good job I'm not allergic," replied Stuart as he stood and unzipped his trousers, letting them drop to his ankles. He pulled down his underpants and his cock sprang free. Hoisting Connie from her seat, he sat down and then pulled her onto his lap. Manoeuvring her by the hips, he positioned her so that his cock ploughed straight into her pussy. As he began to fuck her rhythmically, she unbuttoned his shirt.

"Right, I'm going to select the extra item," said Colin, as he disappeared into the store.

Connie unpeeled one of the bananas and flattened it against Stuart's chest and then began to eat it. When she had finished, Stuart rubbed a banana over her breasts and sucked and licked them, eating whilst still pumping his cock into her. She bounced wildly in his lap as she forced more banana down her cleavage for him to eat.

"I'm back," declared Colin, "and this is what I've fetched." He held up his hand and Connie shrieked in alarm. "Colin! You put that pineapple back at once!"

Colin gave a big beaming smile as he placed the pineapple down on the table. "Only kidding. Brought you this actually," he said and produced a punnet of blackberries from a carrier bag. Connie grabbed the fruit and squished them on Stuart's chest. The dark juice rolled down invitingly.

"If you get that on your uniform, it won't half stain," Ruby commented wryly.

As Stuart continued to pound Connie's pussy the pair of them smeared the other with banana and blackberries and ate it. "Quite a nice combination," announced Connie.

"Well, I've certainly had three of my five-a-day today," said Stuart. "And, now, Connie, you're going to get cream for your fruit." He held her tightly, and grunted and juddered as his load exploded inside her. As they sat panting, they received their second round of applause.

"Bravo," said Ruby. "That was a lovely use of fruit."

"Are you OK?" Damon whispered to me.

"I've never been watched before," I admitted, but as I spoke a thrill of excitement snaked down my spine.

"You'll be fine. Don't worry."

Ruby surveyed the staff. "Now which team is next . . . I think perhaps it ought to be the turn of confectionery. Up you get, Michelle and Tariq."

"Actually, I think I'll lie down," said Michelle. She clambered up onto a table. After removing her skirt and panties, she rolled them into a ball and used them as a makeshift pillow. Tariq dispensed with his trousers and underpants; he was already aroused, his erection standing proud, magnificent but almost menacing in the way it rose rigidly – thick, long and solid.

Michelle daubed the soft, spreadable chocolate over Tariq's brown cock, and then parted her legs whilst he ripped open the packet of popping candy. He sprinkled it onto Michelle's pussy and, immediately, we all heard the sound of the crystals exploding. She started to laugh. "Wow, that's so weird."

"You've got a popping pussy," chuckled Stuart. "That's brilliant."

"And they sell that stuff to kids," tutted Colin. "What a waste."

Tariq crouched over Michelle so that he was facing her feet and his cock waved tantalizingly above her mouth. He lowered his head in order to be able to lick her.

"Tariq, have you ever thought about shaving your bum hole?" queried Michelle.

He shrugged. "I'm Asian, we're hairy."

She wrapped her fingers around his shaft, holding it steady and then, inch by inch, she devoured it. Tariq moaned with pleasure. The room was filled with the sound of cameras clicking and Michelle and Tariq slurping.

"Don't you pair know how to eat quietly?" scolded Colin.

"Too much chocolate," complained Michelle as she sucked and licked with fervour.

Colin shook his head. "I never thought I'd see the day when a woman said she had too much chocolate."

Tariq worked his tongue into Michelle's pussy and the popping sounds became louder and more rapid . . . like the racing of my heart. I was desperate to see them both come.

"Tariq, that candy has turned your tongue blue," laughed Ruby.

"And Michelle's got a blue muff!" exclaimed Colin.

Stuart laughed uproariously. "Seriously, Michelle, your pussy's gone blue. Ha, ha, you look like a Smurf."

"Time for the extra product," said Colin, as he opened the carrier bag. "I picked up a sachet of sherbet." He opened the packet and handed it to Tariq, who dumped the whole contents onto Michelle's quim. A puff of fine powder floated in the air. Tariq took an almighty big lick and spluttered. "Sherbet's a bit fizzy," he wheezed.

I took several photos, but then just stood to watch the action as they sixty-nined each other, busy licking confectionery from each other's nether regions. Michelle took Tariq's cock deep into her wanton mouth, her saliva mingling with the chocolate as she lapped and sucked. He started to moan loudly whilst continuing to lick her powdered pussy. Suddenly, he convulsed and hot jets of spunk splashed over Michelle's chin, neck and the top of her blouse.

"Not quite what I meant when I asked for a pearl necklace for Christmas," she laughed.

When she sat up, I took a photograph of her mouth, which was covered in chocolate and Tariq's come.

"Oh, you messy cow," Ruby chided.

"My cock looks nice and clean," Tariq said admiringly.

Michelle sighed. "Whilst my pussy looks blue and white."

"We have a clean-up job in aisle three," shouted Colin. "Can a member of the cleaning staff make their way to aisle three immediately, but you'll need a big mop."

"You cheeky thing," cried Michelle.

"Time for another team," Ruby interjected, "before things turn nasty."

"I think it should be household products next," Damon said, as he winked at me and passed over yet another shot of vodka. I knew the warm sensation within wasn't from the alcohol; I was incredibly turned on and aroused. I had never seen my work colleagues like this before, so hot, so lustful and just going for it.

"OK. That's me and Ruby," said Colin. "Time to get this uniform off." He took off his shirt and then helped Ruby remove her blouse and bra. He picked up the packet of clothes pegs.

"And what do you think you're going to do with those?" she said, adopting an assumed air of haughtiness.

Colin laughed. "You know perfectly well that people buy these as nipple clamps. You can tell by looking at the customer whether they want the pegs for hanging up their washing outside or for nipple fun inside the bedroom." He rolled Ruby's nipples between his fingers, making them stiff, and then clamped a peg on each. She grimaced.

"Now it's my turn," she said, reaching for the spare pegs.

"Not a chance." Colin grinned. "OK. We have a roll of cling film to use. I might need some help with this." He unzipped his trousers and pulled them and his underpants down to his knees. He bent Ruby over a swivel chair, hitched up her skirt and pulled down her tights and knickers, which she wriggled out of after kicking off her shoes. Between them, Colin and Stuart used cling film to secure Ruby by her wrists and ankles to the swivel chair so that her legs were spread wide. Her pussy was delectably displayed, open and exposed, pink and swollen. Colin stood behind her, positioned himself, and then Ruby gasped as he lunged forward and roughly penetrated her. I could tell by the look on her face that she was really eager for this. Colin leant forward so that his stomach and chest were pressed against her back and then Stuart wound the remaining cling film around the pair of them so that they were bound together. He avoided Ruby's breasts so that they dangled down freely with the clothes pegs still intact on her nipples.

I switched on the video function on my phone as Colin began using his powerful thighs to pump his cock into Ruby who was moaning with delight at each thrust. I couldn't believe I was filming my manageress having sex whilst she was fastened by cling film to a member of her staff and a chair, and with clothes peg pulling on her nipples . . . and she was loving it!

"This feels so strange," said Colin, "being trussed up like a turkey, unable to move apart from doing this with my cock. Although—" he stopped talked momentarily as he banged Ruby several times with real gusto "—I do like my manager tied up. It's good to be shafting her for a change, rather than the other way around."

"Are you criticizing my managerial style?" groaned Ruby.

Stuart jumped up. "I'm just going to get the extra product," he said, as he dashed out of the staff room. He returned promptly with a dishcloth in his hand and, before she could complain, stuffed it into Ruby's mouth.

"Yeah, my manager bound and gagged," panted Colin, who was rather red in the face from all the exertion. "Damn, I hope I don't put my back out doing this."

We cheered him on for encouragement as he continued to fuck Ruby as vigorously as he was able whilst being swaddled. "You won't believe how hot and uncomfortable it is being wrapped up in cling film. Jeez, I'm sweating," he said.

"People pay good money to be wrapped up for weight loss treatment. You could lose inches from your body," observed Michelle.

"I'm about to lose something," muttered Colin as he pounded into Ruby. They were both grunting and then, with a roar, Colin made three lengthy strokes as his come shot inside her. We gave them a boisterous round of applause as Stuart freed them from the chair.

I was smiling uncontrollably – it was the turn of my team. Earlier, I had been worried about being watched but now I was so horny and excited I couldn't wait to start.

"And now," Ruby called out, "we have the manager's special. It's a real bargain, two for the price of one, as lucky old Grace is getting both Curtis and Damon with the aid of dairy produce."

I unbuttoned Curtis's shirt and saw the coal-black skin of his chest.

Damon whispered in my ear, "Do you know why Curtis's nickname is anaconda?" he asked.

I shook my head.

Curtis smiled. "It's the name of a huge snake." He unzipped his trousers, and pulled them and his underpants down. His black cock bounced against his belly and my eyes widened in amazement. Curtis was immense. He nodded knowingly and mouthed at me, *Anaconda*. As I continued to stare at his throbbing cock, he laughed and said, "And, did you know that Damon is known as Donkey Damon because he's hung like one?"

"I guess my jaws are going to ache," I said.

"Not your jaws, Grace," commented Ruby.

Damon had his hands up my skirt and, before I knew it, my panties were around my ankles and I was stepping out of them. Roughly, he yanked my skirt down and I heard the stitching rip. Immediately, Curtis scooped me up in his arms and I wrapped my legs around his waist for support. His straining, bulbous cock was angled correctly and, with one swift push, he forced himself inside me. He had wasted no time at all in spearing me on his massive member.

The opened carton of milk was thrust into my hand and I poured some over Curtis's chest, watching the rivulets run down to form white pools in my lap. "Aah!" I screamed. Something cold and wet had hit my arse. To everyone's amusement, Damon had spanked me with his hands full of strawberry trifle; cold cream, custard and jelly stuck to my skin.

Curtis cupped my messy buttocks in his hands and bounced me up and down the length of his wet pole. Damon grabbed my blouse, ripping it open; there was the sound of buttons pinging off and hitting the floor. I lost my inhibitions. Turning to face my audience, I smiled at their cameras knowing I was being photographed and that video footage was being taken. The thought aroused me intensely.

As Curtis rammed into me, I felt the cold, sticky sensation of yoghurt being tipped down my front and I was hit by the overwhelming smell of raspberries. I poured more milk over Curtis and lapped at it as Damon rubbed the yoghurt over my breasts. He stuck his fingers into my mouth and I licked them clean.

"Here's your extra product," said Colin, as he handed Damon a tub of butter. "There you go, Marlon Brando, time for you to act out *Last Tango in Paris*."

People started to snigger. "You're in for a treat, Grace," said Stuart.

"I've never seen the film," I panted, as Curtis continued to fuck me energetically. I watched as Damon slathered his giant cock with butter. "What happens in that film?" I asked breathlessly, wondering if I had to lick the butter off.

"Pretty much this," replied Damon as Curtis splayed my arse cheeks wide. I felt Damon smear my puckered rosebud with butter and then he sank the full length of his greased member into my arsehole. I screamed as my muscles were forced to take his pulsing girth, but savoured the painful way they expanded and yielded to him and then tightened back around his huge cock when he was embedded deep. He laughed. "Grace, you need butter when you make a sandwich, and you're the filling for our sandwich."

I was trapped between them, impaled on two enormous cocks. To begin with Curtis and Damon alternated their thrusts, so I received one cock and then the other. But, quickly they synchronized their rhythm and banged me simultaneously so each gigantic member slammed into a hole at the same time. Trifle was poured onto Damon's groin and, as he thrust, my buttocks were covered so that, quite delightfully, I squelched as I was fucked. The remainder of the milk and yoghurt was tipped over me and strawberries were popped into my open mouth, along with cream and jelly.

I started to play up for the cameras: blowing kisses, licking cream from fingers, biting the strawberries seductively and letting the juice run down my chin. I loved the fact that Stuart, Colin and Tariq were getting turned on by watching me take two cocks, one in my pussy and the other invading my tight little arse. I was so turned on, and the more that my teammates ripped into me, the sexier I felt and the more I gave my all to them and the surrounding cameras. The lads screwed me for ages, their rampant cocks plunging into me, making me moan from the delectation of being fucked and filled. I was so greedy for it, adoring the way they were driving every single inch of their immense cocks into me. It was slightly uncomfortable, but it excited me incredibly, knowing I was being stretched to accommodate their girth, that both were fucking me at the same time, and that I had given my pussy and arse to them.

"Grace, you know what BOGOF stands for, don't you?" shouted Colin.

"Yes," I panted.

"Butter's out, get orifices filled!"

It felt marvellously sluttish being screwed for an audience, and I was enjoying the voyeurism involved. Curtis and Damon were mercilessly crammed into me and I could sense my imminent orgasm. Although I wanted it to last, I couldn't help myself and my climax ripped through me uncontrollably. I twisted and writhed, but they sandwiched me firmly between themselves as my muscles convulsed and clamped around their cocks. My orgasm brought on theirs and they grunted and groaned as they erupted inside me.

Gently, they lowered me to the floor as the others whooped and cheered. I picked up my skirt; it was drenched with milk, yoghurt and trifle. I wriggled back into it but the seams had split and the zip had broken when Damon had wrenched it off. My blouse was saturated and, due to the missing buttons, I was unable to fasten it. I looked with dismay at my uniform.

"Time to vote for the winning team," cried Ruby. "Which team demonstrated the most innovative use of their products?"

Ruby and Colin were voted the winners.

"That was such a good use of household products," enthused Michelle. "Although, I don't think the manufacturers will be able to demonstrate their wares like that in their next adverts."

"Wow, that's the fourth year on the trot I've been on the winning team," Ruby boasted.

"Yeah, nothing to do with the fact that she's the boss so we all vote for her," Damon whispered in my ear. "Personally, I thought we were the best team."

I nodded in agreement.

"Don't forget all uniforms need to be washed and ironed ready for when we open after Christmas," said Ruby.

As I looked around the staff room, I realized everyone was changing into a spare pair of clothes. "I didn't know I needed to bring a change of clothes," I said to Damon. "I've got to go home, on the bus, in my uniform."

He smiled. "It's done deliberately to all new members of staff, not telling them, but you'll know what to expect next time."

Colin put his arm around my shoulders. "So then, Grace, did you like playing the Bar Code Challenge?"

I glanced down at my wet, messy uniform with its missing buttons, broken zip and ripped stitching and which smelt strongly of dairy produce. Spunk was beginning to dribble out of my pussy and arse. Even with a coat on to cover myself up, I was going to have a very uncomfortable bus journey home.

I looked up at him and smiled broadly. "I loved it. Do we really have to wait until next Christmas before we can play it again?"

Where There's Smoke

Courtney James

I've just sunk below the surface of the tub when the knocking at the door starts. My first thought is to ignore whoever's there. After a long hard week of grading the examination papers that will count towards my students' final degrees, all I want to do is enjoy a little "me time". I've run a bath and added lots of passion fruit-scented gel to create mounds of sweet-smelling bubbles, poured myself a big glass of white wine and unwrapped the present I treated myself to, courtesy of my favourite online sex shop.

It's a long, thick vibrator, its blue plastic shaft of a rippling design that I just know is going to stimulate me in all the nicest ways. More importantly, the thing is waterproof: perfect for a spot of bath-time fun. My pussy has already begun to grow wet in anticipation of the moment when I'll flick the switch and begin to run the buzzing toy over my naked, soapy curves.

Yes, best just to let my unwanted caller think there's no one home. I wrap my fingers around the stem of the wine glass, take a long sip of nicely chilled sauvignon blanc, and close my eyes. What fantasy, I wonder, shall I use to accompany my self-pleasuring? Then it comes to me. Walking home from campus just now, I passed the local fire station and saw a couple of hunky firemen washing down one of their appliances. Watching them at work, their biceps bulging beneath the sleeves of their uniform T-shirts, filled me with all kinds of naughty thoughts, and now I start to think about what it would be like if they decided to turn their hoses on each other – and then on me. I picture them stripping off their shirts, playing the water over their muscled torsos, with their cocks hard enough to tent out the fronts of their baggy trousers. Call it a fetish if you must, but something about the thought of a man who is brave enough to go into a burning building in order to save lives sends my libido into overdrive.

The banging comes again, harder this time, and I heave a sigh, knowing I'm going to have no peace until I answer the door. Living in a private apartment block has many advantages in terms of security when you're a single woman. In theory, random visitors have no way of getting past the front entrance without being invited inside, which protects me from the likes of cold-calling double-glazing salesmen and Jehovah's Witnesses. But that means whoever's trying to get hold of me has to be someone from within the block. Maybe the landlord needs to speak to me about something. Just as long as it's not dull old Malcolm from the tenants' association. He's doorstepped me on several occasions since I moved in, reminding me not to leave food out for the neighbourhood foxes, or inviting me to one of the interminable meetings where he waffles on about rubbish collections and the importance of keeping noise down in consideration of other residents.

With reluctance, I haul myself out of the bath and cover myself with a towel, knotting it hastily beneath my armpit. If it is Malcolm, who might be irritating but makes a virtue out of respecting the privacy of others, I'm sure he'll leave me alone if I greet him half-naked and dripping wet.

When I fling open the door, however, it's as though someone with a hotline to my rudest fantasies has decided to give me a treat. Standing there is the best-looking man I've seen in ages: a broad-shouldered hunk, so tall I have to crane my neck to look up into his bearded, smiling face. If that wasn't a pleasant enough shock, he's dressed in a fireman's uniform, holding his bright yellow helmet in one hand. I can't help it; even though I should be annoyed at the intrusion, my pussy reacts to the sight by rippling with lust.

He regards me with an expression that's somewhere between amused and apologetic. "I'm sorry to disturb you, miss, but we're doing a routine inspection of all the properties in this block. We need to make sure that your smoke alarms are working properly."

Now he mentions it, I seem to recall Malcolm making some announcement about this at the last residents' meeting, though by that stage in the proceedings I'd kind of tuned out in favour of checking emails on my phone.

"I can see you're in the middle of something," he continues, "and I can come back later, if that's more convenient for you."

I should take him up on his suggestion. After all, I have an appointment with a hot bath and a brand-new vibrator, and just a few words of conversation with this gorgeous stranger has provided me with all the fantasy fodder I could need. But instead, I find myself shaking my head.

"No, it's fine. Please do come inside." I stand aside to allow him inside the flat.

He sets the helmet down on a bookshelf, and glances up at the little white alarm that's fastened to the ceiling in the hallway. "So when did you last test this, Miss—?"

"Call me Chelsea, please."

"Nice to meet you, Chelsea. I'm Tony. Now, about your alarm . . ."

I shift from foot to foot, like a student who's been caught cheating on an exam. "To be honest, I haven't tested it in all the time I've lived here. Though that's only been nine months," I add quickly, as if that will somehow justify my lack of interest in my own safety. And yes, I know I should keep on top of these things, but I'm a busy woman and poking my smoke alarm to see whether it bleeps or not has fallen a long way down on the list of my priorities.

To his credit, he doesn't try to make me feel any guiltier than I already am, even though a secret, submissive little part of me thrills to the idea that he might take me over his knee and give me a good spanking for not following the official fire brigade advice to check all alarms on a regular basis.

"Well, let's take a look at it right now, shall we, Chelsea?" Tony glances round the small hallway, made even narrower by the bookshelves that line one side, and I can see him mentally ticking off all the ways in which my flat is a potential death trap. "Do you have a stepladder?"

In the kitchen, I have one of those little stools with the steps that pull out from underneath. Though I'm sure if he wanted to, he could just stretch out one long arm and touch the low ceiling. "Let me just get it for you."

As I make my way back to him, clutching the stool, my big fireman watches me struggle to negotiate a path through all the boxes and bags that litter the hall with undisguised interest. At least, I think that explains away his intent expression, until I feel the towel slip down a little. In my rush to answer the door, I couldn't have tied the knot securely enough. I grab at my makeshift cover-up, hoping to pull it back into place before Tony gets more than the eyeful of my full, round breasts he's already had. But it's too late. The towel slithers to the ground, baring me to him entirely.

I give a little dismayed squeak, and drop the stool, which clatters as its metal legs make contact with the parquet flooring. I need to retrieve the towel, but Tony has already snatched it up. When I try to wrest it from him – which is rather awkward when I'm also attempting to cover as much of myself from his gaze as I can – he just yanks it further out of my reach.

"You want this back, do you?" He grins, and though I feel embarrassed and a little vulnerable at being naked in front of him, I drape one arm over my tits, use the other to cover my pussy, and meet his look with a defiant one of my own.

"That would be appreciated, yes."

"Well, all in good time. First, you need a lesson on being prepared in the event of a fire. I mean, look at this place." He casts his hand around in an expansive gesture, indicating the cluttered hallway. "Just imagine it's dark, the flat is full of smoke, and you're trying to get to the front door as quickly as you can. It's not going to happen, is it?"

"OK, I'll tidy up in here, I promise. Now can I have my towel, please?"

Tony shakes his head sadly, and makes a little tutting noise. "Sorry, Chelsea, it's not going to happen just yet. We haven't even considered the subject of the smoke alarm."

He throws the towel into the living room, knowing his big body is acting as a barrier I won't be able to pass, and sets up the stool. "Now, watch what you need to do, once a week without fail." He climbs the ladder and presses a button on the alarm. It gives a little bleep. "There, that's how simple it is. But as soon as you notice the battery start to go, you need to get it replaced at once. I could give you statistics on how many people are killed in fires every year, and how many we have to rescue, simply because they couldn't be bothered to maintain a cheap little device like this. But you're an intelligent woman; you should know these things." Again he flashes that oh-so sexy grin. "And as you seem to have forgotten them, I'm going to make sure you remember."

"How do you intend to do that?"

"The way naughty girls should always be encouraged to improve their behaviour. With a good spanking."

Part of me can't believe he just said something so outrageous. But deep inside, my body is reacting to the suggestion, flooding with heat at the realization he's so in tune with my own desires. I can feel my breathing start to come a little faster, and my pussy lips are swelling.

"You . . . you're not serious. You can't be."

He says nothing, just sets about putting up the step-stool and placing it against the wall. Then he takes my hand. "Where's your bedroom?"

I gesture with a nod of my head, and he starts to lead me down the corridor. As we pass the bathroom, he catches a glimpse of something through the open door. All the evidence of my planned self-indulgence is laid out for him: the bath, the wine, the vibrator . . .

That last item is snatched up by Tony with a little chortle. "I thought you were a naughty girl. I was wrong. You're a *very* naughty girl. No wonder you didn't want to come to the door. You just wanted to come."

I whimper helplessly, turned on like crazy by his dirty words and the thought of what he's about to do to me. The idea of being spanked is bad enough on its own, but throw a vibrator into the mix and I'm lost.

"You want this, don't you, Chelsea?" he says, as we enter the bedroom and he sits down on my bed. I nod, but he wants me to vocalize my need. "Say it. Say you want to be spanked."

"I want to be spanked, sir," I reply obediently. "And I want you to make me come."

"Now, that we'll have to see about." As he talks, he's stripping off his jacket. Beneath it, he wears a dark-blue T-shirt, just like those two firemen I saw earlier, and it strains across his firm pecs. My mouth waters at the power and strength he radiates, and even though I've never been spanked before and can't help being a little scared by the prospect, I know he'll take good care of me.

Almost before I know it, I'm being guided over his lap, face down with the small, pale moons of my bottom jutting up invitingly. Tony runs a hand over my naked rump. "You have a lovely arse, Chelsea, but it'll look even nicer once I've warmed it up."

He gives me a couple of light taps, measuring the swing of his arm and the resilience of my buttocks. Then he starts to spank me in earnest, using upward strokes that catch the lower curve of each cheek. In response, I give out a series of little yelps, more of surprise than pain.

"You're a bad girl," he tells me, punctuating each word with a slap, and stringing them out so that I don't know exactly when or where the next blow will fall. "Never take risks when it comes to fire safety."

"No, sir, I won't," I promise him.

He brings his arm down over and again, smacking hard against my bare bottom. After each one, he takes a moment to rub the punished flesh, so the sting becomes less concentrated, more diffuse. And I can't help but notice that as the pain dies away, it's beginning to be replaced by a warm, pleasurable sensation.

Tony must have realized that I'm starting to get off on being punished, because he puts his fingers to my pussy, and when he pulls them away, he shows me how wet they are.

"I think you're more than ready for this," he says, and turns on the vibrator. Without ceremony, he places the head of the thing at my entrance, and pushes it up inside me. It slides in with ease, slicked with my juices, and now my delicious torment really begins.

The spanking resumes, only now the force of the blows seems to meld with the fierce vibrations of the sex toy, until the whole of my sex is burning with need. I sob and writhe against the fabric of his uniform trousers. Tony has reduced me to a sobbing,

helpless mess and I'm no longer sure whether I want him to stop
or carry on. Beneath me, I can feel the solid mass of his cock,
and I yearn for him to slide that big, hard tool up my tight little
arse so that I'm filled front and back.

"Have you learned your lesson?" he asks, out of nowhere.

"Yes, sir," I reply with sincerity. "I'll keep my hallway tidy and
I'll always check my alarm."

"That's just what I wanted to hear." With that, he presses a
finger to my clit. He doesn't need to do anything else. On top of
all the other stimulation I've received, the gentle touch is enough
to have me screaming out in orgasm, and damn what boring old
Malcolm says about not making a noise that will disturb the
neighbours.

When I've ridden out the last waves of pleasure, Tony eases the
vibrator out of my pussy. He guides me up into a sitting position
and we share a kiss, long and slow. Somehow, the slight ache in
my tender bottom only serves to make the moment sweeter.

"That was wonderful," I tell him when we break apart, "but
now I think I should repay the compliment."

I'm reaching for the braces on his uniform trousers so I can
unhook them and start the process of stripping him when
there's a sudden, unexpected bleep. I look round, trying to
work out if it's the smoke alarm, but Tony reaches into his
pocket to retrieve a pager. "Damn, I'm needed back at the
station," he tells me, looking at the words on the little screen,
"but don't worry, tomorrow's my day off and I'll be back here
to finish what I started."

We both know that doesn't mean anything to do with checking
whether my flat is safety compliant.

"I look forward to it," I tell him. I'm finally going to have the
chance to check out that big, thick hose of his, and I'm certain it
will be well worth the wait.

He snatches up his helmet and hurries out of the flat, leaving
me on fire for his return.

Life on the Naughty List

Kannan Feng

"So . . . I didn't think elves drank straight vodka . . ."

I glared at Max balefully over the top of my glass, but I didn't speak until I had taken a long swallow.

"Learn something new every day, don't you?" I growled.

I hadn't bothered to do anything except kick the stupid pointy shoes off at the door. I was still wearing the peaked hat, the ridiculous puffy pants and the velvet vest I'd been wearing for the past ten hours. Santa's elves apparently wore extremely close-fitting uniforms; my corset for goth night wasn't really much tighter than the vest.

Max set down his keys. There was a snicker lurking at the corner of his mouth that he was too wise to voice.

"So how bad was it today, Valerie?"

"Two kids peed in the line, someone tipped over all of the reindeer at once, four of the dads asked me if they could be on the naughty list, and someone's little angel somehow managed to drop kick Keith in the nuts."

"Oof, you'd think Santa would get a cup."

"You'd think Santa would get a clue," I retorted, putting the glass down. The vodka still burned in my throat, but I was already feeling a little bit better. It was only for another two weeks after all, and then I could go back to job hunting. At this point, filling out résumé after résumé after résumé was already looking pretty appealing.

I shook my head, standing up. My feet burned and my head hurt, but the vodka was giving everything a pleasantly hazy softness.

"All right, you want to take a shower or . . ."

I squeaked in surprise as Max grabbed me around the waist

and dragged me against him. My boyfriend was a big guy, broad
and strong, and even in the classic short-sleeve button-down
and khakis of the standard IT guy, you could tell he was no
internet-addicted computer geek. Well, he was, but he got to the
gym every few days at least.

I started to say something, but then his mouth was right next
to my pointy ear. I hadn't even bothered to remove the rubber
tips, but I could feel his warm breath as he whispered to me
just fine.

"So those dads who asked to be on the naughty list," he said.
"What did you say to them?"

I licked my lips. When someone was listening, I had laughed
politely and mentioned something about reporting them to Mr
Claus. If no one was listening, on the other hand, it involved
telling them to do something obscene and likely impossible with
a candy cane. A sharp one.

"I . . . I asked them how naughty they had been," I improvised.
"You know. Like for the North Pole records."

"Uh-huh," he muttered. "I don't think I believe that. I think
you wanted to know how naughty they were so that you could
have some fun."

At that, I couldn't help myself and I giggled. He was grinding
his half-hard cock against my ridiculous puffy pants and
quizzing me about Santa's naughty list. It should have been
stupid, and it was, but it was also kind of hot.

"Oh, that doesn't sound like you're taking me very seriously
at all, little one," he said, his voice stern. "Listen to you, laughing
like it's funny."

It is *funny!* I wanted to say, but before I could squeak the
words out, he pulled back and landed a hard swat on my rear.
Those puffy pants provided a lot less cushioning than I would
have thought, and I yelped, pulling away to rub the offended
part hard.

"That hurt!" I protested. "You didn't even warm me up!"

"I don't know how much someone who may be on the
naughty list herself really deserves a warm-up," he said seriously.
Max crossed his arms over his chest, staring down at me. That
laugh was getting ready to come out any moment, and I was
damn sure that I wanted him to break before I did.

"I'm not on the naughty list at all!" I pouted. "I'm a good girl, sir!"

"Hmm, I think you're a little liar," Max responded. "I think you've been getting up to all sorts of naughty things behind my back. Not very professional for one of Santa's elves, is it?"

"I don't know what you're talking about! I've been doing nothing but, um, making toys, and, uh, scheduling drop-offs!"

"I don't want to hear any more lies out of you," Max commanded, and when I opened my mouth again, he spun me over the arm of the couch.

He delivered a dozen spanks to my ass, one hand holding me down by pushing between my shoulder blades. I yelled into the couch cushion, kicking my legs out hard behind me, but it was no use.

I had walked into the hiring office, and it didn't surprise me at all that they had taken one good look at me and said, "Elf!" Even at twenty-four, I am just barely five feet tall and I would only make it up to 120 pounds if I happened to be wearing my steel-toed boots. Even my blonde hair is cut pixie short, and the freckles sprinkled over my nose only make me cuter.

None of my cuteness was saving me from the blistering that Max was intent on delivering, and when he paused, I tried to reach back and rub my rear again. The heat was incredible, and it was affecting more than just the skin of my ass. I was upended over the couch just right and I was already humping the hard surface a little, rocking on it to help soothe the ache that was beginning to develop in my pussy.

"So what've you been doing?" Max asked, and I yelped in alarm when he held my hands behind my back. It made me wiggle and buck harder, which of course turned me on even more. He watched me squirm a little, but then he pinched my rear, making me yelp. "Come on, elf, what've you been doing?"

"Um . . . feeding the reindeer?"

There was another series of hard swats, these aimed right beneath the curve where I would have to sit down. The blows were hard enough that they must have hurt his hand, and I was yelling with pleasure as much as with pain. If I were naked, I'd be soaking the arm of the couch, but, as it was, I was soaking my panties and the ridiculous puffy pants straight through.

"Wanna try again?"

This time I was panting so hard that it took another spank before I could answer.

"Polishing candy canes?"

"Oh you're just asking for it, elf!"

This time, instead of pinning me down, he turned me over so that I was bent like a bow over the arm, and he undid the pants, pulling them and my panties halfway down my thighs. It revealed the white expanse of my lower belly, the narrow tuft of pale hair between my legs, and my upper thighs, which I realized were his next target.

"Oh, oh no!" I yelped, and his hand was slapping down on the tender, untouched flesh. Instead of going fast this time, he spaced the blows out, landing them one after the other. The pain crested and rose higher, and when he paused this time we could both smell how wet I was.

"Gonna tell the truth now?" he asked, slightly out of breath.

I nodded frantically, tears of pain running from my eyes. "Yes, oh yes, I'm sorry, I'm on the naughty list," I babbled, and I was so high on the pain that I was giggling through my ridiculous words as I said it. "I've been orchestrating elf gang-bangs, we've been making dildos and vibrators after lights out in the toyshop, I've been eating Mrs Claus out whenever Santa's on rounds, um, um, I let Santa stick it up my ass . . ."

That last one got Max hard, making him burst out laughing, but it didn't stop him from dragging me off the couch and kneeling me in front of him.

"Dirty mouth on this one," he commented. "Let's see if we can scrub it clean."

That was all the warning I got before he had freed his meaty cock and was forcing it into my mouth, his big hands on either side of head and holding me still. He knew exactly how much I could take before I choked, and he used every bit of it, fucking my face as I whimpered and clung to his hips.

I didn't have to do any work at all. Instead, I just held still and relished the taste of his cock sliding between my lips, the way my ass and my thighs burned, and how my own juices were beginning to slide down my legs and soak into the edges of my red and white stockings.

I heard him groan and he forced his cock into my mouth more deeply. For a second, it looked like he was going to come, but then with a savage sound, he pulled away, letting me drop to the ground.

"I don't think you're good enough to take my come," he growled, and I mewled in protest. Yes I was! I was, I was a perfectly good place to dump his come, and then maybe he would get my favourite vibrator from the bedroom and . . .

He grabbed me by the upper arm and hauled me to my feet. He was big enough that his hand went all the way around my arm, and I loved the way he could just push me around like I was a doll, or a fuck toy, or well, a naughty elf who let Santa fuck her ass.

He dragged me to the window and bent me so that my hands were on the wide sill. Outside, a light snow was falling. We were in a fourth story walk-up, and the window only faced an alley. Across the way, I could see a few people settling in for the evening, and to my immense relief, none of them were looking my way, where they would see a woman in pointed ears and a pointy hat getting all hell fucked out of her.

"Are you worried that all of those people are going to look over and see how naughty you are?" Max said, his voice harsh with need. He was reaching the end of his endurance, and at this point, so was I.

"Yes, yes, yes," I groaned. "Please, please finish up, don't let them see me, sir, please!"

He chuckled darkly. "You're going to stay right there, you bad little elf, and you're gonna take it until I'm done, do you understand?"

I nodded, aware that the hat was still sitting on my head, that the tight vest was creaking at the seams, and that the puffy pants, now around my stockinged ankles, needed to be professionally cleaned before I could bring them close to Santa's Holiday Village again.

He held my hips so hard that I knew there would be bruises there in the morning, and he entered me with a grunt. His cock isn't that long, but fuck is it wide, and I bit my lips around a yelp. Soon he was fucking me like a machine, pounding me as I struggled to hold still. His hips slammed against my tender ass, and, oh God, I was so wet. I started thinking I was going to go crazy unless I got something on my clit, and I begged him.

"Oh, oh God, oh God, please, put something on my clit, I'll be nice, I'll be nice, I'll be so fuckin' nice, I won't be naughty any more."

Bastard that he was, he came, pushing me so hard that I imagined going right out the window. Before I could cuss him out for not giving me anything at all, he dropped to his knees behind me.

I whimpered when his hands spread my cheeks wide apart, and he planted a kiss right on the spot between my asshole and my pussy. Every nerve in my body woke up, and he was working his tongue between the slippery folds. I knew he was tasting me and himself, and I ground back against him wanting more.

He split my pussy open with his thumbs, opening it to his tongue and his lips, and I bent even further forward, desperate for everything he could give me.

At the first touch of his tongue against my eager clit, I yowled, and then he went after it like it was Christmas candy, licking so hard that I could feel the tension run through my body. Soon I was shaking, every muscle in my body tensed hard.

That was when the bastard landed another slap on my ass, and I sobbed. The slap pushed my orgasm back, and when he could feel me shaking all over again, he gave me another smack.

"No, no, no, don't do that, I wanna come, I want to come so bad, Max, please, please, don't spank me, I'll be good, I'll be nice, I'll be so fucking nice, please, I want to come!"

He laughed, and I could feel it, of course I could with his mouth buried in my pussy. I thought he was going to smack me again, but this time, he let the tension build and build until my legs were shaking, and I was sobbing with need. I didn't care if someone across the alley saw me any more, I didn't care that I was still wearing that goddamn hat, I just wanted to come, and just when I thought I couldn't take it any more, I did.

My orgasm hit hard enough that it almost hurt, and this time I did yell. That wasn't good enough for Max though, and he kept licking, drawing out the shudders until I jerked away. I nearly fell over because of the pants around my ankles, and then he caught me and lowered me to the floor gently.

"Did we seriously do that?" he asked when we had both gotten our breaths.

I grinned, reaching up to palm some of our juices from his face to lick at them myself. I saw the way his eyes darkened, and I kicked myself free of the ridiculous pants.

"You started it," I said. "Now let's see if you can finish it. After all, I'm pretty sure I shouldn't have been playing with the candy canes that way. Sounds pretty naughty to me."

Big Top

Lily Harlem

A movie star has a hundred chances to get it right when they are filming. The performers in the circus have one shot or it could cost them their lives.

The empty seats passing by were a blur of red as I concentrated on Diamond's white mane. It was flicking in the breeze, flowing like seaweed in a current, and as always the movement calmed me.

I took a deep breath, tensed my abdomen and stood. This bit was crucial. I had to be sure my feet were dead centre in her back otherwise when she changed pace I'd topple off.

This was only a practice, but still, it was a long way down to the sawdust-coated ring and I couldn't afford to break any bones, not with a packed house tonight.

Arms outstretched, I straightened. The rhythmic steps of canter flowed up from my soles, through my knees to my spine and neck. I smiled out of habit and waved to the non-existent crowd. All felt good, there was no sign of lameness in Diamond's right fore.

I clicked my tongue against the roof of my mouth, letting Diamond know that I wanted her to keep going. Round and round, on and on, legs pounding, head bobbing.

I stretched my right leg behind myself and performed an arabesque. With pointed toes, I then arched my back, grabbed my ankle and touched the ball of my foot to the crown of my head.

Diamond didn't change pace. She kept on going, steady, obedient and calm.

I stood straight again, waved and smiled, then dropped down, riding her bareback.

"Hey, Cina, you making stew tonight?"

I glanced upwards.

Raif was swinging on the trapeze, upside down, holding on by just his bent legs.

"Yes, why, do you want some?"

"Always." He grinned and spun around so he was sitting on the bar. "Save me some."

"I will." I brought Diamond to a trot and a walk and finally to a halt in the middle of the ring. I stood on her rump and jumped into a forward somersault to dismount. Not pausing when I landed facing the audience, I waved and bowed the way I always did. Not that I was wearing my show gear, I was in sweats and a red T-shirt, it was just habit.

Slow clapping echoed around the big top.

I turned and saw Devlin Indigo-Price, ringmaster extraordinaire, standing at the curtained entrance to the circus tent.

I set down my shoulders, buried my hand in the warmth beneath Diamond's mane and leant on her a little. Devlin's presence had the ability to make my strong legs weak and my perfect balance wobble.

"She's back to normal," he said, strolling into the ring, his strong voice echoing around the canvas walls.

"Yes, no lameness, thank goodness."

He propped the handle of his whip on his shoulder. As usual, even two hours before doors open, he was dressed ready for the Greatest Show on Earth.

His ringmaster uniform consisted of tight, black lace-up boots with black trousers tucked into them. Around his waist he wore a silky red cummerbund, and over a white shirt – complete with bow tie – a tailed red coat with golden buttons and embroidery.

He touched his top hat and waved to Raif. "You OK up there?"

"Yes, boss. Just hanging about."

"Yep, keep doing that."

Devlin smiled at me and flicked the whip to his right side. It made a small crack as it sliced through the air.

I glanced away. The whip made my arse tingle. Thinking

about it landing on my buttocks had me clenching my thighs together. He'd been paying me special interest of late – I was nervous that he'd seen the longing I had for him in my eyes.

Nervous but also excited.

I licked my lips and watched as he stooped and ran his hand down Diamond's leg. He rubbed her fetlock checking for heat.

He was kind, caring and loved my horse. It wasn't a pretense his consideration, it was how he was. A ringmaster can't help but be caring, charismatic, flamboyant and masterful.

When I'd joined Billy Boyd's Smashing Circus I'd thought Devlin a little arrogant but now, hearing him talk to the audience night after night, I knew that wasn't the case. He backed up every enthusiastic word with the amazing show he loved being in charge of.

He also held each performer and animal in high esteem. He made sure everyone and everything was OK and held the travelling family together as though he was the glue that bonded us all.

Diamond touched her nose to his back, a gesture of affection, and lifted her hoof.

"I think you're fine," Devlin said, standing. "You're just a mare who wants my attention."

That'll be me.

"I should put her away, so she can rest."

"Yes." He propped the whip on his shoulder again. Its long tail fell down his back and the last few inches coiled on the floor.

Diamond wasn't afraid of the whip. She knew Devlin would never hurt her. Devlin would never hurt any of the circus animals.

But I wish he'd hurt me.

I pulled in a deep breath and took hold of Diamond's head collar. My thoughts of Devlin mastering me, taking command of my pleasure and my need for pain when I orgasmed were beginning to take over.

"Cina."

"Yes." I turned.

"We should talk?" he said.

"Why?" My heart rate picked up and my stomach clenched. Had I done something wrong?

Devlin glanced upwards and then settled his gaze on me. "I think you know."

I shook my head. "No."

"I'll come to your caravan. Tonight. After the show."

"I'm making stew. Do you want some?"

"No, I'm not coming for the stew." He leaned closer, much closer than he usually came to me. "Make sure the stew has gone by the time I get there."

I could smell his cologne – sweet spice, straw and apples.

"But what do you want?" I asked in barely a whisper.

"You."

He turned and the whip flicked past my face.

You?

I opened my mouth to speak then remembered Raif above us and shut it again. What the hell had just happened? Devlin, the ringmaster, wanted me?

I couldn't say no – he ran the show, what he said went.

But I didn't want to say no. I wanted Devlin and I wanted Devlin to want me more than I wanted anything else.

Two hours later, I stood behind the curtain waiting for my slot. Holding Diamond's reins, and now in my costume – sparkly white leotard, soft white ballet pumps and a plume of swan feathers flowing from my headband – I was listening to the clowns warm up the audience.

They seemed like a jolly lot, the audience, and there'd been plenty of laughter and participation. This always made me feel good, because as a performer they were at the forefront of my mind at show time. They'd trusted us with their evening, money and imagination and it made my blood warm to know they were excited, happy and having fun with us.

Devlin stood at the entrance to the ring, chin tilted, chest puffed. This was his moment. He was the voice of the show. Being ringmaster was his calling. It was what he did best, commanding, showing off the aesthetics of the circus, building the anticipation into a frenzy.

Fuck.

I clenched my hands. My nipples were tight, peaking against my leotard. I was a frenzy inside. My imagination was running riot with thoughts of him and his whip in my caravan later. He'd never been inside before. It was my territory.

His whip.

I crossed my legs. My clit was humming with the blood rushing to it. What would it be like to be at Devlin's mercy? Him standing tall, chin tilted like that, telling me that I was his then branding my arse and fucking me. Fucking me till I couldn't remember which way was up and which was down.

He turned, looked at me and set an unblinking gaze upon mine.

Did he know what was going through my mind? No, that was impossible. How could he?

He faced the curtain again. With his free hand, he smoothed the front of his jacket then straightened his hat. In profile, his nose was long and angular, his lips soft and full and his chin a little large perhaps, but in perfect alignment with the rest of his face.

The curtains pulled open. The clowns, red-nosed and gleeful, skipped out holding buckets of torn paper and cackling at the fun they'd had.

Devlin stepped into the ring.

A huge drumroll rang out.

The curtains shut.

The audience erupted into a roar that blasted around the big top.

Show time.

With a commanding presence and boisterous voice, Devlin began the prelude to the show.

"Ladies and gentlemen, boys and girls, please get comfortable, get ready and be prepared for the Greatest Show on Earth."

I licked my lips, peeked through the curtain and watched him strut around flicking that whip.

"We have dancing piglets, a woolly mammoth, lions and tigers, the bearded lady, the first family of the trapeze, dwarfs, the marmalade troupe of hair hangers, and the most beautiful unicorn-riding acrobat in the world."

"What?" That had never been part of his warm-up before.

I was nudged by Diamond pushing her nose on me. I rested my hand on her muzzle and soothed her. "Yes, in a minute.

Then it's us." I tutted. "And look you've knocked your horn." I straightened the long white polystyrene conical that was attached to her bridle.

He'd said he wanted me. Now he'd said I was beautiful. Was it all an act?

"Go, Cina, go." Raif was at the curtains. "Now. You're on."

"Yes. Yes."

With a quick leap, I sprung onto Diamond and sat astride her back. She was frisky and raring to go. A few days off with a bruised hock and she'd missed her admiring audience.

The curtains were rushed open and Diamond went straight to canter. I waved with both hands, not needing to hold on, directing her with my legs.

The audience gasped at the unicorn in the ring, but all I could do was look at Devlin. He always stayed in the centre during my act. It wasn't long, only a few minutes, and he waved his hands, flicked his whip and got the audience riled up before my acrobatic stunts.

Soon I was on Diamond's back, balancing on one leg. Flash bulbs went off as the audience captured me in the elegant pose.

I tried to push thoughts of Devlin from my mind but couldn't rid the sensation of his gaze on me. Had he always looked at me like this and I just hadn't noticed?

I was facing backwards now, standing on Diamond's rump. On and on she cantered and I dropped down and went into a handstand.

The audience clapped.

I spread my legs, star-shaped, and pointed my toes.

More clapping.

Next was a somersault to the floor while Diamond was still at this pace. I tucked my knees in and pushed off with my hands. The harlequin-patterned ceiling of the big top swirled in my vision and I landed on my feet then bowed and waved.

Diamond ran to the curtains, knowing that Raif would be on the other side with a carrot.

"Ladies and gentlemen," Devlin shouted, "please give it up for Cina, the one and only unicorn acrobat on the planet."

The crowd cheered. Devlin took my hand and held it aloft.

"Isn't she wonderful," he said, grinning at me with his eyes narrowed in a sinfully exciting way.

The audience cheered louder.

I curtseyed, tugged my hand from Devlin and ran.

I ran from the ring.

I ran past the clowns.

I ran to Raif who had hold of Diamond outside the big top.

"Cina," he said. "Are you OK?"

"Yes, just a bit . . ." My head was spinning. It was happening. I knew it was. The look in Devlin's eyes had been unmistakable. He was coming to me – with his whip.

"Could you?" I said. "Put Diamond in her stablebox for me? I, er . . . twisted something." I gripped my shoulder. "Just want to lie down."

"Of course, honey. Of course."

"The stew," I said. "It's at Hairy Matilda's. I took it there earlier."

"Oh, OK. Well thanks, we'll all tuck in." He patted Diamond's neck. "Do you want me to bring you some?"

"No, really, no." The last thing I wanted was Raif turning up when things got hot with Devlin. "I've eaten. I'll catch you tomorrow, yeah?"

"Yes, sure. Rest well."

I ran through the night air to my caravan on the outer perimeter of the camp. The grass was damp and soaked through my pumps and the smell of hot dogs and candyfloss filled my nostrils.

After passing a whirring generator and the cage that held the dancing piglets, I reached my home, pulled open the door and stumbled inside.

It was quiet and still and I flicked on the fringed lamp in the living area. Hurriedly, I pulled the curtains, wanting privacy – privacy if I was alone or with *him*.

I slipped off my pumps, wet now, and sat at the table. My breaths were fast and my skin prickled, the small hairs on my arms stood erect.

I reached for my tarot cards and spread them with the palm of my hand finding comfort in the paisley pattern that adorned their backs.

"Cards of Wisdom," I murmured, "show me the way forward with my Master and his whip."

I began to turn cards, the pictures speaking to me, confirming my thoughts, my hopes, my dreams.

The Ace of Cups: love starting as a stream and flowing to a mighty river.

The Emperor: wise, powerful with the ability to shape the world.

The Wheel of Fortune: energy beyond understanding or control, the pull of gravity on the body, desire, need, destiny, the circle of life.

On and on I turned the cards, each one answering the questions in my head.

Eventually, with all cards turned, I rested back and reached for a cigarette. I lit it and drew on the mint-laced smoke then watched it curl in the shadows around the light.

For the longest time I sat. I waited. I smoked. I let my thoughts settle.

Finally, when the chugging generator outside switched off, signaling the show had ended and the performers all turned in for the night, there was a gentle knock on my door.

"Show time," I murmured.

I opened it.

Devlin Indigo-Price stood before me – top hat in place, bow tie straight and long red-tailed jacket undone.

"I have come," he said.

"Yes." I moved back and signaled for him to enter. "Please, get out of the cold."

He stepped in, his big boots banging on the floor of my caravan and the tip of his whip just catching on the frame.

I shut the door and flicked the lock.

He moved through the kitchen area and stood with his back against the cabinet I kept books in. He looked big and imposing in my small space but also totally relaxed.

"You have been reading." He signaled the cards.

"Yes."

"And what did they tell you?"

"That you would be here tonight."

"And the next night?"

"Yes." I nodded. "And the next."

A hint of a smile tugged at the right side of his mouth.

I stubbed out the cigarette I'd been smoking. I then locked my hands behind my back and cast my eyes downwards. "Did the show go well?" I asked.

"Always." He slid his hand down the handle of the whip.

I stared at its long thin tail hanging innocently in front of his body and tickling my carpet.

"Come here, Cina," he said. "Closer."

I did as he asked then stared at the tight knot in his tie. It didn't seem appropriate to look him in the eye.

He tucked the end of the whip beneath my chin – it was hard and cool – added pressure and I was forced to tip my head up.

"Please look at your ringmaster," he said, his breath warm on my face.

"Yes, Master. I like looking at you." I stared into his dark, bottomless eyes. I *loved* looking at him.

"And I like looking at you." He paused. "Now tell me, how long is it since you joined the Greatest Show on Earth?"

"I have been travelling under your command for one year now."

"Yes. To the day."

I thought for a moment. He was right. It was to the day exactly that Diamond and I had left the Surini Brothers' Circus and come to Billy Boyd's.

"The cards," he said, "they told me that my woman, my life love, I would lay my eyes on for fifty-two weeks before I lay my hands on her body."

"And that's today?" I hardly dared believe that I was his life love, though I certainly could believe that he was mine.

"Yes. I have been waiting."

I swallowed and looked at his lips. I loved the way his mouth moved as he spoke. I loved the words he spoke, too. He'd been waiting for this moment the same way I had. Though I hadn't known that there was a night written in destiny for us to finally be together.

"I'm going to kiss you now, Cina."

"Yes." I knotted my fingers tighter behind my back.

"And that kiss will seal our souls."

"Yes. That's what I want." My heart was thumping wildly, my breaths hard to catch. My whole body was screaming for his yet still I was utterly motionless, waiting for him to make the move. We were going to be together, forever.

He lowered his head, lips slightly parted, and pressed them over mine.

A small whimper left my throat and I closed my eyes.

The feel of his mouth, soft and pliant, the taste of him – tobacco and herbs – had my hormones racing. A tug of desire pulled in my groin and I hoped my year of celibacy would soon be at an end.

He pulled back and licked his lips. "Sweet, sexy, Cina," he murmured. "Do you really want it as badly as I think you do?"

"I want you."

He raised his eyebrows.

"Master," I added.

He smiled. "Yes, I am your Master. I will care for you, protect you and make sure you are eternally happy."

"I know you will." And I did. I knew that Devlin could give me everything he promised and more.

He removed his hat and set it aside. His short dark hair was a little flattened where the rim had pressed it down.

I itched to smooth away the dink, fluff it up. But that wasn't for me to do, not yet.

He touched the white feathers that rose up from my headband. I'd forgotten I was wearing them – my race back to the caravan and frantic card reading had stolen my thoughts.

"So pretty," he murmured.

I studied his face. It was bliss to be this close to him. I could see every dot of stubble over his top lip and chin, each individual eyelash and even a small freckle, like a tiny tear, just beside his right eye that I hadn't noticed before.

"Take me out," he said, his gaze suddenly connecting with mine.

I didn't need to ask what he meant. The desire blazing in his eyes spoke as loudly as any words.

"Yes, Master," I said.

He nodded, a little stiffly. "I'll make it good for you," he said, taking the whip from beneath my chin. "I'll make it good for us both."

"I trust that you will."

I sank to my knees. Still wearing just my leotard, the carpet pressed softly into my flesh.

Excitement laced my every breath as I slid my hands around his silky cummerbund. Set in the small of his back was a tiny bow. I tugged it and immediately the material loosened. It fell away and I caught it. After folding it, I placed it out of the way.

His trousers were high-waisted and neatly fitted and there was a thick bulge behind the zipper. I turned my attention to the button, released it then slowly pulled down the zipper.

He was breathing slow and deep, small draughts drifted over the feathers in my hair, tugging the band that sat ear to ear holding them in place. My skin felt super-sensitive, every nerve ending heightened.

When the zipper hit the base, he locked his knees and braced himself against the cabinet.

It was a small movement but I loved that he was excited. So excited that he'd had to ensure he was able to stand while I touched him.

Gripping the material of his trousers where they sat at his hips, I dragged them down to his knees.

He wore small, black underwear. Not boxers. Circus men didn't wear boxers.

My stomach gave a roll of anticipation.

For so long I'd thought only of Devlin. I'd dreamed of having his cock in my hand, my mouth, my pussy. And now here I was, inches from it and moments away from getting up close and personal.

"Please," he said, a note of desperation in his tone. "Cina, I've needed you for so long."

I pulled his underwear down and released his cock.

He groaned and shifted his hips.

I wrapped my hand around his shaft and squeezed. He was at full hardness and as hot as the blood that raced through my veins.

"Ah, yeah." He placed his hand on my shoulder, the one that held the whip and the handle dug into my flesh slightly. "That's it . . . more like that . . ."

I poked out my tongue and swiped it through his slit.

"Yes . . ." he hissed.

I smiled, a little, then opened my mouth and slid his shaft

between my lips. I hugged his length with my tongue and let his tip smooth over my palate.

He moaned and shifted his hips towards me.

I kept on going, taking him as deep as I could.

I shut my eyes, reached beneath his cock and cupped his balls.

"Cina . . . oh, my love, that's more than I dreamed . . ."

He was my Master and to know that he dreamed of me brought tears to my eyes.

I withdrew, sank back down, taking him deep, so deep, and creating a gentle suction that tugged on the very end of his shaft. A salty drip of pre-come coated my tongue.

"Ah, that's it. Please . . . no more." He placed his hands on either side of my head and pulled me from him.

"No . . ." I gasped, bereft.

"All in good order," he said breathlessly. "This first time, we should find our pleasure together."

With his eyes a little glazed, he reached for his underwear and pulled them up, then quickly he did the same with his trousers but he didn't re-secure the zipper and button.

"But . . . ?" My fun had been spoiled, utterly.

He smiled, it seemed his control had returned. "Don't look so petulant."

"I'm not, I was just—"

"Shh. I know what you want more than you do."

Damn he was sexy. Some might think arrogant but I knew him. I knew Devlin Indigo-Price and I knew damn well that his words would be backed up with action. It was supreme confidence shining in his eyes, not superiority or cockiness.

He placed the head of the whip against my sternum and pulled at the low neckline on my leotard.

I glanced down. My small breasts were in view, my neat dark nipples taut and hard.

He sucked in a breath. "Take it off."

I did as he asked, peeling off the scrap of material.

I was naked beneath. I felt even more naked as he was fully dressed – boots and tie and jacket.

He dropped his gaze down my body. Feasting on me with his eyes. His mouth was a little slack and his breathing had picked up speed again.

"I've so often thought of you like this, my love." He let the tip of the whip travel from my sternum, over my belly and to the rise of my hairless mound. "You are so small, dainty, perfectly formed yet also strong and supple and . . ."

"And?" I placed my hands on my hips. I wanted to know what else he thought I was.

"So ready for my whip."

"Yes." I parted my legs. The juncture of my thighs was moist. My pussy felt swollen and needy and my arse . . . I clenched my buttocks at the thought of the whip licking across them.

"Like this." He grabbed my shoulder, a little roughly, and tugged me the few steps to the table that had the tarot cards spread out.

"Over. Bend over." He placed his hand between my shoulder blades and forced me double.

I gasped as my arse stuck out, towards him, and my breasts flattened on the cards. Right in front of my nose was the Tower, it's energy either destructive or creative. For me it symbolized creativity. A welt on my arse, a hundred welts on my arse, administered by Devlin, would rebuild me, take me to him, make me his.

"So sweet," he said, running his hand down my back and over my buttocks. "So unblemished."

I whimpered.

He slipped his fingers through my crack and fondled my pussy.

The scent of my arousal seeped up to my nose. I wiggled, pressing myself onto him for more.

"Oh, yeah, good girl, that's it. Now touch yourself, too."

I snaked my hand down to my clit. I rubbed, fondled and gave my arousal something to concentrate on.

"There's not much room in here so it won't be the full length of the strike," Devlin said, his voice low, almost hypnotic, "but I'll give you a taste of it. A taste of things to come, a treat, something you can think about and decide if you want more of."

"Yes, I'll want more." I closed my eyes and twisted my head, rested my cheek on the Tower.

He gave a gruff laugh. "Oh my, you are a little pain whore, aren't you?"

"Only for you."

His hands left me and so did his body heat.

There was a shift in the air and a crack.

He was warming the whip.

"Please, Master." I shifted on the table. My clit was burning for it, my arse a mass of anticipation. I masturbated harder, faster.

Again the whip cracked, this time nearer to me. I felt the air rush past.

I groaned. I'd waited so long for this. I didn't want to wait another second.

And then it came. A searing, white-hot slice of pain that attacked my right buttock.

"Ah." I jerked, jolted forward and harnessed the agony as it shot over my skin, through my pelvis to my clit.

"Shh." He cupped his palm over the heat. "Is that what you want?"

"Yes. More . . ."

He pressed a kiss to my cheek, the one facing upwards, his nose touching my eyelid. "Hold on then, my love."

I parted my legs, felt moisture amongst my folds, and gripped the edge of the table with my free hand.

Another crack of the whip. This time the sharp tail struck my opposite buttock.

I moaned and let the pain play with my pussy and also my vision. Red, black, green and yellow danced behind my closed eyes.

"Oh, oh," I moaned.

He hit again, each buttock twice more.

It was bliss, perfection. I knew these were baby hits. If we'd had more room I could have appreciated a full-length thrash, but he was right, my Master, this was enough for our first time.

"Oh, I'm going to come," I gasped.

"Wait for me, Cina. Wait for me." His voice was stern.

I eased up on my clit, but the need was so great.

His cock was at my entrance, pushing in – hot and hard and thick.

"Yes," I wailed, opening up for him.

He drove into the hilt, filling me, completing me.

His pubes scratched against the sting on my arse cheeks and his balls pressed up against my pussy.

"I'm going to fuck you now," he said. "My sweet love."

I didn't answer, just him seating to the hilt had tipped me over the edge. I came. With a gasp and a full body tremble, my orgasm raged through me.

The pain, the submission, had taken me to new heights and every spasm and contraction in my pussy was tenfold.

"Yes, yes, fuck, hug me like that," he moaned. His moan turned into a long drawn-out groan and he too came, filling me with his seed, spurting into me and claiming me. "Cina, Cina, Cina," he cried.

I released my clit and panted through the final stages of my climax.

"We fit so well," he said breathlessly.

There'd been no frantic fucking, no wild mating, just the act of joining together had created our climax and stolen our breath.

I opened my eyes and lifted my head. Stuck to my hot cheek was a card.

Devlin took it gently from me and twirled it between his fingers. "Before tonight we had no knowledge of each other's love and our eternal compatibility," he whispered by my ear. "The Fool shows himself now because he's the cause behind all effects, the power behind all manifestations and the seeds sown in every beginning."

"Yes, our love is here." I squirmed a little, my pussy was full of his warm come. "And the seeds are sown."

"My perfect woman," he said, resting his lips against my temple. "Our seeds will grow into a perfect life together. We'll have children, girls who ride unicorns and boys who tame lions. And you, I promise, will never have a sad day that is of my doing. I will love and care for you for all eternity."

Trespass

Annabeth Leong

Alice hauled herself up the last few feet of the near-vertical rock scramble and stood tall atop, looking at a view hardly anyone ever got to see. The valley rolled out below her, fertile and inviting. Fog turned the tree tips below a soft blue color, and she closed her eyes to soak in the sound of rare birdsong.

It had been uncomfortable to climb in the long-sleeved dun-colored shirt and olive-green slacks of a park ranger. In more than a half-dozen trips to national parks across the United States, however, she'd used the outfit to score unquestioned access to trails ordinarily closed to the public – which always seemed to be the ones with the best views.

Sure, this valley would still have looked beautiful from the public vantage point on the other side of this mountain. She wouldn't have heard the birdsong over the packs of squalling children out on school trips, though, and she wouldn't have gotten such a triumphant secret thrill.

The skitter of a nearby rock made her stiffen. She fumbled in one pocket for the tie she'd stashed and prepared herself to act the part.

A few seconds later, a large male hand came into view, followed by the rest of the man. Alice wasn't sure if her heart began to pound from attraction or fear. He moved with animal grace, big muscles rippling like a wildcat's. Other than that single dislodged rock, he'd made no sound climbing, and he moved noiselessly now. He seemed twice her size or more, and his stern expression made her shrink back.

Alice paused in her effort to straighten her tie, her hopes of bluffing another tourist sinking. This man wore the official version of the uniform she'd copied so assiduously.

She offered a nervous smile. "Sorry, I couldn't resist taking a break. I'll get back on duty now. Don't worry about me. I'll report to the visitor center directly."

He folded his arms over his chest and replied with a feral, dangerous smile. His silence made Alice babble. She talked about the weather, pretended to commiserate about rude tourists, and chattered about how she had only recently transferred to this particular park and looked forward to going out with the other rangers for beers.

When he still didn't say anything, Alice rubbed her hands against her thighs. "Well, as I said, I need to get back to work." She took a deep breath and moved to pass him.

He shot a hand out before she could reach the rock scramble, gripping her upper arm. She glanced down at where he held her. Even his fingers were big, and they dug into her triceps hard enough to hurt.

The man began speaking in a conversational tone. "The worst tourists," he said, "the rudest ones, are the ones who think the rules don't apply to them. When I catch one of them on a trail that's been closed to the public, I want to give her a good, hard spanking."

That sounded ominous. If her fake uniform didn't fool this man, she was definitely in some sort of trouble. From the sound of things, that trouble might be more serious than a fine. Alice pictured herself draped over his big thighs as he smacked her ass cheeks until she cried. Beneath her fear, an unexpected rush of arousal made her feel weak.

"A spanking?" Alice's voice came out as a squeak.

"Yeah. Until she begs for mercy and swears never to trespass again." He raised an eyebrow. "Of course, I probably wouldn't be able to trust that she'd learned her lesson at first. That would only be the beginning of what I'd do to her." He propelled her to face him, the gesture apparently effortless. His other hand closed around her other arm, trapping her more securely. "What about you? What do you think should happen to tourists who think they know better than we do?"

Alice did her best to square her shoulders, but her hands had begun to tremble. If she confessed now, it sounded as if she'd be in for a spanking and much more. On the other hand, trying to keep up the facade seemed dangerous. She gave a weak laugh. "I'm not as creative as you. I'd probably just escort the trespasser back to the public area."

"Really? After what you said about rude tourists? Park rangers are creative people. Any real park ranger would have better ideas."

"I'd try to teach them," Alice said desperately. "I'd show them why the trail had been closed."

He smirked at that. "Generous of you. What about if the person you found made a habit of trespassing in national parks?" He released one of her arms and grabbed her tie instead, yanking it and forcing her to stumble a few steps closer to him. "What if she did it by impersonating park rangers? Putting on the uniform you worked to earn under false pretenses?"

Alice gulped. Her mind felt too slow to get her out of this. Her body was way ahead of her, responding to his rough handling with a melting heat that wasn't helping her think any faster. "That's probably something I'd leave to law enforcement."

He grinned at that and grabbed her around the waist, pulling her against his body and letting her feel his impressive erection. "You're forgetting that we *are* law enforcement," he said. He leaned in close enough that his lips brushed her ear. "There are only six rangers working at this park, honey. We all know each other. Believe me, if I'd ever seen that ass of yours before, in any park across this country, I'd recognize it."

Alice knew she ought to respond with something brave and defiant, but she couldn't help whimpering at the way he touched her. It took all her control not to grind her pussy against his cock. The secret thrill of climbing to this secluded spot paled beside the dirty thrill of rubbing against a man whose name she didn't even know.

"Here's your choice," the ranger said. "I can do it your way and take you back to the visitor center. You've been spotted at other parks, so you've got a list of infractions waiting for you. We'll get you into the legal system." He paused. "Or I can confiscate this fake uniform you're wearing. And this fake badge." He moved his hand over the badge she'd affixed to her chest, cupping her breast in the process. The heel of his hand worked her nipple, but there was no need for him to massage it to hardness – her nipples and clit had stood at attention the moment he'd started talking about a spanking. "I think you know what comes next."

There was only one appropriate way to answer his offer – and if she went with him to the visitor center, she could probably enter a complaint about his sexual harassment as she faced her own charges – but that wasn't the one she was considering. Alice was the kind of girl who liked secrets. She enjoyed getting around the system and getting her own way. Right now, being spanked and fucked with this gorgeous view spread out before her sounded a lot better than getting arrested. She knew the ranger would give it to her rough and hard, but if the pulse pounding in her pussy was any indication, that would be exactly the way she wanted it.

She reached up and undid the top button of her shirt.

He slapped her hand away. "Oh no, honey. We're not leaving this shirt in any condition to be worn again." The ranger gripped her shirt on each side of the buttons, his forearm muscles bulging as he clenched his fists. Then he tore it open.

The tie prevented the collar from breaking open, but the rest of the shirt split to reveal her torso. He grinned and popped her breasts up out of her bra. "That's better," he said. "Now you look more like what you are. I think I'll leave the tie on, though. I might need to keep you on a short leash."

The way he talked made it hard for Alice to catch her breath. She stood as still as she could as he tore the shirt away from the collar, then removed her pants and tore away her thong. Though no one besides him could see her, she blushed with shame at being outdoors in nothing but her tie, bra and hiking boots. At the same time, the scent of arousal spread unmistakably from her cunt.

The ranger dropped her clothes in the dirt and kicked them aside. Then he took Alice by the wrist and stepped to the edge of the small plateau where they stood.

She hadn't minded the height while climbing, but she'd been under her own control then. Alice's head spun as she contemplated the long trip down – and she shrieked as he sat with his legs dangling over the edge and yanked her down with him. He spread her over his lap. Alice reached out and gripped a rock with one hand, but she knew she was only inches from a terrible fall.

"You like to live dangerously, honey? Climb trails you're not supposed to? Let go of the rock."

It might not have made much difference to Alice if she had fallen, but she had no real reason to trust this ranger. She couldn't bring herself to release her hold on it. He grabbed her wrist and squeezed, showing his strength. "Let it go," he repeated. "I'll make sure you don't fall."

She whimpered but obeyed. He locked one strong arm over her back, but that only emphasized that Alice was entirely at his mercy.

"You're going to want to make sure you don't squirm," he said. "If you fight me, it'll make it much harder for me to hold on."

Alice opened her mouth to reply, but her words became a squeal as he brought his big hand down hard on her ass. This wasn't the play spanking she'd experimented with in the past. This was punishment. It stung, and he gave her no time to catch her breath before coming in for the next blow.

Cursing, Alice flailed her legs – and the ranger abruptly released the hand that held her secure. Alice froze, heart pounding, dizzy from the height. "I told you not to move. If you want me to hold on, you need to earn it."

"No, please, I'll be good."

"Prove it."

He came at her with a flurry of blows, each one bringing tears to her eyes. He struck the tops of her thighs, each individual cheek of her ass, and both together. Alice didn't dare wriggle. She barely dared to breathe. She remained as motionless as possible as he heated her ass with his blows, holding nothing back, the feeling so intense that she went limp across his lap and sobbed wordlessly.

Only then did the ranger hold her again, tucking his arm securely around her waist. "Thank you," Alice whispered.

"Keep being a good girl. Just a few more. For these, I'm going to want you to spread your legs for me."

Alice did, and the movement made one of her legs dangle over the edge. She gasped, forced to trust herself to the ranger's strength. He dipped a hand into her split. "Wet," he said. "Dripping wet. I told you the outfit you had on earlier didn't suit you. It's much better for you to be naked, showing off that wet cunt."

He emphasized his words with another slap, this one hitting her pussy. She was so wet that she felt beads of moisture splash around his hand and onto her thighs. Alice wasn't ready to beg for mercy, but she was ready to beg for his cock. She worked a hand between their bodies so she could rub his erection through his pants.

"I told you not to move!"

He pulled them both away from the edge so suddenly her head spun. Before Alice knew what was happening to her, the ranger had opened his pants and taken out his cock. Grabbing her by the tails of her tie, he directed her head exactly where he wanted it to go. She opened her mouth just in time to take his cock to the back of her throat.

Alice gagged, and the ranger pulled back and paused. "You can do better than that, can't you? You look like the sort of girl who's done this at least once before. Try again."

She swallowed around him as best she could, took a deep breath, and closed the back of her throat. This time when he pushed in, she managed to accommodate him.

He didn't check to see how she was handling it, though. Still gripping the tie, the ranger controlled Alice's head, guiding her almost all the way off his cock and then forcing her to touch her lips to his pubic hair. In seconds, his ragged breathing made Alice think she was about to get a mouthful of come. She lifted a hand to his tightening balls to encourage the orgasm, but at that he shoved her away again.

"You think you're getting out of this with just a blow job?" He pointed at a rock scramble that led higher up the mountain. "Stand facing that. You're going to want to brace yourself."

Alice wanted to ask what he was going to do to her, but she didn't really want to know. Honestly, she was enjoying the ranger's demands. His unpredictability had flooded her body with adrenalin, intensifying the effects of her arousal. Ass still smarting and throat still aching, she did as commanded and stood to face the rocks. She took the time to find secure handholds because she had a feeling she would need them.

The ranger came up behind her and introduced two fingers to her pussy, pressing in roughly. "You're going to let me fuck you however I want, aren't you?"

Alice was well past the point of denying it. She nodded helplessly and inched her legs a few inches farther apart. Her cunt clenched madly around his fingers. It felt as if she would come if he so much as swiped her clit, and she couldn't wait to take his cock to the root.

The ranger, however, had other plans. He wrenched his fingers from her cunt and trailed them up to her asshole, smearing her arousal over her rear entrance. "A girl like you's not going to be shocked that I want this hole. You've used it before, I'm sure."

Alice had, but only with plenty of preparation, and never with a man she didn't know. She couldn't refuse the ranger anything, though, not with her body thrumming powerfully with its own demands. She rested her forehead against the rock wall and did her best to relax her muscles and let his fingers in.

"Good girl," he praised as he worked a second finger into her ass beside the first. "I knew you'd be good for this." As he finger-fucked her ass, Alice's clit burned with impending orgasm. She tried to slide a hand down to give herself relief, but he caught her wrist and wrenched it upward. "You just can't behave. The moment I ease up, you push your luck."

"I'm sorry."

"You're going to be even more sorry in a moment when you realize I'm not going to let you come." He jerked his fingers out of her ass.

Alice leaned against the rocks, gasping and shuddering. Her pussy dripped onto the tops of her thighs and her ass muscles fluttered. Behind her, a condom wrapper ripped, and she tensed, thinking of that big cock entering her asshole.

Her hand drifted toward her cunt again.

"How many times do I have to tell you no?" The ranger grabbed her arm roughly and twisted it behind her back, forcing Alice to use her free hand to keep herself from falling.

He plunged his cock into her pussy with one rough thrust, and she moaned her gratitude. The ranger pumped hard a few times, just enough to make the orgasm shimmer behind her eyes. Then he pulled out, laughing softly. "That was just for lubrication, honey. You're lucky I'm feeling nice today."

Shifting the head of his cock to her asshole, he pressed her tight against the rock wall, its rough surfaces scraping her skin. A mossy rock tickled her stomach. The ranger kissed the tip of her ear, his breathing harsh. "Let me in, baby."

Alice closed her eyes and surrendered to the situation – the outdoor air rushing through her hair, the humiliating way he treated her, and the hard, relentless cock demanding entrance to her asshole. She exhaled, and he sank in a little way.

"That's right." The ranger began to fuck in and out of her, tiny movements at first, but sinking a little deeper every time. Alice broke out into a sweat from the intensity of it. He had a big cock – under normal circumstances, she wouldn't even have tried to take it in her ass. It overwhelmed her, forcing her to trust her weight to him. She wasn't capable of anything besides breathing, feeling the pulse in her neglected, gushing pussy, and focusing on opening to him.

When he'd pressed all the way in, they rested that way for a moment. Alice heard the rare birdsong again, and something felt right about what she'd found in this out-of-the way spot, a primal experience that she hadn't known she was looking for. This ranger had taken her out of her human experience, making her feel like a simple animal.

Then he kissed the back of her head and began to fuck her in earnest. Again, he gave it to her hard when other lovers would have held back. Alice cried out. His cock held her prisoner against the rock face, filling her ass to the point just short of pain. When he pulled out, the ecstasy of it made her dizzy, and when he thrust in she was forced to give herself up to him all over again.

She hoped he would forget his promise not to let her come, but he never released her. He grunted as he fucked her, lost in his own world, as if a part of him had forgotten that Alice was there. He made her feel like a silent part of nature, a hole for him to explore. He bit her neck as he came, and she sobbed more from the pain of her denied pleasure than from the pain of his teeth.

Pulling out, the ranger was almost tender with her. He stroked a few beads of sweat off her back and murmured that he really didn't see any need to punish her any further. She had clearly learned a good lesson, he said.

Alice bent to retrieve her ruined clothes, but at that the ranger became stern again. Pulling the used condom free of his cock and tucking it back into his pants, he kicked the clothes out of her reach. "You haven't earned those clothes, honey, like I said. I think the outfit you've earned is the one you're wearing."

She looked down at herself, freshly fucked and still dripping arousal, dressed only in remnants. "How do I get back to the parking lot like this?"

He shrugged, a glint in his eyes. "You're good at getting to places you're not supposed to be. I'm sure you'll figure something out. Go on now."

Alice's pussy throbbed, and she knew that the moment she got to her car, she would finger-fuck herself silly, perhaps more than once, and it didn't matter who might see. For the moment, though, she had one more task of obedience ahead. Squaring her shoulders, she righted her bra and checked her shoes. She would have taken off the tie, but the ranger shook his head.

"Don't mess with the clothes. I like the way you look now."

Alice took a deep breath and climbed down the scramble. She was good in the woods, and she was already picturing the maps she'd studied before coming out to this trail. She came up with a path that would keep her mostly out of sight until the last fifty feet or so, when she'd have no choice but to streak to her car in full view of anyone gathered around the visitor center. On the other side of this challenge, however, the orgasm of her life awaited her. She imagined the pleasure that would soak through her and mingle with the lingering ache the ranger's cock had left in her ass.

As she passed out of his sight, she gave him one last naughty smile, because Alice had realized something. He'd spanked her and given her the rough fucking she craved, but he hadn't made her beg for mercy, and she'd never promised to stop trespassing. Her cunt clenched as she imagined what might happen if he caught her again.

Hot Prospect

Louisa Harte

"Sorry, I'm not interested."

I'm about to protest but the line goes dead before I can say anything. Crap, there goes another potential client. I sigh. Story of my life. I remove my headset and glance again at the sales pitch. It's the latest version by Greg, our team supervisor. Seriously, how any of us are expected to sell products with a script like this is beyond me. Bland and uninspired, just like the uniform Greg insists we wear. Another by-product of the fancy business courses he keeps scooting out on. He says it'll improve our performance. Boring black and white, just like the script we have to follow, it could all do with an injection of colour.

I stand and stretch and, right on cue, Greg slides out of his office like a slippery eel, straight down the stairs for another break. Typical. It's all right for him, he can take off whenever he feels like it – while we, the sales team, have to peck away at our work, cooped up in these partitioned, little booths like hens at a battery farm.

But, hopefully, for one of us, all that could change. Greg's offering a bonus to the top salesperson this week. Not a huge amount, but enough to take that mini vacation I dream of – leaving it all behind and sunning it up on a beach for a week or two. Now, with only two days left to go until the bonus is announced, I'd better get stuck into these calls.

I sit back down, don my headset and call the next number on my contact list, a Mr K. Jones. OK here we go again . . . I pick at my nail polish while I wait for a reply.

Eventually, the call's picked up. I lean back in my chair,

holding the sales script loosely between my fingers. "Hello, Mr Jones? Hi. My name's Sam. How are you today?"

The line's quiet at the other end, until finally, a voice replies. A deep, husky, masculine voice. "Well, hello there. I'm fine, thank you. Pleased to meet you, Sam."

Wow. My eyes widen. I'm used to bored, disinterested and even abusive responses, but this is something else altogether – interested, intriguing and downright sexy.

"And how are you?" he continues.

"Good thanks." *Wow, and considerate.*

I cast my gaze back to the script. "Now, Mr Jones, I believe I may have something to improve your life."

He laughs. A rich, low chuckle that makes me tingle. "I imagine you do. Please, tell me more," he says.

Sexy bugger. I stifle a gasp and grab my script again, trying to refocus. *Come on, girl, get a grip.*

"Here at Croydin's Catalogue Clothing we've a range of stunning clothes to suit all tastes," I resume, regaining my composure. "I'm sure I have something here to interest you."

"Oh, I bet." That sexy chuckle again. "OK. I'm listening . . . Oh, and by the way, you have a very sexy voice, Sam."

"Yours is pretty hot too." Crap, I can't believe I just said that out loud!

Damn. Rule Number One – stick to the script!

He chuckles again. Even his laugh turns me on. Boy, I'm in trouble here.

"I'm Kyle by the way," he says.

I clear my throat. Try to sound professional. "Hi, Kyle. Now, I just have a couple of questions to establish your tastes," I say, attempting to get back on track.

"Oh, I'm pretty easy really," Kyle interjects. "But first, tell me, I'm intrigued – what do you look like, Sam? Do you have long or short hair?"

"Long," I find myself instinctively replying, my fingers automatically reaching up to fiddle with my ponytail.

Damn. Rule Number Two – don't get distracted! But as I can't quite tell whether Kyle's being lewd or he's genuinely interested in the pitch, I'm compelled to continue. OK, I confess, I'm just making excuses to see where this goes.

"Nice. And what colour are your eyes?" he continues.

Kyle's voice is hypnotic and instantly I find myself replying. "Green."

"My favourite colour," he breathes.

I smile. "Hey, do you always chat up your callers?"

"No. You're the exception."

Whoa. I feel an unexpected rush of pleasure at his admission. I shake my head. Gee, I need to sort myself out, not get worked up over some sweet-talking stranger. I attempt to resume the script, but instead find myself trying to imagine the body that matches his sexy voice. "What do you look like?" I ask, vaguely aware this is going the wrong way.

"Use your imagination . . ."

Kyle's provocative words hang in the air and the script falls from my fingers. Surely I can digress a bit – this is the best conversation I've had in weeks. And we all assume Greg doesn't monitor our calls, he prefers to prowl around the office, sticking his nose into our work in person. I close my eyes and let my mind wander, playing with ideas until an image of this guy grows clear in my mind. Slim, fit and, of course, well endowed.

"Have you something in mind?" Kyle prompts.

"Yeah," I whisper, savouring the image I've conjured in my head.

His voice deepens. "Good. So tell me, what are you wearing?"

My heart hammers. This is wrong. I could get fired for behaving like this. But with this smoking-hot image in my mind and Kyle's sexy voice in my ear, I'm defenceless. A cheeky smile grazes my lips.

Oh, what the hell. I could do with a bit of fun.

I glance down at my plain white blouse and sensible skirt – hardly seduction material. Still, I'll just have to work with it. "Where shall I start?" I whisper, trying to mask my timidity.

Kyle senses my hesitation and takes the lead. "Start with your top."

"I'm wearing a white cotton blouse," I say, desperately searching for a more erotic description. I've not really had much practice at this sort of thing.

"Does it show off your curves?" Kyle prompts, offering encouragement.

I glance down at the swell of my breasts beneath my blouse. At least I've got that going for me – my male colleagues are often making leery comments about the size of my boobs. "Yeah," I say, determined to work it. "Especially my breasts."

"Good, you're getting into it now," murmurs Kyle. "How tight is it?"

"So tight that if I open a few buttons, my tits'll poke out the top," My initial nerves rapidly fade under Kyle's expert guidance.

"Great. Then open them," Kyle commands.

Ooh, authoritative. I like it. I pause and make sure no one's looking. Then I lean around my booth and check on Greg's whereabouts. Good, still no sign of him. Thankfully, the booths offer a small degree of privacy – goodness knows I need it for what I'm doing.

"Go on," Kyle's sultry voice encourages.

Goaded on by a surge of lust and Kyle's sexy encouragement, I automatically find myself tugging at the buttons on my blouse. As the third button pops open, my breasts peek out of the front of my blouse, straining and pushing against the skimpy bra trying valiantly to contain them. "OK, now what?" I whisper.

"Now undo your bra and take it off." Kyle's formal tone and calm and precise instructions add to the illicit naughtiness of our exchange.

Stifling a giggle of pleasure, I slide my hand under my blouse and unclasp my bra. Easing the straps over my shoulders, I whip off my bra and toss it onto the floor under my desk.

"Done?"

"Yeah," I whisper eagerly, fully complicit now in his game of seduction.

"Excellent." Sensing my compliance, Kyle's tone becomes lustful. "Now feel those voluptuous tits. Touch them how you like to be touched. Describe them to me."

It's as if I can't wait and, like an eager student under the instruction of a hot tutor, I do as I'm told, kinky passion making me reckless. I cup my boobs in my hands and stroke them through my blouse. *This is actually really horny.* "My tits are like two big, soft mounds of dough in my hands," I whisper, excitement fuelling my words. "I'm kneading them with my fingers, squeezing them together, pressing and teasing them."

Kyle sighs. "That's good, Sam. *Very good.*"

His appreciation urges me on. "Now I'm pinching and teasing my nipples through the front of my blouse. They're getting tighter and harder and they ache to be nibbled and sucked."

"Mmm . . . I can picture that," Kyle replies huskily. "You're getting good at this. Now, move your hands lower."

"To my skirt?"

"Yes. Describe your skirt."

I run my fingers over the smooth black material, which now feels surprisingly erotic. It's as if my plain uniform is magically transformed under Kyle's expert tuition and my own sensual touch. Along with the sight of my nipples poking cheekily through the front of my blouse, I feel like a wanton hussy.

And I like it.

"It's tight black linen and it skims the top of my knees. Oh, and there's a zip on the side," I say.

"How convenient," Kyle whispers. I can almost sense the devilish smile on his face. "Pull it down," he orders, his voice becoming breathless.

I quickly check no one's watching. I blush at his suggestion, but my fingers work faster than my mind and within seconds my zip's down and my right hand is creeping under the fabric.

"Good girl. Now, you know what I'm going to ask you to do next, don't you?"

Ha. Beat you to it. One step ahead, I already felt a kinky thrill as I slid my hand to my crotch.

Kyle hesitates. "You're already under your skirt aren't you, you naughty girl?"

Slippery wetness develops between my thighs. It's as if he sees straight into my thoughts.

"Now put your hand in your panties," Kyle instructs.

I shiver with glee and pull my panties aside to slide my fingers into my knickers.

"How do you feel?" he whispers.

"Creamy," I say, my words flowing freely like my slippery juice.

Kyle stifles a groan, his breathing becoming laboured. Sounds like he's almost losing it himself. *Good.* "Now, tell me how you like to be touched," he continues.

I shuffle down in my chair and spread my legs wider to access my hungry pussy. I probe my slit with my fingers, excitement making me bold. "I'm running my fingers over my slit, sliding them around in my juice, moving them towards my pussy."

"Mmm . . . Sounds delicious. Push a finger inside," Kyle orders breathlessly.

Eager to oblige, I slide a finger inside me and stifle a groan of pleasure at the moist heat of my pussy.

"And another . . ." Kyle urges. "Then thrust them in and out," he says, his voice keeping pace with the rhythm of his breathing.

I rhythmically slide my fingers in and out of myself, my heart pounding as the office, work, everything fades in the grip of this hedonism.

"Now stroke your clit," Kyle instructs.

I sweep my thumb over my clit, now hard and swollen and purr with pleasure as I rub it back and forth over the tip.

"Describe what you're doing," Kyle pants.

"I'm rubbing my eager clit with my thumb," I reply huskily, "and fucking myself with my fingers."

Kyle moans. "Beautiful. Now, make yourself come."

Intoxicated by Kyle's words and my thumb's skilful strokes, I feel a huge climax building inside. I increase the pace of my stroking, circling and rubbing my clit as if my life depended upon it. Murmuring my pleasure, I hear Kyle sigh appreciatively too as he pictures me wanking.

Arousal thumps in my veins and pleasure surges through me. I can't hold off any longer and I reach eagerly for a final stroke to bring me relief. My body shudders, my thighs clamp around my fingers as the ripples of orgasm take hold.

"Oh yeah!" I gasp as the juicy climax rips through me. I close my eyes, giving into the powerful sensations consuming my body.

Gradually, as the blissful feelings subside, I open my eyes. Slowly, the office comes back into focus – the hum of voices, click of keyboards. Everything—

Including Greg's face, peering at me over the top of my booth.

Damn. That was a short meeting! Hastily, I button up my blouse and try to distract his attention. "Oh, hi, Greg," I say, trying to look attentive.

"Looking a bit relaxed, Sam," Greg says, arching his eyebrows. "I trust you're working hard."

I suck in a breath and kick my bra further under the table, out of sight.

"Oh, she's working all right," Kyle whispers lustily in my ear.

I stifle a grin and tap the keyboard purposefully.

"That's better." Greg nods. "Now keep it up."

"If only he knew . . ." Kyle whispers.

I want to laugh at that. Somehow I manage to contain it while I wait for Greg to move his arse. Finally, he seems satisfied and moves away to check on my colleagues. I sigh. "Phew, that was close."

"I bet you like an element of danger."

Feeling the flush in my cheeks, I have to admit it. "I guess I do now."

After a few moments of silence, Kyle's voice resumes over the phone. "So, did you enjoy that?"

"What?" I reply, playfully coy.

"Fucking yourself while I listened."

"Yeah. Couldn't you tell?"

"Well, there's more where that came from, if you'll excuse the pun," he says. "Call me again tomorrow."

I can sense the sly smile on his face. "OK. Yeah, why not."

"Oh, and Sam . . ." Kyle interjects. "Dress appropriately." With that, the line goes dead.

What does he mean by that? This uniform's pretty naff, so I'll have to be creative. I take a moment to catch my breath. Gee, that was fun. I grin and zip up my skirt, an image of our naughty liaison lingering in my mind.

I continue smiling as I work my way through the rest of the day's calls. Feeling reckless now, I depart slightly from the script and even shift a few products in the process, which is pretty amazing for me.

And what Greg doesn't know shouldn't hurt him.

I hope.

Early next day, I breeze into the office, a new spring in my step at both the prospect of speaking to Kyle again *and* the feel of the kinky underwear I've donned underneath my uniform. I figure if I can't have some sass on the outside, I'll have it somewhere.

I think back to last night. I'd dissected my wardrobe, trying on sexy undies in front of the mirror – all the stuff I'd bought in the past but hardly got to wear. Finally, I'd settled on something.

And here I am now in the office, wearing my selection. Beneath my sensible uniform, is a hot basque and fishnet stockings. Yeah, it's a cliché, but for good reason, as it does feel pretty horny.

Greg's already in, pacing the floor in front of his office. "Bit early for you, isn't it, Sam?"

My heart flutters. "Thinking of the bonus, Greg," I reply, forcing a smile.

He lets out a low whistle as I strut past. "You look perky today – what's your secret?"

I smile. *Find some hot stud and fuck yourself while he listens over the phone. I can just see that making company policy.* Ha! I'd better keep that one to myself. "Oh, you know, just excited to be back here," I bluff.

That certainly raises Greg's eyebrows. "Well, whatever your secret is, let the others in on it."

Feeling invigorated, I head to my booth. Same routine, but today I feel cheerier than I've felt in months at the thought of what's ahead. Gradually, my colleagues drift in and the sound of voices and keyboards clattering replaces the silence. I pull on my headset and set to work, continually sneaking furtive glances at Greg's office to check for a good moment to call Kyle. It makes me feel powerful to be monitoring Greg's movements for a change, and in turn I take other risks, like departing further from the sales script, my anticipation about speaking to Kyle fuelling flirtatious banter, which even results in a few significant sales. *Not bad.* Especially given that it's bonus day today. Not that I stand a chance of getting it, but hey, a girl can wish.

Finally, I get the opportunity I've been waiting for. Greg announces he's popping out for a meeting and could be gone until midday. I wait till he's gone and then dial Kyle's number.

This time, I don't have to wait long before I hear that familiar velvety tone in my ear. "Hello, gorgeous," Kyle says.

"How did you know it was me?"

"Lucky guess. How are you feeling today?"

"Horny," I reply. Something about Kyle just brings out my brazenness. "Last night, I couldn't stop thinking about our chat yesterday."

"Only thinking?" Kyle teases.

My cheeks flush. *He's perceptive.* "No, not just thinking."

"What else?"

"And playing with myself," I confess, recalling how I'd recreated our steamy exchange, at home in bed.

"Kinky girl. And did you enjoy it?"

"Yeah, but, it wasn't as good as hearing your voice."

Kyle chuckles. "Let's see what we can do about that, shall we?"

I smile shamelessly. Whatever he's got in mind, I'm up for it.

"Tell me, Sam, did you follow my instructions today?"

"You betcha." I smooth my fingers over my skirt savouring the steamy thrill of the kinky undies beneath.

"Good," Kyle replies. "So what are you hiding from me?"

I close my eyes to heighten my senses. "Under my blouse, I'm wearing a sexy black basque. The laced-up-front is struggling to confine my boobs."

"Mmm, I can just picture that," murmurs Kyle.

I grin. I'm getting the hang of this more and more with each day that passes. "And under my ever-so-sensible skirt I'm wearing not-so-sensible stockings." I run my hands over my thighs. "They're black fishnet stockings and they feel deliciously sexy against my soft thighs."

Kyle takes in a breath. "Mmm lovely . . . and does dressing like this turn you on?"

"Yeah." It's true, I love the way the stockings clutch my thighs, emphasizing my curves. Plus I love the fact that I could bend over at any moment and reveal my secret to whomever I choose. "It's pretty kinky."

"Do you know how you sound?" Kyle says playfully.

I giggle. "Like a slut?"

I can sense the smirk on his face. "Yes, like a slut. And what should I do with a slutty woman like you?" His polite tone is laced with promise.

My eyes flick open. Heats prickles my skin and I undo a few buttons on my blouse. *Can I do this?* Tell my fantasies to a complete stranger – and at work? But the fact that he *is* a complete stranger makes this all the more possible and with images already filling my mind, along with the thrill of the illicit environment, I've got to go for it. After a furtive check no one is looking, I close my eyes again and whisper, "You should spank me."

Kyle chuckles sexily. "Yes, I should," he replies. "Let me tell you what I'd do."

I settle back in my chair, letting Kyle take the lead and indulge my fantasy.

"First, I'd tear off that sensible blouse of yours and I'd run my hands up the sides of your basque, savouring your curvy waist. Then I'd run my hands over your boobs and you'd whimper, begging me to unlace the basque and free your big tits."

"Oh, would I?" I taunt. I cup my tits through my blouse, in keeping with his imagery.

"Yes, you would. But I'd only unlace a few notches, enough to expose the top of your glorious tits."

My nipples harden at the thought. *Horny.*

He continues. "Then, I'd push your skirt up around your waist and bend you over my knee. I'd run my hands up over your fishnet stockings until I reached the curve of your arse."

I like it. My pussy contracts at the thought and I slip a feverish hand under my skirt to satisfy my craving. "And then what?"

"I'd pull your panties down, inch by inch."

"What panties?" I interject, my fingers connecting with the curls of my mound.

"Oh, I see, like that is it?" Kyle adopts a more strident tone. "Well, I'd have to punish you for that. I'd unbuckle my leather belt and curl it in my hand."

I hear the sound of a belt slipping through its clasps. I gasp. Damn, this guy is good.

"Then, I'd touch the belt to the curve of your butt," Kyle resumes, "before raising it into the air and then . . ."

"*Yes . . .*" I prompt, my body tingling in anticipation of what's to come.

Whack!

It's all I can do not to cry out with passion as he imitates the sound of his spanking. The image of me lying across his lap, my butt cheeks turning pink under his smacks makes me hungry with lust.

"Do you think that would teach you?" he whispers.

"No." I groan, my fingers gliding to my slit.

Whack! "Then I'd spank you again," he continues, sounding breathless. "And, each time I spanked you, you'd buckle and your tits would press against my knees, bulging and begging to be set free from their confines."

I slide my other hand under my blouse and squeeze my erect nipples through my basque. "And then what would you do?" I ask, eager for more.

"I'd slide my other hand between your legs and finger your pussy."

I gasp and drive a finger into my pussy to mimic the fantasy. "But, I'd want more," I beg, feeling my juices seep over my fingers.

"Then I'd tease your clit with my fingers and spank your arse until you came."

I moan at his horny description and rub my thumb over my clit, feeling a huge, juicy, climax building inside.

Kyle lowers his voice. "But all that spanking would make me horny."

"How horny?" I encourage.

"*Very horny.* My cock would press against my trousers, aching to fuck you."

Ha. A wicked smile curves my lips. I enjoy hearing Kyle lose his trademark cool. "Good," I goad. "I'd want to be fucked."

My words have the desired effect. Kyle's breathing deepens and I hear the sound of a zip being lowered.

Feeling reckless now, I heighten my own pleasure by taking the reins. "Let me tell you what *I'd* do. I'd jump up off your lap and turn to face you. Then, I'd unlace my basque and brush my tits against your face."

"Oh, would you?" Kyle goads.

"Yes, I would," I say, enjoying the thrill of vocalizing my fantasy. "Then I'd rip off your trousers and pull out your cock."

"And then what?" Kyle's breathing quickens.

"I'd slide my fingers up and down your prick."

I'm sure I detect the rhythmic stroke of his fingers over his cock. The thought of us both wanking turns me on even more. "Then, I'd straddle your hips and slide my eager pussy onto your dick." My words flow freely, fuelled by lust and the climax I feel building inside.

"Slowly at first." I listen to the fervent strokes at his end, enjoying my power, controlling his pleasure with my words. "Then, faster and faster," I say, my own hand working beneath my skirt, increasing the pace of my rubbing to mirror the image of us fucking. "And I'd grind myself down onto you . . . over and over again . . ."

"Yeah." Kyle sounds desperate for me to continue.

"*. . . until your fat cock exploded inside me.*"

That does it. That final image renders me powerless to hold off any longer. I groan. My body reels and shudders as my orgasm takes over.

I hear the sound of frantic pumping and I'm soon rewarded with Kyle's own guttural cry. The image of him coming sends another surge of euphoria racing through me.

Slowly, the heady feelings subside and my attention returns to reality. I open my eyes.

"Well, that was entertaining." Kyle's voice is raw. "How was it for you?"

I sigh, flopping back in my seat. "Pretty damn good." I grin at the irony. This guy beats anyone I've fucked in real life. "And you?"

"Fantastic. Couldn't you tell?"

I laugh. "Well, there were signs. Anyway, I bet you do this kind of thing all the time."

"Actually, it's my first time. Well, second, if you count our conversation yesterday."

I curl my fingers in my hair flirtatiously. "Well, I think you're hot."

"Glad I live up to your expectations."

My pussy quivers. Oh, he does that all right. *And more.*

"Well, I suppose I'd better buy something now, hadn't I?" Kyle asks slyly.

I laugh. "I think it's the least you can do after distracting me so thoroughly."

"Good, because I want to. What do you recommend?"

I grin and flick through the catalogue on my desk. "For a hot guy like yourself, I'd recommend our classy navy pinstripe suit. It's same day delivery, so you'll get it today."

"Sounds good, I'll take it."

I sigh. Listening to Kyle's seductive voice is becoming addictive. "Can I call you again sometime?" I ask, tentatively.

"Sure, I'd like that."

I'm surprised how elated how I feel at his reply.

"Oh, and, Sam, before I go . . ."

"Yeah?"

"Those undies sound sexy – keep wearing them."

I smooth my fingers over my stockings. The sexy material does make me smile. "OK, I will."

"Until we meet again." With that he's gone.

I listen to the dial tone for a while after he hangs up. I feel a bit wistful after our conversations. I hope I'm not getting sappy, but there's something about him that makes me smile. I gaze at the catalogue and picture Kyle's imaginary physique in the smart navy suit. The heat of our exchange warms me through lunch and the rest of the day. And, hey, I even make several more sales.

Time passes surprisingly quickly and I'm right up to speed on the day's calls when Greg's secretary, Kiera, interrupts.

"Hey, Sam, Greg wants to see you in his office," she says, leaning over my booth.

I swallow nervously. Greg doesn't call us into his domain unless there's good reason. "Know what it's about?"

"Nope. Just get your arse there pronto if you know what's good for you," Kiera adds, before disappearing back off to her office. Damn. What does Greg want? Must be serious for him to send Kiera to get me. I gather my paperwork, clutching it to my chest like a shield and nervously make my way to his office.

"You wanted to see me?" I say, peering around the door.

"Yes, come in. Sit down."

I enter Greg's office and perch on the edge of a chair facing Greg across his desk.

Greg takes in a deep breath. "Now, be honest with me, Samantha."

My heart sinks. He's using my full name. Not a good sign. "Sure," I croak.

Greg leans over the desk towards me. "Have you been departing from the new script this week?" he asks. "Perhaps, ad-libbing a bit." He narrows his eyes at me.

My mouth falls open. *Oh, hell. How does Greg know?* But from his expression I can see there's no use lying, he's obviously on to me. I meet his gaze. "Yeah," I mumble.

"I thought so," Greg says. Then, a smile flickers on his lips. "Because I've never seen a salesperson shift so many products in two days."

I lower my paperwork, scanning Greg's face for signs of a wind-up.

But his smile just gets bigger. "Congratulations, Sam, you're this week's top seller." He hands me an envelope. "The bonus is yours."

I gape in shock as he passes me the envelope. "Really? Are you sure?"

"Of course I'm sure. And, not only that, I want you to rewrite our script. I thought my version was good, but you must be doing something better. You've outsold the rest of the team put together this week."

I slowly begin to smile as Greg's words sink in. Come to think of it, I have done quite well in the last couple of days. I turn the envelope over in my hands, visions of my beach holiday filling my mind.

Greg continues talking as I digest the news. "I've been inundated with callers praising your attitude." He hesitates. "One client in particular was very complimentary. He was impressed with your technique and praised you for being so attentive to his needs."

"He did?" I say absently, still fiddling with the envelope.

"Yes. A polite, well-spoken gentleman."

I swallow thickly. The envelope falls still in my hands.

"He even wants to thank you in person."

My heartbeat drums in my chest as Greg rises to open the door. The door opens and a tall, slim guy steps into the office. He has dark tousled hair and liquid brown eyes. *Hot.*

"Hello, Sam," he says.

His voice is distinctly familiar and, as I scan his lithe figure, my breath catches in my throat at the smart suit he's wearing. *A navy pinstripe suit.*

"Sam, this is Kyle Jones. Do you remember speaking to him?" Greg blusters. He ushers Kyle forward to meet me.

Shakily, I stand. *Oh boy, do I remember him.* "Pleased to meet you . . . Kyle," I stammer, wishing my legs didn't feel like jelly. With his sexy smile and intense dark eyes, he's better than anything I'd ever imagined.

Kyle sweeps his gaze over my body. A cheeky grin flickers on his face, getting me wet all over again.

"Pleased to meet you too," he replies in that husky tone.

"She's our star performer," Greg waffles on, throwing a proud arm around my shoulders.

"Oh, she's that all right," says Kyle, his gaze burning into mine.

"Whatever it is you're doing, Sam, keep it up," whispers Greg.

I stare lustfully at my illicit lover. As more fantasies fill my mind, I simply nod and smile.

Happy to oblige.

Dogging the Law

Giselle Renarde

Even in the darkness, he could see her eyes bulging when he tapped gently but firmly at the window. Rolling it down, she asked, "Is there a problem, officer?"

"I was about to ask you the same thing. You haven't broken down, I hope?"

"No, no." She shook her head. "The car's working just fine, just fine and dandy."

When she said nothing further, he remarked, "Well then, I must say, I'm wondering what a nice lady like you's doing out in a nasty park like this in the middle of the night."

"I . . . oh . . . I . . ." She stared unapologetically at his badge, which gleamed in his cruiser's headlights.

"Ma'am, this place is crawling with lowlifes who wouldn't think twice before stealing a nice lady's innocence."

"Oh." Her knuckles turned white as she gripped the steering wheel. "I'm sorry, officer. I swear I didn't know."

Cocking his head, he squinted at her. He wasn't so sure she was telling the truth. "Maybe you're waiting for someone?"

"Waiting for someone? Ha, ha, ha." Her laughter sounded nervous and forced. She gripped the wheel tighter. "No. Me? No, I'm not . . . hahaha . . . waiting for someone."

"Hmm." He pushed his top lip up with his bottom one, letting his thick moustache scratch the bottom of his nose. "Only, some nice ladies come down here to meet their secret lovers while their husbands are, oh, say, putting in a little shift work up at the factory."

"Me? No. Lover? No, not me. No."

He hooked his thumbs through his belt loops, rocking from

his heels to the balls of his feet. He always liked the way his holster thwacked his thigh. The weight of his weapon aroused him far more than it should, and he wondered if the woman in the car took notice.

"I'm not meeting anybody," she said, and when her gaze drizzled down the dark surface of his uniform, her cheeks blazed. "I promise. I swear. I'm not lying to you, officer."

"Well, there are other reasons a woman might drive down here in the middle of the night," he replied. "But those women . . . well, they're not *nice* women like you."

"That's not a very charitable thing to say." She looked up into his eyes through the partially open window. "You're talking about . . . Are you talking about . . ." She lowered her voice and whispered, "Ladies of the night?"

The officer tapped his nose with his index finger.

"Well, It's not very open-minded of you to say those women aren't nice."

"They sure aren't very nice to me," he said.

"That's only because you're trying to arrest them."

Hmm, feisty.

"I'm sure some have had a rough life. If not, they probably wouldn't be out here in a scuzzy park. They'd be selling their services in penthouse apartments. Wouldn't you say so, officer?"

Oooh, this encounter was getting mighty interesting. "I'd say that if they were truly nice women they wouldn't be selling their services at all. They'd be at home in bed, with their husbands."

The driver's pink lips pursed until they turned as white as her knuckles. She was obviously fuming, because her head shook so adamantly her shoulder-length curls bobbed and bounced. In the harsh lights from his cruiser's headlamps it was difficult to tell if her hair was sandy or blonde or even dotted with greys. She was certainly older than most of the girls he picked up. In fact, she was more around the age of the johns.

"So if you're not here to meet someone and you're not selling any services," the officer went on, "maybe you're down here selling something else."

Her eyebrows shot halfway up her forehead. "Like what?"

"Well, what do you think gets bought and sold in this park after dark?"

It must have dawned on her what he was suggesting, because her expression changed from irate back to doe-eyed in an instant. "Drugs? You're talking about drugs?"

"That's right," he said, calm and confident. "Ma'am, have you come to this park for the purpose of buying or selling drugs?"

"No!" she squealed. "I've never done a drug in all my life! I wouldn't even know how!"

Considering her gravely, he leaned his face right down into her window. After he'd gotten her trembling in the driver's seat, he offered an appeasing, if somewhat smarmy, smile. "Yes, ma'am, I'd say you look straight as an arrow."

"I can assure you that I am."

He lingered in her window just a moment longer before standing upright. Placing a fist on each hip, he jutted his chest out, hoping she'd admire his physique. "So if you're not here to meet someone and you've got nothing to sell, the question remains: why have you come here at all?"

Staring straight ahead, she let both hands fall from the wheel. When they rested dejectedly in her lap, she said, "Well, you were right about one thing, I guess. My husband does work nights. He has for years. It isn't easy, being home alone. I miss him dearly."

"That still doesn't explain what brought a nice woman like you to a dangerous dive like this."

Batting her tear-laden eyelashes, she said, "The truth of the matter is that I like to watch things happen."

Looking over his shoulders, the officer asked, "Watch what? I don't see much of anything going on."

"Well, I know, but that's just because you're here. Usually, this lot is dotted with cars all full of couples kissing . . . and more."

"Why, goodness me!" the officer exclaimed in a mocking tone.

"And not just people in cars. There are lots of guys who meet in the woods. If I use my binoculars, I can get a pretty good look at what's going on."

Setting one hand above her car window, he leaned forward, looming over the woman who looked smaller by the moment. "Now why would you want to see a thing like that?"

"I don't know," she admitted. "I guess I find it exciting. I'm not doing anything wrong, not really. I just like to watch while . . ."

"While what?" he asked.

Gazing beyond his big body, she said, "I don't want to talk about it too loudly. Maybe you should get in the car so I can close the window. Then I won't be so worried about anyone overhearing."

"Well now, ma'am," he said. "This is most unusual."

"I know it is, but I want to explain myself. I don't want you thinking I'm a creep or a pervert."

"How could I think a thing like that about a nice lady like you?" he replied, in a tone somewhat more mocking than it needed to be.

Looking him straight in the eye, she said, "Just get in the car."

No need to argue with a request like that. He walked calmly around the front of her car, and by the time he arrived on the other side she'd already popped the passenger door open. Swiping her binoculars off the seat, he eased himself into her spacious vehicle. Ooh, that upholstery felt good. Much cushier than the cruiser.

"So, you wanted to know why I come here?" she asked, cranking the window closed.

"I must say, I am mighty curious." He shifted in his seat, looking for the perfect position of comfort. "A nice lady like you. Doesn't make much sense."

"Even a nice lady like me's got some curiosities," she replied.

He inched closer to the driver's seat. "Curiosities about what, now?"

She took the binoculars from him and held them to her chest. "Curiosities about what other people do when they get together. It's not like I can go around the neighbourhood peeking inside bedroom windows."

"So you drive down here in the middle of the night and peek inside car windows?"

"I don't peek," she said, in a rather haughty tone. "I stay inside my vehicle at all times. I keep my doors locked, I'll have you know. But I do bring my binoculars, as you can see." She set them on the dashboard, and they slid down the slight incline towards the windshield.

"Well, ma'am, I supposed we all have our . . . curiosities."

His erection throbbed inside his dark uniform, drawing her eye downward. She didn't need binoculars to spot that stiffy, oh no. This lady liked to look, and she did so unapologetically, staring at his bulge as it twitched, as it punched away at his fly.

"Take it out," she said.

He looked at her face, but she didn't look at his. She kept her eyes on the prize, even when he said, "Now, ma'am, that would be most ungentlemanly of me."

"Not if I'm asking for it." Her fingers found his thigh, walking towards the thing she so obviously lusted after. "Please, officer. I'm begging you. I want to see it."

Glancing over his shoulder, he looked into his cruiser's headlights, which burned his retinas. When he blinked, he saw the world in reverse – black became blazing white, white became a neon sort of black. For a moment, he couldn't tell up from down, and in that moment the nice lady in the driver's seat found his cock with the flat of her hand.

"Why, ma'am . . ."

She rubbed up and down his shaft, just the right combination of care and commanding. What was all this? He was supposed to be the big strong man, and here this nice lady's showing him how it's done? He almost wanted to take over, show her who was boss, but he couldn't resist her wonderful touch.

"What do you think you're doing, there, ma'am?"

"I'd have thought it was pretty obvious." She raised an eyebrow, and that was all it took to get his fingers moving. He peeled open his belt and pants for her as she told him. "I've seen some things out here . . . Hole-e-e Moses, you'd blush just hearing about 'em."

"Oh yeah?" His cock sprang out the V of his fly. "Like what?"

Grabbing his hard-on by the root, she made a fist and squeezed most satisfyingly. "Well, I've seen plenty of this." She moved her hand up and down his shaft in an expert motion, which told him she was not afraid of a good cock. As she stroked, she said, "It ain't easy to fuck someone in a car."

Her language made him gasp, not because of the word itself, but because it came from such a pretty mouth. "I can imagine."

"Most folk don't even try, especially if they're bigger, you know. It was easier when vehicles had them huge back seats, nice long flat surfaces. Then you could really sprawl, you know? There was almost room for a young man to get down on that floor while I leaned back against the door and tossed one leg up on the back seat. You remember those days?"

"Why yes, I surely do," he replied, though it was hard to speak with his arousal nearly choking him. "My, you are good at that."

"Well, thank you!" She smiled sweetly, as though he'd complimented her peach pie. "You know, I recall this one time when I was nothing but a young slip out with my boyfriend, and, oh, he was skinny boy back then – he's my husband now, but back then, why, we weren't married – and I wouldn't let him go all the way with me, you see, no matter how much I wanted to."

"You don't say . . ."

"I do indeed. And he'd get down on them running boards and I'd hike up my skirt and he'd plunge his face between my legs. There was that much space in cars, back in those days! Everything's different now, you see?" Still stroking his cock with her mighty fist, she glanced into the back seat. "You'd never fit a man down there, I tell you."

"No, ma'am." He watched her left hand join the right one as she stroked his cock double-fisted. That sight alone nearly set him off, but even if he couldn't see what she was doing, the sensation would have brought him close.

"After a while, I stopped wearing panties out on dates," she said, nearly causing an eruption. "Just too much trouble, fiddling with them, getting them off in a car. No thank you. Anyway, I liked opening my legs for that scrawny young boyfriend of mine and seeing the look on his face when he saw how glossy my thighs were with juice. That was just from us kissing. He got me so turned on like that."

"Did he, then?"

"Oh yes, he certainly did."

"And does he now?"

Her hands slowed around his erection, as though they were pondering along with her mind. Moulding his firm flesh like clay, she said, "Things are different now. Bound to be, after so many years together. Takes a lot more than it used to, I'll tell you that much."

When she slid both hands up his shaft and closed them tight around his wet tip, by golly, he just about lost it!

"Sorry," she said. "Too much?"

"No, no. Keep on going." He brushed a bead of sweat from his temple with the back of his hand. "Who'd'a thought it? A nice lady like you . . ."

"A nice lady like me's got a nasty lot on her mind." Her hands moved faster, up and down his shaft. "Nice lady like me loves to watch men unbutton blouses and slip their fingers inside. So much the better if a girl gets so turned on she tears that blouse wide open and pulls her perky young tits out for all the world to see."

"All the world that's watching through binoculars."

"Still," she went on, "if they're doing the nasty in their cars in a public park, I mean, they know they might get caught."

"Maybe they have no place else to go," he reasoned, though reason was never his forte when he was so thoroughly aroused.

"Maybe they want to get caught." She rubbed harder, one fist around the root of his cock, the other around its red-hot mushroom head. "Maybe they find it exhilarating, the idea that someone could be watching, someone could be taking enjoyment from the sight of them fingering a lady, or sucking another man's dick, or hiring someone to choke 'em while they come. I've seen all sorts, out here. I've seen all—"

Rap-rap-rap on the window, and timing couldn't be worse. Just as the glare of a flashlight shot through the glass, he exploded like a geyser, filling the nice lady's cupped hand with hot cream. And, because one explosion was never enough, he came again and again, until the cream leaked from between her fingers. She'd gotten him so hard it hurt, and the eruption came as a major relief. All the same, he stole his waning erection away and shoved it discreetly inside his pants, zipping and buckling and panting and sweating while the woman poured his come into a tissue from the glovebox.

Unrolling his window, the officer asked, "What seems to be the problem? I'm busy obtaining critical intel from this nice informant here."

"Sorry for the interruption, but a call came in. Looks like we'd better skedaddle."

Turning to the woman in the driver's seat, the officer said, "I suppose you'll have to finish telling me what you've seen around these parts another time."

"You know where to find me," she said, cleaning come from between her fingers.

When they got back to the cruiser, the deputy asked, "How's the missus, sir?"

"Fine and dandy," the officer replied. "Or I should say fine and randy? That lady's got some mind for creative lovemaking, I tell you what!"

"I'll say," the deputy shot back. "Not that I was watching or nothing, sir. I wouldn't go spying on you."

"I wouldn't pay no mind even if you were, young gun – and the missus would love it."

The deputy offered a faint smirk. "I'll bear that in mind, sir."

A Bad Habit

Sarah Veitch

Charlene reread her credit card bills in the hope that somehow the amounts owed would become smaller. It reminded her of her student days when, despite being too busy to shop for groceries, she'd peered hopefully into the empty fridge. Now she was twenty-two and working as a publishing assistant in an upmarket part of London, work which was prestigious but poorly paid.

Maybe she could find an evening job? She turned to the back pages of the local free sheet and the advert almost leapt out at her: "Strip-O-Grams wanted for classy agency. No nudity. Full training will be given."

The following Saturday she arrived with five other hopefuls for the interview. They were shown a film then given a short talk by Germaine Garson, a tall, broadly built woman of around fifty. It was obvious that she was one of the dominant ten per cent.

"We're in the entertainment agency – we're not porn stars," she said firmly. "So if anyone tries to take it further than an arm around the waist or a kiss on the cheek you must politely pull away." She added that anyone booking a Strip-O-Gram had to sign a contract in which they promised not to maul the guys and girls.

"We offer a limited number of roles – mainly police and fire officers," she continued. "They're governing positions so it's easier for our employees to maintain the upper hand."

Moments later, she asked to see each girl individually. When the first girl came out, she was smiling. Charlene walked in next, answered a few questions about her employment and availability, and walked out smiling too. Germaine had said that she planned to expand the business so was taking on several new candidates.

Four of them returned the following week and were put through a three-hour training session with Germaine's assistant after which they were good to go.

That Saturday, as she returned from a morning's shoe shopping (she was celebrating getting the Strip-O-Gram job) the phone rang and it was Germaine.

"Can you perform at a pub in Soho tonight? A gentleman has booked a policewoman for his brother's eighteenth at the last moment. Apparently they were supposed to visit him at his university in Oxford but he turned up in London unexpectedly."

"Do I need to bring my own handcuffs?" Charlene asked with a laugh.

"No, we'll supply you with a grey plastic set. They're better than the metal ones as they don't require a key!" She sighed. "You'll have to call in to the office to collect the uniform as I don't have time to bring it over to you."

What a thought. Still, the money was good. Charlene had a quick freshen up, ate a banana from the fruit bowl (the fridge was still bare) and took the bus to Germaine's agency. There she was given a surprisingly realistic policewoman's outfit, truncheon and cuffs.

That night, she showered lengthily before smoothing wisteria-scented oils all over her body. After slipping on a cosy dressing gown, she pinned her hair up in a loose chignon. She would take off her policewoman's cap after making the fake arrest and let her tresses tumble down her back in sexy curls.

Now, just where was that policewoman's outfit . . . Charlene's heart suddenly leapt and she momentarily stopped breathing, the way that a woman does when she's lost something valuable like her purse. Oh my God, she had no memory of bringing the carrier bag with her into the flat, must have left it on the floor of the bus. Racing to the Yellow Pages, she looked up the number and phoned the company but an answering machine said that they were closed for the night.

What the hell could she wear? Germaine had said that it had to be classy so that ruled out adult schoolgirl or prostitute. It was then that she remembered the nun's habit that her cousin, whose mother was a dab hand with a sewing machine, had once brought round to wear to a fancy dress party. At the last minute they'd had a better offer in the form of a music gig so she'd never even tried the outfit on.

Now she did so and felt slightly disappointed that it reached all the way to her ankles: after all, her legs were her best feature. Still, she'd be whipping off the habit in due course to show her black briefs, stockings and suspender belt. She'd have to wear her own underwear now, of course, as the agency's was still in the bag with the policewoman's uniform.

Charlene hung the outfit's rosary beads from the habit's tie belt and spent a few moments practising removing her nun's headdress and letting her hair down in a single sexy gesture. She glanced at the clock and did a double take. Now that the moment was drawing near she felt terrified. After swigging down half a bottle of cooking sherry left over from the Christmas trifle, she hastily called for a taxi, a legitimate business expense.

The agency had assured her that the guy who'd organized the gig had red hair and would wave to her as she entered the pub. She'd then pretend to arrest the birthday boy, his brother, before the pub landlord put on the classical stripping music and she got out of her police uniform and down to her bra and pants.

Hiccupping a little, she walked into the pub, but no one hailed her. It was only when someone said that they didn't realize the Salvation Army still collected from pubs that she remembered she was dressed as a nun. Glancing around the room – she felt drunkenly high now that the sherry had mixed with the adrenalin in her bloodstream – she saw a redhead in the corner and sashayed over. No one put on any music so she began to hum the stripping music out loud.

"Da, da, da, da. Da, da, da, da," she chorused, taking off her headdress and shaking out her long hair before pulling her habit awkwardly over her head and draping it around the birthday boy. Only when the redhead said, "What on earth?" did she realize that she was serenading a short- haired girl.

"So whose birthday is it?" Charlene asked woozily.

"I think all of yours have come at once," someone said.

Glancing down, she realized that she was wearing her stockings and suspenders but had forgotten to put on any pants.

"What on earth are you doing?" the pub landlord asked, racing over and hiding her bare buttocks with a somewhat undersized tea towel.

Charlene swayed and grabbed hold of his waist for added support. "Well, I'm hardly the ghost of Mother Teresa. I'm the Strip-O-Gram."

"We were told to expect a policewoman and that she'd only strip to her underwear. This is a family pub," the man replied.

She felt angry male fingers manhandling her back into her habit before she was hastily marched to a room at the back and given a black coffee by an equally angry landlady. She put on her headdress herself, keen to hide her flaming cheeks from prying eyes.

A short time later, Ms Garson arrived.

"I've apologized to the birthday group, refunded their money and given them an extra fifty to say no more about this," she said, stony-faced. "I've also paid a sweetener to the pub."

"I'm so sorry," Charlene muttered, beginning to sober up.

"You're going to be," Germaine Garson said, flexing her large right hand. "My car's outside," she added. "We're going back to the agency so that you can fully make amends."

Neither of them spoke on the short journey back and all too soon the middle-aged matriarch was parking in her designated parking spot. They must make an odd couple, Charlene thought, a no-nonsense businesswoman (with the build of a businessman) and a small, sheepish nun.

They entered the moonlit office and the older woman got behind her desk. Charlene sat contritely facing her.

"There are two ways we can do this," her employer said. "The first involves you paying back all of the money I shelled out and never setting foot in here again . . ."

Charlene gulped. She was already close to applying for a payday loan, hated the thought of adding the agency to her list of debts.

"And the second?" she asked softly.

"I give you the thrashing of your life but forgive the debt and you continue to work for us."

Was she suggesting corporal punishment? Charlene cleared her throat. "By a thrashing, you mean . . . ?"

"I mean I'll give you a sound spanking before moving on to the implement of my choice."

She wanted to keep this job, to live long and prosper. Charlene looked embarrassedly at her lap and muttered, "I deserve to be spanked."

"Come over here and tell me that," Ms Garson said, pushing back her chair.

Deeply shamed but determined, Charlene shuffled over and stood to one side of the older woman.

"Lift your habit above your waist and go over my knee, you naughty girl."

The heavy material slipped twice through her fingers, but eventually she caught the hem and pulled the material up to expose her stocking-clad legs and all-too-bare bottom. Going over the older woman's knee took even more courage but she forced herself to do so, hating the enforced flesh on flesh. The material sat in folds on her back and made her even more aware of her naked buttocks and their innate vulnerability. It felt especially shaming to have a woman staring down at her arse.

The first spank was measured and she thought to herself that this wasn't too bad. The second was equally bearable. But, as the tattoo continued, Charlene's tender cheeks began to heat up. They felt sore and then bruised and then very bruised and she kicked her legs and squealed for her employer to stop.

"Stop now? I've hardly started. Why do you think they call it punishment?" Ms Garson said and spanked on and on and on.

When she finally ceased, she warned that she was just resting her arm.

"Go and look at your punished bottom in the mirror."

Holding her nun's habit above her waist, Charlene skulked over to the full-length looking glass and peaked over her shoulder at her chastened flesh. Her buttocks glowed with fingerprint marks overlapping on her cheeks and upper thighs and looked larger than she remembered. She put her palms protectively over them and was surprised at the heat.

"Strip for me completely," Ms Garson said, hitting a button and causing the familiar stripping theme to echo through the agency.

Feeling ridiculous, Charlene walked over to her and began to sexily remove her nun's headdress and let loose her hair. She slid the headdress over Germaine Garson's blouse-covered breasts and watched as the woman's breathing quickened and her face became infused with lust. Ah, so her employer liked to have sex with women. If she seduced her, the rest of her punishment would hopefully be forgotten or at least delayed . . .

She peeled off her habit before kneeling at Ms Garson's feet and kissing the toes of what must be size seven or eight black leather shoes. She kissed on up the woman's right calf and thigh.

"We could lie down on the chaise longue," she murmured, hoping to get away with copious caresses.

"Or you could please me right here with your tongue," Germaine Garson replied.

"I've never . . ." Charlene muttered. She'd yet to even go down on a boyfriend.

"Then it's about time that you learned." So saying, the older woman pushed up the skirt of her business suit, removed her white cotton panties and sat down again, splaying apart her thighs.

Think of your many debts . . . Determinedly, Charlene tried out an exploratory lick of the woman's pinkest parts. Her employer shuddered and lifted her pudenda. Charlene continued to tongue at the increasingly slick labial lips, pretending to herself that she was licking an ice cream. As the cunnilingus continued, she began to enjoy the feeling of power that it gave her, liked hearing Germaine Garson's little sighs and groans.

Eventually, the older woman's sound effects intensified and Charlene felt her grab at her hair as they reached a crescendo. Obediently, she licked every last second of pleasure out.

Sorted! Charlene spat out a pubic hair and rested her head on her employer's lap, hoping that her chastisement was over. Her bottom still felt wildly overheated and she longed to put on her protective habit again.

"Now for your caning."

Charlene opened her eyes wide as she heard the words. "But I thought . . ." she muttered.

"You thought that a few licks from your tongue would undo all the damage you caused tonight? My agency's reputation has been tarnished and we could have faced public ruin if anyone in that pub had called in the police or tabloids – and that's before we get to what you've done to my bank balance in these recessionary times."

Put like that she deserved hanging, Charlene thought miserably. But she still balked at the thought of the cane.

"Doesn't the rod really hurt?" she whispered.

"A great deal, so I'm told, but it imparts a lifelong lesson. And I think you need that as you are constantly living beyond your means."

"After this I'm going to totally sort my life out," Charlene said, meaning it. "I'm not going to buy any more clothes or shoes till my debts are repaid."

Ms Garson nodded. "It's fitting in a way. After all, historically nuns have caned their errant pupils so now an errant nun is having the tables turned."

She smoothed Charlene's damp hair out of her eyes before taking a slender key from her bag.

"Go over to the ebony cabinet and use this to unlock the top drawer. You'll find six canes and a rather fetching bullwhip. Choose the one which you think will best teach you how to behave."

So her employer had done this before. Stalling for time, Charlene walked slowly over to the cabinet and took her time unlocking it. She pulled out the drawer and stared at the curve-handled rods, each of a different material and different thickness. Assuming that the thin one would cut the most deeply, she chose the chunkiest of the six. It was fashioned from a light bamboo-like wood, had black binding around the handle and felt comparatively heavy in her hands.

Her steps continuing to drag, Charlene returned to where the matriarch sat. She wished again that she'd been allowed to put on her habit. Her total nakedness made her feel even more vulnerable, especially in contrast to Ms Garson's business suit.

"Where do you want me?" she muttered, looking warily at the desk.

"Oh, I punished a naughty girl across the desk last week. I think we'll go for the footstool this time."

"What did she do?" Charlene muttered.

"She started contacting clients independently so that the

agency didn't get the commission. She used our name but didn't maintain our high standards, was renting her friends out as Roly-Poly's and Glam-O-Grans."

"Makes me losing my policewoman's outfit seem fairly innocuous," Charlene said, feeling momentarily superior.

"On the contrary. Unlike you, she didn't get drunk and naked in public," the older woman said.

"I really am sorry that I . . ."

"Your bare bottom is going to be even sorrier," Ms Garson said.

She kicked the large cube-shaped footstool into the middle of the floor and stood back, flexing the cane in both hands.

"You've caused me a lot of trouble tonight and I'm really looking forward to hearing you beg."

"I could just beg without the caning . . ."

"Oh no, I much prefer to hear a naughty girl sing for her supper," her employer replied.

Maybe this would put her into the agency's good books and she'd get lots of work. Resigned to her fate, Charlene knelt and bent over the footstool, placing her hands flat on the carpeted ground. Every iota of her attention was now focused on her raised rump, served up and awaiting punishment. She trembled as Germaine Garson tapped the rod against her extremities, urging her to raise her buttocks higher in the air.

"I'm not a monster so I'm not going to draw the rod back over my shoulder or anything draconian," she said matter-of-factly. "But even a modest caning will make sure that you don't sit down for a week."

Seconds later, Charlene felt the rattan connect with her arse. Squealing and holding her punished bottom, she jumped up and began to hop up and down.

"Five to go," her employer murmured.

"It hurts! It really hurts!" Charlene protested, continuing to hop from one foot to the other. "I don't know if I can take another five."

"Arousal helps diminish pain," the older woman said, going over to another locked cupboard and bringing out a strange black plastic contraption. She took it into the adjacent dressing room, urging Charlene to follow her there.

At first, Charlene mainly took in the mirrored walls then she realized that Ms Garson was indicating a plinth in the centre of the room to which she was attaching a jet-black dildo. The woman flicked a switch and the machine began to vibrate.

"Hands behind your back," her employer said.

Wondering what was going to happen next, Charlene obeyed her. She felt the handcuffs snap into place then the woman pushed her gently towards the plinth.

"Straddle the machine so that your thighs are wide apart and your hot little hole is touching the dildo's tip."

Charlene blushed. Presumably this sex toy was going to make her come but no one had ever looked at her face as she orgasmed because she made a point of hiding it in the pillow or burying it in her lover's shoulder. And her lovers had always been male . . .

"Remember, if you get turned on it will help you to endure the rest of your caning. And, after you've paid the piper you'll reap your rewards with the agency."

Did the woman have to speak in clichés, Charlene thought then reminded herself that she was not here in her role as publishing assistant. Now she was merely a disgraced Strip-O-Gram who had to make amends. She looked helplessly at the mirrored walls, seeing her red face and even redder buttocks reflected back as she got onto all fours, hovering just above the glossy black rod.

Its vibrating tip touched her entrance and she let out a breathless half-squeal then glanced at Ms Garson, hating her look of smug satisfaction. She'd try not to show future signs of pleasure, didn't want to be in thrall to this oversized toy. But the oscillations continued to send ripples of lust through her pudenda and lower tummy and soon she was squirming in place. Worse, her writhing had caused her body to sink deeper onto the dildo so that it was now buried in her increasingly wet and wanton cunt.

"Time for further cane strokes, I think," her employer murmured, suddenly switching off the machine.

Charlene looked up at her dazedly. "But I'm so close, Miss."

"Stay there and before long I'll switch you on again," the woman said, leaving the dressing room briefly and returning with the cane. "Kiss it and ask nicely for the rest of your punishment," she said.

Whimpering, Charlene kissed the rod, which had so recently warmed her buttocks.

"Please punish me, Ms Garson, and let me come."

With her hands cuffed high up her back and her naked body suspended on the dildo she had never felt more vulnerable in her entire life. She cried out loudly as the cane striped her waiting posterior but, due to her position on the plinth, had to stay obsequiously in place.

"Ask for stroke three and tell me how much you deserve it."

Desperate to orgasm, Charlene said that she'd been a very wicked girl and deserved a very sore backside then cried out and drummed her feet against the ground as the rod connected with the sweet spot where buttock meets thigh.

"Let's just give you a little more pleasure before delivering a lot more pain," the matriarch said, turning on the vibrations again.

Charlene groaned in mingled shame and ecstasy, grinding herself against the black phallus, as her sex got increasingly slick.

She again got deliciously close to orgasm before her employer switched off the vibrations and brandished the rattan.

"Just give me all three quickly please then let me climax," Charlene begged.

"Oh, I don't know about that. Half of the fun of administering a punishment is prolonging the agony."

"I could lick you again," Charlene whimpered and her boss whipped off her panties for the second time that night and pushed her naked pubes into her very flushed face. The woman was wet, wet, wet and clearly enjoyed having a naked acolyte at her mercy. She came quickly under the ministrations of Charlene's tongue.

"Can I come now?" Charlene asked raggedly.

"As soon as you've had your last three strokes."

"Please cane me again, Miss," Charlene said as she lay exhaustedly over the dildo, but the sudden fire in her backside caused her to jump and squeal.

"Ask me to lay on the fifth."

"Please . . ." Charlene said brokenly. "Oh, please . . ."

She cried out again as the rattan connected with her helpless posterior and wriggled about like a butterfly on a pin before steeling herself for the last character-strengthening stroke.

"I deserve the last of this six of the best," she whispered with hard-won submission and was grateful when her employer didn't lay on the rod with especial strength.

"Now let's take your mind off of things," Germaine Garson said, sounding kinder. She switched on the vibrations and Charlene was soon squirming in place.

"I want you to remember what it feels like when you let yourself and other people down. I want you to look at your hot bum and your hot face in the mirror. Is this the sort of state that a career woman should get herself into? Is this the future you see for yourself?"

"No, Mistress," Charlene mumbled, wondering why that particular obsequious term had popped into her head. "I promise to mend my ways."

She closed her eyes but could tell that the older woman was staring at her, drinking in her ignominy. Being watched both thrilled and shamed her, adding to the heavy lustful sensations pulsing through her crotch. Various taboo images flashed through her mind of her getting naked in the pub in front of innocent strangers, of being made to lick her boss and of lying, bare-bottomed, across her knee. The images took her over the edge and she climaxed strongly, grinding her groin into the machine.

"You needed that," her voyeuristic boss said with relish, but Charlene was too spent to reply.

Half an hour later, she sat gingerly on one side of her hip in the passenger seat of her boss's car as the older woman drove her home.

"You'll think of this every time you sit down at the internet to make an unnecessary purchase," Germaine murmured.

Charlene groaned. "I don't think I'll ever sit down again."

"Oh, you will. In a few weeks, the tenderness will fade and you'll need a refresher course. That's how I keep my girls in line and run such a tight ship."

"I'm never going through that again!" Charlene said with feeling.

"That's what they all say at first and then they make a mistake at work or need a payday loan and suddenly a sore arse is a small price to pay."

She'd be the exception to the rule, Charlene told herself firmly as she climbed the stairs to her apartment, but her backside twitched as if it knew differently . . .

Filthy Mary

S. J. Smith

The tale I'm about to tell may appear from the outset as something of a tired old cliché, involving as it does the oft trotted out saga of the tradesman arriving at the home of the bored housewife and the sexual high jinks that follow. I don't doubt you've heard it a million times before, trotted out as the flimsy backdrop to every bad sex movie that's ever been made.

Good afternoon, madam, I'm here to mend your washing machine.
My, what an enormous tool you have.

Etc., etc.

You may well think that such stories belong firmly in the past – nailed to the masts of long sunken ships. But I swear to you every word of it is true. And perhaps if I were to claim this tale was *retro* rather than merely outdated, then you might just give it a second glance.

Let's find out.

A few years ago I landed myself in something of a fix. I'd suffered a calamitous run of bad luck on the card game front, and had simultaneously managed to incur the wrath of a very influential man after being caught in flagrante with his wife. I had no money, owed a small fortune in debts and none of my friends were speaking to me. For the first time in many moons I found myself in a situation I wouldn't be able to cheat and swindle my way out of. There was no way around it – I was going to have to get a job.

Now I don't like jobs and jobs don't like me. I wasn't cut out to be a working man – my tongue and my cock have always been my bread and butter. But I found myself applying for gainful employment with a dubious company named Handymen Ltd, who promised in their various advertisements that in exchange for an exorbitant monthly fee they would dispatch a tradesman to the home of their customers *within the hour*, should some domestic catastrophe take place. A broken-down boiler, a smashed window, a blocked drain – whatever the emergency, Handymen Ltd would see to it that everything was put right with as little fuss as possible, provided you kept up the payments.

After lying about my qualifications and sweet-talking the interviewer, I was given a few days' expert training in how to extort yet more cash from unsuspecting and vulnerable people, and provided with a crisp white Handymen Ltd uniform and an ageing white Handymen Ltd van. I spent a week going here, there and everywhere pretending I knew how to fix things. I probably did more harm than good, if truth be told, but I was earning a wage and keeping out of trouble, and things seemed to be going OK.

But, of course, scandal and debauchery never seem to move further than a stone's throw away from my life, and it wasn't long before I had my encounter with a woman named Mary Newton.

Mary had gained something of a reputation amongst the employees of Handymen Ltd. The girls who answered the telephones in the office thought the whole thing was hilarious, but the chaps who did the call-outs were less than amused. They were married men with families, they argued. They shouldn't have to put up with this kind of thing – it bordered on sexual harassment. And the girls in the office only laughed harder.

Filthy Mary they nicknamed her, the suburban scourge of Handymen Ltd. She called up every single day with some new problem – the front door wouldn't lock, the radiator in the parlour was leaking – and demanded a nice young man be dispatched to her home forthwith. What happened next depended on who you spoke to and how much they'd had to drink.

Terry claimed she'd got down on her knees and started unbuttoning him, declaring she was going to give him a blow job he'd never forget, before he'd managed to politely extricate himself from the situation. Mike meanwhile insisted he'd actually had to make a run for it, fleeing her bedroom as she came after him bearing a carpet beater in one hand and a pair of handcuffs in the other. Both of them swore they'd never set foot inside her house again.

With more names being added daily to the list of handymen who were refusing to go to Filthy Mary's assistance, I knew it wouldn't be long before they turned to me. I'd sworn to myself I would never touch another married woman – not after what had recently happened – but old habits die hard, and I won't deny that the idea of spending an afternoon with my cock inside some bored housewife – *and* getting paid for it into the bargain – was not without its appeal.

The inevitable phone call came during a quiet lunchtime. I was sat in my van eating a cheese and pickle sandwich when my mobile rang and Katrina from the office told me that I was to go number thirty-six, Elm Lane. She was sniggering as she spoke, and I could hear the other girls giggling in the background too. "Filthy Mary is having trouble with her plumbing – you'll probably have to shove your *plunger* down her *pipe*." She barely finished the sentence before they all cracked up into howls of laughter.

I smiled and ended the call. Finally, I was going to get to see what all the fuss was about. Elm Lane was twenty minutes away – I had an erection before I got halfway there.

Filthy Mary's place was a big detached townhouse, with a well-kept front garden full of rosebushes and a black BMW parked in the drive. Rumours insisted she was married to some nervous wreck, who spent two-thirds of his life away on business, earning the cash to keep her in the lifestyle she'd become accustomed to. I only hoped he was elsewhere that afternoon – I wanted Filthy Mary all to myself. I sloped up the path and rang the bell, and a fragmented shape appeared on the other side of the frosted glass window.

The door opened and there stood Filthy Mary herself. She was early to mid-fifties, on the short side and rather chubby, with a huge pair of tits that competed for attention inside the black see-through negligee thing she had on underneath a short pink dressing gown. Her hair was bottle blonde, done in a bob, and she wore a thick layer of make-up – heavy on the mascara and lipstick. Her eyes were shining blue – she looked first at my face and then down at my crotch.

"Hi there, Mrs Newton, my name is Steve and I'm from Handymen Ltd. I understand you reported a problem?" I had to recite that opening line every time I encountered a customer, – even though it was patently fucking obvious who I worked for. The company's yellow and red logo was embroidered across the left breast pocket of my uniform, as well as being plastered all over my van which was parked directly behind me.

"You got here very quickly," she said with an alluring smile, and she leaned against the jamb.

Of course I'd got there quickly. I'd driven across town at speeds far in excess of the limit, urged on by my throbbing cock, but I didn't think I should mention this just at that moment, and opted instead to quote more gobbledegook direct from the Handymen Ltd big book of bullshit. "We aim to answer all calls within one hour." I stared unapologetically straight at her tits, and then looked her right in the eye. "I'd hate to keep you waiting, Mrs Newton."

"I'm very impressed." She adjusted her dressing gown, loosening and retying the cord to *accidentally* flash me a hint of what lay beneath, then moved inside the house and beckoned me to follow with a single finger. "Would you mind taking off your shoes?"

"Only my shoes?" I tipped her a cheeky wink as I bent down to unfasten my laces. There was no point beating about the bush. We both knew why I was really here. We might as well move directly along to the intense flirting.

"For the moment, yes. You can keep that nice uniform on until I tell you otherwise." She returned my cheeky wink with interest, and licked her lips. "I should warn you that my husband is away at some damned conference or other, so I'm all on my lonesome. I trust I can rely on you to behave like a gentleman."

Wow. Filthy Mary was exactly how I hoped she'd be – a lecherous, brazen woman who knew what she wanted and wasn't afraid to show it. She was old enough to not give a fuck, but young enough to still be hungry – she didn't crave flowers, or poems or compliments, just a big juicy cock to sit on.

Her house smelled of furniture polish and bleach, and was decorated in the manner of someone who liked to keep up with the Joneses. I followed her down the hall, appreciating the sway of her lovely big arse cheeks underneath that skimpy pink dressing gown. "So, what seems to be the problem, Mrs Newton?"

"It's the lavatory – it simply won't flush," She paused at the foot of the stairs. "God knows what's wrong with the ridiculous thing. It's the third time it's broken in two months."

"I'll soon have it working, Mrs Newton. Don't you worry."

"Call me Mary."

I gave her a five-step head start as she climbed the stairs, and was treated to the sight of a pair of black lace stocking tops stretched tight around a pair of generously proportioned creamy white thighs. I fought the urge to wolf-whistle, even though I'm sure she would have loved it.

She showed me into the bathroom, which was all marble and natural stone, and pointed at a dainty white toilet over in the corner. "There's the sodding thing."

I put on my plumber's hat, hoicked the lid off the cistern and peered down into the gubbins. The metal bar that held the ballcock in place was twisted violently out of shape. If I were the suspicious type I would have sworn she'd deliberately sabotaged the loo, just to get me out here.

It was a five-minute job to fix, but as I had my plumber's hat on, I decided to spin a few plumb lines. I blew out my cheeks and said, "I can see the problem, but I'm not sure if I've got the right parts in my van to fix it."

She scowled at me. "How long will it be before it's working?"

I rubbed my chin. "Ooh, well, if I can get the parts it might only take a couple of hours, but if I have to order them special from the depot it might not be until tomorrow."

"Well that's no good." She put her hands on her hips. "I'm desperate for a wee-wee. If you don't fix the loo I'm liable to wet myself right here and now." She was clearly testing me, seeing just how far she could push the situation before I buckled. But I've never been the buckling type, especially when it comes to carnal relations with ladies, and I decided to push back just as hard.

"I'm afraid, Mary, that you'll just have to do your wee-wees in a bucket."

"A bucket? How dare you? Ladies of my social standing do not use buckets."

"Then you'll have to hold on."

"But I'm *desperate*." She crossed her knees and gritted her teeth.

I looked around the room for some form of receptacle, and spotted a cut glass vase full of fake flowers sitting on the rim of the bath. I grabbed it, and upended the flowers onto the floor. "Here – you can use this."

Filthy Mary rolled her eyes. "I don't suppose I have much choice in the matter."

"Trust me, I'm a qualified plumber." I gave her a knowing look and waved the vase under her nose.

She shrugged off her pink dressing gown, and I saw straight through her see-through negligee: big pink nipples and big pink tits, a big round belly and a pair of sleek black knickers, which came tumbling down to reveal a wide triangular nest of scratty brown pubes. She climbed up on top of the marble counter, squatted down on her haunches, pulled up her hem and parted her meaty curtains with manicured fingertips. "Quickly," she urged. "It's coming any second." I rushed over and held the vase ready in place beneath her cunt.

She spread her thighs a little wider, and a tiny trickle erupted from her pee hole, which quickly became a ferocious jet that sang a high-pitched note. My grip on the glass turned cool to hot as her piss filled the vase, swirling around the base like a whirlpool. There was a dreamy look on her face, and her cunt flaps wobbled delicately as the stream rushed by. Eventually it slowed, and the last few drops rolled down her fleshy lips and dripped from her arsehole.

"I told you I was desperate," she gasped in relief.

"I can see that you were." I held up the vase to show she'd almost filled it.

"But now I can't reach the loo roll. How am I supposed to wipe myself?"

I put the vase of piss down on the floor. "Allow me, Mary."

I got on my knees and shamelessly licked her clean. I lapped up the rivulets that ran down her thighs, and dug deep into the crevice of her arse to make sure no wee-wee escaped out the back door. I sucked her drooping flaps between my lips, parted them with my tongue and probed her piss hole to devour the last few drops. She gripped the back of my hair and pulled me deeper between her thighs. She called me a dirty bastard and rubbed her clit against my nose.

I stood up straight and unbuttoned my regulation trousers. "I'm afraid I'm going to have to fuck you now, Mary."

"Do whatever you have to." She dug her legs out from underneath her round body and leaned back on the counter.

Her pussy was so saturated that I glided in without touching the sides. I yanked the straps of her see-through negligee off her shoulders and rolled the flimsy material down her body to form a hula hoop, which I clung on to like a horse's reins.

"Don't come," she insisted between grunts, "I want to taste your cock."

"You'll get what you're given and like it." I hauled on the reins and buried myself deep into her squelching cunt, sending her rapturous face into the frenzied delirium of an orgasm.

She was glowing red and sweating, her former air of pomposity now reduced to tatters. Her hands went creeping, searching for something to cling on to, and she wrapped her fist around the silver shaft of the hot water tap that hung down over the basin. Her mouth formed an "O" shape and she bucked and writhed and came twice more before I showed any sign of relenting. Feeling my own orgasm rapidly approaching, I pulled myself out of her hole, wanked my slippery prick to a frenzy and shot my load all over her saturated pubes.

After we'd got our breath back, she made me a cup of tea and I mended the toilet. The air of lust that had hung in the air upon my arrival was blown clean away, and our interaction normalized accordingly. I was now merely the plumber, and she was the homeowner anxious to have me off the premises as quickly as possible. The very second I demonstrated that the loo was up and running she ushered me away out the front door. I bid her farewell and went on my merry way, thinking that would be the last I'd see of Filthy Mary.

But next day at half past nine in the morning I got a call from Katrina in the office. "I don't know what you did to Mrs Newton yesterday, and frankly I don't want to know, but she's been on the phone this morning asking for you personally to go to her house as soon as possible – she has another plumbing problem."

Another plumbing problem? Jesus, some people just didn't know when to leave well alone. Some things are meant to be one-offs, vivid encounters that are over and done with long before there is time for things to stagnate and turn as rotten as they inevitably do. Filthy Mary and I had both got exactly what we'd wanted from our encounter, and I felt absolutely no need to go back for round two.

But go back I did. Back to her suburban townhouse where I parked my van in the same spot, slouched up the drive and rung the bell exactly as I had done the day before. Yesterday's air of titillating anticipation was gone, I knew exactly what I was going to get – or at least that's what I thought.

What I was certainly not prepared for was the sight of Filthy Mary opening the door dressed up in full Nazi regalia. She wore a black peaked cap, a black leather corset, which squashed her huge breasts together to form a cleavage I've seldom seen the like of, and knee-high black leather boots, all of which were liberally sprinkled with swastikas. All she was missing was an inked on Hitler tache to complete the picture. I must have done a double take, as she laughed and said, "We're playing Camp Commandant," by way of explanation.

My ears pricked up at her use of the word "we". Did she mean the royal "we" as in herself, did she have someone else in there that she was about to introduce me to, or was the other person in her "we" equation going to turn out to be me?

I followed her inside, not at all sure I liked where this was going. "To be honest, Mary, I was surprised to find out you wanted me to come back."

"Oh, it wasn't my doing." She closed the front door behind me and flicked down the deadbolt. "It was my husband – he was so impressed with your efforts yesterday he wanted to see you come back and finish off the job properly."

This was getting stranger by the second. "You told me your husband was away on business."

"I lied." She smiled matter-of-factly and raised her eyebrows. "He was actually in the next room, watching us from behind the two-way mirror. He enjoyed your performance, but felt the climax was a bit of a damp squib – he'd been hoping you were going to take me all the way."

I gaped at her, unable to find the words to express myself.

"Would you like to come up and say hello? He's in the bedroom."

What the hell had I got myself involved in this time? I followed Filthy Mary upstairs into her plush bedroom, where I was greeted with the sight of a wrinkly, skinny, pale man tied to the wall with his arms and legs spread in an "X" shape. He had a ball gag in his mouth, and was naked apart from a tiny pair of red frilly women's knickers, which his erect cock had burst clean out of. I nodded to him. "Um, good morning, Mr Newton."

Filthy Mary stomped across the room and administered a hard slap to her husband's penis with the palm of her hand. "Put that thing away. Nobody wants to look at it." She rearranged his flimsy panties so they just about covered his throbbing rod. "That's better. Sissy wears her knickers like a good girl."

Mr Newton grunted. His wide eyes were staring straight at me. I didn't know where to look.

"Now then." Filthy Mary got down on her knees and unbuttoned my trousers, and reached her gloved hand inside my underpants. "Let's have a look at this nice big cock of yours." She found my length, took a firm hold and said, "Well, hello." Although I'm ashamed to admit it, I had a raging rod on, and it came springing out into her face as if it were on elastic. When confronted with seedy, perverse circumstances that might make a more well-adjusted person run for the hills, my own reaction has always been to get immensely aroused, even if I don't always want to. An ageing man in panties with a hard-on and a dumpy woman dressed as Hitler shouldn't really be doing it for me, but I'm afraid to say I was getting massively turned on.

She spat on my cock and massaged the moisture into my end until it glistened. "We have to get it good and wet so it'll slide straight up my botty." The peak of her cap hit me in the belly as she slid her lips down my shaft. She turned her head to the side so her husband could watch her tongue flick back and forth across my bell, then spat on me again, and draped a ribbon of sticky drool along my length. "There, that should do the trick."

Filthy Mary climbed onto the bed and got down on her hands and knees. She yanked down her SS panties and spread her bum cheeks wide. A black butt plug was protruding from her

anus, complete with a red and white swastika stamped on the
end. Nothing more really needed to be said. I got into position,
took hold of the greasy plug and dragged it slowly out. Her bum
hole puckered and winked at me. I put one foot up on the bed
and guided my cock inside her smooth, slippery tube.

Mr Newton watched while I fucked his wife up the arse. She
yelled at me to do it harder, and furiously rubbed her cunt while
she watched her husband watching. I ploughed in and out,
pushing deeper with every stroke, and then just to tease I
withdrew my cock completely, leaving her bum hole yawning
wide open as if silently screaming for more. I obliged, driving it
home all the way, until my balls were slapping her pussy lips.

She grunted and gasped, clutching fistfuls of the duvet cover.
Her peaked cap tumbled from her head, and bounced along the
bed in time to my thrusts, before toppling over the edge and
falling to the floor. I couldn't keep this going for much longer – I
was going to lose control any minute and fill up her shitter with
spunk. But still feeling aggrieved by her description of my
previous ejaculation as a "damp squib", I pulled out of her arse
and clutched the base of my cock to hold back the explosion for
a few more seconds. "Where do you want it, Mary?"

Rolling over onto her side, she disentangled her black panties
from the pointed heels of her boots, and tossed them away.
"Over here," she panted, and led me across the room to stand in
front of her husband. Kneeling down between us, she took Mr
Newton's cock in her right hand and mine in her left, and,
aiming both tips towards her waiting mouth, she spat on us and
jerked us off hard.

We came within seconds of each other, as if this had all been
perfectly choreographed, and Filthy Mary caught a double
whammy all over her face. Spunk splattered across her cheeks
and nose, and a pool of white formed in her cupping tongue,
before overflowing and dripping from her chin onto her
enormous breasts. She made noises like a rutting animal and
milked the last few drops out of my spent cock. I staggered
backwards while she licked her husband clean.

And that was the last time I saw Filthy Mary. I tiptoed to the
door, put my prick away and quietly let myself out. I drove away,
light-headed and soporifically content. It was odd, but I got a

feeling that in doing what I had just done, I had paid some kind of penance, and things were going to be OK again.

Within the hour, I ran into an old friend, who loaned me the cash to pay off my debts, and helped me disappear across the Atlantic to hide for a while.

And you wouldn't believe what happened to me in New York.

Peeping Thom

Landon Dixon

The complaints were flooding in faster than the Foam River come spring thaw: women and girls were getting "peeped" all over town, a perverted voyeur on the loose in our small, habitually respectable community. And the cry rose up like the wheat come summertime: what was I doing about it?

"I'm only a one-man RCMP detachment at the moment," I tried to explain to the good Mrs Fister, the reverend's surprisingly attractive wife, in the biblical and all other senses. "Bill Roscoe and Jeb Towers are both out of town laying track for a month. With the Depression and all . . . there've been cuts. The boys have to supplement their part-time policing wages."

Rosemary Fister sniffed with her delightfully upturned nose, the twin orbs on her chest bobbing deliciously beneath the tight, black cotton of her dress. The woman was in her mid-twenties, had the face and body of a whorehouse first-stringer, but the moral sensibilities of a cloistered nun. That, I assumed, was what led her to hitching her wagon-like derrière to our local minister, a man more than twenty years her senior.

"Well," she huffed indignantly now, "this . . . 'intruder' has to be caught, and punished. Before he compromises yet another innocent female citizen of our fair town."

I leaned slightly back in my swivel chair and spread my uniformed legs under my wooden desk, my oxblood leather riding boots creaking. Giving my boner more room to breathe, and do its business. Rosemary Fister's combination of saintly demeanour and sinful build never failed to elicit a hallelujah out of my nether regions.

"Tell me again – what happened," I prompted, picking up a

pencil to keep my sweaty hands from jumping down onto my groin; my ears open and eyes focused on the busty, big-bottomed minister's wife.

She sighed, allowing her humps to put on another show. Then she ribaldly regaled me with, "Well, I was taking my bath, in the parlour of the rectory. I was sitting in the tub and, um, scrubbing myself, when I decided that I needed more hot water. So, I stood up in the tub."

Her pretty face reddened appealingly at the cheeks, and she demurely bobbed her head down to the pair of hands writhing in her warm, dewy lap. "I . . . well, I was completely . . . nude, you see. Since my husband was out tending to a member of the flock . . . and I was taking my bath. Just some soapsuds on my body, not really covering me. But I badly needed more hot water, you understand."

I saw and understood, all right. In my dirty mind's eye, at groin level. Rosemary Fister's lush, heated, moist body fully exposed, her tits and pussy dripping in the tub in her parlour. A sight that would make even a church deacon kick a hole in a stained glass window (and I knew what the "staining" would be). "Go on," I urged, my cock a truncheon of pulsating steel between my legs.

Rose dabbed at her nose, her big violet eyes avoiding mine pinned to her tits. "Well, I stepped out of the tub, to go to the kitchen to get more water. I didn't think to put on my towel, since it was such a short trip, and I was all alone. But when I glanced at the parlour window . . . I saw a face just outside – looking in at me!"

She shuddered at the remembrance, making her big knockers enticingly shiver. I stiffened to even more rigid attention, bending the long, hard pencil between my clutching, twitching fingers.

"Well, it wasn't a face exactly – that's what shocked me so badly. Along with the violation of my privacy, of course. It was a gas mask, you see. Someone wearing one of those Great War gas masks. It looked absolutely hideous – staring in at me just outside my parlour window."

"And what did you do!?" I rasped, leaning forward and leering slightly, squeezing my throbbing tool with my thighs.

My face was redder than the scarlet serge tunic covering my heaving torso.

Rose licked her plush, flower petal lips, darted a shy glance up into my glaring orbs. "Well, I screamed, of course. And then I . . . well, I tried to cover myself up. I forgot all about the towel on the loveseat—" the big-titted tease, I thought nastily "—and flung an arm over my chest, like this, and a hand down onto my . . . legs, like this."

Her breasts bulged quarter-hidden behind her lithe arm, her pale, delicate hand fluttering just above her juicy cunt. The pencil snapped between my fingers and the rod went off between my legs. I grunted and bucked, blowing a hot, sticky load in my federal government-issue pants.

"I'll . . . I'll get right on it!" I gasped, fighting to keep my eyes open and my moans closed. As I spurted into my drawers I was riding the high of Rosemary's story, desperately trying to keep from soiling my reputation like I was my pants.

I didn't get up when the lady rose to her feet, or see her out of the small stationhouse. I had a right to defend myself against self-incrimination, after all.

"So . . . that's Mrs Fister, Steamboat Hilda, and the girls' field hockey team now," Lorraine said to me, after I'd cleaned myself up and reported back for duty out in the reception area of the stationhouse.

Lorraine was helping me out while the boys were gone – routine paperwork and correspondence. She'd just come back from two years' finishing school in Moose Jaw, and I thought it'd be a good way to get reacquainted with my now grown-up distant cousin. As well as toss a few dollars her way.

I parked my haunches on the corner of her wooden desk and dropped my hands down into my lap to muffle the stain and my scent. "And don't forget Granny Oakley," I added, with an involuntary shudder.

"That's right!" Lorraine yelped, holding up a pencil of her own. "The peeping Tom peeped at Granny Oakley when she was doing her business out in back of her farmhouse."

I gave out another shudder. Granny Oakley was a wizened old hag of ninety or more, with tits that dragged the earth like harrows and varicose veins that resembled the roots of a tree. She lived with her succulent doll of a nineteen-year-old granddaughter on a farm just outside of town and had reported her voyeur violation two days before.

"We've got a serial peepist on the prowl, Lawrence. No woman or girl is safe in this town at night any more – in their own homes!"

"And elsewhere," I added. The girls' field hockey team had reported being ogled en masse in the basement of the local high school, when they'd been changing after a particularly perspiring game under the prairie evening sun.

"I'm getting worried myself," Lorraine said, looking up at me. "I'm one of the few women who hasn't been eyeballed by the gas-masked gaper."

"Give it time," I joked, looking down at the cutey.

Lorraine had really "developed" during her two years away from home, in more ways than one. With her flaming red hair and twinkling blue eyes, pert nose and dimpled cheeks, burgeoned chest and flared hips, lithe arms and legs, she'd attracted a flock of suitors, ever since she'd returned.

She frowned at me now, deep in thought. Then the pencil came up again, along with her eyebrows. "Hey, I have an idea how we can catch the snooper!"

"Let's hear it. Because my only brainstorm is to issue blackout curtains to everybody housing a female in town."

Lorraine licked her full lips, batted her bright eyes at me. "What if we set a trap for the peeping Tom? A 'honey' trap, to catch this fly in the night."

"Coat everyone's windows in flypaper?"

"No. Just the opposite. Urge every woman and girl to keep their shades drawn, as you suggest, except for one house – housing one gal. Me."

I stared at her. "What!?"

She grinned. "Sure. I'll be the bait. And when he comes sniffing around my house, you can nab him. I'll lure him in, and you spring out of the shadows and clap him in nippers. Case closed!"

I didn't think much of the idea, and said so. Lorraine was living in a lonely shack all by herself on the outskirts of town, which I also didn't approve of. "You're not a full-fledged member of this detachment, you know," I pointed out. "I only hired you to—"

"I don't mind! If it'll help you out – help out the town."

The girl was showing way too much enthusiasm for exhibiting her body for the purview of perverts. I had a familial, as well an official duty to protect her. "Let's not get you mixed up in this just yet. I want to roust a few citizens first, see if I can't crack this case the old-fashioned way – by busting some heads."

Lorraine sighed, pouting her pretty lips.

I rounded up the usual suspects, put them through the routine ringer. Doyle Calabash, the town drunk, an Irish immigrant who celebrated Saint Patty's Day 365 days of the year. I collared him outside the Harvest Tavern, shook him until he spilled tears out his red-veined eyes and puke out his red-rimmed mouth. But he didn't cough up any confession.

Nor did "Five-Fingers" McGee, the reigning town pervert and avowed bachelor. The septuagenarian Scot had a penchant for flashing little girls under his raincoat in dry weather, and an affinity for going on the lamb, bestiality-style. But when I hauled the dirty old man out of Joe Preston's pigpen, he claimed he'd given up females of the human species. "Too fickle," he drooled at me through the three teeth he still mouthed. And from the way he'd been cuddling with Gertie the sow, nursing one teat after another, I had to accept his stinking claim as the truth.

It was later that night, when I was making my rounds, that I noticed the blazing lights on in Lorraine's small shack. It was half past midnight, and the rest of the town was shuttered up like they were expecting a zeppelin attack. I hustled down the boardwalk of the one-horse main drag to Lorraine's house on the outskirts, my anger rising at what I suspected her of doing – against my stated wishes.

But then it was more than my anger that rose, when I looked in through the naughty girl's bedroom window.

She was standing next to her bed, looking at herself in the full-length, tiltable, gold-framed mirror positioned against the wall, dressed in just a pink slip. I skinned off my flat-brimmed, felt campaign hat and pressed my nose and hands to the glass, peering in at the woman.

She thought she was being clever, with her bedroom lit up like the first of July (Dominion Day), putting on a show for the town peeper. I could see, among other things, that she had the large oval mirror strategically stationed so that she could look at the reflected window, to presumably catch anyone looking in at her.

But she didn't seem to see me – yet, anyway – as she lifted her dainty little hands up to her hair and pulled out the pins. It was like a follicle grenade going off, her lustrous red hair streaming down her back. She shook it out, throwing her head back and thrusting her chest out. Her well-developed breasts swelled out the front of her slip, two hard indentations at the tips of her tits clearly visible, poking out the slick satin.

Lorraine brought her hands slowly down from her head, caressing the palms over the swollen sides of her breasts, along her breath-taking curves, onto her flared hips and then the ripe, round mounds of her buttocks in back. She dug her fingers into her satin-sheathed butt cheeks, licking her lips in the mirror, her breasts bobbing and nipples pointing.

It was a stimulating sight for any man, perverted voyeur or not, perfect stranger or police officer. My rod shifted position in its underwear holster, locking up and loading with hot blood. Lorraine was no longer the gangly, awkward teenager she'd left town as; she was now a more-than-full-bodied young woman, openly displaying her very adult assets. I unhooked my Sam Browne leather gun belt and drew my sex weapon out of my uniform pants and started jacking for semen, undeniably turned on by the sexy sight.

And it was right then, as I was pumping my shooter, beating off to the breath-taking picture of Lorraine in her slip in her bedroom, that she spun around and shrieked, "Ah-hah! I've got you!" And then she charged at the window with both breasts a-barrelling.

I didn't turn tail and run. Instead, I tucked tool and stood my ground, excited by the prospect of tail.

"It's me!" I yelled, when Lorraine splatted her face and fingernails against the windowpane and gaped out at me. "I'm coming!"

Her face dropped with disappointment, but her tits held their own. And, as I marched in through the front door and down the hall to her bedroom, I vowed to hold them myself. My sexual adrenalin was pumping in my prick. I wasn't going off half-cocked; I was fully cocked.

"Oh, hi, Lawrence," Lorraine sighed, plopping down on the edge of her bed.

I dropped down next to the girl, swung my arm around her slumped shoulders. "It's a good idea, Lorraine." I cheered her up. "You just have to add some more honey to the pot."

She jerked her head up and looked at me, her pretty face perked up, her beautiful eyes sparkling. "You think so?"

I stroked the soft, silky, ginger hair draping her shoulder, breathing in the sweet perfumed scent of the woman, basking in the heat of her lush, curvaceous body so close. It'd been a long time between night shifts with a woman for me, actual close-contact sexual combat, and my wick was burning with a short fuse, eager to be dipped into the molten wax of a lady-candleholder.

"Sure," I soothed, stroking Lorraine's hair, landing my other hand on her soft, silken thigh and squeezing. "You just have to sweeten the pot, make the bait even more tempting."

She was eager to follow my lead, thinking she was going to break the case, not suspecting this RCMP officer was intent on breaking her cherry. I gently pushed her slip strap off her right shoulder, then reached up and slid the other strap off her other shoulder. The sexy garment dropped down, then hung up on her jutting nipples.

Lorraine looked down at her heaving chest, up into my blazing eyes. I pulled her slip all the way down, and her nipples sprang free and her bare tits burst out.

We were both breathing hard. "Now, stand up," I huffed, my body flushing with heat like my face.

She stood up and the slip glided right down the curves of her nubile body, puddling at her bare feet in a whisper of sex. I swallowed like a bullfrog clearing his throat, staring at Lorraine's large creamy-white tits and protruding pink nipples, the mound and cleft of her pussy outlined against the tight satin of her pink panties.

"And . . . And . . . should I take off my panties," she breathed, "to better attract the peeping Tom?"

She was bait, all right, but not jailbait. I nodded the eager affirmative.

Lorraine gulped and hooked her trembling fingers into the waistband of her panties, and then slid them down her long, sculpted legs. She stepped out of them, completely naked before me. Her pussy was a soft, seductive triangle of ginger fur, her pink lips visible just beneath, glistening – it seemed to me – in the bright lights of her bedroom. Her tits joisted up and down with her ragged breath, nipples bobbing along for the awesome ride.

"That's good, very good," I croaked. "But now you should, uh, position yourself – to really entice that midnight voyeur."

Lorraine gave me a warm, shaky smile, glancing down at the tented front of my trousers. I was stiffly saluting in my uniform pants, from the seated position, no hiding my excitement. She drifted by me in a haze of beauty and scent and slid onto her bed, stretched out on her back. She flung her arms up over her head and bent her legs and arched her chest.

I scrambled around to gape at her. It was a boudoir scene of the bawdiest – the beautiful woman sprawled out nakedly temptingly for me, the cop (and cock) of the walk. "Is this good?" she murmured, her voice quivering like her splayed tits.

"Glorious!" I exulted.

I jumped to my feet and ditched my tunic, boots, pants and underwear with the fervour of a convert to the crooked side; all pretences of law-abiding behaviour lost in the lustful rush to be joined with Lorraine. And I knew she felt the same subversive way, by the way her nostrils flared and lips parted and eyes widened when my cock jumped out from my loins right in front of her, pressurized and stretched to the spurting point. She reached out and gripped my hell-fired cock, pulled me down onto her heavenly body.

We passionately kissed, hungrily chewing on each other's lips. Her mouth was soft and dewy, her body burning against my flaming form. My cock pressed into her belly and my chest flattened her tits, her hands on my shoulders and mine in her hair. I was fresh-mounted and ready to gallop on a musical ride!

Lorraine slid her hands down my back and onto my buttocks, dug her nails into my quivering haunches. I wedged my hands in onto her chest, took up her tits and groped the soft, fleshy mounds, tweaked the hard nipples. Her tongue leapt into my mouth with a cry of delight and I accepted the compliment, swirling my tongue around hers, giving further voice to our lust.

I pumped my cock into her belly, kneading her breasts and torquing her tongue. She striped my clutching buttocks with her fingers, undulating her wet pussy into my wood, heaving her tits up at me, capturing my tongue between her blazing white teeth and sucking on it like it was a flesh-pop. We melted together, molten on fire; my duty to uphold the legal and moral standards of the small farming community totally forgotten in the heated, head-spinning rush to judgement and joinment.

Lorraine gave dirty words to what we were both filthily thinking, sucking her lips off my tongue and hissing, "Make love to me, Lawrence! Fuck me!"

I was never one to abandon a damsel in distress, or a damn fine dame out of dress. It was one of the reasons I'd gotten into the policing racket. Now, I got into Lorraine, lifting up and grabbing onto my pole, probing the bulbed, leaking head into her bush. She grasped the shaft and shot my cap and cock right into her cunt.

"Yes!" I groaned, plunged deep into a Turkish bath delight of steamy sensation. The girl was as tight as a hatband, hot as a forge, wet as a Nehi. I rutted around in her juicy pink depths like a dog burying his bone.

"Fuck me, Lawrence! Fuck me!" Lorraine screamed, her pretty face screwed up, her fingernails back on my butt meaning business.

The window curtains were still wide open and the bedroom lit up like a crime scene, for any wandering voyeur to catch a view of the local constabulary engaging in raging carnal relations. But we didn't care, me and Lorraine. The cherry was busted and I didn't give a tinker's damn if I was, too. I pumped my hips in a rhythm as old as dirt, and just as filthy, fucking the beautiful redhead.

She moaned, and writhed, her tits jumping in my gripping hands, her hands spurring my ass cheeks on harder and faster.

I clamped my wet mouth to hers, swallowing her cries of passion and regurgitating a few of my own. I thrust deep and hard and quick, drilling my lover. We were both quickly coming up gushers.

Lorraine shuddered beneath my frantically humping body. I suddenly felt even hotter juices baste my groin, bathe my thundering cock with still more lubrication. The look on Lorraine's lovely face was pure erotic bliss. I hammered home my own personal feelings and then was jolted with joy, myself; my love gun going off in the girl's velvet holster and blasting her womb with my blazing wads.

We lay together on the bed after the sensational lay, panting for breath and pawing one another. "I hope no one saw us," Lorraine gasped, glancing at the lit-up window. She giggled into my neck. "Like the town peeping Tom, for example."

I squeezed her tight. "I don't think this town will be bothered by that perverted peeper any more," I stated with confidence, gently burrowing Lorraine's thigh with my dick.

How could I be so cocksure? Simple, *I* was the voyeur everybody was harping about – Constable Lawrence Thom of the Royal Canadian Mounted Police. I'd been masking my face and peeling my eyes at the ladies after hours on my late-night rounds, pumping my cock solo in lieu of a real love interest. But now that I had beautiful Lorraine to discharge my flammable passions into, I had no need to peer into boudoir windows any more. The pervert would be safely sealed up behind closed doors from now on.

Net Profit

Georgina Jephcott

I was one of five women getting ready to serve food to a billionaire called Petre. It was a dinner party for one. We were part of the menu, sitting naked on a long bench waiting for our costumes in silence. When the big woman next to me hissed, "Federico's coming," everyone tensed.

Federico bustled in, steering a dress rail. He was an impossibly gorgeous gay in jeans and a pink vest. "Put this on," he said flicking a brown bundle at me before continuing down the line.

"This" was a chocolate-brown fishnet body harness which might as well have been a bunch of elastic bands it was so stretchy and tangled.

I struggled to find a way into mine but the others were having little or no trouble, making it even more obvious that this was my first time.

"Hurry up, Second," Federico yelled, trundling the empty rail back down the line. I realized he meant me. I was Second Dessert.

I started to panic, a fish caught by necessity, I so needed this gig.

The big woman next to me was the first to "dress" – a giantess with a wonderful voluptuous shape. Thanks to her patient skill, the creamy tight net now defined her figure.

She caught my admiration. "Hi, I'm Gloria, First Dessert. Need help?"

I cancelled my automatic "no" just in time, replacing it with, "Thanks."

"You're the new girl?"

I nodded.

Gloria took the mess from my hands, sorted it deftly then

offered me a "leg" to step into and then another. "First you must find your feet."

She coaxed the net up over my legs, concentrating. Her eyes were big, brown and calming. Luxurious hair befitted her figure, expensive perfume matched her elegance.

"Good to be nervous," she said, as her fingers arranged the net up around my crotch. "This is the top gig, right, just getting here means you're in the big money. But it's the Chosen One tonight who gets the big-big money and the rest live in hope of another chance."

It would take at least two more of these gigs to get me out of debt. But if I got "chosen" tonight I guessed there'd also be enough for an air ticket to anywhere.

A question got free before I could stop it. "What happens to the Chosen One – something pretty damned bad, yeah?"

The quickly guarded splendour of her smile revealed it was something pretty damned good.

"Turn around." She turned me round anyway and with quick assertive tugs made sure the net defined my buttocks above and below and between.

"Why does it have to be so ridiculously tight?"

When she pulled me back round, her eyes were as cold as her tone as she yanked the net up over my breasts. "Listen, you've got debt? You want to come back, right? Well, advice, honey, if I could make my net even tighter, I would."

"Why?"

She smiled, wisely. "To find out, you have to get chosen."

Gloria turned away, giving me a doubtful look, but I reached out, touched her. My whispered, "Thank you," opened up the uncertain possibility of friendship. She frisked me off as Federico returned.

I sat down realizing that she might see me as a threat. This inspired me. I was in with a chance.

Federico dumped chocolate-brown-coloured boots, bra and pants at my feet and moved on. Gloria's was a delicious creamy yellow, perfect for her dark skin. She was the obvious winner, I thought.

My boots and underwear were not just outrageous and rude – they were expensive, never worn and a perfect fit.

Federico hustled us to the dining room.

We stood in line, the five courses of the meal. Even in such beautiful company, I will admit, I felt competitive.

It would have been easy if he had been a fat billionaire with a greasy face and fake hair. But Petre was a gorgeous young man, appraising my body, and I cursed my heart for racing.

When his dark eyes eventually found their way to mine I was caught. This high-cheekboned, square-jawed, beautiful young man had me right there in his eyes.

The pale long hair should have looked awful and would have but for that soul-connecting darkness in his eyes. A schoolgirl pain needled me when he looked away.

Federico stood behind Petre like a butler.

I recalled the splendour in Gloria's smile and sensed she'd "known" Petre and that the chances were I never would.

As "Second Dessert", I had to wait my turn but it gave me time to think what to do to impress him.

Each course was delivered and placed on a table behind us.

I watched the others serve him one by one.

The starter girl had a pear-shaped bottom, cruelly latticed by the avocado-coloured net, but he didn't seem interested in either her or the salad, not even taking in her "As-Seen-On-TV" walk as she retreated.

The main course was steak. Her net was blood red. She wore big white knickers with bloody fingerprints on the crotch and the butt. Her bra, what there was of it, was mustard coloured. As he put mustard on his steak, he flicked a glance at her perfect breasts before waving her away.

I was getting more and more nervous. Creative ideas formed and died in a blink. I could trip up Gloria the Gorgeous Giantess when it came to her turn and knock her out of contention or I could go home and pretend I didn't want to solve the mystery in his eyes.

Gloria's walk was her own as she carried her tray to him.

She stood alongside so he had to turn his head to see her as she served scarlet berries one by one into a virgin white dish. To accompany the fruit – cream. She poured it into a mixing bowl with slow deliberation and began to whip it vigorously leaning forward a little. He watched her trembling breasts and seemed mesmerized by the wonderful look of concentration on her face and the subtle movement of her lips as the cream slowly stiffened.

It was clear this was something new to him, something she'd created especially for tonight.

When the cream had stiffened, she let a heavy drop fall in its own time on each berry in the dish.

I couldn't tell if it was sleight of her hand or just sheer luck but in her exertion a nipple had escaped her bra only to be caught and emphasized by the net. Gloria turned away seemingly unaware, but he stopped her. "You missed one."

Her realization seemed genuine. I watched in awe of her presence of mind as she smiled a half-smile, reached into the bowl and covered her nipple with a cap of cream. She paused just long enough for him, and me, to think she might be about to let him take that "berry" into his mouth.

His eyes were on her butt as she walked away and I knew that as far as me being the Chosen One was concerned, it was over already.

As she returned even I was tempted by her nipple and felt a guilty pleasure.

But I had to concentrate. Even if not "chosen" I still had to do well to get selected for next time. When he appraised Gloria walking away it was as if he'd been watching a moving work of art. I liked him more not less.

As he put each cream-laden berry into his mouth, appreciating each one so sensually, it came as a surprise to me that my nipples were stiffening in response.

Suddenly it was my turn. I walked forward with my tray of chocolates and truffles, along the sharp edge of his gaze.

I leant forward, aware of him taking in the delicious chocolates on display and not my breasts. My best and only hope was that his beautiful eyes would find my lips and realize that my eyes were interested in his lips alone.

Every chocolate on my tray had its own little label. Of all the varieties offered only one was "me".

His fingertips reached out for ... a strawberry crème. Nobody I know selects strawberry crème first. I watched his teeth break the skin and his tongue explore the centre. He might as well have been sliding his love finger between my legs, parting my lips.

I concentrated on his lips and refused to meet his gaze.

There was one more strawberry crème on the tray. I took it, reckless, certainly, suicidal, perhaps. I saw a twitch of annoyance at the corner of his lips, heard the merest breath of surprise from Gloria behind me.

Daintily, demurely I hoped, I curtseyed deep enough to place the tray on the floor then straightened. I broke the crème, took a half in each hand between ballet fingertips and licked out the centre of the first as slowly as I could, giving the other half time to melt between my fingertips.

He watched as I applied the second half as if a lipstick. I walked around the tray, turning my back on him and bent over to pick it up. Neither dainty nor demure, I hoped to move slowly enough to give him an eyeful and quickly enough to make him wish I'd allowed more time.

I retrieved the tray without mishap, but got caught for a moment on the spike in Gloria's eye as I walked back towards her, blinking her away, concentrating on not licking my chocolate lips. I turned to face him again.

My inconvenient arousal, caught in the net of the body stocking and bound by the G-string "pants", made concentration on anything else but his beautiful lips difficult.

After me, it was the turn of the coffee girl. She had an enviable perfectly proportioned figure, tastefully concealed and yet almost revealed by a cappuccino bikini. His fingers waved her away. His eyes were still on me.

The chocolate on my lips was setting.

When Petre stood up I realized how tall he was – he and Gloria a perfect fit. He picked up a golden drawstring purse and moved towards us.

When his lips swooped to suck the melting cream from Gloria's nipple, I knew she'd won.

But when he kept hold of the purse and moved on to me, I closed my eyes. He did not kiss me but held his lips next to mine long enough to warm the chocolate and for me to melt. I hated wanting him but I wanted him.

Petre placed the purse in my hand, took hold of my free hand

and led me away. I sensed Gloria and Federico following us. My heart hit warp speed, money-numbers racing. I'd been Chosen.

When he led me into what was obviously a dungeon my heart dropped.

I knew exactly what lay ahead. The last time I got whipped I said to myself never again no matter what the money.

He stood me in the centre, took the prize from me and held it up. "Because you won this contains three times the amount you expected."

I tried my best to suppress a smile but failed.

"Congratulations," he said softly, looking at my lips. "May I?"

I nodded and felt my legs weaken as he cupped my face in his huge, delicate hands and meticulously kissed the last of the chocolate from my lips.

He let me go and stepped back. "If you choose to continue now you earn another one just like it."

Six times the amount I'd expected would see me free and clear. I could travel. No matter what happened I'd never have to come back here or anywhere like it ever again.

"Do you choose to continue?"

I looked him in the eye – the inky darkness tempting me in deeper. I know it was stupid but the thought *just how dangerous can a man be who asks permission just to kiss you?* clinched it and I in my melted state nodded. He smiled.

It wasn't until he said the words, "Tie her up," I remembered Gloria and Federico were also in the dungeon.

Gloria avoided my eyes but I could see she was still disappointed at losing. Federico's attitude towards me was one of disdain and impatience.

They got to work with brisk precision, stripping off my bra, pants and boots with an insistent efficiency. The net remained; there was no relief from its relentless grip.

They buckled cuffs around my wrists and ankles, attached long ropes to each and then stood either side at the end of them. On his nod they stretched my arms out wide, securing the ropes.

Again waiting for his signal, they picked up the ankle ropes. I expected to be stretched wide, but they coaxed my legs apart gradually, with him watching my body as they pulled. A flick of his finger stopped them on the merciful side of discomfort.

There was no cruelty in those eyes – eyes so dark you had to let your own eyes become accustomed before you could even attempt to read them. I saw enough to make me think for an incredible shooting-star second that I could be a work of art in his gallery.

When the ropes were tied, he beckoned Federico and Gloria back to him. He withdrew two wooden kebab sticks from his dinner jacket. They took one each and stood either side of me, threading the sticks through the fishnet – Federico on a line level with my buttocks and Gloria level with my breasts. He nodded. They turned the sticks, tightening and tightening until I gasped, until I cried. A graceful flick of his finger made them stop; a snip of his fingers told them to cut. He handed them scissors and started licking my tears away then kissing me, chocolate soft and urgent hard, every casual brush of his arousal tantalized.

When he stepped back, eyes on my lips, I was breathless and wanting.

"Gag her," he said softly.

The silk of his voice alone was enough to shut me up, but Federico stuck tape over my mouth, pressing hard using his thumbnails to define my lips. Anger and jealousy lit his eyes and I knew for certain that Federico knew Petre just as Gloria knew Petre.

I felt like the impossible fourth point of a triangle.

Free of the net, I gradually became aware of every line left on my skin, a strange but not unpleasant feeling.

"Heat the oil." It was a whisper not an order. Federico moved to obey.

"Blindfold her."

Gloria did this and as she did so whispered, "Congratulations, honey."

Speechless, helpless and blind, I welcomed this darkness, his darkness.

From the silence emerged the soft sigh of clothing falling to the floor on the breath of his scent. The unmistakable sound of a zip confirmed his undressing.

His oily fingertip found the lower edge of my right shoulder blade and the muscle responded involuntarily with a log-on cat-shiver ripple of pleasure.

This wonderful fingertip surely belonged to a hand that would not slap or punch.

His penis glided into me as an entirely new thought.

I was almost glad to be helpless and to be "blind" but not to be—

He might have read my thoughts because the tape was ripped from my lips. He kissed me with an intense but subsiding violence, which tumbled into a surreal gentleness I simply couldn't cope with. My sensitized lips giddied me into desire.

The fingertip wandered blind yet certain over the plains of my back, meandering along the criss-cross tracks and time slowed.

The feeling between my legs – unique – a ripe heaviness constantly aware of his presence inside me and wanting, wanting, wanting to close my legs, squeeze and push against him. I groaned with frustration.

Gloria intruded, gagging me again, pressing the tape so hard against my lips, her expensive perfume so suddenly cheap.

Petre grabbed my butt and started fucking me. There was nothing I could do about it and for once-in-a-forever it felt so wonderful.

But when his traitorous hands left my cheeks I was still impaled on him and wanting. He withdrew. "Remove the blindfold," he ordered softly. "Warm the oil again."

I took a breath from the depths of frustration and opened my eyes. The light of the room had become a soft yellow bordering on dusk. He was standing in front of me, erect, confident and seemingly unselfconscious. His eyes were on my breasts.

Everywhere his oiled fingertip had touched was now champagne tingling – all over my back, my butt, down the backs of my legs. I felt a quiver of expectation, wanting this feeling all over me, all at once.

I recalled Gloria saying, "If I could make my net even tighter, I would" and now realized why – so the grooves would be deeper and last longer.

Petre washed his hands in the oil. His elegant fingers fascinated me as he applied it first to his lips and then his penis.

Federico watched and I sensed in a last lucid moment that in this dungeon it was Federico and Gloria who were being tortured, not me . . .

Petre ripped the gag off me, replacing it with a violent winter kiss. Words such as "No" and "Stop" were just two white words in the blizzard. Hot-ache screams of pleasure howled all through my inner cathedral.

He broke the kiss, left me shivering as if from the cold.

In the lull it was as if winter's wind had dropped from the sky and lay on the ground, hiding.

My lips were incapable of speech as the tingle effect began to riot over them.

Now he was behind me, hands roughly kneading my breasts at first but then fingertips finding and exploring the tracks all across them, above and below and between.

His penis slid inside me. I closed my eyes and had to let go. I wasn't sure if I was meant to climax or not but had to anyway. It was almost private, almost silent.

A private orgasm? His dick, like some note-taking detective, deep and dark inside me, knew.

He touched my nipples, fertilizing the seed of the next climax. If he'd been rough with them . . . but the cruelty of his gentleness, exploring and testing their rude hardness, made me squirm against the ropes.

A slow involuntary trembling between my legs gathered speed. I was surfing an impossible rising curl of pleasure and if it weren't for the ropes holding me up I'd be on the floor, gasping for breath and only imagining what might have been.

Moments before the third climax, a silent darkness kept me in breathless expectation until the implosion happened. I realized my feet were leaving the ground and I was wriggling on his penis, screaming silent arias as he kept me on the tip of the spike. The inevitable tumble rolled me down a mountain, an accumulating snowball.

Of course, I smashed into a barrier. There is always a barrier. Hot snow exploded and a million raindrops posed for two moments in a shocking rainbow.

A fourth and final climax raked deliciously all through me as he took his pleasure. I sensed the enormity of his strength as he hugged me from behind and danced me rough and sure all the way back up to the top of his personal mountain.

We stood together at the peak. He used no words and that was good. I don't trust words, not one of them. But if he had whispered, "I adore you," at that moment, I'd have believed him. That's how dangerous he was.

He left me and I regretted the loss.

All the ropes loosened. I felt myself crumpling to the floor, which seemed a very long way away. I caught a glimpse of diamond sincere tears in Federico's eyes.

Gloria must have caught me, her perfume no longer cheap but priceless. I hoped she was carrying me off to a bed somewhere and loved the idea. But a black cloud thought assured me she was taking me off to some quiet place where she would beat me up for being chosen and boot me out the back door with enough bruises to keep me out of his sight for a couple of months at least.

This spawned the stabbing "where's my money" thought but once she'd put me on the bed my hand was encouraged to find the purse.

Drunk on sex and already swimming through sleep's early shallows, I slept, tingling.

When I awoke my hand closed on the purse, a quick tug opened it up and revealed clean cash. I counted wonderful numbers.

I heard footsteps. Gloria came in wearing flat shoes and a boring floral overall. She could've passed for a cleaner. She was carrying a tray. "Sleep well?"

I smiled, sitting up and stretching, the unexpected prospect of breakfast in bed a true luxury.

She extended the hidden legs of the tray and set them astride me. Buttered toast; marmalade available; bacon, sausage, fish and rice – all offered in mini portions from an exquisitely designed dish.

"Enjoy. I'll bring you hot coffee and chilled orange juice."

By the time she returned there was little left. She cleared away, poured coffee for two, and sat on the edge of the bed. "What are your plans now, Fleur?"

"Pay everything off and run. Catch a plane."

"Searching for what? What you've just discovered here?" She gave a knowing smile looking at the marks on my skin.

The thought of not getting on a plane now that I had the

money was brand new. The ripe pleasure-aftermath between my legs was also new. My lips were tender, sensitized by the brutality of the gags and his outrageous kisses.

The criss-cross sparkle all over my skin tickled mischievously but was fading. "Who is he, exactly?"

She shrugged. "He's your average billionaire, on a plane right now and might not be back for a month or more. This is usual."

"When he returns – there'll be another—"

"Dinner party?" she interrupted. "Perhaps, he likes the dinner party. But we might have to be lifeguards or nurses or dominatrices. Petre decides. As a winner you're guaranteed another chance. In the meantime all I can offer you here is work."

I wanted to wear the naked net again, wanted the oil, wanted his uncomplicated dick again . . . but in all honesty also found myself seriously wanting Gloria's lips on mine.

What was the point of chasing all over the world when what I wanted most was right here? Gloria was right.

I sipped on coffee and the look in her eyes. Without Gloria's help I'd never have been chosen. If I kissed her now to say thank you it would be nothing more than an excuse just to kiss her. "What kind of work?"

"Everyday hard work, this is a big place to clean."

"Clean? You want me to clean? And you are . . . his wife?"

She smiles. "No, my dear, I'm his cleaner and I need help. Federico is his gay wife, though they've never married."

My turn to give a knowing smile.

She said nothing just watched my eyes waiting for me to speak again.

"What was in it for Petre, then?"

She shrugged. "He's a genuine bisexual with an ego the size of a planet. The dinner for one is an occasional ceremony Federico is forced to attend as a punishment."

My extreme pleasure was Federico's torture.

"What's in that oil?"

She looked at the marks on my skin and said quietly, "All of your expectations and a secret ingredient only history and he knows. Do not waste even one more tingle on your skin."

In my head, logic gathered everything together: the money,

my feelings and my future. I managed to sound tough. "Kiss me goodbye, Gloria, I'm heading for home and then the airport."

The soothing shock of her kiss quietly folded my words up and put them to one side. The coffee cups clattered to the floor.

Eager to touch her through the thin cleaner's uniform, I found a body harness and the lines of the straps led inevitably between her legs where I touched a dildo held upright against her belly.

I broke the kiss, pretending to be outraged at the discovery, pushing her away. "Take it off."

With only a moment's hesitation, she stepped back from the bed and pulled the overall zip down. A shrug revealed her with a hint of her wonderful perfume and the "offending" dildo held upright against her by tight floral knickers, matching the cleaner's uniform.

"Take it off."

As she took down her knickers the dildo flopped out, ready, a tempting me-size.

"Take it off," I repeated, as if irritated and on the verge of anger.

She unbuckled the harness and handed it over.

"So this is what you had in store for me? What else?"

She walked to the bedhead and revealed a rope tied to the corner.

"You were going to spread me? Why?"

"Because you won?" Her tone implied she hoped this would be explanation enough.

I shook my head. "Try again."

"Because I hoped."

"Hoped for what?"

"To get to this moment."

"So you could tie me up and fuck me?"

"Yes, if you wanted that or whatever it took because I want you to stay and I have to tell you for your own sake those marks on your body must not be wasted."

Truth was in her eyes – that naked honesty.

I handed back the harness. It wasn't because I believed a single word she said – it was because I felt each one of them. "Put it on me."

She obeyed.

The difference in our sizes caused many adjustments and tugs and I loved every one. "Get on the bed." It came out more bark than speech.

Gloria obeyed, guiding the dildo when I put it between her legs. She tried to touch me, but I caught hold of her wrists and forced them above her head, pinning her down easily as if I was stronger than her. I kissed in anger and kept the dildo at its deepest point inside her. Pretend struggles, mewing, whimpering sounds were pleasing even though I was wise enough to know she was wriggling to get her clit into a better position.

And then with a smile and a twist of her wrists she was free. This wasn't pretend and in a breath I succumbed, resistance collapsing as she held me tight against her with one arm and returned my kiss with overwhelming violence.

In the strawberry crème aftermath I knew I was deliciously helpless.

With her free hand, she stroked the small of my back and when her fingertip traced along a mark left by the net it activated all the others, fizzing them up into a riot.

Her strong hands encouraged me to sit up, keeping the dildo in place. "Fold your arms behind, honey."

I obeyed. The action pushed my breasts out, tightening the skin. I gazed down into her eyes in anticipation. She made me wait, but when her fingertips began to trace the tingle-tangle lattice marks already mapping my breasts, I groaned with pleasure.

Gloria knew that dildo as a friend and how to make me work it.

In return, she made my nipples ache with pleasure.

I was lost and found and I'd travelled life years to get here.

We came together, with eyes closed, falling through pleasure clouds, trusting in each other's arms, hoping the bed would still be there to soften the landfall.

It was.

Our eyes opened together.

In the mixed up afterwards, in the dreamlike smoke of memory, I felt everything all over again and knew that every last trace of the net had left my body except for one.

She slid her hand between my legs and her love finger between my lips in search of my clit and, with its gentle touch, the shock of ecstasy made me scream without sound. I shuddered and jerked on the tip of her finger endlessly until I begged in a whisper, "Please let me come."

It took just one rub of her finger to break me into a million sparkling fragments thrown up into a black pleasure sky and left to drift down to earth.

She cuddled me until there was nothing left but the superb afterglow.

"All done, all gone," she said quietly, getting off the bed. "You can go now. I was being selfish asking you to stay. I can offer you nothing except a cleaning job. I have no oil. It could be months before Petre gets back and you might not get chosen even then."

She left the room.

The old clear-your-debts-get-to-the-airport movie ran but in faded colours.

I showered, dressed, stuffed the money into my shoulder bag, got my heels on and walked, but I had to pass the dungeon.

The scent of jasmine furniture polish stopped me in the doorway. Gloria had her back to me polishing Petre's dining table. It seemed that nothing could stop her rhythm.

I noticed an unwrapped uniform draped over the back of his chair.

The whisper of her uniform as she polished Petre's dungeon floor found me out in my wanting and what I wanted wasn't going to happen anywhere else in the world but here.

I stripped off in silence, padded over to the chair, in front of her now, but she didn't look up. I broke into the packaging and put the knickers on. With the sound of the closing uniform zip, Gloria looked up and smiled. Kissing her smile was the best thing I ever did.

Trolley Dolly

E. C. Cutler

"Let's make a bet on it," Matt said, looking up at the TV screen in the crew lounge. I should have known then that the wager would have some kind of sexual component. If I lost, would he want me down on my knees, sucking his cock, or maybe putting on some kind of show with baby oil and a dildo in the privacy of his hotel room? We'd become good mates since we started working together, but I'd never quite been able to shake the feeling that he had the hots for me. And even though I don't look at other guys in that way, there were times when I wondered what I'd do if he ever made a move on me – then wondered why I wasn't immediately dismissing the idea out of hand.

"What have you got in mind?" I took another swig of my much-needed beer – we'd hit some serious turbulence on the way to Miami, and had to spend half the flight calming down anxious passengers – and turned my attention to the TV. The bartender, who appeared to have no immunity to Matt's twinkly Irish charm, had switched the channel to coverage of the Scotland–Ireland rugby game at his request.

He gestured to the screen with his bottle. "If Scotland win, I'll borrow a uniform from one of the girls and wear it on the flight back to London. If Ireland win, then it'll be you dressing up. Sound fair enough?"

I considered the scoreline. Scotland had a slender lead, but with only five minutes to go I reckoned they could hold out. And if it meant the rest of the crew were treated to the sight of Matt teetering along the aisle in a skirt and high heels, then it would definitely be worth it, given some of the in-flight pranks he'd played on them in the past. Payback had been long overdue in some cases, and it would be sweet when it came.

"OK, mate, you're on." My tone confident, I held out a hand for him to shake.

It didn't take long for that confidence to shatter. Ireland had come on strong, and converted a last-minute penalty to win the game. Matt clapped me on the shoulder and grinned. "Hard luck, Alex. But if it's any consolation, I think you'll look fantastic as a woman."

The flight back to London wasn't for twenty-fouor hours. Normally, I'd have enjoyed a day's layover in Miami, lying by the hotel pool or window-shopping in the glamorous surroundings of Miracle Mile, but now all I could think about was the forfeit Matt had in mind for me. Maybe it would have been easier if he'd asked me to pleasure him sexually in some way – at least then my humiliation would have been kept between the two of us, rather than being witnessed by the whole crew.

But would it be humiliating to find myself down on my knees before Matt, my mouth crammed full of his hard, salty dick? A small, treacherous part of me didn't shy away from that image. If anything, it welcomed the thought of being placed at my friend's mercy, his to command in whatever way he chose.

Still, those fantasies didn't make things any easier when I answered a knock at my hotel room door to find Matt standing there, with something in a protective plastic clothing cover in his arms.

"The shuttle bus will be coming to take us to the airport in an hour," he said. "Just enough time to get you ready . . ."

"Look, Matt, I'm really not sure this is a good idea," I stuttered, the reality of what was about to happen hitting home as he started laying the uniform out on the bed. "And where did you get that anyway?"

He grinned. "Big Cheryl was only too happy to lend it to me, once I told her what it was for. Now come on, get your clothes off."

My heart sank even further. That meant at least one other person already knew what had been planned for me. Given that Cheryl was one of the biggest gossips on the Swift Fly staff, it wouldn't be long before the whole crew had wind of my impending transformation.

I stood where I was, ignoring Matt's request to undress. "How about we forget the dressing-up thing, hey? How about I buy you a bottle of single malt instead – the good stuff?"

"Welshing on a bet, Alex? I'd have thought better of you." Matt's tone and stance told me he had no intention to let me do anything other than dress in Cheryl's borrowed clothes. Knowing I didn't have any other choice, I quickly stripped out of my T-shirt and shorts, and reached for the uniform.

"And the rest," Matt ordered.

"What?" I stared at him blankly.

"Boxers off, too. You didn't think I'd let you keep your own underwear on, did you? Not when I got you something really special to wear."

Feeling my cheeks flush, I pulled down my shorts and tossed them at him. Matt appraised me slowly as I stood there naked, fighting the urge to cover my groin with my hands. Under his intense scrutiny, my cock began to twitch and lengthen. Despite everything, being placed in such a bizarre situation was turning me on.

"Getting a little excited there, Alex," Matt commented, his lips quirked upwards in amusement. "I think you ought to do something about that before we go. Don't want a big bulge spoiling the line of your pretty little skirt, do we?"

"Please, Matt, don't." I knew exactly what he wanted me to do. Instead of doing anything to quell my rising erection, the thought of having to wank in front of him was just getting me harder.

He said nothing, simply stood with hands on hips and an impatient look on his face. The only way out of this was to give him what he wanted. Normally, I'd have taken things slowly, lubing myself up with hand lotion and getting into the feeling of my hot fingers as they grasped my shaft. But this was about getting myself off hard and fast, ready for the next part of the humiliating process Matt had in store for me. So I just spat into my palm and took myself in hand, all too aware of my friend's gaze on me.

Even if I'd wanted to string the pleasure out, I doubt I could have. From almost the first sweep of my fist from base to tip, I was on the edge: balls drawn up tight, breath coming fast and tense. Glancing down at Matt's crotch, I saw the telltale straining in his trousers that told me he was more affected by my performance than he attempted to make out. If only he had his cock out, too, so I could see whether it was as big as it appeared. With thoughts of him lying sprawled on the bed, dick gripped in his fist as we wanked in rhythm, I let out a groan and my come spurted out over my fingers.

Matt handed me a tissue, and I cleaned myself off. Then he presented me with the underwear he expected me to put on, bursting out laughing at my reaction. I'd expected something bikini style, maybe; nothing like this. The coffee-coloured panties were pure silk, trimmed with cream lace around the leg holes. No one who saw them could doubt I was wearing women's undies.

I shook my head, not wanting to know where he'd got these. I couldn't exactly see Big Cheryl giving him free rein with her scanties. "I can't . . ."

"You can. More than that, you want to."

He was right. Pretend as I might, I wanted to know how it would feel to have that soft, delicate material against my skin. Aware that time was pressing, I did my best to feign nonchalance as I stepped into the panties and pulled them up my legs, as if I did this sort of thing all the time.

I suppressed a shudder of pleasure, hoping Matt hadn't noticed my reaction. Somehow, the silk cradling my cock and balls felt right, as though I was being seduced by the fabric. Why had I never thought to try on any of my girlfriends' panties before now?

Matt distracted me before my thoughts could run away with me, which was just as well because my erection was threatening to come back with a vengeance. "Very nice." Was there a slight catch to his voice? For the first time since he'd arrived with the uniform, I wondered quite how deeply this scene was tapping into his own secret fantasies.

He tossed me a pair of tights in the unappealing tan shade, which was standard wear for Swift Fly's female flight crew. Knowing any protests were futile, I sat on the edge of the bed and rolled them carefully up my legs, half afraid I would ladder them before I even had them on.

After that came the white shirt and navy jacket that weren't so different from my usual regulation uniform, and the matching navy skirt that so clearly was. I couldn't look at Matt as I put them on, or look in the direction of the free-standing mirror, in case I caught a glimpse of my reflection. The jacket felt a little tight across my shoulders, but apart from that, everything was a pretty good fit.

"I have to say one thing, mate," Matt commented as I slipped into the unexpectedly comfortable kitten-heeled shoes he'd provided for me. "All the girls are going to be jealous of how good your legs look in that skirt."

"Shut up," I snapped, even as I basked in his compliment. "Now, let's go downstairs so I can get this over with."

"Not yet." It seemed Matt had one last surprise for me. He produced a make-up bag he must have been concealing beneath the uniform when he brought it into the room, and a black, shoulder-length wig. "You still look too much like Alex. Now, sit."

This was the final humiliation, but again I meekly did as he instructed. Once Matt had finished applying foundation, mascara and lipstick, and placed the wig on my head, he brought the mirror over so I could admire my transformation. And admire I did. With his powders and paints, Matt had disguised my beard line, defined my cheekbones and given me slick, pouting lips. If I hadn't known better, I'd have sworn a woman was staring back at me.

"Fuck," I murmured, half to myself.

"Meet Alexis." Matt had a satisfied smirk on his face, clearly pleased with the results of his handiwork. "She's a stunner, isn't she?" He glanced at his watch, seeming to realize just how long he'd spent working on me. "The bus'll be here any minute. We'd better go down and check out."

When we walked into reception, the whole flight crew were already down there waiting for us. I held my head high, certain I looked ridiculous but still feeling that undercurrent of sexual excitement as the silk panties caressed my most intimate places.

"Alex won't be joining us on the flight back," Matt said, revelling in the moment. "Alexis is coming with us instead."

There was a round of catcalls and applause. Our pilot, who

I'd been working alongside for three years, grinned and said, "Oh, Alexis, if only I wasn't a married man . . ."

I had to put up with ribbing and suggestive comments all the way to the airport, and even though there was no malice behind it, I was already plotting the many inventive ways I would get my revenge on Matt. A couple of times I looked over and caught him staring at me, and I was sure it wasn't only my imagination that made me see desire in his gaze.

When the time came for the passengers to start boarding our flight, the rest of the attendants made sure I was standing at the front of the plane, welcoming everyone and checking their passes. I felt stupidly self-conscious, but although a couple of passengers gave me a curious second glance, most seemed to accept me for what I appeared to be – a statuesque, long-legged woman.

Luckily, on this trip, I was charged with attending to the passengers in the first class section, which was half empty. Matt was assisting alongside me, and a couple of times as we fetched drinks or answered a call, our hands would touch or we would brush against each other. I'd have put these touches down as accidental, if it weren't for the fact that when Matt bumped against me, I felt the solid ridge of his erection poking at my thigh.

As we tried to manoeuvre in the cramped space of the galley, a sudden pocket of turbulence made us bump together, and again I was all too aware of his excitement. "Am I making it hard for you?" I murmured, unable to resist the urge to tease him. He'd had enough fun at my expense, after all. Then I went on my way with the requested glass of champagne for the Cuban businessman in Row C who'd been flirting with me throughout the flight.

Matt waited till dinner had been cleared away, the lights had been dimmed and the majority of the passengers had reclined their seats so they could try to sleep before making his move. We were back in the galley, stacking plates, and he came up behind me, enfolding me in his arms. His voice was an urgent purr in my ear. "God, Alex, you don't know what it's doing to me, looking like you do right now."

I pushed back against the hard cock that butted up against my arse. "Oh, I think I do." Turning to face him, I asked, "So what was this bet of yours all about? Giving the rest of the crew a few laughs at my expense, or fulfilling some sordid little fantasy of your own?"

"There's nothing sordid about it. I just thought you'd look spectacular *en femme*, and you do. Though seeing you in those little panties, that big cock of yours threatening to spill out of the silk – well, that was fucking fantastic just on its own." He lowered his voice further. "And I bet it's doing just that right now, isn't it?"

"I don't know what you're talking about," I replied primly, even though he was right. I'd been fighting not to get an erection for most of the flight, but now, pressed up tight against Matt, my cock was so hard I feared it might poke a hole through my underwear.

"Don't you now?" As Matt spoke, he ran a hand down the front of my skirt, grinning in triumph as his fingers settled round the contours of my hard-on. A whimper escaped my lips as he rubbed me through the layers of fabric. I should have been pushing him away and going back to my duties. After all, I didn't sleep with other men. Never had. But right now, I wanted him more than I had anyone.

Still he kept on stroking and teasing me. "How much of this can you stand before you come in your panties, Alex?"

"Please, Matt, don't. Someone could walk in and catch us at any moment."

"They won't care. You know damn well half the crew have fucked each other before now. According to Cheryl, Lucy spent the night with Captain Marriott."

"And him a married man, too." But Matt's words did nothing to assuage my fears.

"OK, let's become Mile High clichés and take this to the toilets, then."

This time, I didn't object. By now, I was so turned on I was hardly thinking straight, but Matt's words had some logic to them. Plane toilets are hardly the most glamorous of locations, but at least in first class they were roomy enough to accommodate both of us. In any case, this wasn't going to be any kind of slow seduction. We just needed to act on our lust for each other.

The area by the toilets was deserted. I took a quick peek through the curtains that led to economy, but that, too, was quiet. Most people had reached the stage in the flight where all they wanted to do was grab some sleep. I couldn't see Cheryl or Lucy; they'd probably taken a seat somewhere and settled in for one of their regular bitch-fests about the other attendants.

We let ourselves in to a vacant cubicle and locked the door behind us. I only had a moment to register the clean, modern fixtures and the vague chemical tang in the air before Matt was on me, his lips pressing against mine. I'd never kissed another guy, but any doubts I had were quickly forgotten as our tongues twined together. His mouth was soft, and tasted of mint. I closed my eyes and lost myself in the sensation.

He tugged at my skirt, undoing the zip and sliding it down, then helped me out of the restrictive tights. God knew how women coped with wearing them all the time, but I reckoned I'd have been equally fazed by dealing with fiddly suspenders. So much simpler just to undo your trousers and guide them down to your ankles, as Matt was now doing.

I thought he might pull down my panties, but he left them in place, content to stroke me through the thin silk. By now, my cock was at full mast, the head poking up over the waistband. He rubbed his thumb over its tip, smearing pre-come as he went, and I almost lost it.

"I always thought you'd be big, but wow . . ." His voice trailed off, and I did my best to suppress a pleased smirk. Catching sight of myself in the mirror, I couldn't help but register the contrast between the feminine face staring back at me and the obvious maleness below my waist. Was that what Matt got off on? I didn't know and, at that moment, I didn't care. My dick was in his grasp and he was wanking me with steady strokes that almost had my knees buckling.

"No more of that, please," I begged. "If I'm going to come, I want to do it in your mouth."

"So the little slut has fantasies of her own, eh?" Matt chuckled. "Of course, but only on the condition you're willing to return the favour."

"Of course."

"That's all I needed to hear." With that, he pushed me back

against the faux-marble unit that contained the sink, and went down on his haunches. He pressed his lips to my silk-covered cock, lapping at it with little flicks of his tongue. As the material grew damper, it clung even more deliciously to my flesh. But even that thin barrier was too much; I needed to be buried in Matt's mouth.

"Please . . . please suck me," I begged. I could hardly believe I was uttering the words, but Matt responded with a knowing smirk, pulling down the front of the panties so they bunched just below my balls. Then he took my dick with one big, greedy gulp. As soon as he began to run his tongue over my helmet, I knew I was lost. Nothing could have prepared me for the sensation of being engulfed in his hot, urgent mouth, and I gripped hard at the unit behind me, my hips thrusting at him with almost unconscious movements. He didn't object as I stepped up the pace, fucking his face in earnest, even though he must have been fighting the urge to gag every time my cockhead bumped his palate. He must have known this first time would be almost overwhelming for me.

Almost before I was aware of it, my spunk was gushing into his mouth. Matt never missed a beat; he swallowed it all down, then rocked back and let me slip from his lips. He smiled up at me as he dabbed a finger at the corners of his mouth, then licked it clean of the come he'd wiped up.

My legs could barely support my weight, and I panted as though I'd run a marathon. But I was ready to give Matt a taste of what he'd just given me, even though I knew my oral skills would be pitiful in comparison to his.

He sat on the closed lid of the toilet, spreading his legs wide and inviting me to get between them. I didn't need any more in the way of invitation. Kneeling in the apex of his thighs, I fumbled at his belt and the zip of his uniform trousers. Reaching into his opened fly, I discovered he hadn't bothered with underwear, and my hand closed around hot, gently pulsing cock-flesh. It didn't seem wrong to be caressing another man's shaft; if anything, there was something wonderfully right about enjoying the way it felt in my palm. I traced a finger down the thick vein, hearing the breath catch in his throat as I touched him.

I could have spent forever playing with his dick, but time was short. We had passengers back in the cabin who might be in need of attention and wondering why no one was responding to their calls. So, clutching Matt's length by the base, I steadied myself before plunging my mouth down on to it. I registered the hot, salty taste of him, and the silkiness of the juice that seeped from his tip, thinking how different the sensation was to running my tongue over a woman's slippery folds.

"Go on, suck me. Suck me hard," Matt instructed. I did my best to comply, my cheeks hollowing as I applied what I hoped was the right amount of suction to his cock. As I mimicked what he'd done to me, I heard him groan low in his throat, and knew I must be hitting the right spots.

Just as I'd been, Matt was clearly on a short fuse. He shifted on the toilet seat, seeking to lodge himself deeper in my throat. Then he grabbed my head, careful not to dislodge my wig, and held me in place. With my mouth crammed full of his meat, all I could do was breathe through my nose and prepare for his impending explosion. It wasn't long in coming; a few urgent jabs of his dick and I tasted the bitter tang of semen.

Matt pulled out of my mouth and quickly zipped himself up. "That was fantastic, but I think one of us needs to get back to the cabin before anyone realizes how long we've been gone." He tossed me something from his pocket and as I caught it, I realized it was a tube of lipgloss. He grinned. "In case you need a touch-up."

And just like that, he was gone: letting himself out of the cubicle and leaving me to repair my smudged make-up. As I stared into the mirror, I couldn't help thinking that, despite everything, I'd enjoyed my first outing as Alexis, and I wouldn't object if Matt wanted me to dress for him again. But there was still the small matter of revenge. I was sure I could make a bet with Matt that he'd be certain to lose. When he did, there were so many filthy, wonderful things I could make him do for my pleasure. With this game, I knew the sky really was the limit.

The Post-Woman's Victim

Zorba Tocks

Bronwen Moore was a woman with a serious mind and a driving ambition to become a notable journalist. Unfortunately, the magazines and newspapers she sent her submits to were not of the same opinion and, consequently, she filled reams of paper with words that never reached the public, to remain a hardworking person at the end of her tether and frustrated as hell.

She wasn't fond of her name, which was given by her Welsh mother who was forever wishing to spend her life by the sea reading Gaelic mythology; hence she was named after the daughter of Llyr, the god of the sea. Her mother had been cruel at times, denying her the emotional stability and love she craved and she often thought it was the reason why she'd never been able to keep a man for long and disbelieved she'd ever find the right one, because unfortunately she'd inherited the same traits, especially rewarding people for her neglect in the same way her mother had treated her. "Don't bother me, child!" Mrs Moore would say; and later: "Oh, sorry, dear; here, take this fiver and get yourself something nice."

There came the day when Bronwen's boredom reached a bursting point after years of living alone while she was brushing her long, blonde-dyed hair in front of a mirror before tying it into braids that she'd pin to the back of her head. She was not aware that men viewed her neck and shoulders akin to a graceful swan; nor was she aware that her prominent boobs, indented waist and pear-shaped butt caused a stir when she bent over to look at merchandise in the stores. All she saw was an unsexy and unspectacular looking woman.

Her only joys were her own secrets and in-house activities, for she had no one to talk to and therefore no one with whom to discuss her fantasies. And her fantasies were simple: a good-looking, faithful and honest man who would adore her welcoming cunt and fuck her near to death every night and do other things to her that would cause gossip and scandal in the village if they knew.

"Knew what, exactly?" she asked herself unsmiling, talking out loud to the ordinary reflection she saw in the mirror. "That my only consolation was stroking my own clit in my own cold bed or sitting on a vibrating dildo, grinding myself onto it furiously until I'm raw? Or would it be my lonely orgasms that'd inspire their gossipy tongues? They would, I'm sure, if I yelled loud enough! And boy, that damn vibrator can really make me yell sometimes!"

She remarked on that because she lived in the small, quaint village of Huntley, with 1,012 inhabitants, near Gloucester in the district of the Forest of Dean, which has an old church, dating from the eleventh century dedicated to St John the Baptist and the one school next to it. The community used to have its own post office as well, but it was closed.

But the lack of communicating was a problem and she decided that day to get a part-time, fairly well-paid job where she could meet people and maybe get some ideas for new stories. So the following Saturday, she bought a copy of the *Gloucester Citizen* and an ad for postmen and post-women with the Royal Mail caught her attention. All she needed, she read, was a current driver's licence.

"Hmm," she said out loud, "twenty hours per week, good pay with twenty-two days holiday to start, contributory pension scheme, childcare – useful if I had kids – and various corporate discounts."

She applied and was hired. After her recruitment and training, she found herself the driver of a Matra, a French-manufactured electric car with a range of ninety-five miles fully charged, speeding along at tops of sixty mph.

"You're a lucky one, Bronwen," Hawk, her new colleague said. "Those bubble cars pull a small trailer for the mail. They were first an experiment in Oxford. It's a fluke you got the only one in this district."

"Yeah," another named Abbey piped in. "It must've been your figure what got the Super's eye, ha, ha!"

"Now then, Abbey, don't start," Hawk cautioned. "She doesn't deserve your tongue pulling her leg just yet."

"Humph! Someone senior should've got it! Me, for instance," she insisted. "I've a mind to speak to the Union about this!"

"There you go again, woman!" Hawk teased. "The reason you're always running to the Union is because you want the #1's dick up your bum and don't think I don't know, either!"

"Fucking disgusting you are, Hawk! You're the one who fancies his dick up your bum, not me!" she retorted. "More the pity for you if he does, because it'd be a fucking waste!"

"There you go then." Hawk smiled in triumph. "I knew you wanted him!"

"Oh, go suck it!" she spat. "Anyhow, we know what happens at number fourteen!"

"What do you mean?" he asked with a grin. "I only make special deliveries there."

"Yeah, especially juicy ones!" She giggled, looking at him with begrudging fondness without seeming to have much respect. "Dirty sod! Let's be having you then!" she said.

Hawk whispered in Bronwen's ear: "Don't worry, luv; *she* lives at number fourteen."

Unknown as to their purpose, he and Abbey fled to the back of the delivery room for a quickie out of view behind a stack of boxes. Without preliminaries, she dropped her uniform pants to her knees and bent over with eager desire to be fucked, while he jacked-up his dick to accommodate her. She liked it rough and he jammed it into her slightly moist cunt with the unpleasant disposition of a lout mounting a whore, because neither cared for the niceties of sexual protocol. Get it in and get it out was their unrefined attitude, but that tone of belief became irrelevant when he spurred to greatness as she pushed backwards upon his rampant rod effectively to a powerful finish.

"That was a good 'un, me beauty," he chuckled with enthusiasm and she punched him in the gut and slapped his butt violently as a reward for not giving her an orgasm.

They sped back to the delivery room looking guiltily innocent. "Bronwen, look out for the recluse!" Abbey shouted before she left unabashed and none the worse for wear, while Hawk scratched his nose, relishing the stings on his rear while admiring Abbey's fuckable arse and wishing they'd had more time.

Bronwen wasn't sure what'd happened between them but had a good idea and was too shocked to ask what she meant by "the recluse". She quickly learned her tasks and soon got used to her little bubble vehicle and its quiet hum as she made her rounds.

Several weeks passed, and she stopped to make her first delivery package at a pleasant cottage about a mile outside of town to a customer addressed as: Alastair Scott, Scott's Corner. She noticed the garden was well trimmed but had swathes of wild flowers and flowering weeds, which looked perfectly normal in the setting with hazel, elm and birch trees standing randomly to the sides.

She rang the bell admiring the thick clinging ivy covering the front facade and, hearing the shuffling of feet, waited for the door to open.

"*Good Lord!*" she said amazed. "I . . . would you mind putting something on, sir?"

It was all she could say when confronted by a tall, suntanned, smooth-bodied man totally naked with a slack cock dangling between his legs, hands on hips and smiling at the world as if nothing was amiss.

"Yes, I do," he answered with a wide, cheeky grin. "I like naked. What have you got?"

"A registered Royal Mail package, sir," she said, trying her best not to scan his manhood. "Please sign for it."

"Aha, that must be my erotic hard copies – splendid – and thank you, ma'am," he said excitedly, ripping the package open, eager to read more about what he desired to stir his mind that was denied him in reality.

"You're welcome," she muttered before scampering away.

When she returned the vehicle at the end of her shift and plugged in the electric charger, Abbey was waiting as usual to rib her and saw her looking out of sorts. "So," she drawled, "looks like you met Mr Alastair Scott today."

"Who? Oh . . . yes . . . the one who lives out of town you mean?"

"Yeah, Bronwen, the one with the big dick, duh! Did you get any of it?"

"Don't be ridiculous! Honestly, Abbey, why do you think dirty all the time?"

"Because that's all there is to think where we live. Anyway, did he give you some?"

"Certainly not!"

"You daft dummy! I'd go for a bit given the chance. I'm married to a boring wacko nincompoop I have to wallop regularly to warm us up, which I revel in anyway and let Hawk fuck me between times, but so what? And to spank that tight recluse's ass – oh, my – can't you imagine him over your knees, smoothing his hard buttocks then digging in your nails before applying lots of rapid smacks and then lovelier harder smacks with all your energy until his cock gets so stiff you could walk on it?"

"You're immoral with a terrible mind!" Bronwen retorted, yet mentally agreeing the man had a fine arse and a finer cock, which would be much lovelier inside her than spanking him.

"I'm not! I just do what comes natural!" Abbey replied huffily and added: "How do you think I keep my men in trim?"

"You're joking," she said. "No man would allow that!"

"You're naive, that's your trouble," Abbey insisted. "Some men need it."

Bronwen shook her head. "I don't believe you; I'm going home."

Meanwhile, Alastair opened and closed one of his new books, his mind distracted by the new post-woman and what he'd like her to do to him and him to her. *Risky*, he thought. *I like the look of her and if I don't act soon I'll never know.* He went outside, tempted to cut a hazel twig, whip himself to a frenzy and then wank off, but it was never completely satisfying. He was fed up and frustrated tending to himself and vowed to achieve something more.

Driving the vehicle, hopping out every few minutes, carrying the mail and driving elsewhere continually from 8.30 a.m. to 12.30 p.m. was surprisingly active and Bronwen poured herself a glass of beer and headed straight for the shower.

It wasn't a large bathroom, but a full-length mirror was fixed against one wall, which gave the room depth and made it look bigger than it was. She toweled herself dry and stared at her figure reflected in the mirror as she smeared body lotion on her hot skin, playing with it on her nipples, applying it to her legs and butt, a gentle rummage in her anal passage, ending with her fingers rubbing her clit, then reaching for her treasured implement.

She had a selection of dildos, but a favorite was a six and a half inch long vibrating jelly corkscrew model that sent spiral vibes along its bumpy shaft. She'd bought it on Amazon the previous year in blue to match her eye color. It had a suction cup base that was ideal to fix onto any flat surface to enjoy its buzzing penetration and arousing feeling. She'd dubbed the white plastic stool she kept in the bathroom her "milkmaid's stool" and activated the switch, then plonked the corkscrew suction end upon it and straddled, plunging it into her sodden, bearded oyster with a deep sigh, tensing her inside muscles as she'd taught herself to do to increase the sensations.

Suddenly, a thought of the recluse opening the package of erotic books confronted her. An image of him taking one of them had his eyes flicking speedily across the pages, his cock immediately erect with its plump, hard red bulb throbbing impatiently for her to spread her legs. Her cunt wept as she dreamt it was him with her eyes closed, the vibrator and image spurring her on until she grabbed the stool's sides for balance, screaming from a powerful orgasm. She'd never had an orgasm like that one. It seemed that Mr Scott was maybe more interesting than she'd thought.

It was another month before she had to make the trip to Scott's Corner and its attractive owner again, but this time she was mentally prepared for his nudity. She didn't expect anything to happen, because who the hell would find her a ravishing goer anyway in a drab uniform without make-up to make her look ravishing when she wasn't even beautiful in the first place? Or so she thought.

She rang the bell and waited. The door opened and there he stood again in all his naked grandeur.

"Oh," he remarked obviously pleased. "I've been dreaming of you, you know."

"Yes, quite, sir; I've a busy morning, so would you sign for the package, please?" she asked, wanting to say she'd imagined him with her as well, but not daring.

"Eager to be off, are you?" He smiled, showing white, even teeth and inviting lips, making her wilt as she thought of him kissing her and chewing her clit. "I'd like to invite you for dinner cooked by yours truly – nay – catered to be safe, because I'm lousy in the kitchen unless the food is raw. Do you like raw? Raw sex for instance?"

Bronwen's face went crimson with embarrassment. "I don't think it's a good—"

"But it *is* a good idea," he interrupted enthusiastically. "You're the most beautiful woman I've ever met! Why waste yourself living alone when you can couple with me?"

She didn't question how he knew she was single; the village knew everybody and everybody's business.

"I was told you're a recluse," she said lamely.

"Really – huh – I wonder why? I dress to travel and go shopping you know, but in my own home I'm my own person. People *think* I'm a recluse, but I'm just a lazy guy who doesn't have to work they *think*, although I *do*. I'll bet *you* think I'm naughty playing pranks greeting you au naturel, right?"

"It was rude and shocking, but—"

"Aha," he interrupted again, "but you don't mind!"

"Yes – no – I wasn't going to say—"

"Good." Now irritating her. "Can you be here for eight? Please wear your uniform and keep your hair pinned up; it's sexy."

She gazed at her work clothes and shoes, wearing no hat because she had too much hair; he had to be kidding, but he wasn't.

"Please," he said. "It'll be fun after we eat."

"What do you mean by fun? I hope it's only sex – I mean, *that* I'd like," she said boldly, adding with a slight stammer: "If . . . if that's what you meant."

"I do," he answered. "I'm betting you look fabulous underneath. Do you like my body?"

She was gobsmacked. *Of* course *I like your magnificent body,* she thought, *and I can't wait to feel your stiff cock pounding into my aching cunt!*

Instead, covering her astonishment, she muttered in shy acceptance: "Yes and I'll be here at eight o'clock with a bottle of wine."

"Get a Bordeaux Saint Emilion if you can, then we'll have two. They'll loosen up our shyness."

She nodded and toddled off, eager to return. She got the correct wine and back home had a shower, wondering what he saw in her that she didn't, shoved her uniform in the dryer with a scented sheet, washed and brushed her hair tying it back up again as Alastair had requested, let out a deep sigh and crossed her fingers.

She walked back to his house, sensibly taking the precaution of not having to drive after too much booze, and tentatively rang the bell, this time with a shaky hand. He opened it and to her amazement was dressed in a black kimono. The aroma of whatever he'd ordered for food smelt heavenly to her nose as he greeted her.

He led her into the dining room where a table was set with his bottle already breathing. She saw an old-fashioned besom hanging from a hook against a wall, the type her grandmother had used, with a handle made of hazel wood and a bunch of birch twigs tied at the end with wire, assuming it was a pseudo antique among the haphazard paraphernalia decorated around it. She noticed he smiled quirkily when he followed her gaze but didn't think to wonder why.

"I'll keep the food warm while we toast our good fortune," he said, raising his glass.

Then followed the getting-to-know-you question and answer period and she explained honestly how it felt to be an unsuccessful journalist, while he told her he played the money market on the internet and knocked off working each week when he hit ten thousand profit.

She liked him and wasn't discouraged by his endless erotic knowledge, thus the evening progressed well and she began to loosen up. His sexy demeanor and odd humor had her in stitches, quoting from his erotic books: a vagina – a sugared almond, cherry pop or passion fruit and a penis – a purple-headed womb broom or blue-veined piccolo, all amusing slang that's seldom used, but she cut him off when showing no enthusiasm in spanking and whipping from some of his descriptions:

"Did you know that an over-the-knee spanking with both parties naked is regarded as the most intimate of all disciplinary positions? That's in one of my books," he said hoping to impress her.

"Gosh, no – truly, eh? It's strange that people should write those stories!"

"Well, they do. Did you know," he continued pointing to the besom, "although fairly effective, dried twigs will break; and to make a good switch bundle one needs to cut them fresh from the stem and trim the twigs and leaves, because otherwise they would lessen the sting? It doesn't matter really what the tree species is; I mean, it doesn't have to be a birch tree to make a birch and a thorough whipping is most effective on a bare bottom and—"

Bronwen cut him off again. She didn't like the inference of welts and cuts on anyone's arse and that was the end of it: "Horrific to use one, I'd say. Shall I pour more wine?"

After the meal they cleared the table and moved to the lounge, sitting quietly together on a sofa, allowing the warm effects of the wine to filter through their bodies, both of them feeling relaxed and comfortable. He put an arm around her with a worried look in his eyes.

"What do you do for sex?" he asked abruptly.

By now she had the courage to tell him without embarrassment that her secret friend was a battery-operated vibrator with a bumpy shaft and how she used it and had trained herself to do the Indian trick.

"What's that?"

"You read erotica and I've only read the *Kama Sutra*, which details what needs to done. Training my muscles to grip is my expertise, but the truth is I haven't tried it with a man."

"Some competition then," he remarked unperturbed, "but it so happens I keep a supply of ribbed condoms, which should do the trick for you. I know you'll like it and I want that *Kama Sutra* thing."

Inspired by the promise of raunchy rollicking, she made her move and kissed him, which he returned by tenderly placing his hands against her cheeks and sliding down to discover her hard nipples, which he massaged softly through her shirt.

Then the worried look returned to his eyes.

"Is something wrong with me, Alastair?" she asked concerned.

"No, it's me," he answered. "I'm not straightforward."

"I don't follow you."

"Well, it's . . . oh, it doesn't matter," he said morosely.

"Tell me," she urged with a nudge.

"OK," he decided. "I'm naked beneath this kimono and . . ."

She giggled and gently began to caress his cock, which didn't react. "You're usually naked anyway," she said squeezing it harder, "and I don't wear underwear, either."

He closed his eyes and exhaled a deep breath. "When I saw you the first time through the window – before I opened the door – I took a chance and purposely stripped to shock and aggravate you, but you kept your cool, which impressed me. So I took another risk and got you here tonight, thinking you might be the right person to handle me."

"That sounds pretty straightforward, but you *have* received your mail like that before because a colleague told me," she whispered encouragingly, not minding that he'd flaunted the body she desired to have and to hold because she knew Abbey had failed to entice his attention. "Is that all?"

"No, it's not." He blushed. "The reason is I'm trying to be naughty, and OK, I'll admit it wasn't the first time, but the woman didn't appeal to me. It was devilment, nothing else."

"All right, you're forgiven," she said. "You're naughty then, so what?"

"So what if you got innovative and tied me hand and foot naked to the bedposts and—"

"God, no . . . *spank* you?" she blurted too soon, suddenly recalling what Abbey had inferred. "I *can't* do it!"

"I wasn't going to say that, Bronwen," he lied weakly, because he silently wished she'd redden his butt with the slipper and then fetch the besom from the dining room; better still if she'd order him to cut a bundle of switches beforehand. Instead, he said: "Please tie me up tightly as a punishment and I'll be at your mercy. Then do with me what you will."

"I'm not keen on hurting you, Alastair. I want romance and

loving. What did you say? Oh, yes; I want your blue-veined piccolo to fuck my sugared almond and fuck it as many times as you like!"

"I told you I wasn't straightforward," he said miserably. "I'd like the same, but if you want to call it quits before we progress, well, maybe that'd be best for both of us."

She considered his proposition and decided there didn't seem to be anything threatening in it. Besides, she was sure she had something going here and had no intention of leaving, to abandon him without first tasting the thrills and passions he might offer in addition to her first cautionary stab at mild kink, not to mention the possibility of quitting her job to enjoy his ten thousand a week income.

"All right, you naughty man. Get naked." She sighed and shrugged in resignation, yet curious for the experience; "but don't ask for anything kinkier than that – OK?"

He let the kimono slide off his body and led her to the bedroom, insisting again that she keep her uniform on, which she was eager to discard. Out of a cupboard he retrieved a large box and revealed the contents – ropes, cuffs, studded collar and belt, blindfold, a ball gag, a curled-up innocent-looking quirt – a short, vicious whip commonly used by South American cowboys, a polished leather slipper worn from age and several packets of condoms.

"I hope you haven't used all of these," she remarked quietly.

"Honestly? No, they're merely a fantasy collection, except the slipper that belonged to my mum, who used to make me cut a switch as part of my punishment and gave me an over-the-knee spanking with this slipper beforehand." He didn't tell her he whipped himself occasionally or about his desire to experience recall of his youth.

"I wouldn't keep it if someone used it on me," Bronwen stated. "Will you get on the bed, or do I have to force you?"

He got on the bed and she used the ropes to fasten his limbs. Apart from a condom, the rest of the stuff she ignored and left in the box.

A thought entered her mind with peculiar suddenness. "Do you want me to be sadistic?"

"I wouldn't say no," he answered.

"Tell me your definition of the word then."

He paused to think. "It's someone who gets sexual pleasure inflicting mental or physical cruelty and pain upon others."

"Hmm, that's precisely correct. I think I'll demonstrate its true definition after we've fucked." He neither understood nor questioned her meaning.

She complied with his request not to shed her uniform and only lowered her pants and opened her shirt to let her boobs sway freely, while he was stretched out immobile licking his lips. Sitting astride his legs, she raised her butt and leaned forward to suck his idle cock, which had begun to rise from the sight of her, but it didn't get up to full strength. He kept murmuring how sexy and great she was and gradually she believed him, yet worried that he wasn't expanding to an impressive hard-on.

"Oh, I see," she said, as the whole scenario dawned on her, and she lowered her mouth to bite the inside of his thigh. "I need to innovate, right?"

She kicked off her pants and quickly went to fetch the besom, whipping it through the air as she re-entered the bedroom, collected the leather slipper from the box on the way, watching his eyes widen from the prospect of a lashing pre-empted by a spanking.

After untying him, she folded a pillow and directed him to lie on his stomach upon it and then re-tied him tightly as he wished, this time with his hands and ankles together so she could twizzle him on his back again at will. She took the slipper and smoothed it over his skin, slid it along his crack, around his balls and over his butt, which waited, waited and waited for a stroke to land, and then only patted it lightly on both sides, teasing him to tense himself, relax and tense again, as she raised her arm with great pretense of a beating that didn't happen.

With heightened nerves, he almost begged. "Aren't you going to thrash me?"

"Shh, be patient," she hissed before biting his mounds and digging her nails into his buttocks delicately, sliding her tongue along his spine, wetting his crevasses, kissing him gently on his shoulders, nipping his neck and smacking him repeatedly with the slipper like a butterfly landing on a flower.

She took the besom, driving him crazy from the sound of the

twigs swishing through the air, watching with evil glee as his buttocks continually tensed with expectations, which provoked him into thinking it's coming, coming and then annoying his temperament and emotional turmoil to endure suffering the cruelest pain of denial – when, when, when?

The besom scratched his back slightly as she guided it down and across it and then laid it playfully on his still white butt dying to feel the lashes ripping into it. All he received was gentle flicks of the wrist and harmless twitches, which began to arouse him with unrestrained intensity, and his imagination did all it could do, only imagine, as his thoughts swirled with hopeful questions – What if? Why won't she? Will she? *Please!*

Then, between his legs, she stared amazed at the miracle of his cock going full out underneath him, his erection topped with a plump, hard red bulb, throbbing for her to relieve, and the perfect specimen she'd pictured before, an irresistible temptation she couldn't avoid.

With her arms primed from daily exercise humping the Royal Mail, hurriedly she twirled him easily onto his back, took his prick in her mouth, sucking and tantalizing its tip with her hungry tongue, making him arch his back from the glory of his senses. He was smiling. "You're the wickedest person in the world; a bloody teaser and strong, too, hefting me like that! *Aagh!* You're killing me!"

"Shh, keep quiet or I'll give you another severe whipping," she cautioned, smiling back while slipping on the condom. "This ribbed masterpiece looks wonderful on your incredible shaft, my man, and I can't wait any longer to . . . *ooh Jeez, It's nice!* There'd better be plenty more where that came from! *OOH!*"

She moved speedily upon it, slowed down and gripped her vaginal muscles, doing her Indian trick and it was his turn to be shocked and writhe from the utter pleasure.

Then, overcome with exhilaration, she couldn't stop herself from battering her cunt faster, riding upon his slithering rigidity up to the limit of its length and plunging down hard, forcing it to reach and stimulate her G-spot, grinding herself relentlessly to orgasm as he came, heaving his tethered body and grunting with satisfaction.

"I'm very wet," she said and crawled to place the loveliest cunt belonging to the most beautiful woman he'd ever seen onto his mouth. "Lick me."

He obeyed – well, he didn't have a choice – not that he wanted one.

Afterwards, released and inseparably drawn towards each other, both knew they'd found the right person.

"So," Alastair began after pouring the last of the wine, "that was an example of your idea of sadism, was it?"

"Perhaps, but it worked, didn't it?" She grinned. "And it'll all depend on how good or naughty you are. You'll have to wait and see, won't you?"

He stared at her, mentally calculating the odds and thought: *Maybe, maybe the real action might happen one day. I can't deny I've fallen for her and the kind cruelty of her treatment did me well. Yes, I'll give her anything in the world, be her slave and do everything she demands.*

"Does that mean we're going to couple up and you'll move in?"

She laughed. "Alastair, my poor tortured victim, are you sure you can afford me?"

He laughed in return. "You'll have to wait and see, won't you?"

Four Days on, Take it All Off

Kannan Feng

June was in the shower when the fire alarm started to ring, and the only garment she could grab was the thin silk robe hung up by the door. Swearing, she shoved her arms into it and managed to get into her flip-flops, before stumbling her way out the door.

There was a time when she hadn't taken fire alarms in the building that seriously. It was always someone who couldn't cook, filling their apartment with smoke, or some smoker who had decided that they were too lazy to go down to the smoking patio on the ground floor.

That time was long past, and Brady made it very clear to her what she was supposed to do when that alarm rang.

"You get your rear down the stairs, and you go stand across the street," he said sternly. "I don't care if the alarm goes off because of steam from some guy's shower, if you hear that alarm, you get the hell out."

He must have seen the bit of mutiny on her face, because he pulled her close.

"Come on, Junie, I wear that uniform, and you're gonna fight me on this one?"

Brady's tone – wheedling and maybe just a little scared – convinced her, and when he saw that she would listen ("even if it's just a burned pizza!"), he had grinned and made sure that she got plenty of . . . positive reinforcement to keep it fresh in her mind.

June crossed the street to the little park across the way, thankful that it was a warm August night. Her neighbours were filing out of the building, and she grabbed a spot on a stone bench to watch. She wrapped her arms around her waist, holding her flimsy silk robe closed, and she waited. People were milling around, grumbling about the nuisance, but it took less than ten minutes before the sirens could be heard.

She grinned when the fire truck roared to a stop in front of the building, and when the men in black and yellow jackets streamed into the doors, she tried to see if she could spot Brady. He was taller than most of his fellow firefighters, but they were moving so fast that she gave it up for a bad job and simply waited.

Four days on, she reminded herself.

That meant that he would be home tomorrow night. They could grab the odd Skype call here and there, but he had responsibilities at the firehouse. It was sometimes hard to reconcile her sweet, goofy boyfriend with the strict man he was when he was on duty, but whether he was cooing in her ear or pausing the call to bark orders at the new guys, she missed him.

June held the robe a little tighter around her body, aware of how little there was between her bare skin and the air. Her short black hair was already drying, fluffing out like dark, slightly curly feathers, and she tucked her bare legs underneath the bench. She was short and slender, but the robe was short, keeping her modest by the barest inch.

Just when she was starting to feel vulnerable in the open air while wearing so little, the all-clear was sounded, and she started heading back inside with the other tenants.

The fire truck was still parked in front of the building, and she saw a knot of firefighters discussing something next to it. June slowed her steps to see if she could spot Brady, but they were being so serious that she sighed to herself and gave it up.

Four days on, three days off, she reminded herself. After tomorrow night, he was going to be all hers and, by God, she was going to make the most of it!

When she was back in their apartment with the door locked behind her, she could let her thoughts run free. She could imagine how his firehouse T-shirt stretched tight over his broad shoulders, the way his thickly muscled arms would wrap around her. At more than six feet tall, he towered over her, and when he got that white sharp grin on his face, she knew that they were going to have some fun . . .

The idea of those teeth on her shoulders, her neck, and travelling down, made her smile, and without even really thinking about it, she seated herself on the couch. She was naked underneath the robe, and now she let it fall open. June dragged the palms of her hands over the gentle rise of her hip bones and the flat plane of her stomach before bringing them up to cup her small breasts. It wasn't much like having Brady's big rough hands on her, but she could squeeze them the way he did, gentle at first, and then harder, drawing on her pink nipples until she mewled with pleasure.

She heard a strange squeaking sound, but now she could almost conjure him out of thin air, the way he would move her body like a toy, the way he raised himself over her, the way he laughed . . .

June sat up suddenly, because that *was* his laugh that she heard, and then she nearly shrieked at the sight of the man in the doorway.

She had almost never seen him in his fire response gear, but there he stood, the helmet hanging carelessly from one hand, while the other reached to unbutton the black and creaking jacket. That must have been the squeaking sound she heard, and she blushed.

"How long have you been standing there?" she asked.

He shrugged, his blue eyes as bright as stars. "Long enough," he drawled. "Long enough to see that maybe we missed something hot when we did our sweep."

June giggled, and instead of bouncing up to give him a hug the way she was going to, she lay back on the sofa, letting the robe fall open to either side.

"Oh really?" she asked. "Something hot, huh?"

"Hmm, yeah," he murmured, stepping a little closer and tossing the helmet aside. "Something that really, really shouldn't be missed.

"Hm, hot enough that you should call some of the other guys back?" she asked innocently, and Brady grinned in response. Something about that grin always sent a curl of heat right through her body, and without thinking about it, she straightened her legs in front of her, spreading them just slightly.

"You'd like that, wouldn't you?" he commented, shucking the jacket with practised ease. He tossed it on the couch beside her, and she briefly thought about how heavy it was, how strong he had to be to wear it through fire and tumbling brick. Then he was standing between her feet, and she could look up at him.

He was a big man, broad through the shoulders and narrow-hipped. His dark hair was cut regulation short, but there was a scruff of stubble on his face. June wondered if he didn't shave when he was at the firehouse, if that was something he did just for her, but then every thought flew out of her head when he knelt between her legs.

He laid one large hand on her thigh, looking up at her with those big blue eyes.

"You're so fucking hot," he said, and there was a reverence to his tone that made her blush a little.

"Bet you'd love it if I radioed the guys and got them back here, huh? Maybe we could put that fire out for you . . ."

"Just you," she found herself saying, and she was rewarded with a wide smile that held as much love as lust.

"Pretty big order," he murmured, sliding his hand up higher. When his fingertips grazed the trimmed dark hair on her mons, she sighed, but he was only there for a moment, gliding up towards her breasts.

He covered one breast entirely with his hand, and he leaned close, close enough that she could feel his breath on her lips. Brady smelled clean, and there was a rubbery scent as well, one that came from the coat next to them. He was still dressed; the protective trousers were held up by suspenders over a clean white T-shirt, and June, June was practically naked. She shivered at how open she was, how vulnerable she was to him, and he smiled.

"Let's see if I can do something about all this heat," he murmured, and then he was kissing her, sliding his tongue between her lips and taking her mouth with the pure assurance that came of having known her and loved her for more than a year.

She gave herself up to the kiss completely, wrapping her arms around his neck and pulling him close. June couldn't resist sliding her legs against his, relishing the harsh feel of his trousers against her most sensitive skin.

"I want you," she broke away from him long enough to say, and he grinned.

"I know, I can smell you," Brady said and, before she could protest, he was slipping down her body. She was only aware of the loss for a moment before he started planting a burning line of kisses on her belly, and then he was settled between her legs, his hands underneath her thighs and pulling them further apart.

"This . . . this is the fire I've been thinking about when I'm at the firehouse," he said, and he leaned down to give her a precise and deliberate lick up her slit. She had been damp before, but she moaned when that hot tongue slid along her pussy, pushing the lips open just slightly.

"You been jerking it in the shower?" she asked breathlessly. "Where all those other guys could watch?"

"Fuck no," he responded. "You think anyone but you gets that show?"

She giggled, but the giggle turned into a groan when he licked her again. She twisted her fingers into his hair, tugging, trying to bring him closer, but he kept doing that, licking her over and over again, never hitting her clit as hard as she wanted him to, never entering her at all.

"Please," she finally said, her voice soft and breathy. "Please, I need more than that, please, Brady, I do!"

He laughed, and she could feel it straight through her body. That was all it took. Suddenly he was sliding his thumbs along her soaking wet slit and opening her up for his insistent mouth. June cried out in desperation when it seemed like he was going to pause, but then his tongue slid snugly against her clit, curling over it with intense expertise, and his lips were working against her.

Her pleasure rose up like a tide, but just when her legs were shaking and her body was shivering hard, he pulled back.

"Oh what the hell!" June wailed, and with a laugh, he went back to work.

Soon she was twisting again, tugging on his hair hard. His hands kept her in place, but she was still trying to ride his mouth, thrusting her hips up as far as she could. She was almost there, she could feel the way the heat coursed through her body . . .

And then he stopped again.

"You son of a bitch!" she swore. "Fuck you, oh fuck you, I wanted that, I was so close."

"Yeah, you were," he said, grinning up at her with his face wet. "Well, who knows, maybe third time's the charm."

It wasn't. Neither was the fourth time nor the fifth time and, after that, June's eyes were wet with need and rage.

"Goddamn you, don't you dare . . ." she cried, and he shook his head.

"Come for me, sweetie," he murmured.

This time, he licked her clit so hard she nearly came off the couch, and her body, strained and longing for such a long time, lit up like a fireworks display. Her orgasm swept over her, making her shake and making her cry out. Her hands tightened convulsively in Brady's hair, refusing to let him up, refusing to let him stop tonguing her.

"More, more." She realized she was moaning, and his talented mouth never stopped, never stilled. The sensations faded rather than stopped entirely, and all that June knew was that she was still shuddering hard when he pulled away gently.

She made a noise of protest when he withdrew, but then he was there again, sitting on the couch next to her and kissing her softly. She did her best to return the kiss, but she knew that she was slow and shaky with pleasure. Instead, she let him make a mess of her face, smearing her juices over her lips and her chin.

I smell good, she thought blankly, and she let him cradle her in his arms before lifting her up.

"I'm useless to you," she murmured into his chest. "All worn out, nothing left."

"I don't know about that," he said, a teasing note in his voice. "I'm pretty good at finding sparks."

She didn't protest when he lay her down on the bed, and she stirred briefly when he positioned her on her belly over two pillows. Somewhere along the way, she had lost the robe, and now she was entirely bare, open to his eyes, to his hands, his lips and his body.

"Let's see what we've got," he murmured, and June felt him

pull her legs apart with gentle care. The thought of him fucking her when she was this worn was delicious, and she loved it right up until the point when his fingers started to push into her swollen folds.

"Ow . . . ow, no, that hurts," she grunted.

He pulled away immediately. "Too sore?"

"Yeah," she said, glancing over her shoulder at him. "Some asshole thought it was a great idea to keep me on the edge for hours."

"Forty minutes," he corrected her briskly. "And I'm sorry if a really great orgasm made you sore."

"Liar," she retorted, and then she frowned when he slid to the edge of the bed. "Where do you think you're going?"

"I'm gonna take care of myself in the bathroom and then I'll come back . . . No?"

June was shaking her head. "Nope. You can't have my pussy, but you can have my ass."

Her blunt words were like an electric shock. She grinned as Brady sat up straight, and, before she could say another word, he was in the nightstand, rummaging around for the bottle of lube they kept there.

"You are the best girl," he crooned, "my best, my favourite girl."

June made herself breathe as his slicked fingers pressed gently against her tight ass. She loved it, but it took time, and she wondered if he was a little too turned on to be as patient as he usually was. Something about that turned her on even more, and she got her knees underneath herself, shoving her rear even higher.

"Am I tight, honey?" she murmured. "You gonna fuck my tight little ass?"

"Yeah, yeah I am."

His voice was thick and heavy with need, and his fingers were inside her, two instead of starting with just one. She knew that coming made her looser, and she could enjoy his fingers moving inside her.

"Stick your cock in," she said suddenly, and he paused. She usually needed three before she could take his cock, but today was different. She needed him, and she realized that she needed him in her ass.

"Come on," she said, when it sounded like he wanted to protest, and that was all the encouragement he needed.

He was still half in his gear. Now he undid the fly and knelt behind her, close enough she could feel the cool rubbery material against her thighs.

She squealed when the tip of his blunt cock pressed against her hole, but there was nothing she could do when he started pushing, nothing she wanted to do at all besides let herself be forced open.

"Oh God, oh God," she wailed, and when he would have stopped, she grabbed his hand. "Fuck me," she grunted. "Fuck my ass, come on, show me how you want to do it."

His large hands closed over her narrow hips, and he pushed his cock the rest of the way in. When his hips were snug against her ass, he paused, drew almost all the way out and slammed it back in.

June's sharp gasps turned into one long, unravelling cry as her boyfriend pounded her, and, through it all, she was dripping wet. She could feel how big and hard he was, how desperate his movements were. He wasn't going to last long, not as tight as she was and with how she was moaning underneath him, and when she could find words, they were filthy.

"Oh, fuck me, yeah, fill me up, fill me up with your come, come on . . ."

With a final savage groan, he did exactly as she said, pumping into her with one last rough thrust, which practically put her on her face. She lay shivering underneath him, wanting to climax again, but knowing she couldn't.

"Tomorrow," he promised her when they could both speak again. "I'll do that again tomorrow, and we'll strap that little silver bullet to your clit when I fuck your ass, how's that sound?"

"Like way too much right now," she said with a groan. "Help me to the shower."

Under the hot steamy water, they washed each other and kissed slowly, something that they had overlooked during their more energetic fun.

"Do you have to go back?" June asked wistfully.

Brady nodded. "Sorry, sweetheart, I just got a couple of hours here because one of the guys owed me. Tomorrow though, OK? I'll take you out for dinner, we can go to a movie."

"Sure, sure," June agreed, but she was already thinking ahead to a bed with fresh sheets, a bottle of lube on the nightstand, and a man she loved bending over her . . .

Chelsea

Brian K. Crawford

Chelsea came out of the Green Park tube station and blinked in the bright morning sun. The wide paths were crowded with tourists and she heard a dozen languages on the short stroll. She arrived before the palace and found the fence lined with eager tourists snapping pictures and hoping for a glimpse of the Royals. A sign said the next changing of the guard would be almost two hours. She sighed. She had no interest in royalty and thought the whole thing an expensive anachronism, but it was her first visit to London and she was determined to see the sights. She circled the Victoria Memorial and idly read the plaques. Then she walked along the fence, peering in at the guards standing rigidly at attention.

She thought their huge bearskin hats looked ridiculous and must be intolerably hot. But the crisp red coats and white belts were very striking and the young men looked very military and masculine. They stared straight ahead, their faces completely impassive. Tourists made fools of themselves, calling out and gesticulating, trying to get a guardsman inside the fence to react. She stepped up into a gap at the fence to see how the guard reacted, and she could not look away.

He was the most handsome man she had ever seen. He had a square chin with a marked dimple and a strong determined jaw that contrasted with full, sensitive lips. But what caught and held her were his eyes – an icy blue so pale it was as if she could see through them to the mind behind. Tall, broad-shouldered, obviously very fit – he was everything she was attracted to in a man. It was a wonderful opportunity to be able to look him over without having to be discreet. Impressive as the uniform was, she had a sudden image of him standing there nude, his broad chest and strong legs bare in the sun. And of course, since it was her fantasy, he had a huge erection, the tip bouncing against his belly – and all because of her irresistible beauty.

Wow! Her knees trembled and she gripped the bars of the fence to steady herself. He was staring straight into her face, but she didn't know if he was even seeing her. Had he seen her reaction? As if in answer, he suddenly snapped to attention and brought his rifle across his chest, then on his shoulder. With three high ceremonial steps, he turned to his right and marched across the entrance of the building. He took fifteen steps, arm swinging high, made another turn, and returned. He brought his rifle smartly down to his side, separating his feet to parade rest. She could have sworn there was the tiniest hint of a smile at the corner of his lip as his eyes met hers. This time she was sure he was looking at her.

For some reason she found his little exercise extremely sexy. She was normally not much into marching, drill teams, that sort of thing. But he was so precise in his movements, every detail perfect, controlled. His rifle, a large automatic weapon with a huge curving magazine, was impressive and clearly heavy, though he handled it as if it were a baton. She mused that a man with that strength, discipline and control might be spectacular in bed. Sometimes she liked her lovemaking a little rough, nothing violent, but the idea of him picking her up and throwing her sprawling across a bed got her juices flowing.

But there was no way to communicate with him. He couldn't move an inch, much less exchange numbers with her. That idea set off another fantasy: what if she were inside the fence with him; what if she knelt before him and reached up under that bright red coat, pulled down the zipper on those pants with the razor creases? She imagined taking him into her mouth with all the tourists gaping at her. She imagined his stoic stare wavering, those icy eyes closing in pleasure. She could imagine the cobblestones under her knees, the length of him sliding into her mouth, down her throat, her blonde head bobbing against that red coat as the tourists' cameras clicked and whirred behind her. Now there's a video that would go viral.

Oh my God, she was dripping down there. Looking up from his crotch to his face, she was sure he was meeting her eyes, hers alone. It was as if he knew what she was thinking. She pulled herself against the fence, letting one of the square metal bars press hard against her breast. She rocked gently from side to side, letting the bar bump across her nipples, hard as gumdrops beneath her thin cotton top. *Good thing there's a fence here to protect you, soldier boy*, she sighed to herself.

Chelsea had never wanted a man so much. He was perfect. She was sure that expressionless stare hid a passionate nature. As he stared impassively at her, was he having fantasies about her? Oh God, what if they were the same as hers? What if his cock was stretching toward her mouth just as she was yearning for it?

There was a clash of noise off to the side, and the crowd all craned to see an officer and four soldiers parading toward them. Shit, had she been standing here that long? They were coming to relieve him. She'd never see that gorgeous man again! But what could she do? Impulsively, she fumbled in her purse and pulled out a piece of notepaper. She quickly jotted down her first name and her number. But how could she get it to him? She folded it into a small square and slid it into a crack in the fence, on the inside, with just a tiny corner protruding. No one would notice it, she was sure. But had he seen her hide it? He was standing not ten feet away, staring right toward her – he must have seen what she did. But his face was as impassive as ever, his eyes staring as if unseeing.

A moment later, the detail approached and stopped before him. The officer barked out a command. He marched forward; another guard took his place with a great deal of stamping and shouting. Her guard joined the detail, and they marched away with that peculiar arm-swinging step. They turned a corner of the palace and he was gone.

She felt let down. It would have felt like that old post-coital relaxation, except she was anything but satisfied. She was still as hot as blacktop on a summer day. Normally these momentary erotic fantasies quickly faded, pleasant little lifts in her day, but she couldn't get that man or her fantasy out of her head. She found a public loo, ducked in, and brought herself off in seconds. She washed her hands and face, but the erotic sensation wasn't gone. She fancied she could still feel his cock in her throat.

That was how it started. For twenty-four hours she wandered around London seeing the sights – the jewels in the Tower, the Millennium Eye. But her heart wasn't in it. Twice during the afternoon she returned to the palace, studying the guards, but he wasn't among them. They all looked like callow boys playing soldier, with that curious mottled pink and white skin she associated with the British. They had none of that masterful confidence that "her guard" exuded.

She was walking toward London Bridge when her phone rang. She stepped out of the current of pedestrians and fumbled in her purse. Of course, it wouldn't be him. Her mother, most likely, or one of a half-dozen friends who knew she was in England.

"Hello?" she said.

"Chelsea?" It was a deep baritone, rich and vibrant like an actor's or singer's voice – and an English accent. Her heart started pounding. Her steps slowed.

"Yes? Who is this, please?"

"Oh, you're American," he said, sounding surprised.

"Yes, I am. Does that matter?" There was a pause, and she was suddenly terrified. Oh, God, what if he hates Americans?

"Only if it means you're leaving soon," he said after a long moment.

"I have three more days." She chewed her lip. Would that be bad news to him, or good?

"Oh, right. Well, that should give me enough time."

"I beg your pardon? You're very sure of yourself."

She heard him smile. "Yes, Chelsea, I suppose I am. My name is Ian, and I'm the Life Guard."

"You . . . you're a lifeguard? You mean at a swimming pool? I'm sorry, there's—"

He gave an easy laugh. "I'm a member of the Queen's Life Guard, Chelsea. I'm a soldier sworn to protect the Queen. The one you were ogling yesterday with lust in your eye."

"I wasn't—"

"We don't have time for that, Chelsea. You left me your number so we could fuck, did you not?"

She stopped dead on the sidewalk, staring up at the face of Big Ben ahead of her. A young man walked into her back, grumbling something rude as he slipped past her. People streamed past on either side.

"Well, yes," she whispered. "I suppose I did."

"That is it, isn't it?" he asked, concern in his voice for the first time. "You're not writing a book or doing a travelogue or making a documentary, are you? You're not going to blog about the Life Guard you shagged? Tell me you're not."

"No, nothing like that, I promise." She fancied she recognized a Liverpool accent in his voice – he sounded like a Beatle. She couldn't think what to say, so she just blurted out, "I just saw you standing there, looking so masculine in that gorgeous uniform, and I . . . I wanted to . . ."

"What? What did you want to do, Chelsea?" He must have his mouth right on the phone; it was as if his lips were against her ear.

She watched the clouds drifting behind Big Ben, oblivious of where she was, her eyes seeing only that wonderful image, her head bobbing back and forth, her nose pressed against that crimson coat.

"I wanted to suck you," she said. "I wanted you in my mouth." A woman gave her a startled look as she passed, but Chelsea never saw her.

He didn't miss a beat. "While I'm in my uniform?" he asked. "Standing as if I'm on guard?"

"Yes."

"With you on your knees?" How did he know all this?

"Uh-huh."

"With people watching?"

She considered, twirling a strand of hair in her free hand. "Wouldn't have to be, I suppose."

"But it would be better if there were?"

She couldn't believe she was having this discussion on a crowded sidewalk. "Yes."

"Lots of people?"

"I don't know. They don't have faces, really. They don't really matter, just their eyes. On me, on what I'm doing."

"What about my A2?"

That stopped her. "I'm sorry. Your *etude*?"

He laughed again. "I don't think we'll need music. My L85A2 assault rifle. Do I need it?"

"No. I'm not really a terrorist, Ian."

"I didn't think you were, miss. I thought maybe it needed to be part of the scene – for you, I mean. For the air of danger, perhaps?"

"Oh, I see. Would it be loaded?"

He paused. "We could go with 'Yes', 'No', or 'Surprise me'."

"No! I'm terrified of guns."

He chuckled. "Are you sure you're really American? You're not some daft bird from Leeds with a fake accent?"

She had to laugh in spite of herself. "No, really. I'm from Boston."

"Yours or ours?"

"The one in Massachusetts."

"Not the real one, then. So that's all right."

"What do you mean?"

"Never mind. It's too late for tonight. Go out tomorrow, take in the sights. Tomorrow night at nine, meet me."

Her heartbeat went up even more. This was it. She could hang up; pretend this conversation never happened.

"Where?" she asked.

"I'll text the address to you – easier to get it right, and you can put it in your GPS so you don't get lost in the big city."

"OK." She stood there, holding the phone to her ear, listening to him breathe. He seemed in no hurry to hang up. She couldn't think of anything else to say. "Where are we going?" she asked at last. "I mean, what should I wear?"

He laughed. "Wear what you like. It's your fantasy, luv. Bye."

"Bye," she murmured. The phone went dead. She stood there, still staring vacantly at the clock tower. A moment later her phone beeped. It was a text message from Ian, with an address, followed by "9 sharp. Don't let us down."

As she started walking again, she wondered if that "us" was that quaint Liverpudlian plural first person – "Give us a kiss, luv" – or not. What had she gotten herself into? She was going to meet some strange man with a gun. What was she thinking?

Well, OK, she knew exactly what she was thinking. But was this incredibly stupid? How could she trust him with her life? Then she chuckled. Hell, the Queen did. She could hardly ask for better references than that.

She shook her head, trying to clear the strange spell she was under. She was famished, and soon found an excellent Indian restaurant. The British Empire had that to say for it at least.

She passed an uneasy night and the next day she dutifully made the rounds of "the sights". She avoided the palace; she wasn't exactly sure why. She rented a boat and rowed the Serpentine – the slowest boat on the lake, for she was deep in thought. Half a dozen times she thought of changing her mind, simply not going. But each time she saw him standing there, his rifle – his A2 – against his thigh, that absurd bearskin right down to his eyes. And there she was, kneeling, reaching up under his red tunic, feeling the length of him straining against her palm. Oh, she'd go all right.

At last the afternoon of the Longest Day ended and she returned to her hotel. She took a long luxurious bath, and fixed her hair and make-up. Still there were two hours to wait. What should she wear? A sexy strapless evening gown that left her shoulders bare and showed off her breasts to best advantage? He could look right down her front while she . . . or maybe a British schoolgirl outfit, with short skirt and knee socks and straw boater on her head? She realized she had no idea what Ian would like. They hadn't discussed his fantasies – he seemed fine with hers.

Of course her options were limited by what she had in her suitcase. Perhaps the day would have been better spent shopping. But in her fantasy she hadn't noticed or cared what she was wearing. It wasn't about her uniform, only his. In the end she chose the outfit she'd brought if she went clubbing – a yellow tube top and a short white cotton skirt, with nothing under. "If he doesn't like it, fuck him," she said, then giggled at herself in the mirror. Damn, she was getting giddy. She'd have to watch her drinking. Her phone alarm chimed. It was time. She crammed her wallet and lipstick into the tiniest clutch purse she had, and went out.

She'd downloaded the directions and had no trouble following them on the Underground. When she emerged at street level, it was still fully light though only a few minutes before nine. It was a respectable residential neighborhood. She hadn't a clue where she was. She walked two blocks and found herself before a six-story building – perhaps condos or apartments – flats, they called them here. She went into the deserted lobby and went up in the elevator (lift, she reminded herself) to the fourth floor. She was in a short hallway with a marble floor. Between her and a potted plant at the end were four doors, two on each side. The far one on the right was ajar. She walked down to it, her heels clacking on the floor. She checked the time – just nine on the dot – took a deep breath, then pushed it open and walked in. She stopped and stared in amazement.

It was a large unfurnished room, perhaps twenty feet square, with no one in it. There was a closed door in each of the other three walls. But what caught her attention was that the far wall was painted to look like the outside wall of a stone building. A narrow wooden box with a peaked roof stood to one side, glossy black with gold trim on the outside, white inside. Suddenly she understood. It was meant to represent a portion of the palace, and the box was one of the sentry posts. How the hell had Ian set all this up so quickly? And where was he?

The last question was quickly answered, for the door beside the sentry box opened and there he was, in full uniform, looking as gorgeous as ever. He marched toward her, made a ceremonial turn, and stopped in front of the box. With three high steps, he turned again to face her and came to parade rest. His eyes were focused just above her eyes, unseeing.

She stood staring at him, wondering what she was supposed to do. She was reluctant to speak to him – he seemed just as rigid and professionally impersonal as if he were really guarding the Queen. But the sight of him standing there ignited the old fire in her. His firm jaw, icy eyes, and motionless pose made him seem like a robot. But she was much closer now than she had been at the palace. In spite of his close shave, she could see a shadow of his beard on his cheeks and a drop of sweat on his lip. She wondered about that. Was he hot in that uniform and bearskin – or was he thinking about her and what she had told him she wanted to do?

Well, he obviously wasn't going to move. It was completely up to her. She gathered her nerve and took one cautious step forward. Suddenly she heard a noise behind her and spun around in alarm. One of the side doors opened and a young man walked into the room. What the hell? Before she could speak, four more people came in behind him. Most were like the first – young fit, upright, and clean-cut in a way that could only be military. But then a girl entered. They lined up across the back of the room. No one spoke, but each looked closely at her, openly looking her up and down. Then Chelsea understood. They were here to watch, just as Ian had proposed. They knew exactly why she was here, and why they were. Her heart quavered, unsure if she could really do this with people watching. She assumed the men were fellow guardsmen, but who was the girl? Chelsea looked at her – about her own age, slim and pretty. Their eyes met and the girl smiled, a small, secret, almost sisterly smile. Somehow that smile communicated to her that the girl understood exactly why Chelsea wanted to do this, and why she wanted them there. She wasn't judging Chelsea or thinking she was demeaning herself. She knew about fantasies, and wanted to participate, to help Chelsea achieve what she wanted. Chelsea felt grateful for her presence, and her uncertainty vanished. She turned back to Ian, still standing motionless, as if he were totally unaware of anything happening in the room.

The rustling and shuffling of the people behind her stilled and the room was silent, and all she could hear was her pounding heart and her ragged breathing. It took a moment to draw her mind back to the fantasy. She walked slowly toward Ian, watching his eyes to see if he was watching her. His eyes never flickered, even when she stopped just a step from him. She hadn't realized how big he was. Of course the huge bearskin hat and uniform made him imposing. But now she was this close she realized that he was a very large man. Her head didn't come up to his shoulder. His broad chest was a huge expanse of scarlet woolen cloth.

She knelt in front of him, her bare knees nearly touching the tips of his mirror-polished shoes. Right before her face was his white belt with a large gleaming buckle. Feeling like a supplicant before a statue of her god, she hesitated to touch him. But nothing was going to stop her now. She reached out tentatively and pressed the sword-sharp crease down the front of his trousers. The crease crumpled under her fingers, and she could feel his thigh beneath. Not a statue – there was indeed a man beneath that iron shell. She lay her hand against his thigh, feeling the muscles taut and hard. She reached out with her left hand and grasped his other thigh. Then, leaning her head far back to look up at him, she slowly ran her hands up the front of his thighs. Her hands disappeared under his coat and slid up to his hips. She couldn't see his face, but she thought she saw his nostrils flare.

She wanted to take hold of him right then and there, but she postponed the pleasure. She slowly brought her hands together, finding a button where they met. With her hands pinned under his coat, she had to work to unfasten the button. She thought could feel the pressure of his cock against her right hand, but she forced herself to concentrate on the job at hand. She found the tab of a zipper. She pulled it down with a sound that must have been audible to the audience.

Now for that awkward bit of getting his erection out of his underwear. Sometimes the man had to assist there, and that didn't seem likely here. She tugged his fly open wider, and her problem resolved itself as his cock lunged out and rose through the slit in his coat like a steel wedge splitting a log. She gasped as the object of her lust suddenly bobbed before her astonished eyes. What a cock the man had! More than proportional to his size, and as thick as her wrist, heavily veined, the head was shiny and nearly purple, like a plum just reaching its juiciest ripeness.

She took it gently in both hands and pulled it down toward her. She stared down at the tip. A drop of clear liquid sparkled at the opening. Lubricant – just what she needed. She leaned forward and touched the drop with the tip of her tongue. Was that a shiver she felt transmitted through his cock?

Holding the head cupped between her hands, she started licking it like a little girl with an ice-cream cone – first this side, then that; a slow circular swirl all the way around, a tickle in the opening. She put her mouth over the whole tip and brought her lips together, squeezing it from between her lips, feeling the smoothness of the skin against her tongue. Surely there is no smoother, silkier skin anywhere on the body.

She drew her head back to admire it, sliding her hands down to circle it at the base. He was so hard that it curved up and pressed against his belt buckle. She could just make out her own distorted refection in the gleaming buckle; her dark staring eyes and her mouth gaping as if she were waiting for a wafer to be placed on her tongue. She could smell him too, that unique musty scent of a clean man's cock.

That's all it took. She pulled it down toward her again and sucked it hungrily into her mouth. There was so much of it – her mouth was full to stretching, but she had no more than a third of it in. She sucked hard, feeling her cheeks compress around his cock while her tongue never stopped stroking it. She could feel him leaning against her, pushing his hips forward. But she wanted more.

She shuffled back a foot, never losing contact between her mouth and his cock. Clutching his hips to support her weight, she could lean toward him. Tilting her head back as far as it would go, she let her throat relax. The massive head pushed hard against the back of her throat once, twice, then her throat popped open and he slid down her throat like a python down a hole. While she was still trying to accommodate it, she felt his hands twining in her hair, pulling her head toward him, ramming himself down her throat. Her nose pressed into his pubic hair and still there was more of him.

Finally, her face was crushed against him, feeling as if she had been impaled like a sword swallower. He pulled back, but only an inch or two, then drove forward, filling her again. She felt his balls swing heavily against her chin. She could barely breathe, but already she was teetering on the edge of an orgasm. She drew her head back, felt his head pop out of her throat, and sucked it hard.

God, how she loved giving head! She loved fucking too, of course, but there was only so much a woman could do with her cunt – and it was so far away. Motion there was controlled largely by the man. In her mouth she could give him pleasure in a hundred ways, with her lips, her tongue, her teeth, her throat, even her voice, and she could see his cock and feel every tremor, every twitch. She could see it sliding in and out, slick with moisture, rigid with desire for her. She had a front row seat.

That thought reminded her she had an audience. She turned her head, still running her tongue up and down the side of his shaft, and peered over her shoulder. Their air of impassivity was completely gone. Two of the men had their cocks out, stroking them as they watched. The other two stared as if hypnotized, watching every move that Chelsea made. Chelsea looked at the girl, and saw that she was as turned on as the men. She clutched one of her breasts in one hand, and the other was rubbing her pussy through her thin skirt. The sight of the others so excited raised Chelsea to new heights. It was her lust, what she was doing, that was turning them on so. It was her fantasy that was getting them all off. She went back to work on Ian's cock, squeezing and stroking with her hands, licking and sucking it in harder and faster. She felt Ian's hands on her head and let him shove his cock down her throat again. She purred and moaned around his huge cock pistoning into her mouth.

Short of breath, on the verge of choking, her face pressed into his hair, she could see and hear nothing, was aware of nothing other than his cock and her mouth and the pleasure flowing between them. It went on and on, until she was barely conscious. Suddenly he withdrew from her mouth with an audible pop. She cried out like a child whose toy is snatched away and reached to pull him back, but Ian was too strong for her, too fast. He reached down and pulled her to her feet. He had thrown off his bearskin at some point, and his face was red and sweating, his eyes and nostrils wide with lust. She looked up at him in surprise, wondering why he had stopped her.

She didn't wonder long. He grasped her shoulders and spun her around to face their audience. All the men were jerking off now, their hands pumping almost too fast to see. The girl had opened her blouse and her breasts were exposed. She was holding her skirt up around her waist while her right hand rubbed furiously between her legs. It was the most erotic sight she had ever seen. As she stared, Chelsea felt her own top tugged down to her waist, her breasts spilling out into the light. She glanced down as Ian's big hands closed around them and gave them a fierce squeeze. But then his hands left her tits. One slid around behind her, bending her over. The other lifted her skirt and threw it up over her back. She felt a fumbling between her legs, then he rammed deep into her so quickly she cried out and would have fallen if he were not holding her hips.

He slammed into her, her body shuddering with the impact, filling her to overflowing with each stroke. She heard hoarse, guttural groans, but wasn't sure if it was Ian, their audience, or her own orgasm rising within her. She felt Ian coming, boiling hot into her, his hips slapping loudly against her ass. That sent her over the top, and she melted into the longest, hardest orgasm she'd ever felt. She ground her ass against Ian's hips, wanting more and more of him inside her. He gripped her hip bones and pulled her against him until she thought his cock would burst from her belly. With each thrust, she felt him spurting again, and each time she came again. Finally, he was drained and the last of her own orgasm ceased shuddering through her like electric shocks. She stood up panting, and leaned back against Ian's chest, feeling the buttons of his tunic against her bare back.

She glanced at the others. Most had apparently already come, but one of the young soldiers was still pumping his cock feverishly. As she watched, he groaned and a thick white jet shot out and spattered on the floor. The girl's languid eyes were locked on Chelsea's as one hand cupped a breast and the other soothed and stroked her pussy.

Ian leaned down and nuzzled Chelsea's ear. "Well, I think we'll have to make you an honorary Beefeater," he whispered.

Mr Greenline

Kay Jaybee

It hadn't taken Ellie long to work out which of the drivers walking around the bus station was the one she'd heard so much about. Even if Sara hadn't nudged her in the ribs, and none too covertly pointed him out, she'd have known he was the one.

His swagger-like walk was enough to give him away. The blaze of his eyes as he surveyed the queue of people waiting to board his bus underlined the point. Then their bright searing sparkle emphasized it, and went on to highlight it in bold capital letters.

"What do you think?" Sara was speaking to Ellie, but her eyes never left the back view of the man unlocking the double passenger doors of the number 43 Greenline bus.

"He appears to be everything rumour claims."

Sara nodded. "Is that a yes, or a no?"

Not replying for the moment, Ellie watched the tight neat outline of his fitting black trousers. The guy hadn't let his sitting-down job let his body run to fat, that's for sure; but then he couldn't have been more than twenty-three years old, and if the shape of his arms as they appeared from just below the elbow of his short-sleeved was anything to go by, he probably worked out. She ran a critical eye over the breadth of his shoulders, and smiled to herself as she took in the epaulettes on each one – she'd always had a thing about those, no matter what the uniform. To Ellie they suggested a very obvious type of fun . . .

"That's a yes, but on my terms."

Sara laughed. "I knew you'd say that. You getting on the bus then?"

Again Ellie took her time to answer. The man she had referred to as Mr Greenline was sitting in his bus's cab now, sorting out the money for the fare machine. Suddenly he looked up, and Ellie knew he'd seen her checking him out. His lips turned up at the corners, and his eyes shone in her direction. She could almost feel their heat radiating into her through the thick windscreen glass of his cab, and across the station forecourt.

Ellie shifted her gaze to the queue forming outside his door, and their visual contact was broken. She didn't tell Sara that in that moment she had been helpless to prevent her heartbeat double and her chest feel as though someone had secretly come along and encased it in a bra two sizes too small.

"He needs taking down a peg or two. Do we know his name, or is he always just 'Mr Greenline'?"

"Always Mr Greenline. I guess if I did what he did, then I wouldn't use my name either."

"Fair point."

Sara dragged her eyes away from the bus driver. "And let's face it, Ellie, I know you're craving a man fuck. If you didn't, you'd never be contemplating catching a bus to a destination you don't need to go to. Right?"

Ellie said nothing. After all, Sara knew her better than anyone. It would have been pointless to deny it.

"So, remind me how the system works?"

"According to the girls in my office, you get on and say you want a ticket that takes you all the way."

"That is so corny. I hate that."

"And yet, you'll still do it."

"And what makes you say that?"

"Because I know you very well, and I can feel the horny vibes bouncing between you and that bus already."

Ignoring the second statement she couldn't possibly deny, Ellie frowned. "And the bus company really have no idea?"

"Can't have, or he'd have got the sack."

That fact intrigued Ellie. What was it about the man that stopped all the women – rumour had it – he'd shagged at the back of his bus from reporting him? Was he that good?

The doors to the bus opened, and the usual crush of party animals, some drunk, some tired, some pumped up on life, some high on more dubious substances, surged forward. The majority of the women were the usual late-night clubbing uniform of miniskirts and low-cut tops, all wanting to spare their high-heeled feet from the walk home. Some of them, Ellie suspected by the way they were blatantly sizing up Mr Greenline, had another agenda altogether.

With her shoulders pushed back, her chest forward, and her red-streaked chestnut hair flowing around her, Ellie made sure she briefly caught and then dropped his eye line. Turning to Sara, she said, "Stay here. And the moment I get in front of him, phone me."

Striding away from a puzzled Sara, Ellie joined the queue. Moving one step forward, she edged toward the vehicle, her phone clasped in her hand.

Stepping up into the bus behind the penultimate queuer, Ellie could sense the potential apprehension of sexual tension bouncing around the gaudy orange and red fabric covered seats. Turning to Mr Greenline, finally face to face, Ellie felt his hazel eyes holding her own for a fraction longer than necessary as he shrewdly regarded her. "And where may I take you?"

Leaving his innuendo hanging in the air, every instinct in Ellie told her that this man and his assumption should offend her, and yet somehow it didn't. Mr Greenline's expression wasn't telling her that she was his for the taking; it was telling her that she was sexy. That he found what he was looking at attractive, rather than that he was just a hunter on the continual quest for tasty prey.

Fixing her eyes on his, Ellie replied, "Where would you suggest?" Her expression silently challenging him, until, on cue, her phone rang. "Then again, maybe not."

Flashing him a non-committal smile, Ellie retreated.

Mr Greenline called after her, "Maybe you'll take my trip another time."

Tilting her head back in his direction, Ellie asked, "Are you worth it?"

"So they tell me."

"Do *they*." Ellie twinkled her eyes at him once more, just to make sure he'd got the message, and disappeared back into the crowd of Friday night travellers.

It had been a challenging two weeks. But it had taken time to decide how best to act. Ellie, already turned on by the thought of what might happen later that evening if all went to plan, found her whole being responding to Mr Greenline's stare as she climbed aboard the bus at exactly the same time of night, in the same clothes as she had a fortnight ago. Her breasts felt tight again, and a flutter and buzz of sexual anticipation stirred in the pit of her stomach as she reached the front of the queue. "May I buy a ticket please?"

His eyes sparkled. "To the very end of the line this time, or will your phone ring again?"

Her pulse stepped up a pace. So, he had remembered her. Just her? Or did he just have a brilliant memory when it came to all women who he sensed could give him a blow job in the back of the bus? Remaining sceptical despite the spiralling state of her physical need in this man's presence, Ellie kept her expression as neutral as possible. "I'm not expecting a call tonight."

"So is that a yes to the end of the line then?"

"It all depends what's there."

Mr Greenline pressed the button that shut the automatic doors. "I need to start the bus. End of the line ticket?"

"Why not." Without allowing herself to glimpse in his direction again, Ellie took the proffered ticket and went to sit down. She wondered if the driver had realized that he had asked her to stay on the bus, and not the other way around? If Sara's reports of local gossip were to be believed, then it was generally the women who made a play for him.

There was no doubt that it was a game. A game of nerve.

Which women would stay on the bus to the end, and which would wimp out and get off before the end of the line? Some of the travellers were obviously genuine passengers, but you could tell from the glances a few were giving Mr Greenline, courtesy of his rear-view mirror, that she was not the only one who had bought a ticket to the end of the line. What did he do, take it in turn, pick one or two and send the others away, or did he just sit in his seat and wait for the women to give up and leave one by one, until only a single female remained?

Casting her eyes around, Ellie pinpointed five possible contenders, all aged between nineteen and thirtyish, all of whom were fixating their vision on the back of Mr Greenline's head. Did they perhaps think that by staring hard at him he would pick up on their desperation and choose them to play with?

She felt ashamed of her fellow women, but at the same time had to acknowledge that she was just as bad – worse maybe, as she'd been planning her return so carefully. Ellie had thought perhaps that she had simply not noticed his arrogance the first time. Any man who did this must be arrogant and full of himself. But again she didn't feel that vibe. Ellie just got the sense that he saw himself as performing a public service – a lift home, and then a trip to heaven and back?

Having purposefully kept her own vision averted from the front of the bus, Ellie finally glanced up, and caught sight of the driver's face in the mirror. He was looking straight at her. Ellie felt her pussy twitch in instant response. Sara had been right. It had been way too long since she'd had any cock.

Travelling through the city seemed to be taking forever, as they stopped and started, letting people on and off the bus.

If she had done her research properly, then Ellie calculated that there would be two more stops before they reached the overnight bus park where Mr Greenline would declare the end of the line. This meant there was only one more official stop to go.

Using the mirror at the front of the bus and the reflection from the windows to aid her, Ellie counted that six people remained aboard. Two were men, and one was an elderly lady who was already gathering up her belongings in readiness to disembark. That left two women of about twenty-five years old – one blonde, one dark-haired – plus herself.

The bus pulled into the last proper stop and, as predicted, the men and elderly woman got off. So did one of the younger women, who, by the look of regret on her face, had intended to stay on, but had chickened out at the last minute. Or perhaps the other woman had persuaded her to leave? Having seen the determined expression on the blonde's face, Ellie was sure that was the case.

No one else got on. It was just her and the woman at the back. Ellie took a bottle of water out of her handbag and swallowed some moisture back into her throat. Ignoring the hint of perspiration that was dotting the back of her neck, she swept her hair up into a high ponytail and, as the bus slowed, Ellie got up and walked up behind Mr Greenline.

"You aren't supposed to stand up while the bus is moving."

"And you do know that you aren't supposed to have sex with women on this bus."

His laugh was deep and gravelly, and for the first time Ellie wondered if he was a smoker, although she couldn't smell any hint of nicotine about him. "This is true, but I never make anyone stay on the bus if they don't want to."

"I'm sure you don't."

Mr Greenline pulled up outside the bus's overnight shed. "End of the line ladies, time to get off."

Ellie's fellow passenger rose to her feet and came to stand next to her by the driver. "Or you could drive into the shed right now, Mr Greenline? That is what they call you isn't it?"

"Ummm, yes." The driver gave his other passenger a dazzling but wary smile. "And you are?"

"Sara."

Ellie detected a flicker of doubt on his previously self-assured features as he asked, "And you both want to go into the shed?"

"I believe we both paid for tickets that would take us to the end of the line. This isn't the end of the line. That is." She pointed to the shed.

His eyes narrowed as Ellie took Sara's hand. "Ah, I see."

Ellie watched as the hard-on that had already started to make itself visible beneath the material of his black trousers, tented with no subtly whatsoever.

For the first time Ellie began to wonder how much of the local gossip had been true. She had no doubt he'd had many women in the back of his bus, but she had the feeling that this was the first time two women had come to him together.

"So, are you going to drive the bus to the end of the line?" Ellie kept her tone even. "Sara and I have heard so much about you. I find it difficult to believe that, if the rumours about Mr Greenline are true, you would even hesitate."

"Unless of course—" Sara ran a finger across Ellie's chest "—you don't think you can handle a double dose of these all at once?"

The engine to the bus sparked back into life, and the driver, whose erection was becoming more evident beneath his uniform by the second, drove into the large dark shed. Operating via sensors, a series of harsh strip lights came on, showing that theirs was the last bus to return that night.

The purr of the engine had barely stilled and the key had only just reached Mr Greenline's uniform pocket as he climbed off his seat, when Ellie took hold of one of his shirt's shoulder epaulettes, and Sara looped a finger through the other. "So, Mr Greenline, what is your usual first move?"

The bus driver licked his lips nervously, but there was no denying the lust that radiated from him now, as he was faced with the opportunity to live out a real-life fantasy. "I ask my final passenger if she would like to stay, or if she would like to leave."

"Always the gentleman."

"I don't want to keep someone here if they've changed their mind."

"Very commendable, and yet you always hope they'll stay. Expect them to stay even." Ellie nodded towards his chest. "There's no disguising the square-shaped outline in your shirt pocket."

"They often stay. I take them to whichever seat they wish, and then we have fun."

Whatever uncertainties had clouded his judgement for a moment, the driver had quickly knocked them aside, as he placed one hand on each of the girls' hips. "And where would you two like us to go?"

Pulling at his epaulettes, the girls led Mr Greenline to the middle of the narrow bus aisle. "I believe here would suit us perfectly." Ellie let go of her side of the shirt, confident that he was far too far down the road of arousal to make a run for it, and opened her handbag.

With a nod to Sara to begin their well-rehearsed plan, Ellie took out two long pieces of gold cord. "I always think epaulettes should have gold braiding of some sort, don't you, Sara?"

"Certainly." Taking one of the lengths of cord from her lover, Sara copied Ellie as she threaded the cord around the shirt's epaulettes twice, and then fastened the ends around the handhold attached to the top of the adjacent seats.

"What the—"

Ellie snapped out her interruption. "If you want to keep that mouth free so you can taste the delights we have to offer you, then I suggest you remain quiet. After all, you don't want anyone outside to hear you do you? This could cost you your job, couldn't it?"

His eyes blazed, but he closed his lips tightly as he was secured, via his uniform's shoulders to his own bus seats.

"Sara, if you please?"

Beaming broadly, Sara stood next to Ellie in the confided space and, after a long lingering kiss that sent a groan of appreciative longing from the bus driver, took off her skimpy T-shirt, rolled it up, and used it to fasten his hands behind his back.

Undoing his shirt buttons slowly, keeping her eyes locked on his all the time, Ellie asked, "How many times have you wanted this to happen, Mr Greenline? How often have you fantasized about the women on your bus turning the tables on you, and giving you a treat, rather than the other way around?"

He swallowed, but said nothing. He didn't need to. The expression on his face said it all.

"I see." Ellie ran a palm across his chest. It was firm, and as toned as she'd predicted it would be on her first trip to the bus station. It had a spattering of hairs near the top, but was otherwise smooth, and she enjoyed the warmth of his flesh under her fingertips. "You've always wanted it to happen, but it never has. Till now. Right?"

"Uh-uh."

Sara derailed any further comment as she'd taken off her bra, and she was dangling it provocatively from one finger as if she was a stripper in a cheap downtown show. "You like what you see?"

"Stupid question." He flashed Ellie a knowing look. "I take it you've seen her tits a good many times before."

"Seen them, licked them, bit them, fucked them."

His breath was becoming more ragged by the second, and abruptly Ellie was done playing. If she didn't hurry up the action he'd have spunked his load inside his uniform before anything interesting had happened.

Taking off her own top and bra, Ellie let him gawp for a

second, before standing with Sara, so close, that their nipples brushed together in a way that tripped shots of electricity through her, and sent her already slick pussy into juice overdrive.

Then, with no warning, Ellie ripped off her girlfriend's skirt and panties, sending a grunt of desire from Mr Greenline, who moved a step forward, but got no further due to his corded restraints.

Removing her own clothes, Ellie did the same. "I believe it's time, Sara."

Sara instantly vaulted over the nearest seat, and stood behind the driver.

"Can you feel her, Mr Bus Driver? Can you feel my girl's big tits being pushed up against your uniform?"

His reply of "Yeah" was throaty at best.

Ellie moved closer. Her nipples were buffered against his chest, and her mouth, although not kissing his, was speaking directly into his lips. "How does it feel, being a bus driver sandwich?"

"Unbelievable!"

"Good." Ellie ran a hand down his front, cupping the bulge of his cock in her palm, squeezing it through his trousers. "I see your dick agrees with you."

"What are you going to do?"

Ellie placed a finger over his lips. "That would be telling."

Placing both her hands on his shoulders, Ellie hooked her thumbs through the epaulettes under the cord and then wrapped her hands into Sara's, whose joined hers there. Then, with their faces meeting to the right of the driver's head, the girls locked lips, pressing their naked bodies up against his.

Keeping their hands in place, the women acted as if Mr Greenline simply wasn't there. Rubbing and grinding him from behind, Sara exaggerated every move she made as she writhed against the cotton of his shirt back, and the smooth polyester of his trousers, as they stretched over his taut arse.

Ellie tilted her hips forward, making sure that her every gesture teased, touched or thrust against his groin, while simultaneously teasing the gap of torso visible from between the two sides of his open shirt, with brushes and presses of her breasts.

Using his epaulettes as leverage, the women kissed each other deeper. Helpless to do anything but feel and listen to his passengers as they attacked each other with their mouths, tongues, lips and teeth, Mr Greenline's moans were becoming more deep-throated and husky. His hands moved constantly as he tried to loosen them from where they were pinned – held captive not only by Sara's shirt, but by the squash of her body.

The blonde could feel his scrabbling increase. Breaking away from Ellie with a wink, she breathed her words into his ear, her own tone panting and breathless. "How badly do you want to touch us?"

"You've no idea."

Ellie silenced further comment with a kiss to the lips, savouring his masculine taste and firmness, after the sweeter, delicious flavour and aroma she'd got from Sara. Then, with her head tilted in enquiry, Ellie asked, "And when you do get your hands free, which bit of us will you touch first? So much flesh to choose from." She liberated the condom packet from his shirt pocket and tapped it between her fingers. "Sara, if you please."

Reaching around the driver's waist, Sara undid his belt and zip fly before Mr Greenline had managed to form any sort of coherent response. Then Ellie shot a hand forward and freed his cock from his boxers before it burst free from the fabric all by itself.

"Nice." Ellie weighed the length in her hands. "You should feel this, Sara; it's good. Nice width, nice length, nice smell. It's gonna feel great on the inside."

With her hands still on the bus driver's shoulders, Sara leant as far around his body as she could, the friction of his wrists working hard to become free of her expert binding, sending shots of fresh arousal through her own body.

Grinning in teasing agreement with Ellie, Sara said, "Oh yes, and just think, it's been inside so many passengers, so many women who aren't getting their kicks at home."

Ellie massaged the bus driver's cock harder, "Is that the service you provide at the end of the line, Mr Greenline? A place for cougars to get their rocks off when they're neglected or bored at home? Bus driving is a public service after all; why not expand the facilities on offer?"

"Something like that." His hands were almost free. Mr Greenline wriggled his shoulders a little, testing how tight the bounds around his uniform were, and soon found that only the removal of his shirt would set him completely free.

"So—" Ellie gestured to Sara to come around to join her in front of their male companion, and stood playing with her girlfriend's nipples as they looked at the semi-tied man, "—where will you start?"

Mr Greenline stared from one of them to the other and, without replying, brought his finally free hands round in a whirr of activity. With Sara's shirt still hanging off one of his wrists, the driver grabbed each of the girls' right tits. "I think that's a good place, don't you?"

"Can't argue." Ellie placed a hand of her own over Sara's free breast, and Sara followed suit, so that every hand was full of soft pliant chest. Bringing a bare foot up, Ellie wrapped her toes beneath the base of Mr Greenline's shaft, massaging his balls in time to the movements of their hands until all three of them were in dire need of extra attention.

"Now!" Ellie and Sara acted fast, and in a way that told the driver they'd been practising this.

The condom was on his length, his trousers were around his ankles, and Sara had unhooked the cords from the tops of the seats in less than five seconds, and Mr Greenline found himself being ushered to the back of his bus by the women.

"OK, bus driver man, time to prove to us exactly why no one has reported you."

Sara knelt on the floor of the aisle, with her elbows resting on the middle of the couch-like backseat. Before Mr Greenline's eyes had got their fill of the butt and sodden pussy she was offering up to him, Ellie had climbed astride her lover. With her long, high-heel-enhanced legs straddling Sara, Ellie completed the gorgeous two-tier system of female honey that was suddenly right before him.

"Fuck us, Mr Greenline. Fuck us. Prove you're worth it."

With the expression of a child who'd just been given every Christmas present he'd ever dreamt of in one go, Mr Greenline dived his length inside Sara, while his hands steadied himself by massaging Ellie's breasts.

Then, desperate to discover if Ellie's channel felt as wonderfully fitting as her girlfriend's, he swapped his cock to her body. His large smooth palms grabbed at Sara's hips until he felt secure enough to start a rhythmical thrusting from one girl's mound to the other and back again. Ellie then Sara, Sara then Ellie; his breathing was speeding up in time to his pumping groin as the driver barked, "Do each other as well! I want to hear you coming. I want you to love this!"

The women didn't need telling twice. Ellie slid a finger over Sara's clit, while Sara rocked awkwardly from side to side, pushing up against the weight above, until her thumb found its way to her girl's nub.

"Girls ... oh hell ... I ..." Mr Greenline got no further. His thrusts between the women were becoming a blur, and each time he left one feeling neglected, while the other was beautifully full, he got closer and closer to the end of the line.

Muffled by the seat against which her head was pressed, Sara's cry of "I'm coming," was only heard by Ellie, who felt her own orgasm trigger at the twitch and spasm of her lover's pussy. Her channel, currently full of cock, clenched Mr Greenline tightly, and Ellie climaxed against him, driving Mr Greenline headlong into an orgasm with her.

Untangling their arms and legs a few moments later, the women gathered themselves quickly. Picking up the cords that still hung from Mr Greenline's epaulettes, Ellie yanked them downwards, hard, so the driver had no choice but to drop to his knees. "Nice?"

"Oh yes."

"Good." Ellie glanced playfully towards her lover, who sat on the chair before the driver, her legs spread open. "So tell me, Mr Greenline, now you've proved what an excellent public service you've been providing the women of the district, there is one more thing we need to discover.

"I can see why you've never been reported. I imagine every woman who has been to this shed with you wants to purchase a return ticket, but tell us, Mr Greenline, was that the end of the line, or is there just time for one last stop?"

The bus driver looked from one woman to the other. Their eyes gleamed with continuing desire as Ellie, still holding the gold cords, pushed his face closer to a now seated Sara's wide-open legs. The message was unspoken, but clear. *Start licking.*

Mr Greenline smiled as he inhaled the gorgeous scent of sex before him. He always had time for an extra stop. Or maybe even two.

Uniform Of The Day

Felicia Fine

Saint Patrick didn't rid Ireland of all its snakes. One very nice one lay next to me when I awoke. It was attached to my latest lover. Even though it was the day to wear the uniform jersey of his favorite team, I had never felt any more naked than this. My legs lay open like a flower in full bloom begging for pollen, open for either his cock or his mouth, whichever he chose to invade me with. This time it was his tongue. It tickled my clit and got my juices flowing. He sucked my inner lips into his mouth, rimming and probing, before he dipped into the wet slit of my pussy with a manly suck, the tactile feel of his day-old beard against my thighs providing an exquisite moment.

Shawn certainly knew his stuff. He'd perfected the subtleties of tonguing the labia, gently prying back those tender petals, and priming the little man in the canoe. He rested his chin on my pubis and listened to my tummy gurgle.

"You should teach a class on how to do that," I sighed, completely comfortable with his smiling face beaming at me through the valley between my breasts. "Muff-diving, you call it. Not to split hairs, but how many euphemisms do you men have for the female organ, anyway?" I asked, as my legs lay open in case he wanted more.

"Probably no more than women have for our cocks," he answered, admiring my vagina with its close, clean shave. "I like the phrase, 'muff-diving'. It sounds like a sport in addition to a sexual act." His tongue flicked at my clit again until I came once more. My thighs squeezed his head like a vise until my tremors ended.

It was the start of the Irish rugby season so the comparison of sex with sports could be understood. In addition to falling for me, Shawn loved his rugby and his bar mates with equal vitality. He was more sexually playful than usual on game days before hitting the pub.

"I hope eating me out is more fun than watching a ball game with your mates."

"I've always wanted to combine two of my favorite things – rugby and lovemaking – at the moment the lads score a try."

"Hmmmm. Let's give that some thought." With Shawn, I had become more adventurous than I thought possible. "If you want to stay home for a change and watch the game, my titties can be your goal posts, my pussy your playing field."

"That might just be the ticket, but now that you're muff-less, I guess I'll be skinny-dipping rather than muff-diving."

"Come up and lay next to me. I want to charm that snake of yours. Besides, after what you've done for me, I think it's your turn to be scrutinized."

This time Shawn spread *his* legs. I was starting to feel hungry and going down on his cock was the best appetizer I could think of.

We just happen to live in the Irish town of Limerick, the home of infamous sayings set to Irish song. Any weekend in an Irish pub can have the frivolity similar to what Americans reserve for that one day of the year known as Saint Patrick's Day. And when the limericks and the singing begin, women beware.

I've spent some time at a quaint little tourist attraction pub known as Durty Nelly's. I'm good enough at darts to go unchallenged by the men who watch me. I'd met Shawn there. He was man enough to accept my tossing skills to be better than his, although he could get the better of me at billiards. But we proved to be equals in our lovemaking, offering our honor and honoring our offers. His smile was quick and his laugh richly masculine. His conversation and his gestures were affirmative yet gentle. Our discourse flowed easily, sliding comfortably into suggestive gibes at one another. A month after our meeting, I moved in with him. He'd been a part-time athlete not so many years ago, so he had a nice body to go with his sense of humor and his proclivity for all things sexual.

Before Shawn, rejection of all inhibitions had been as illusive as an honest barrister. His kisses proved to be as fiery as his words. Our romantic sessions remained hot and heavy, not for the inhibited or faint of heart. We made each other feel attractive, sexy and wanted. We felt each other up at every possible passing. I loved the way his erections rubbed against the front of his breeches until he could get out of them. Sometimes Shawn led me to the nearest open space in the house and fucked me on the floor. I loved being an instrument of his pleasure.

The disheartening problems of the world outside assaulted the senses less when such satisfying antics were taking place inside. I had never been able to masturbate in front of a partner before Shawn, but I got over that. I could pleasure myself in front of him without embarrassment, move my fingers over my lips, find my clit and feel the hardness of the little marble, roll it between my fingers while he watched . . . and sometimes let him finish me.

I asked him to masturbate for me as well. He said he considered it a waste of good semen, but when I suggested he aim at my breasts, he complied. I felt it important to know how a man touches himself and found I couldn't keep my hands off myself when he yanked his wanker for me. His technique was to flop it this way and that between his thumb and forefinger until it started to harden. He jiggled his balls for a bit before grabbing his shaft and began the long strokes, starting at the stem and stretching it out toward me where I perched between his thighs. His breathing became heavier as his fingers wrapped around himself and began to pump the burgeoning blossom up and down. When he said he was ready, I moved my chest over his genitals. His creamy spunk spurted between my breasts and landed on my neck. A second volley hit the underside of a breast and dripped back onto his tummy. The result was to agree that I enjoyed watching, but I preferred his issue to wind up within me rather than without.

Then there were my pink footballs, (what he called my tits). Sometimes he hid his cock in the valley between them. He liked to push my breasts together, forcing the nipples as close to each other as they would go, like a cross-eyed Mr Magoo, so he could get them both in his mouth at the same time. I didn't mind such antics. Actually, I could have spent hours just watching him suckle.

He was also fond of bringing home lingerie from Victoria's Secret, but I never stayed in them for long. He liked me best naked.

The day of the rugby game we were to watch together, we made plenty of time for a pre-game warm-up. He stripped me naked, eyeballing me up and down with a healthy leer before his gaze returned to my face, which always turned the no-longer-inhibited me on. He shaved his face and my twat. My pussy was already holding its breath for its eventual adventure. He owned his favorite team's rugby jersey so I helped capture the flavor of the day by donning it, but nothing more.

He had a few rules about our watching the game. When his team captured the ball, he would position me so that he could make a rear entrance in the event the ball crossed the try line. If they scored, so would we. He promised me a climax before each ensuing scrum. Additionally, an extra try would earn me a lick from clit to arse before I straightened up and pulled his jersey back down over my fanny. If a field goal was made, he planned to turn me around, raise my legs, and pound his balls between my uprights.

"When in Rome," I playfully replied. "My Irish puss is smiling."

In my opinion, every play in the game was pretty much the same. A lad runs with a ball and tosses it to another lad and so on before getting knocked down. Ho hum. I thought a camera in the dressing rooms before the game started could have enhanced the experience immensely. Without Shawn's excitement at the proceedings, I would have opted for a day of shopping, but after two pints of ale, I was totally into the action.

When his team got within striking distance of a score, he dropped his shorts. Penis already at full attention, he maneuvered me into position for the impending score. A penalty delayed the match and I wondered if his desire could hold out. Worse yet, what if they didn't get in? But they did, and Shawn said, "I've fantasized about this a hundred times, Kathy. Every sports lover's dream." Then he popped that wily, stiffened Irish prick inside me.

I thought agreeing to this fantasy might make me feel a little like an amusement ride being safety-tested, but I had to admit I liked the tries and rooted for his team to score early and often. I selected a nobler image for the proceedings – that I was a large-breasted carving on the bow of a sailing ship guiding its captain through rough seas.

By halftime, Shawn's team had come away with one goal, one try and one field goal. Good to his word, he plugged me twice and pussy-kissed me once. I didn't have the heart to tell him I'd only climaxed one time because he was giving it his all with more gusto than the men in their striped shirts and short shorts, it seemed to me.

During the second half, his team started out slowly and he decided to change the rules. We should have sex when either team crossed the midline. I went from liking, to loving that midline. Shawn convinced himself that having sex while the enemy was running for a score was not a traitorous act.

"Is this good for you?" I asked, knowing the answer but wanting to hear it.

"Better than the exotic special on a Chinese menu," he answered.

There were no more pithy remarks or sport bar epithets as a team moved close to pay dirt. The excitement of going for his own score stole his words. During these midline-crossing sessions, I looked over my shoulder now and then. I could see a vein throbbing in his neck and the beads of sweat along the upper edge of his lip. They would be salty. It made me think of one of the more infamous limericks I'd heard about a fellow shagging his girl from behind, thrusting exuberantly as if he'd caught hold of a shepherd's lamb languishing amidst the clover.

Shawn looked as driven as a shark about to take a bite out of some plump swimmer's arse. Sometimes he reached forward and grabbed my dangling footballs, hardening my nipples against his palms, and curling his fingers around them. Another delicious treat.

When he grunted and hollered, "Goal," I knew he was about to squirt his jism into me. He was like a starving man and my body was the banquet.

"Oh, yes," I repeated. "Please. Fill me up, make it good."

And he always did, his body jerking in spasms as hot semen shot out of his masterly cock. "Are you OK?" he would say.

"Of course. Absolutely, positively perfect. I'm humming inside.".

Throughout the game, he endured my inane commentary about the inbred violence of it all, and I never told him I'd kept my eyes shut through most of the contest.

Shawn's team won. After the interviews were over, Shawn said, "You look so hot in my jersey, why don't I take some pictures of you in it? You look a whole lot better in it than I do."

I could see no reason not to. I was up to a nice mixture of wine and ale by this time. "Just cute, or naughty?"

"Both."

"I don't want you taking any tush photos then showing them around at the pub."

Shawn laughed. "They will only be for our amusement."

"Okey-dokey, mate."

I enjoyed the photo shoot more than I expected. We did *Playboy* shots, some with me wearing the jersey, some without, but always wearing a teasing expression. When I pulled the jersey over my head and stood naked before Shawn, the look on his face was almost reverential. I felt a bit like Botticelli's *Venus* on the half shell. I even let him write "GO MUDWAMPS" just below my tits. With him in the buff as well, it was satisfying to watch Shawn snap off pictures as his cock alternated between flaccid and semi-erect depending on how erotic my poses were.

Then he stopped shooting, overcome by his own arousal. I was flattered and wanted him again.

"Oh hell, let's stop this and screw," he finally said.

"Goal or try?"

"Missionary. I've got to get my mitts on those pink footballs of yours."

Not to forget his team's victory, he donned the Mudwamps uniform jersey as I sat on the edge of our bed and motioned him over.

"Before we fuck, I'll take my sporting pleasure," I told him.

Shawn was a coaxable man when it came to my wants and I can be very controlling when my turn comes. I enjoyed giving him head more than I had any of my former lovers. Before, it was something to please my partner without being totally into it. But with Shawn, I wanted to be an oral service slut.

Whenever I looked at his penis, I recalled the first time we'd made love beyond the safety of our flat. It was on a southern beach in County Cork. Shawn and I had finished a long walk along the beach. We hadn't encountered any other beachcombers that day and I was feeling quite randy. I came right out and told him I wanted to suck his cock before the western sky turned from orange and purple to black.

He led me back to a spit of dry sand and pulled down his trousers. I removed my sweater. His prick and my pendulous breasts danced in anticipation. From my knees, I held up the crown of his penis with one hand and messaged his shaft with the other. His dickhead grew toward my face as the wrinkles began to smooth out. It was a truly handsome dick, if "handsome" was the right word. It always reminded me of a prize courgette from my mother's garden when it was fully aroused and ready for me. I shoved his shaft against his stomach and licked its underside from balls to cloven tip. After a few moments of this tease, I wanted more. I needed no clit foreplay. My juices had been flowing since we started our stroll on the beach. I was more than ready. We kicked out of the rest of our clothes. Shawn lay out the garments so we could lie on them.

"This fucking sand gets in everything, but these will help," he said.

While I desperately wanted him, there was enough of a romantic in me to recall the scene from that old movie where Burt Lancaster and Deborah Kerr made out on the beach. Then lust prevailed. I raised my legs in the air. The pads of my feet could watch for ships at sea. Shawn's friendly weapon slid into my slit with the ease of a finger up a goose's arse, as my swarthy dad might have said. He was slow and easy. It must have been a laid-back, no-rush-to-climax, beach thing.

Any attempt at staying sand-free was a losing proposition. I could feel the grains crawling up my moist butt. Shawn's equally wet nuts were banging the particles into my crack with every plunge. Sand grains on Shawn's torso shifted between his chest and my breasts. It was oddly stimulating, a reminder that this loving communion was taking place beneath a fading sky in a natural environment before twilight claimed the glorious scene. The flopping sound of the water played a duet with the slapping of Shawn's nut-sac against my bottom.

The ships at sea would have to seek some other beacon besides the bottoms of my feet. Shawn grabbed my heels to raise the tilt of my cunt so that he could delve even deeper into my ocean depths.

I felt blissfully disheveled. And primal. I started to erupt with provocative little cries of rapture. "Oh, fuck me until I scream," I beseeched.

"Can't do that, unless you want the Gardaí to show up and arrest us. Just grit your teeth and hiss when you come."

"Yeah, OK. Just don't stop."

Then our sexual worlds collided. My eyes squeezed shut as the tidal wave of pleasure consumed me. I clenched my teeth as he'd instructed. "Oh Christ and all the saints," I whispered. My legs went as straight as a mannequin's as I allowed my climax to run from my insides to my extremities. He continued to fill me up as if I was a race car with the petrol hose pumping me full of petrol. I could take more. I wanted to be filled until semen splashed from my tank.

Then I'd heard distant mumbling. An elderly couple stood at the water's edge watching our cavorting, and at the moment of our release, no less. I didn't try to jump up or to get Shawn off of me. There was no point in scrambling for our clothes in embarrassment for there was no more to see. You can't imagine my relief when the elderly man gave Shawn and me the victory sign with his fingers before the couple ambled along, arm in arm and smiling.

"Maybe they'll find their own section of beach," Shawn teased.

"Or maybe they did long ago."

Back inside our flat, the sight of Shawn's purple-headed cock, bobbing on its stalk, already beaded with pearlescent anticipation brought me back from my reverie on the beach to the moments following the photo shoot. I felt I'd come to know his appendage as well as I knew the likes and dislikes of the man it was attached to. I wanted this to be a particularly special blow job to celebrate his giving up a game with the lads.

I penis-slapped my face then poured crème de menthe over his thirsty cock, turning it into the national color. I licked my lips. My mouth opened and took him in. My stiff nipples rubbed against his hairy legs. At the moment, I wanted this big, blue-veined, crème-coated prick to be everywhere – in my pussy, up the Hershey highway, in whatever orifice came to mind. I was overcome with thoughts beyond physical pleasure, waiting for the magical moment when his balls would give up their load and pass through this hot rocket and into my mouth in creamy ecstasy. Ummmm good. So compelling was the feel of warm cock-meat impaling my head, I almost came before he did. His goo-stick had become the temporary pivot of my world and he was vulnerable to each tongue-licking whim. I felt like a snake charmer. What's more delicious than to undo a man in this way?

While one hand held his shaft steady and the other teased his ball sac, I looked up and fluttered my eyelashes. While my lips retreated and held on to the ridge of its tip, his pleasure brought me mine. I never ask for a critique. The fullness of his organ told me everything. I craved his body in all its moods, be it sports fanaticism, cunt fetishist, or *Playboy* photographer.

Admiring his pubic tangle, I slurped and smacked and sucked his cock as if it might be our last connection, a final communion, until he begged to put it back inside of me, but I wanted his load now and he finally gave in to my desire. When he told me he couldn't hold it any longer, I removed my lips and jacked him off so I could watch his ejaculate spit at me.

I thought about the mythological Greek fertility god, Priapos, as Shawn's engorged penis rose proudly. I opened my mouth for I was about to be honored with the nectar of the gods. He squirted. My uvula took a direct hit and my tongue took another. I quickly closed my lips over the crown until he was drained, all his tremors passing quietly into the twilight. I sucked on him gently even after the discharge, a slow, soothing suck, interrupted occasionally by my choosing to flog my face with the spent dick and rub it under my chin. Eventually, he was once again ready to take me the old-fashioned way.

"Looks like you have one final score left in your loins, the veteran ball-handler coming back during the final minutes to put his team over the top?"

"Pull out a last-minute victory?"

"Win one for the Gipper."

Shawn raised his eyebrows. "Hey, you know something about American football."

"No, just caught an old flick on cable TV one night."

"You've put me in position to score, lady. Goal to go, here we go. One more shot at glory."

"Missionary, I think you said."

"If that's all right."

"Compromise is love's secret ingredient," I said and meant it.

I rubbed the wet tip of his helmeted avenger against my clit before I lay back so he could squeeze my tits and fuck me as long and as hard as he chose. I idly wondered if *Playboy* photographers wound up screwing their subjects. At the very least, there was Hef's infamous grotto to frolic in, but our flat was more than satisfactory. Any place was shag heaven with my rugby stud.

But Shawn didn't go for a goal right away. He began a journey across my body first. He stroked the delicate arches of my feet then moved to my ankles and calves, kneading away any stress the bent-over position during the ball game might have caused. By the time he re-entered me, I was as relaxed as a simmering noodle but ready to be lavished with the steady motion of his heat-seeking prod, slow then fast then slow again. I bit my lip in pleasure.

"You're smokin' hot, lady."

I told him he was just horny from the suck-fest.

"You have the cutest, bitchinist arse I've ever banged my balls against."

I told him he was high from drink and the photo session.

"I thought I'd have an affair with Catherine Zeta-Jones eventually, but she got mixed up with Michael Douglas and that kind of soured me on her, so I had to settle for you. Nevertheless, you're beautiful."

I laughed. His ramblings were OK too. "Poor lad. I had no idea you were a star chaser. Now talk dirty to me."

"There once was a miss from Mantises, who had tits of two

different sizes. One was so small it was nothing at all, but the other was large and won prizes."

"Ah, a limerick for old Saint Patty by Shawn, the poet. I trust my tits are worthy?"

"Prize winners for sure, Kathy. Now spread wide so that I may grouse in your goodie."

With that bit of fluffy dialog we began our mating dance again. A small little corner in my brain opened with the randy thought of Shawn setting me on a table in the pub with my legs spread wide apart to give him access and to see my pink lips glisten, and then shagging me while all his friends watched. I embellished the image by picturing my unbridled breasts bouncing to and fro while others looked but couldn't touch.

The thoughts continued until our orgasms approached, and he brought me to a climax that rocked the teeth in the back of my head. We both cracked up like two kids at summer camp when he coaxed a pussy-fart out of me.

The strength of his body and the powerful beat of his heart above my cheek turned the lust into something deeper, something more meaningful than just two bodies in heat. He lay next to me and tweaked a lock of my hair, a sweet gesture of thanks. I pulled his hand to my cheek then turned my face into his palm.

It would take some doing to outdo this day, but I vowed that I would try. We stayed naked the rest of the evening, entertaining ourselves with Irish ballads, enhanced by Irish whiskey shots that led to continued revelry. Shawn sang "Roll me over in the clover and do it again" without guitar accompaniment, thank heavens. We raided the fridge and fed each other in bed. Shawn froze some green grapes to put in our wine glasses and in my vagina. We ate and came until our flat smelled like sex and contentment.

After making love for the umpteenth time, we slept in each other's arms. I conked out, satiated and glutinous, happy that we had played our game with humor and energy and passion. *Hail to the victors valiant. Hail to the conquering heroes. Hail, hail.*

"No, honey," I told Shawn before his team's game was on TV the next time. "You get together with your mates, but I hope you'll think of me when your team scores."

I made a point of having plans on rugby days after our session, but I did find a way to partake in the festivities in a different way. I ordered a sheet of mascot decals from a bookstore. I wanted to get him before the playing field did, so every night before a game, I adhered one of the decals to a different spot on my body like a temporary tattoo and urged him to find it at bedtime. With the season just getting underway, I had plenty of spots in mind to keep it interesting.

When he located the decal, he'd kiss the spot until the mascot started to disintegrate into a wet blob. Then his mouth would make me breathless as he twirled a French kiss into my lower lips, which lay perpendicular to his.

"Oh God," I'd whimper and pull his head against me, unconcerned about his ability to breathe.

As I reached each orgasm, creative language failed me again. "Oh Christ," I'd murmur and explode in a gush. And, strangely enough, I would think of that silly game and want Shawn to score another goal in my field of play.

At present, Shawn and I are still happily sharing our lives together and continuing to explore each other in many ways. I love standing nude on our balcony on cool nights in the moonlight. It's an awesome feeling before either winter or summer close in, that ultimate mix of elegance between hot and cold. "I'd like to grow my muff back next winter," I told Shawn on one such night. "It'll make me feel more secure on cold days during those brief periods when your body isn't covering me up."

He joined me on the balcony and rubbed himself against my backside. "No problem, Kat. I'll keep it trimmed nicely for you. Never know when we might want to do another photo session. I'll even shave your pits if you'll let me."

"You think I could deny you anything? Whatever you like. You're the Irish Wizard of Ahhhs. I can click the heels of my emerald slippers and you can take me where I want to go." I rose on the balls of my feet and bumped my bare heels together to demonstrate.

He ran a slow finger along the crevice between the while globes of my behind. "The Wizard of Ahhhhs. I like that," he said.

He told me he had enough hot air, blown into the right opening, to lift me off the ground, the creative little bugger.

After showers together, Shawn likes to blow-dry my hair too, but he's a perfectly, wonderfully normal, active male in every other aspect. If I have a fetish, it must be shoe shopping. But is there a woman in the Western world who doesn't have that weakness?

And there's one more thing. As a result of the rugby decal experience, I've decided to get a small shamrock tattooed near my pubis to permanently honor Shawn's love of fixating on places where hair normally grows.

Erin go Braugh, or in my case, Kathy go braless.

Lovely Rita, Meter Maid

Emily L. Byrne

She was pulling away from my illegally parked car on her scooter when I got there, her stern back turned away from me. Her blonde hair was wrapped in a tightly controlled bun that coiled just under her magnificent hat and seemed about to strike out, to send a reproof all by itself. I scarcely needed the gift that she had left on my windshield to know that I was not in her good graces.

But she had left me something! Officer 267 had left me a love note, full of restrained passion and barely contained longing. I pressed it to my lips and imagined that her round and solid calf in its gray cotton armor lay beyond it. I hugged it to me and grinned cheerfully at the drizzly day around me. I hummed a few bars of the Beatles song. Perhaps if I didn't pay it, she'd come and arrest me. The vision of her putting her cuffs on my meek and pliant wrists was almost more than I could bear.

I wanted to take my fantasies beyond that, to imagine myself naked and handcuffed to her scooter while she paced around me in her gray second skin. She would read each of my unpaid tickets aloud to me in a stern voice, then insert it up my ass or in my pussy. The paper would be crisp and harsh for a moment, perhaps two, before the heat of my body melted paper and flesh alike into a thick stream of juice.

I would beg her for forgiveness, for absolution, until she permitted me to come, drenching her scooter with the fuel of all my longings. Perhaps then she might permit me to touch her, to stroke and fondle her body through her uniform, the armor of her daily administration of justice. But that might be too much to hope for. I could only pray that she would make of me an example to all scofflaws who haunted the parking spaces, legal and otherwise, of a city that she made her own.

If only I dared to follow my desires! Instead, I tucked the latest ticket reverently into my shoulder bag and moved my car. Some whim made me follow her for a few blocks before I became worried that she might think me a stalker or one of their ilk and I turned off before I had to watch her dismount from her motorized steed to bestow a new ticket on some other fortunate recipient. I envied them, especially if they got to see her while she wrote it out.

I had been lucky enough to watch her face three times, to watch her mouth thin into a tight, determined line, her eyes narrow suspiciously, her cap tilt forward, as she spotted some new violator of the codes that she so rigorously enforced. I imagined that I could see her broad shoulders tighten, muscles firm under the soft roundness of her flesh. Or what I hoped was soft roundness.

It wasn't as if I could dream convincingly of actually touching her naked flesh. I simply could not imagine her without her uniform. She and it belonged together. If she were ever to really notice me, I didn't think I could bear it if she took it off. It would be like defacing a piece of art. Some part of me wondered if I would even recognize her in civilian clothes, no longer an awe-inspiring figure, the personification of law and order.

For a brief shuddering moment of arousal, I wondered what it would be like to desire a regular police officer, with a gun and a bulletproof vest under her uniform. The vision terrified me. Officer 267 was the woman for me, and already more than I could aspire to.

But aspire I would, at least in my dreams. When I got home, I was off to my bedroom, box of tissues in one hand and parking ticket in the other. I inhaled what I imagined to be her scent from the bland paper: a slight perfume, like cinnamon. I knew that it was a smell that must permeate her clothes, her armor, in my mind at least.

I imagined the indescribable joy of being able to plant tender kisses on her black leather shoes, tonguing each of their laces in turn. My fingers were inside me as I stretched out on my bed and rubbed frantically at my aroused nerve endings. I wondered if she would permit me to touch myself, in the unlikely event that I should ever be so fortunate as to be in the compromising position of my dreams with Officer 267.

Not that any compromise would be involved, at least not on my part. Her stern frown, her set lips, this was the only expression I had ever seen on her face. Picturing her smiling was both beyond me and unnecessary. I needed her stern, wanted her fierce for me. Wanted her to own me, to make me grovel and beg for forgiveness for my sins, my crimes.

I wondered how many more unpaid tickets I could accumulate before she would have to arrest me. My breath caught in my throat at that picture. I wondered if traffic patrol ever got to do strip searches. Then I wondered if Officer 267 would want to strip search me, outside of her normal job duties. My limbs quivered all over in ecstatic anticipation of fulfillment and I crammed the parking ticket inside my dripping wet self, reveling in the pressure of it balled up inside me.

In a moment, Officer 267 was frowning down at me, her cap tilted forward as she stood above my bed, and I gave myself to the moment. Fulfillment, even of a most illusory and imaginary kind, was glorious and I reveled in it and its aftermath.

Yet, within that aftermath, I found my resolve. I would need to be brave and resolute if I wanted any of my fantasies to come true. If Officer 267 was truly what I wanted, and I knew that she was, I needed to act. But I was no risk-taking outlaw, not by nature; what was I to do?

Perhaps if I parked my car on a sidewalk? Took up two parking spaces until the meter expired? My brain spun through fantasies of parking infractions that I could commit in hoping of attracting her attentions. So far, I had already exceeded my time at several parking meters and bent up one edge of my license plate holder to block the annual sticker.

But if I wanted more of her than this, I still needed something far more creative and more unusual than anything I had attempted before. And I needed to find a time to do it, whatever it was, when we could be alone on the street or somewhere nearby. Or . . . in my car.

The thought alone was enough to send my eager hands back between my legs, rubbing and thrusting into each orifice until I came with a muffled bellow into my pillow. I grinned at the gray pillowcase, chosen because it matched Officer 267's uniform color exactly. I liked to imagine myself wrapped in her authoritarian arms each night as I drifted off to sleep.

That was probably what inspired me the next morning when I woke, still sleepy and sticky from my exertions. I went from the shower to my computer, searching until I found exactly what I was looking for. Imitation would be the sincerest form of flattery, or so I hoped.

Work passed in a meaningless blur. I managed not to get fired but left on feet far nimbler than my brain had been all day. The costume shop would only hold my order for another hour and I had to get across town to pick it up. Part of me wished that Officer 267 handled moving violations as well, but I knew that was too much to hope for, and I kept my driving strictly legal as I navigated through traffic.

I arrived at the shop with fifteen minutes to spare. Which gave me plenty of time to try my rented outfit on, then wear it outside, claiming that I was going to a masquerade party that night. It was not, strictly speaking, an untruth. Once I left the shop, I sat behind the wheel of my car and adjusted the cap, pulling it down over my forehead and trying to look stern. I was very nearly successful: there was something about a gray cotton uniform that could make even me look like a stern purveyor of parking tickets.

Then it hit me: I couldn't hold a candle to her and it wasn't a real uniform, but I could pass for traffic control if no one looked too closely. I was wearing the armor that the woman of my dreams wore each day she worked, or as close to it as I thought I was likely to get. The wave of arousal that washed over me then left me trembling and wanting behind the wheel of my car.

I closed my eyes, wondering if I dared to send my hand back between my legs, to use my fingers to drive myself to temporary ecstasy here in full view of rush-hour crowds and traffic. I trembled with longing as I tried to find the courage to do it, to throw caution to the proverbial winds and indulge my fantasies. My fingers caressed my pants, tingling a little at the harsh touch of the fabric.

The sharp tap of knuckles on glass almost launched me

through the windshield. Officer 267 had stepped out of my dreams and was standing next to my parked car. My hand trembled as I hit the button to lower the window. Her eyes were an icy light blue that seared and burned me with a frigid blast of winter.

I could see her expression shift as she took in my uniform, the twist that I had made with my hair under my cap. Emotions I couldn't read moved across her face and my desire was replaced with an absolute terror. "C-c-c-costume party," I choked out, gesturing at my clothes, my armor. I felt like a complete fraud.

She frowned at me and it sent shivers down my spine. "Meter's expired. I'll need to give you a ticket for that unless you're moving along. Right now." She glanced down at her watch. Then at my car. Then, she walked around to look at my license plate.

For a wild moment, I thought about gunning the engine and fleeing before she confirmed her suspicions. But I was no longer anonymous; no matter what happened next, she would remember me. No more skulking about, letting the meter expire on my car. No more watching her from afar, lusting over her prowess with her scooter and her wicked pen.

But she didn't know that I had been doing those things. Or so I thought until she walked up to the passenger side of my car and got in. "Drive." It was an order. I would have asked what our destination was, but she was already keying it into my car's GPS. Was she taking me to jail? I couldn't bring myself to ask.

In fact, I couldn't bring myself to say a word. The uniform that I admired so much on her rounded curves was like a stone wall between us now, blocking me out. I was one of the scofflaws, and nothing more. The charming veneer of secret admirer dropped off me until I could have torn my uniform costume from my body in disgust. This was the difference between my fantasies and grim reality.

She didn't say anything either and the silence filled the car like a fog. I hoped that it would hide me until the sound of her abrupt command, "Turn right after the light," shattered me, broke me into a thousand pieces. I didn't even notice that I was leaving the city until I turned into a park. She directed me up to a deserted outlook and told me to stop.

"Get out of the car." Her voice had taken an odd purr, one that rattled my bones and shook free my desire. She wasn't arresting me; so why were we here? She got out of the car and looked around then, seemingly satisfied that we were alone, she turned back to me. "Arms on the hood, legs spread."

My heart was threatening to pound out of my ears, with my pussy on its tail. What was she planning on doing? I did as she ordered and waited, trying not to tremble. Officer 267 stalked around me like a tiger around a gazelle. "You've been watching me for weeks, maybe longer. Parking illegally, letting your meters expire, making my life unpleasant. And why? Because you like me? I don't think so." She stepped up very close to me, breasts pressed against my back, her lips nearly at my ear. "It's the uniform, isn't it? That's why you were driving around tonight dressed in one like it and hoping to get my attention. Well, you've got it." She reached down and pinched my ass, making me yelp.

She slipped her hand between my thighs, letting it rest on my leg just below my aching slit. "Unbutton your shirt. Slowly." She stood right behind me, body pressed lightly against mine. I could feel every breath she took as my fingers shook on my buttons. When I had unbuttoned the last one, she leaned in closer, her breathing a bit faster. "Take it off. And your bra."

I gasped and not just at the light chill of the early evening wind against my naked torso. Officer 267's hands were on my breasts, caressing and kneading. "I like you a lot better out of uniform," she growled softly against my ear. "Take your pants off."

I fumbled my way through unbuckling the belt and unzipping the pants, letting them drop to my ankles, then kicking them free. She yanked down my panties and I stepped out of them before going back to the same position against the car hood. It took every ounce of control I possessed not to rub myself against her leg, not to give in to every impulse of my burning clit.

"So what's your fantasy? We get here and I spank you? Do I fuck you myself? Or do I let you do it while I watch?" She ran a finger over my clit with each question, pulling away at each question mark.

"Tickets," I choked out, my vision clouded by my fantasies.

"Tickets? We have to account for those, darlin'. I'm not wasting tickets on you until I know it's worth my while. How are you planning on showing me that? I've felt soaking wet cunts before, right here in this very spot. This isn't anything special. You think you're the only one aching for a piece of this?" She gestured at her uniform and grinned.

I closed my eyes and gathered all my courage. "I'd like to do . . . whatever you fantasize about, Officer. As long as you don't take your uniform off. Or push me off the outlook or something like that." I opened my eyes at her soft chuckle.

"Good to set some limits on that, I suppose. Lucky for you I'm not likely to do anything like that." She inserted her finger into the bottomless chasm inside me and watched me squirm against it. She added two more fingers and thrust into me, forcing my back to arch as I groaned with unsated desire. "Pretend they're tickets," she growled before licking my ear lobe and running her tongue down my neck.

Her hand drove into me faster and faster, pounding me against the car. "Rub your clit. Now." I stuck my hand between my legs and rubbed furiously, eager as she was to see me come. When the first wave hit me, I shook until my legs felt like spaghetti. I could feel my juices squirt from me and she stepped back a little to avoid getting wet.

She let me collapse against the car, quivering and gasping like a fish out of water. Then she gave me her next command. "Up. Sit on the hood of the car with your legs spread. Wide as you can get them. Straighten your back. Uncomfortable? Good." She frowned and I quailed. What kind of ticket would this parking infraction be worthy of?

Officer 267 crossed her arms over her breasts and frowned down at me. "You," she said slowly, "are the kind of criminal that I joined the force to stop. The kind who engages in petty crimes for the thrill of it. That is what you're doing, isn't it? You see this uniform? It makes me responsible for stopping people like you." Her eyes raked me from aching ankles to throbbing pussy to beet-red face.

"I'm s-s-sorry," I stammered, wondering if I should get off the car, go put my regular clothes back on.

"I didn't say I was done, now did I?" She tilted her head to one side. "Would you even want me if I wasn't acting like a drill sergeant and wearing this?"

I looked down, choked out some nearly inaudible apologies, expressions of desire and longing and admiration. She let me run on until they were merely noises, hardly words at all. And I was still wet, soaking, aching for her, in that uniform, through it all. I wanted her to take me again, here, on my car. I wanted to scrape the paint off in a giant design in the shape of my pussy to remember this night forever.

Not like I was going to forget it any time soon, of course. Officer 267 leaned forward, her face between my legs and inhaled deeply. She grinned, the expression making me wary with its unexpected glee. "But the thing of it is, I like this part. I like having someone like you looking at me like I'm the most amazing creature alive. And the hottest. Even if it's not for the right reasons."

I could feel her hand between my legs again and I took her into me with a groan. Her thumb rubbed my clit as she thrust into me, her eyes locked on mine. Her stare engulfed me, holding me trapped and suspended, so overwhelmed with desire I wasn't sure that I could come. But she rubbed harder until the sensations were too much and I gave myself to her, over and over again.

When she pulled out of me, I had nothing more to give and lay spent and exhausted on the hood of my car. She disappeared for a moment, then came back with something in her hand. Officer 267 dropped a parking ticket on my quivering, naked breasts. "Same time next week?"

Brothers of Mercy

Steve Gee

"Don't just stare down at us for fuck's sake!" Gary was angry but was doing his best to contain himself. It was obvious by the way he was standing with hands on hips and speaking through clenched teeth. "Do. Something. Useful."

"Yeah," agreed Marty, standing near his friend and looking up too. "Sean, go and get something to get us out of here."

"Like what?" Sean peered down from the broken skylight at his two friends staring up at him, standing among the shattered glass on the shop floor.

"Like a ladder. Duh!" Marty was being a tad more patient with the youngest of the trio but even his patience was running thin.

"I can't see one up here," said Sean, his head bobbing up as he looked round.

"Fuckwit! You won't find one out there on the roof will you?" stormed Gary. His hands on his hips were fists now.

"Sean, listen. Climb down the way we got up and look for one. We'll wait here." Marty folded his arms, avoiding adding they didn't have a choice but to wait. Breaking into the shop was supposed to be a good idea "for a laugh", but they hadn't reckoned on the drop from the skylight being so great. Now they couldn't reach up to get out. They'd need a ladder, definitely.

"I could find some rope," said Sean, looking back down.

"For what?" Marty spoke before Gary could explode with some comment about Sean hopefully going to hang himself.

"I could drop it down and you could climb up. Like we used to do at school. In the gym."

"Shit for brains," snapped Gary.

Marty was speaking slowly now, as you might to a small child. "Sean, look around you. Is there a rope lying on the roof? Yes or no? If there is, can you see anything to tie it to? I don't think you are strong enough to haul us up on your own, do you?"

"No, there isn't one," said Sean. With his head framed in the patch of blue sky he looked unhappy. "I'm not sure where I can get a ladder on a Sunday."

"Steal one!" Gary shouted. "It isn't hard, is it?"

Sean looked as if he was going to say he didn't like stealing things, but he had come along with his two friends to see what they could steal from the row of shops near their home. The way it was going, it looked as if taking a ladder would be the only thing they'd get from this adventure. "I'll go and find one," he said and disappeared from the broken skylight.

"Get one long enough," called Marty after him. "Not some little stepladder, OK?"

"He'd never get a stepladder up on the roof," said Gary, sounding a little less fraught. "I'm not sure he'd be able to get a ladder up there either."

"Give him a chance," said Marty. "He's not *quite* useless."

Gary stared at his friend and shook his head, though it wasn't clear whether he was indicating if he disagreed with Marty's assessment or if the situation was too hopeless for any of them.

"We could look round for a table. Drag it over here and climb up. Use a chair too to reach up. We can make it out, I bet." If Marty was being his usual optimistic self, it wasn't coming across that way. "Or we can smash our way out of the front window."

"That will bring the cops running," said Gary. "And look around you: there isn't a table in here. Only the counter thing at the front and that's glass."

"We have to try." Marty set off for the counter. "If it's plate glass it'll hold our weight," he added.

It was soon clear that the counter was screwed down and wasn't going to move. The plastic seat behind the counter – the only furniture in the shop – didn't help at all either. There wasn't even the consolation of any money in the till. The only other thing was a storage room of some sort at the back of the shop. Locked, and if there was anything in there that would aid their escape it was soon obvious they couldn't shoulder the door down. "Fucking well made of iron, this thing," said Gary, rubbing his shoulder.

"Steel, not iron," said Marty. "Iron'd rust."

"Whatever," grumbled Gary. "Anyway, what the hell do they sell here?" Gary frowned as he stared at all the racks of clothes.

"They don't sell. They hire," said Marty. "I came in here once, years ago. For Kenny Dwight's party I think. It's all fancy dress. You know, pirates and stuff for Halloween. Zombies and witches."

Gary sighed as if the detail was irrelevant. "Where the hell is that idiot Sean? Fuck knows why we brought him along."

Marty wanted to say, *Fuck knows why you thought it would be fun to break into a fancy dress shop of all places*, but he kept his mouth shut. Gary was bigger and quick to anger. Sometimes it was best to let him come to that conclusion himself.

After a while, Gary hopped up to sit on the counter and after a few more minutes he said, quietly, "I should have thought which shop was worth breaking into. I thought this was the one that sold watches. Rings, too."

"That was the one with the steel grille over the skylight," said Marty. "Like the chemists had. And the off licence."

"OK," said Gary irritably. "So we were unlucky. We got a clothes shop."

Marty avoided reminding his friend he had already said it was a fancy dress hire place. He watched as Gary jumped off the counter and head to a rack of clothes. "Cool," said Gary, rifling through the various clothes. "German Army uniform! I could be that bloke, Rommel."

"Or Herr Schicklgruber."

"Dunno who he is." Gary had moved on to what was clearly a centurion's costume. "Why'd the Roman men wear skirts?"

"Dunno," said Marty. He had moved over a rack of clothes. "There's a Heidi outfit here. Oh, and one made of bandages. Mummy, I suppose."

"Mummy! Ha ha. Yeah, trust you to go for the girly things."

"Like the Roman Army wearing skirts, right?"

"Is that a nun's outfit you got there?" Gary had dropped the centurion outfit on the floor and headed to where Marty was.

"It's plastic," said Marty. "Far as I know nuns don't wear plastic habits."

"Bet they got some dirty habits though, hey?" Gary snatched the black-and-white plastic outfit from his friend. He held it up to the light. "Cool," he added.

Marty stared at his friend. He'd never seen him look as interested in anything as he did right now, but thought it better not to say anything in case he somehow spoiled the moment.

"I can wear this," said Gary emphatically, as he examined the thin plastic black-and-white outfit. "It'd fit me."

"You aren't a woman," said Marty.

"Nah, but I can pretend to be." Gary grinned. "And you can too."

"What?"

"Women. Like lesbians. Yeah? You can dress as a woman like me and we can be dirty lesbians having fun." Gary chuckled as if it was one of the best ideas he'd ever had.

"Gary, we're stuck in a place we shouldn't be. If the police turn up—"

"Relax, they won't. There's no alarm, is there? Anyway, if they were coming they'd be here by now."

"And what exactly do we say to Sean when he arrives with a ladder?"

"Seriously, you think he'll be back anytime soon? He's lucky if it takes him less than an hour to find his bum when he goes to the bog."

"Perhaps, but I'm not sure putting on these fancy dress clothes is going to help."

Gary sighed. "Look around. You see anything else we can do here while we wait? No, I didn't think so. We may as well enjoy ourselves."

"Bit silly really. I mean they're just clothes and outfits and uniforms." In spite of trying to be dismissive, Marty gulped. "What if I don't want to wear women's clothes?"

"Then dress as a man. Be a Roman soldier with a skirt!" Gary laughed. "I bet we can have more fun if we pretend to be lesbians, OK? That'd be more fun."

"I have no idea what lesbians do," said Marty.

"Liar," said Gary, smirking.

"Lesbians don't have dicks," said Marty, aware his own cock had started to stiffen in his pants. The idea was having an effect on him and he prayed it didn't show.

"They have strap-ons, dickhead. We saw them in that porn movie Sean's cousin had, and don't pretend you don't remember. So we say our cocks are like strap-ons, right?"

Marty felt himself blushing and turned away. "Dunno why you think I might wear women's clothes."

"Come on! You do already," guffawed Gary. "Your sister Denise told me you like to wear her panties when you think no one's looking. Pervert!"

"I don't," snapped Marty, then as he blushed some more, he added, "Well, I did when I was a kid."

"Yeah, like last week she told me. An' her suspenders and stockings. She knows."

Marty felt desperate. "So what? Lots of blokes do it."

"Then you wouldn't mind wearing this. It's like mine but its red, not black." With his free hand Gary held up a similar nun's outfit. It was red plastic instead of black. The matching wimple hung off the hanger too, complete with a white apron at the neck and with a Velcro fastening so it could close up round the throat.

"What if it doesn't fit me?" Marty snorted, feeling this was going to a place he didn't want to visit. "Anyway, nuns don't wear red. Just black. Or blue maybe."

"Ooh, you seem to know a lot about them," chuckled Gary. "Fancy them do you? They probably don't wear plastic either but what the hell? So, try it on. See if it fits. I'm going to put the black one on. I'll be Mother Willie."

Marty felt embarrassed but it was easier just to go along with this rather than have any more discussion about wearing his sister's lingerie. *Thank God*, he thought, *Denise doesn't know about me wearing her bra, that really would be trouble*. He'd do it, Marty decided, albeit with one condition. "If I put it on then it's only for ten minutes. Max. Then we get out of it. Be normal again."

"Fine." Gary shrugged. "You want to get that underwear over there?" The young man nodded to a display with a white basque and fishnet stockings on the wall nearby. "Don't worry, I'll help you into them. Probably the cup size will be OK for you. Small tits like your Denise." He sniggered again.

"Gary—" began Marty.

"Yeah I know, you don't do things like that. Just try on your Denise's bra, right, when you think no one's around?"

"Oh God," whispered Marty. There was no hiding place now. He went to get the basque and the stockings, glad at least to have his back to his friend, who was already stripping his jeans and T-shirt off.

To get what shred of modesty he could, Marty positioned himself behind a rack of clothes. He could hear the rustle of plastic from Gary and hastily Marty got out of his own clothes. The red nun's outfit was draped over the end of the rail and Marty could see there was a long slit in it. He was meant to show his leg in some provocative way. That was why Gary had demanded – his light-hearted banter hadn't disguised the seriousness of his tone – Marty wear the fishnet stockings. *I'll look ridiculous*, Marty told himself, but he was aware his cock was hard and he was trembling more with excitement than fear. He got into the basque, rejecting the call from Gary that he'd come over and help fasten the hooks at the back, and swiftly pulled the stockings on. Then he slipped the long red plastic habit over himself and even paused to put the wimple on, though he wasn't sure it was right. But then, this wasn't serious, was it?

Cautiously, Marty moved out of the protection of the clothes rail. He was aware that his erection was making a strange bulge at the front of his shiny habit and the slit up to the top of his thigh was, no matter how hard he tried, showing far too much fishnet-covered leg. "I feel stupid," he said as he emerged, and then gasped. Gary was just like he was, but in black plastic. He had an erection as well and didn't look the least troubled about it. He even had stockings on too and his slit was just as provocative.

"You knew about all this, didn't you?" Marty felt his face redden anew as the full force of the realization hit him. "You knew what this place was. The break-in wasn't a game . . . You knew they had these . . . these dresses." He indicated himself, aware that his own cock was if anything slightly harder. He swallowed loudly. "You tricked me."

"Yeah, but think of the fun we can have." Gary was smiling as he stepped forward, arms out and his cock stiff.

Marty didn't resist when Gary took him in his arms and pulled him close. Marty could feel his cock pressed flat between their bellies, but more crucially could feel Gary's impressive erection against his own. It felt strange, and more exciting than he could ever have imagined. "I'm not, you know . . . gay," he whispered, as he felt the unmistakable heat of Gary's passion radiating through the thin, shiny nun outfits.

"Really?" Gary laughed gently, and planted a kiss on Marty's lips. More, Gary's tongue probed forward, parting Marty's unresisting lips. It was a long kiss too, and Marty even moaned a little as his friend's tongue began to work round his mouth. They broke after what seemed an age.

"Uh . . . Gary . . . What do we do now?"

"What do people do who wanna fuck?" responded the young man in black plastic, eyes twinkling.

"They fuck," said Marty, barely above a whisper. "But we can't. I mean, what if Sean finds a ladder and comes back?"

"He will in about two hours. Even the dork knows where I put the ladder ready."

"So he's in on this too?"

"Not like this. Not yet anyway," whispered Gary, and kissed his friend again. Open-mouthed, just as long, just as passionately as before and this time Marty used his tongue too, including a little bite on Gary's tongue. A gesture returned that bit harder. Then Gary turned the nun in red plastic round, pushed him easily into a bending position and slid Marty's habit up to his waist. He gave his bending friend a small but sharp slap on the young man's smooth arse. "Ready or not, sister, I'm coming," he said quietly and hauled up his own habit to let his thick cock spring free.

"I've never done this before," said Marty and then gave a small cry as Gary's hard cock pressed against his exposed anus. The tight, puckered entrance resisted for a moment and then began to give way. "Don't hurt me," he managed to say and gave another, louder gasp as the first fraction of Gary's hard prick entered him.

"It's OK, it won't hurt if you relax," said Gary. "I lubed up when you weren't looking. Don't worry, the plastic won't show the stains."

"I'm not worried. Only . . . next time, Gary, can I wear a red basque to go with my dress, please?"

"If you're a good nun," said the nun in black plastic. He began smoothly and steadily pumping his hard cock in and out of his friend's relaxing rear hole, hearing the rasp of his stockings on Marty's fishnet-covered legs and the gasps from the bending young man. He gave Marty's bum another slap, called him a whore and then the Mother Superior drove in harder, deeper and faster.

Gary would have come in his friend's arse if the shop door hadn't clicked open. He froze, cock lodged halfway inside his friend's rectum. Marty for his part gave a small gasp, and not one of pleasure, though he didn't move from his bending position. Although they were hidden by racks of clothes, whoever it was who had come in was sure to look round if they heard a noise. Gary kept quite still and Marty did too. Even Gary's impressive cock in his friend's rear began to wilt a little.

"Whoever is there," said a man's voice, "you can come out now. Unless you are busy." The man chuckled.

Gary shot a scared look at his friend. His plastic habit creaked as he moved his head and he wished he had kept still.

"Look," sighed the man. "I know you are here and I know there are two of you. I can also imagine you are dressed up, right?"

"Yes," said Marty, realizing that if this was the shop owner he was about to call the police. "But we can explain."

"Really?" The man came round the end of the clothes rack that had screened the two young men. He was older than the fetish-clad nuns but not much older. He stared at the motionless pair and then laughed. "You know, it's funny how men go for the nun look. You'd be surprised how popular. Almost as popular as women's underwear. Basques especially, with stockings."

"Back off! We've got friends. Dangerous friends," Gary said sharply, trying to be tough.

"That surprises me. I mean, I thought you got everything you wanted from each other. Shared interest, cross-dressing, anal sex . . . You *were* having sex, weren't you, when I interrupted?

Never mind. You in the red, you can straighten up now. I think the one in black has finished with you." The man paused. "Was he good?"

"Don't know. He didn't finish," said Marty.

"Not my fault!" Gary glared at Marty, then calmed. "You gonna call the cops, mister?"

"Call me Jake. Oh, I could. As I can see there is criminal damage as well as breaking and entering. Also threats against me. Something about dangerous mates I believe you said." Jake took out his mobile phone. "Three nines, isn't it?"

"Please ... Gary was joking," said Marty. "Look, we're harmless. This was just for a laugh, and we're sorry. We'll pay for the window. And the clothes. But we didn't get anything on them. Honest."

"Gary, the one in black?" Jake nodded. "And who are you in red?"

"Marty," came the response.

"Well, Marty, it isn't just the damage, and yes the outfits do clean up nicely. I sometimes think all the clothes I hire out should be in plastic, given what young men do in them. Drinking, throwing-up, having sex with each other. Oh, don't look so surprised! There is something about a man in uniform that tips women into wanting sex and apparently a lot of men too."

The two friends stood, heads hanging in shame at all this, but Marty looked up. "We won't make trouble. We will be regular customers," he said. "If that helps."

"So you can fuck each other senseless while dressed as women?"

Marty looked embarrassed. "I don't think I get to fuck," he said and looked sideways at Gary.

"Go on, admit it, Gary," said Jake. He still had his phone in his hand, thumb poised over the keypad.

Gary looked alarmed but he nodded. "I thought I'd be the one who did it," he admitted, quietly.

"That's not exactly fair is it, Gary?" Jake shook his head. "Life is about give and take, I always say. Giving and receiving."

"You don't mind us having sex?" Marty seemed suddenly alert. Jake raised an eyebrow at the nun in red plastic and waited for him to continue. "Um, I mean, Jake ... You saw what we were doing and you didn't scream or call the police then. You're OK with us doing it."

Jake shrugged but didn't say anything. His thumb had moved from above the keypad on his phone.

Marty took a deep breath and pressed on. "Anyway, how did you know there were two of us here?"

Jake smiled. "I came across a young man struggling with a long ladder at the back of the shops. He didn't look like a window cleaner. I asked him what he was doing and he said he was trying to rescue his two friends in a shop. Naturally, I thought of my place."

"Where's Sean now?" Gary wanted to know.

"Poor Sean. He looked quite lost, if I'm honest. I gave him ten quid and, providing he told me some addresses, he could bugger off. He did, and now I have three local addresses. I checked with a few phone calls, and they're genuine."

Marty nodded. "Then you know where we live and who we are. OK, what do you want with us?"

Jake grinned. "I wondered when you'd catch on. Right, this is what I want." The man put his phone away. "You will let me fuck you both, in my storeroom. No doubt you've tried the door but couldn't get in. Well, I have the key and you can go in there with me and let me do what I want to you."

Gary gulped and blushed. "You . . . You fuck us both?" he asked.

"That's what I was getting to. I get to choose what you wear in there, you both get to bend over and do whatever I want."

"And in return you don't call the police, or tell our families," said Marty.

"Pretty much," said Jake.

"You want us dressed as women," said Gary.

"My, you do catch on fast," laughed Jake. "Oh, and I didn't tell you. I will be filming you having sex, just so I can enjoy it later."

"That's blackmail," said Marty.

"Nope, blackmail is when I do something with it to gain money or influence. As you probably have neither, the little movies are for my own pleasure. Later, of course."

Gary and Marty exchanged a long look before Marty spoke.

"What about Sean, our friend? He knows what Gary was going to do to me."

"The would-be ladder carrier? If you can persuade him to join in another time, then fine. For now, you two cross-dressing nuns will be enough for today."

"That suggests there'll be other times. How often is this going to happen?" Marty wanted to know.

"Good question. Every Sunday. Plus bank holidays if you are good."The man produced a key and went to open the storeroom door. "Oh, and try not to be too surprised by what you see in here. I think you'll find it's all for my pleasure. You might even get to enjoy it too."

"So what did they say, Uncle, when they got in here?" The younger of the two men – the one in the starched white nurse's uniform – looked up from the double bed to the profusion of whips and chains and handcuffs adorning the walls. "I bet they were gobsmacked."

The older of the two men lying entwined on the bed chuckled. "They were. They would have hightailed it and run if they could have but, well, a promise is a promise. I'd promised them fun and sex and the chance to wear more clothes from the shop. Naturally, they took it."

"Like me." The younger male grinned and licked his lips seductively.

"Like you, Nephew."

"So you got to fuck them both. Did Marty get to fuck Gary?"

"Yep. They screwed each other, then I screwed them, then they used their mouths on each other's dick and on mine and I captured it all on tape. When I've edited the movie you can watch the highlights of two plastic nuns having the time of their lives."

"And you chained them up too, like you do to me?"

"Yeah. I needed to recover so I lay here on the bed while they stood by the wall, chained with hands over their heads.You know what I'm like."

The nurse-clad young man laughed and nodded. He moved as much as his handcuffs would allow and wriggled deeper into the older man's arms. The naked man let him get more comfortable and then reached for the hem of the nurse's white skirt. He hooked it up to reveal stocking tops and taut black suspenders as well as a stiff cock. He put his hand on the hard penis and teased it gently.

"Please, Uncle, make me come," pleaded the handcuffed nurse.

"In a short while," sighed the older man. "It never does for you to get too much too soon."

"You want me to play stupid, like I do with the others?"

The older of the two males laughed and gave the nurse's erect cock a sharp slap, which brought a good-natured groan from the younger one. "Naughty nurse, knowing my weakness. No, not now. Later, when I fuck you then I want you to play the gormless kid."

"That'd be wonderful," said the nurse and wriggled in closer.

"It's the least I can do after what you did. Getting me two new fucks means you get to have a reward too. I thought one Sunday you might like to be the mysterious masked Wonder Woman who gets to fuck my two new slaves."

"And they won't know who I am?"

"'Course not! But they won't be in a position to object much anyway if they are gagged and tied, bent over the padded horse over there with their whipped bums on display. I think they can wear naughty maid outfits, with lots of frilly petticoats and oh-so-short skirts."

The nurse gurgled a laugh, and then caught his breath as the naked man began to rapidly stroke the rod-like cock. "Please, let me come now," the nurse whispered. "I'll do anything."

"I know you will, Sean. Time to come hard for your Uncle Jake."

Wet Nurse

Landon Dixon

Blossom could hardly bear it. She desperately wanted to bear it – babies that is, lots of them – but her husband, Greg, was both sterile and impotent. Sterile due to physiological factors; impotent as a result of psychological issues. So, Blossom could barely stand it.

She'd always felt that she'd be a good mother. And so she'd married Greg in the expectation that they would have a large family one day. But five years into their wedded bliss, nature intervened with a plan of its own.

Blossom's hormones started raging and her breasts started swelling, then leaking. Suddenly, the attractive young woman was full of mother's milk, jumping from a B to a D cup – a damp D cup. Her mental desire to give birth had manifested itself overtly physically. She was wet all the time, up top and down below, her breasts prepped and percolating.

Greg tried to accommodate his wife's dripping need. But after three months of concerted effort and exertion, the futile results came back from their family doctor that while Blossom was a lush, fertile body of baby-making capabilities, Greg was as sterile as a dried-up desert water hose.

The news had been devastating for both of them, but even more so for Greg. He wasn't particularly partial to Rubenesque women. He'd liked, loved Blossom slim and trim and small-breasted. He hardly recognized his moon-faced, well-endowed wife any more. It was almost like she was already pregnant, no thanks to him – a constant reminder of his own infertility. It all combined to render Greg impotent. He couldn't even make love to his bursting-with-life-and-love wife any more.

Turning what should've been a wonderful situation from bad to worse was the fact that the couple couldn't adopt a child, either. Blossom wanted, needed a baby to suckle at her overloaded breasts, relieve both the physical and emotional tensions that were driving her wild mood swings and crazy food choices. But her husband was saddled with a criminal record thanks to his chequered past, and thus they couldn't, by law, adopt a child.

The sticky situation looked hopeless. Greg became withdrawn and sullen, hardly wanting to be around his wife any more. While Blossom alternately cried and laughed constantly, the woman tottering on the thin line of hysteria, her enormous breasts adding to the seemingly insoluble problem of keeping her upright and functioning.

And then the solution came to her, out of the clear blue sky, in the most unlikeliest of places – a discount chain store parking lot. It was a warm, bright spring day, and Blossom was bubbling over with joie de vivre and breast juice. She was dressed in a white top and white pants, white sneakers, wearing a white cap with a red St George's Cross on her head.

She parked her car and stepped out into the sunshine, then threw back her arms and stretched with delight. Her tight clothing stretched with her, straining mightily to contain the twin mammoth mounds thrusting out from her chest, the almost equally large, rounded hills pushing out at her back below the waist. A man wheeling a shopping cart brimming with pet food stopped cold twenty feet away from Blossom, staring at the blazing-white, stunning display of voluptuous womanhood and verging motherhood.

He let go of his shopping cart, and it wobbled slowly away. His eyes were locked on Blossom, on her beaming face and burgeoned body. He was drawn to her by a force that he couldn't control – a breast man to a pair of more-than-ample boobs.

"Do you know you're leaking?" he asked politely, pointing with his finger at Blossom's chest.

She abruptly dropped her arms at her sides and looked down at her overhanging breasts. "Oh, no," she sighed, seeing the familiar twin wet spots staining her tight white T-shirt. Even her bulging bra couldn't soak up the overflow.

"Oh, yes," the man breathed, openly gaping at Blossom's breasts, watching in wonder as the discs of damp at her pointed nipples expanded right before his eyes. "You look beautiful," he murmured. "I envy your husband and children."

Blossom didn't consider that last comment rude at all, but it did cut her to the quick. She lowered her head and shrugged her shoulders, making her breasts (and the man's agog eyeballs) surge up and down. "I don't have any babies," she whispered.

The man wore a cowboy hat and denim shirt and jeans, snakeskin cowboy boots. He was a local car dealer, persuasive in business but henpecked at home. He had two dogs, and his wife had a menagerie of cats, but no children. He was middle-aged, slightly chubby but jovial, with a strong chin and tanned face and bright blue eyes.

Now, he stepped closer to Blossom and, still staring at her tits, said, "Name's Willard. Could I be your . . . baby – for a while?"

Blossom jerked her head up so fast her chest humped, her nipples oozing more nurturing liquid with the friction. She'd never considered *that* solution to her problem before.

She looked at the man looking at her boobs. And her breasts shimmered in the sunlight with even more feeling, her always jutting nipples almost busting right through the constraining white Lycra of her heavy-duty bra under her T-shirt. "You . . . You'd be my . . . baby?" she gasped, her pussy tingling in her panties.

Willard glanced up at her face, briefly. "Yes. For a fee." He stared back down at her wet T-shirt, Blossom's nipples sticking out almost straight into his widened eyes, so it seemed. "You look just like a nurse dressed up like that – a wet nurse." He added shyly but expressively, "Could I . . . nurse on you?"

Blossom clasped her hands together and leapt to her toes, exulting at the proposition. Then she rushed into the man and threw her arms around him, her hands almost meeting at the back, her breasts piling up against and almost bowling Willard right over. He hugged her tight, equally ecstatic.

Willard led Blossom over to his white Hummer parked thirty feet further down the lot, his eyes glued to Blossom's breasts as they bounced and bobbed, and bubbled. The man's shopping cart drifted out into the traffic of the highway beyond, completely forgotten.

They scrambled up into the spacious back leather bench seat of the Hummer. The vehicle's windows were heavily tinted, so nobody could see inside. Willard scooched all the way over against the far door to make room for Blossom and her breasts. And then he gaped with renewed awe, as she quickly pulled up her twin-peaked T-shirt and peeled it right over her head.

Blossom's cap came off with her shirt. She shook out her short dark hair and flung her T-shirt and cap into the front seat of the vehicle. Her bared breasts bounded out into the open, the dampness at the protruding tips broadening from coaster to compact disc-sized. She was bursting with excitement, elated by the prospect of having someone finally suck on her breasts, eager to nurse a "baby", of sorts. She jumped her arms back and wrestled with the fatigued hook holding her bra together.

But Willard stopped her, reaching out and grabbing onto her shoulders, gently but firmly pulling her arms back around. Then he retrieved Blossom's stretched-out-of-shape white T-shirt and her red-crossed cap from the front seat, handed them back to her. "You look just like a nurse," he repeated, staring at her breasts. "A wet nurse."

Blossom instantly and instinctively understood, as only a wannabe mother can. She squirmed back into her T-shirt, but left the hem up above her breasts. Then she screwed her cap back on and popped her left bra cup down, allowing a beating, wet-nosed boob to spill out into the stuffy air. She took Willard's hand and drew his head into her lap, fed her thick, red, milk-dappled nipple into the man's open mouth.

Blossom cried out and shuddered when she felt the hot, wet, strong tug of Willard's sealing lips on her overburdened tit. She'd craved this so long; it felt so glorious – a mouth suckling hardily on her swollen nipple, drawing milk out of her swollen breast. She surged with pleasure from head to toe, shimmering body and soul with the sweet, strange sensation of her rich, delicious milk being sucked out of her boob by her baby.

She cradled Willard's head in the crook of her left arm, reached down with her right hand and grasped the rigid outline of the sprawled-out man's cock in his jeans. It seemed the most natural thing in the world – tugging on his erection while he sucked on her boob. As natural as sex or childbirth, or breastfeeding. Getting and giving pleasure, lusty woman and needful adult baby.

That first session didn't last long. Both Willard and Blossom were too keyed up by the sheer spontaneity of the nursing event. Willard quickly spasmed and bit into Blossom's spouting nipple, his cock going off in her warm, maternal, stroking hand. Blossom gasped and spasmed herself, the combination of the man suckling her breast and his elbow pressing into her clit setting her off like she'd never experienced before. The Hummer shook on its stiffened suspension, Blossom's milk-laden tits giving birth to ecstasy for both her and her "client".

Willard plucked two hundred dollars out of his wallet and gave the money to Blossom, as he wiped off his mouth and watched her re-bra the gleaming nipple and glowing mass of her motherly breast.

Willard was the first of "Nurse" Blossom's babies. He'd showed her the way, the solution to all of her problems – physical, emotional and monetary. While her husband was away at his low-paying fry cook job, Blossom opened up a "nursery" in the spare bedroom of their modest home. Greg figured it was just another manifestation of his wife's maternal obsession and didn't give it a second thought.

But he didn't see Blossom in her crisp, starched, white nurse's uniform: white low-heeled shoes, snow-white stockings, ruffled thigh-high white skirt, tight white collared blouse, and white cap with red cross on the front. Nor was he witness to the steady stream of nervous but determined men who showed up at the back door of the house and were ushered inside and down the hall into the "maternity ward", to be ministered by wet nurse Blossom and her enormous, milk-bloated breasts.

Blossom soon had a string of adult babies on the side, married and unmarried men thirsty for her tits, she hungry for their mouths. Both parties perversely benefited, Blossom lucratively, the babies liquidly. Her bank account and their lust were nourished. And for Blossom, the added benefit of her wet pastime was the joy she both gave and received, her raging nipples, clit and hormones sending every session over the top, setting loose more than just her hot breast juices flowing.

Diapering, wiping, spanking, cuddling, bouncing and burping were all extras, of course.

Two of Blossom's favourite babies were Jim and Evan. The cute redheads really looked like twins, although actually they were just college room-mates and close friends. They did everything together, including visiting wet nurse Blossom to indulge in their passion for a mother's warm touch and taste.

The first time, Blossom wondered if maybe she'd taken on too much, even for her ample equipment. But she was more than willing in spirit and spigot to try to feed the two babies at once, as they desired.

She plopped down in the middle of the leather couch in the nursery, in her uniform; then watched as the two boys excitedly stripped off their T-shirts and shorts. They wanted to be as naked as "newborn babes", and Blossom had no objections. In fact, she admired their lean, smooth bodies and their hard, bobbing cocks, as she slowly opened up her blouse and pulled down her bra.

Jim and Evan stared at Blossom's huge, creamy-white breasts and fat, rosy-red nipples, stroking their cocks. Blossom leaked at the turgid tips, eagerly putting on a show in appreciation of the show she was getting.

The men dropped down on the couch on either side of her. And with nothing more than her mothering instincts and perverted natal lusts to guide her, Blossom arranged the two babies so that both of their red heads lay in her lap, while their nude bodies and upright cocks stretched away on the couch on either side of her.

She'd had babies fondle her free breast before, squirt milk out of the jutting tip with their squeezing hands as they sucked on her other engorged tit; but she'd never had two babies feed on her two breasts at the same time. So Blossom shivered and gasped, when Jim and Evan sealed their plush lips tight to her nipples and then vigorously pulled.

It was exquisite, amazing. She was quickly awash in sensation as her babies were in milk. Her brimming breasts and pussy surged, the heavy, heated twin tug on her tits making her head spin and body shimmer.

She only wished she had more breasts, could feed more

babies. She contented herself, and thrilled her two babies by reaching out and grasping the pair of throbbing cocks sticking out from Jim and Evan's ginger-pubed groins. They jerked, biting into Blossom's nipples ever so briefly. Then they happily, gloriously gorged again, gulping great mouthfuls of milk straight from the teat, as Blossom jacked their cocks in perfect rhythm.

Blossom's chest burned, her breasts blazing, her mouth-sunk nipples flaming. She pumped the pair of cocks faster and harder, to match the urgent pull on her tits, the gush of milk from her nipples. And her babies sensed her excitement, wriggling with theirs. They bobbed their red heads in Blossom's lap, rubbing her swelled-up clit with their pressing curls. Blossom spread her legs wider and pulled on the two cocks with the superhuman strength of a truly aroused mother.

Her babies jerked in her lap and on the couch, semen spraying out of their cocks into the air, to the torrid tug of her hands. They inhaled as much massive tit as they could in their ecstasy and sucked with pneumatic intensity, milking marvelled Blossom like a pair of machines. She screamed and arched, spasmed, utter and udder joy exploding in her overwhelmed pussy and breasts. Nurse Blossom turning wetter than any wet nurse has a right to be. Her babies squirting up their sheer delight.

Blossom had never been happier – with her life, her work and, yes, even her marriage. Greg's sterility had given birth to more babies than she could ever have imagined nursing, more gushing joy than any woman and mother had a legal right to. And when he closed his eyes and she gave him a handjob, Blossom could still provide a dry-fuck to her loving husband's satisfaction.

Room 8

Nicole Wolfe

She thought it would pass, but it only got worse with each mile.

Sheila was trying to get to Tulsa, but a detour and a washout had led her to a long stretch of Route 66 that no one had repaved since the eighties. She had seen the storm coming, but didn't think it looked that bad and she was in her Range Rover after all.

The clouds stretched over her like the hand of Thor in just a few miles and a wall of water almost sent her off the road before the Rover regained its footing. She flipped on the radio. There were tornado warnings for three counties, but she had no idea if she was in one of them or driving into another.

The wind lashed at the Rover and the sound of falling hail drowned out the tornado warnings just as they'd announced a funnel cloud spotted on the ground. It was downright dangerous now. She hadn't seen a car for miles and that meant no one to help her if she wrecked.

She needed cover. A lightning flash illuminated a sign to her right. She yanked the steering wheel and cut a hard turn into the lot of the A.O.K. Motel – "Where Everything Is A-OK!"

She pulled up to the office, took off her seat belt, watched the rain, decided it wasn't going to stop, and then ran for it. It was only six running steps but she was almost soaked by then. The office door was stuck. The rain stung her neck. The thunder pounded her back.

She banged the door open with her shoulder and stumbled into the small lobby. It smelled of citronella and dust. The lightning outside was the only way to see anything.

"Hello?" she said even though she knew it was futile. No one had been there for decades.

The door whacked against the wall as the wind whipped in and chilled her wet legs. As she shut the door she noticed it hadn't been stuck. It had been locked and she'd broken the old doorframe when she'd rammed it with her shoulder. The office, despite the dust, was immaculate. The furniture was late seventies. The AAA calendar featured a couple smiling as they cruised in their 1976 Mustang. There was a rotary phone on the wall and an empty cigarette machine next to the check-in counter. The office behind the counter was empty apart from an old desk, copies of *National Geographic* from 1973, and a row of key hooks. Each of the fourteen hooks held a key to one of the fourteen rooms.

The thunder boomed. The office door flew open again and rain came in sideways. She knew getting back on Route 66 would court death. She looked at the motel layout on the office wall and saw rooms one and eight were on either side of the office. She remembered what happened in room one in *Psycho*. She took the key for room eight.

It was like unlocking a time capsule. The tan shag carpet still held its color. The air was stale but she was surprised at how little dust was in the room. The lone chair, its companion table, the nightstand and the bed were covered with sheets. Towels still hung on the bathroom rack and a small unopened bar of Dial was on the edge of the sink. She turned one of the taps and was rewarded with a dribble of rusty water.

She backed the Rover to the front of the room, receiving another soaking as she got her suitcase from it. She opened it once she was back in the room and sighed in relief when she found her clothes, toiletries and everything she'd brought for the lecture dry and neat.

Her wet shoes made sucking sounds as she pushed them off her pruned feet. She hung her dripping shirt, soaked bra and sponge-like jeans on the shower curtain rod. Her black thong was the only dry piece of clothing thanks to its tiny size.

She folded one of the towels dusty side down so she could dry her hair. She walked back into the main room as she rubbed her head and felt a sneeze building in her nose.

"What are you doing here?"

Sheila screamed. She hadn't seen the state trooper in the

doorway. She clutched the towel over her breasts and tried to focus on the trooper but he was silhouetted behind the piercing beam of the flashlight held over his left shoulder. His raincoat hung around him like an Old West duster and rain dripped off his plastic-wrapped campaign hat to the floor. His right hand held his gun, a wicked black semi-automatic, by his side.

"Ma'am, you'd better have a damn good reason to be in here."

"It's not what you think," Sheila said. "Really."

He, no, *she*, stepped into the room. She was a couple inches taller than Sheila and looked like she could pull a truck driver from his rig by his ear. Despite her strong presence, Sheila noticed feminine touches. The trooper had long eyelashes and freckles were spread out on her beautiful face. A delightful scent came from her, which mixed with the smell of the storm to produce something that warmed Sheila's belly.

"Ma'am, I'm going to handcuff you for your safety and mine until I figure out what's happening here. Drop the towel and put your hands on your head."

"But I didn't—"

"Drop that towel and put your hands on your head right now." Her voice was like a Doberman's growl.

Sheila obeyed. Her breasts perked up as the cool storm air swirled over them. Her bottom lip shook. She couldn't believe it. This was not how things worked in her world. She always did the handcuffing. She wasn't used to the metal on her wrists or her clit buzzing as the cuffs click-click-clicked shut.

"Have a seat on the edge of the bed," the trooper said. Sheila sat. "If you get up before I tell you, there's going to be trouble."

Sheila almost said, "Yes, ma'am," but caught herself. She wouldn't, couldn't, let that happen. How could *she* be trembling? Why were her thighs rubbing together? She was a professional dominatrix who taught classes on how to turn your mate into the sub they wanted to be. She made her living swatting men on the cock with a riding crop and putting chip bag clips on naughty housewives' nipples; and now this Oklahoma state trooper had her cuffed and shaking like a new bottom on her first day in a dungeon. Is this what her subs felt like when she walked in wearing her rubber cop outfit?

The trooper braced her gun hand atop her flashlight arm and

checked the bathroom and then under the bed. Once she was satisfied no one else was there, she stood in front of Sheila for what seemed like a full minute. Neither of them spoke. Sheila couldn't even if she wanted. A couple of drops of rain fell from the trooper's hat and onto Sheila's left foot.

"I have an out-of-state Range Rover outside, a broken office door and you making yourself cosy in a place where no one's stayed or worked in a long time," the trooper said. "This looks like it could be a burglary in progress."

Sheila found her voice. "No, no, no. I pulled in here to get out of the storm. I don't know my way around. I thought this place was open and the office door was stuck but I didn't know and I just wanted some place dry to sleep out the storm." Sheila groaned inside. She sounded like a little girl explaining how she'd broken a juice glass.

The trooper put her gun back in her raincoat pocket. Sheila heard the holster under the coat snap shut. The trooper looked around the room and saw the open bag.

Fuck! Sheila thought. *Everything's in plain view!*

Sheila tried to distract her. "How do I know you're a real cop?"

The trooper stopped cold. She turned in a slow half-circle. The movement oozed menace and made Sheila feel like she'd shrunk to the point where she could sit on a dime and swing her legs. The trooper popped open her metal-snapped raincoat in one Clark Kent-like motion that almost made Sheila soak her thong.

The trooper pointed to the equipment on her belt. "Real radio, real taser, real gun." She jutted her thumb at her shiny badge. "Real badge, real fucking cop. Trooper Lang of the Oklahoma State Police. Are you clear?"

Sheila was so hot, her pussy ached so badly, that she couldn't help it. "Yes, ma'am."

Sheila brought her eyes back up when she heard Lang ask, "What's all this?"

Lang stood next to Sheila's open bag and held the ball gag and Sheila's pair of handcuffs.

"It's my stuff for work," Sheila said as she looked back at the floor.

Lang pulled out the lube and the rippled butt plug. "This too?" Sheila nodded. Lang pulled out a handful of vibrators. "These?" Sheila nodded again while her knees bobbed out of control.

Lang found the thick blue strap-on. "And this? This is for work?"

"Yes," Sheila whispered.

Lang walked forward, tapping the strap-on in her hand like a truncheon. "What's your name, ma'am?"

"Sheila Neal." Her heart thumped at the bottom of her throat. She teetered between fear and excitement. Lang towered over her and slapped the strap-on into her hand. Sheila looked at Lang's boots as the tap-tap-tap of the toy cock in Lang's hand seemed louder than the rain, wind and thunder.

"Tell me something, Miss Neal," Lang said. She put the strap-on under Sheila's chin and tilted her head up to look at her. "Are you a bad girl?"

Oh God, she thought, *she's playing the game.*

"Yes," Sheila said. The word was a sweet release. Soft warmth rippled over her body and the look in her eyes changed from apprehension to eagerness.

Lang tapped Sheila's cheeks with the strap-on. "Do you have anything on you I need to worry about, Miss Neal?"

Sheila shook her head, but Lang grabbed her lower jaw and forced her mouth open. "Let's make sure."

She shoved the dildo into Sheila's mouth. She gave a brief muffled protest, but relaxed and let Lang stuff her cheeks and fuck her throat. Lang brought her to the point of gagging but backed off before things got dangerous. She slid the toy cock from Sheila's mouth, leaving her tongue out and drool hanging from her bottom lip.

"Get up and turn around," Lang ordered, as she tossed the dildo onto the bed. Sheila did as she was told. Lang pulled Sheila's thong down to her ankles and then shoved her forward onto the mattress. "I need to check everywhere."

Sheila knew what to do – face down and ass up. "Please, officer. I didn't do anything wrong."

Lang grabbed Sheila's damp hair and slid two fingers into her wet pussy. "Is that what you think? You think you're a good girl?

Are good girls burglars? Do good girls break into other people's property to fuck themselves?"

"N-No," Sheila said, as she pushed back on the fingers in her pussy and the thumb nudging her asshole. She looked back at Lang with the frightened doe eyes she'd seen from so many housewives, nurses, teachers and even a judge. "But I'm not—"

Lang cut off her protest with a hard spank. "Do you know how much trouble you're in? Do you know what I could do to you?"

She did, and the thought almost made her come.

"Do you know what those dykes would do to you in a women's prison? Do you know how many fists would be shoved in your cunt? How many asses would be on your pretty face? I can put you there anytime I want. Maybe you need a harder lesson, is that it?"

Sheila tried to say no, but it came out as a loud moan. Lang stood up and started removing her gun belt. Sheila played with her ass and slipped in a finger now and then, wanting to please Lang. The sound of each piece of clothing hitting the floor and the rip of Velcro on Lang's protective vest helped push Sheila's fingers deeper into her.

"Bring that cock over here," Lang said behind her.

A shudder ripped through Sheila as she looked back. Lang was naked in the chair with one leg draped over a chair arm. Her freckles were spread over her tits, arms and legs. She slowly fingered her pussy with one hand. She snapped with the other and pointed to a spot on the floor before her.

Sheila picked up the strap-on with her teeth and stood up. Lang almost came out of her chair. "On your knees," Lang said. "You might try to escape otherwise. Or was that your plan, bad girl?"

Sheila shook her head. She dropped to her knees and shuffled forward on the old, rough carpet. She wanted to run over there and rub her face and tits on Lang's cunt, but she knew that would bring trouble.

Lang stopped Sheila by putting a foot on her chest. She pinched Sheila's nipples with her toes. Sheila groaned. She wanted those toes in her mouth or . . .

Lang's foot dropped so her toes could play with Sheila's clit.

Sheila rocked her pussy on Lang's foot and whimpered for more.

"Do you know much pussy a pretty girl like you will be eating in prison? Do you want to be gang-banged in the shower? Do you want the guards to take you to the soundproof cell? Do you know what happens in there to pretty bad girls like you?"

Lang leaned forward and snatched the toy cock from Sheila's teeth. She let Sheila lick the sole of her foot and suck her come off her toes. Lang grabbed Sheila by the hair. Sheila winced.

"You'd better start practicing," Lang said. She pulled Sheila's face between her legs. Sheila sighed, delighted to be given such a treat. Lang held her head while Sheila licked her clit. She took her time. She wanted to spend the whole evening there.

Lang pulled her away. "You're pretty good at that," Lang said. "I think you've done this before, which makes me think you really are a bad girl. Are you, Miss Neal?"

Sheila pouted, gave her the sad puppy eyes, and then nodded.

Lang nodded back. "I thought so." She pulled Sheila back to her hot cunt and stroked her hair. "I'm glad we can come to this understanding. It's good that you can accept what has to happen, that bad girls get their asses punished."

Sheila whimpered into her. As delicious as Lang's pussy was, all she wanted now was to be spanked, fucked, or, preferably, both. Lang stood up and bent her over the chair. Sheila's shoulders tingled from her arms being behind her back for so long. She jumped as Lang slapped the head of the strap-on against her clit. She yelped as Lang's hand cracked her ass and the strap-on plunged into her from behind.

Lang held her by the hair and the handcuffs as she rode her hard. The back of the chair was against the wall, so Sheila couldn't escape. She was there as long as Lang wanted to have her.

Sheila felt the lube from her bag being drizzled on her ass. She shook her head a bit, still playing the game.

"Now, now," Lang said and then spanked her with a lube-slick hand. "You know what happens to bad girls."

Sheila's eyes clenched as a hot pressure built deep inside her cunt. Each inch Lang pushed into her ass cut her cries shorter and shorter. She was rigid and breathless by the time Lang had filled her ass. Lang leaned down, her warm tits pressing into

Sheila's back. She pinched Sheila's clit and licked the edge of her ear.

"OK, good girl. You can let go."

Sheila screamed into the chair. She squirted girl-come onto Lang's thighs and pushed back so hard that she forced Lang to sit on her heels.

Her arms were chilly. She realized the cuffs had been removed. She was on her belly on the floor. It was still raining, but she was wet with sweat, lube, and come instead of water. She rolled over a bit too quickly and had to focus to make out Trooper Lang back in full uniform and towering over her.

"You look tired, Miss Neal," she said.

Sheila nodded as she found her breath. "Yes. I'm worn out."

"I wouldn't want you to drive in this weather while you're tired, Miss Neal. I'm willing to believe you didn't realize this place wasn't open. You can sleep here tonight."

Sheila got to her feet but stumbled back to the chair. "Thank you. I think that's a good idea."

Lang bent down and kissed her. It was wonderfully gentle with little darts of her tongue on Sheila's lips. But then she yanked Sheila's head back by the hair, making her wince.

"But just tonight," Lang said. "I get off work at six and I drive by on my way home. I'm going to see if you're still here. If you are, there's going to be trouble for you, bad girl. Do you understand?"

"Yes," Sheila said. Lang left without looking back.

Sheila grabbed her BlackBerry and set her alarm clock. She could still smell their musk in the room.

She turned off the BlackBerry.

Basic Training

Lucy Felthouse

Kerry flopped onto the uncomfortable single bed with a relieved sigh. She'd survived yet another day of gruelling basic training, and was one step closer to being a fully fledged soldier in the British Army. And she'd do it, too, of that she had no doubt. She was too stubborn not to.

It helped that she and her room-mate, Adeline, were the sole females in the group. Granted, they took a lot of teasing from the lads, the occasional inappropriate comment, but the fact that the two of them were expected to be bottom of the class only made them more determined to claw their way to the very top. They'd worked harder, pushed harder with each consecutive task, until the boys had realized they were being left behind. The stupid remarks and borderline sexual harassment stopped, and were replaced with grunts and curses as they fought to keep up.

In the rare downtime they all had, the sarcastic comments, the barbs intended to wind her up, had been replaced by invites to dinner and grudging compliments. Turned out that even in this day and age, women in the Army – or trying to be – had to fight to be seen as equals. And now she'd gained respect, she was also gaining admirers.

Unfortunately for those admirers, though, they were barking entirely up the wrong tree. Kerry's preference was, and always had been, women. And, right at that moment, she kind of wished it wasn't. Her libido was reminding her of the lack of orgasms she'd had since starting the fourteen-week training course. At least if she liked men she'd have been able to take one of them up on their offer, sneak off somewhere and scratch that particular itch. But, as it was, she hadn't had so much as a solo climax in far too long, and her body was beginning to protest.

Maybe she could sneak one in now? She'd seen Adeline heading off in the opposite direction to their sparse, functional accommodation when they'd been dismissed. Perhaps she was off for some fun of her own with one of the guys. She'd had just as many propositions as Kerry – and they were just the ones she knew about. Between them, she supposed, they covered most bases in terms of what men found attractive. Where Kerry was tall and thin with small breasts and a mop of short brunette hair and brown eyes, Adeline was shorter, a little curvier with shoulder-length blonde hair and blue eyes. If there'd been a third girl in basic training that was a redhead, they'd truly have something for everyone.

Adeline was pretty cute, actually. Kerry had thought so as soon as they'd met, but had immediately pushed the thought out of her mind. Just because there was only one other girl around, one lot of eye candy, didn't mean she should start perving on her. Especially since they were room-mates. Inevitably, over the weeks, they'd seen each other in varying states of undress, and Kerry had done her best to avert her gaze every time Adeline was less than fully clothed. It had been tough, but she'd managed pretty well so far.

Still, as she lay on the thin duvet, resisting the temptation to undo her belt and stick her hand down her combats, slices of imagery popped into her head. Smooth buttocks, breasts that would fit perfectly in her palms, a neat dark blonde bush, lips to die for . . .

Ah, fuck it. Opening the mental floodgates, Kerry let the delicious pictures flow in, with her imagination doing a more than ample job of filling in the gaps. Soon, her imagination took over entirely, and she was vaguely aware of her hands releasing her regulation belt, undoing the button and fly and delving beneath the material, as her brain disappeared into Dirty Fantasy Central.

There, she and Adeline were kissing and groping, though the latter was hard work through the thick uniforms they wore. It was immediately clear that the camouflage gear had to go. Lips parted and they tugged and pushed at their garments until they were both naked. Then they reached for each other again, mouths meeting, breasts pressing together, hands wandering across bare skin.

Kerry couldn't keep a lid on her urges – after having a nice long squeeze of Adeline's delectable backside, she brought her hands around to touch those perfect tits. Cupping them, she quickly realized she'd been right about them fitting perfectly in her palms. Weighing and caressing them, she then paid attention to the pert nipples – small and pink beneath her fingers. Moans escaped the blonde's throat and were immediately swallowed into Kerry's mouth. She thrilled at the fact she was turning Adeline on, pleasing her, and after continuing to tease the other girl's nipples into hard points, she then moved on to her next prize.

Forcing herself not to rush, she cupped Adeline's breasts once more, then slowly stroked down her stomach, tracing its slight curve before dipping lower. Soon, wiry curls met her fingertips and she smiled against the blonde's lips as she prepared to touch the pussy she'd been fantasizing about for weeks—

"Hey, Kerry. Oh shit, sorry! I'll come back!"

Kerry hadn't heard the door to their room open, but she sure as hell heard Adeline's exclamation. Snatching her hand from her crotch so fast she probably got friction burns from the rough material of her combats, she resisted the temptation to wipe her wet fingers on the duvet. It'd only emphasize what she'd just been caught doing.

"Adeline! It's OK, come back!" She called out just before the door slammed closed. Pausing for a moment, she waited to see what would happen next, whether her room-mate had heard her.

Apparently, she had, as a couple of seconds later the door opened again and Adeline's head peeped through the gap. "I'm sorry, Kerry." She looked as embarrassed as Kerry felt.

"Get in here, Adeline. You've got nothing to apologize for."

As the other girl moved into the room, then turned and closed the door behind her, Kerry hurriedly put her clothes back to rights.

"I'm so sorry—"

"I should be the one apologizing—"

Their words mingled, then they both stopped speaking with an awkward laugh.

"Seriously," Kerry said firmly, running a hand through her hair, realizing too late it was the one she'd had down her trousers. Now her hair would smell of girl juices. Just as well a shower was next on her to-do list. "I'm the one that needs to say sorry. It's just it's been a while . . . if you know what I mean, and I was feeling a little antsy. I thought you'd gone off with one of the lads and wouldn't be back for a while. I should have locked the door. Sorry. I didn't mean to embarrass you."

Adeline's face screwed up into a frown, and Kerry tried not to notice the cute way the sides of her nose wrinkled up as she did. "Don't worry about it. I'm just sorry I interrupted you. You looked like you were having rather a nice time. And what do you mean, you thought I'd gone off with one of the lads?"

Now it was Kerry's turn to frown. OK, that wasn't the response she'd been expecting. Deciding to ignore the first part of what her room-mate had said, she answered her question, instead. "Well, I'm sure you're probably feeling pretty antsy, too, so I figured you'd gone off to, er, scratch the itch with one of the lads. God knows there's enough of them to choose from. And not one of them would turn you down."

"Ah, OK. I get you now. But you couldn't be more wrong. I wasn't with one of the lads. And I never will be, either."

"Hey, there's no need to be defensive. I wouldn't blame you if you had been."

"No, no." Adeline held up her hands in supplication. "You misunderstand me, sweetie. I'm not being defensive. I'm just saying, I won't be with any of them because they don't float my boat."

"You don't like squaddies? Or soon-to-be squaddies, anyway?"

"I like them fine. I just prefer them with different . . . equipment." She took a step closer to Kerry, whose brain suddenly started to piece things together.

Did she mean . . . ?

"I'm not talking guns, either," Adeline continued, moving right in front of Kerry now. "I'm talking breasts and a pussy, rather than a cock and balls. Do you understand what I'm saying?" She grabbed Kerry's wrist and brought her hand up to her mouth. The hand she'd been masturbating with.

"I . . . I . . . think so."

"You've gone all bashful on me, sweetie. Why? Just minutes ago you were frigging your clit like crazy and now you look like you want the ground to swallow you up. Tell me, what were you thinking about as you touched yourself?" Her warm breath had whispered over Kerry's fingers as she spoke. Fingers which no doubt smelled of Kerry's pussy.

Christ, why did she have to ask that! "Oh, er, nothing much," she lied.

"Tell me the truth, Kerry. Tell me what you were really thinking about and I'll suck your fingers. Taste your juices. You want me to taste them, don't you?"

Kerry's brain short-circuited. Her mouth went dry, and her brain refused to supply a single thing to her mouth. She nodded. Then, remembering what she'd been asked, she finally choked out, "You. I was thinking about you."

A wicked grin took over Adeline's lips, and a fresh bolt of lust coursed through Kerry's veins. She realized her knickers were wet, much wetter than she'd been while she'd been touching herself.

Blue eyes widening, Adeline opened her mouth and popped one of Kerry's fingers inside. Then she licked and sucked, slowly and deliberately, as if fellating a cock. Or that's what Kerry imagined one would do to a cock, anyway. She had no wish to find out.

Adeline's eyelids fluttered closed, and a hum vibrated around Kerry's finger. A pleasurable hum, if she wasn't mistaken. The deft tongue, warm mouth and soft lips continued to tease her relentlessly, until she was convinced she'd end up with a wrinkly finger pad, like she'd been in the bath for too long. Not that she cared – she'd put up with a great deal more than wrinkly pads for Adeline.

Suddenly, the blonde popped Kerry's finger from her mouth and grinned again. "You taste delicious." Then she stuck Kerry's middle digit between her lips and repeated the process.

Kerry didn't think it was even possible, but still she grew

steadily wetter as the girl she'd been wanking over just minutes before licked her pussy juices from her hand. Her labia and clit filled with blood, getting heavier and heavier, until they throbbed and ached with the need to be touched. The need to come.

"Please . . ." Kerry hardly realized the word came from her until Adeline's eyes narrowed and she stopped what she was doing.

"Please what?" she asked, dropping Kerry's hand and raising an eyebrow. "What do you want, sweetie?"

Kerry could tell by Adeline's tone and body language that she was willing to play around, draw this out if she couldn't answer the question directly. So, clenching her fists for strength, she gave a tight smile, then said, "I want you, Adeline. I've wanted you since we met. I want us both to get naked and fuck until we're exhausted. Then do it all over again."

Adeline's response was to turn and walk towards the door.

Kerry's heart dropped into her boots. Seriously? All that teasing was just that . . . teasing? Fucking bitch! She opened her mouth to let some vitriol spill forth when she realized the blonde had flipped the lock, then spun on her heel again.

"So," Adeline said, "I really like the sound of that. Now I've made sure we won't be disturbed, shall we have some more fun?"

Kerry couldn't help the grin that spread across her face. She probably looked like the Cheshire cat, but she didn't care. Not only was she going to get off in the near future, she was going to get off with the hottest girl she'd met in ages.

Screw the shower – tasting Adeline's pussy was next on her to-do list. "Sounds good to me, gorgeous. Now let's get out of these uniforms!"

The only sounds for the next few moments were their breaths, the occasional low grunt as they pulled and tugged at their camouflage gear, and thumps as the heavy material hit the thin carpet. Their underwear quickly joined their uniforms, discarded on the floor, then there was a second of silence.

"Your bed or mine?" Kerry said quickly, eager to move things along.

"Doesn't matter," Adeline chuckled, "they're both crap! I just hope they can hold up under the strain."

"I'd say we'll take it easy . . ." Kerry tailed off, letting her wide smile finish the sentence for her.

"No—" the blonde shook her head, stepping forward "—lets not take it easy. Not at all." Reaching out, she gave a gentle shove, and Kerry let herself fall backwards onto her bed. The cheap bedcovers didn't feel nice against her skin, but she barely noticed as Adeline pulled the tie out of her hair, letting the blonde tresses tumble down around her shoulders. Then she joined her on the narrow mattress and moulded her delicious body against Kerry's.

Tangling her fingers into Adeline's soft blonde hair, Kerry used it to tug the other girl's face to hers. Their breath mingled briefly, whispering across their lips, then Kerry moved in for another kiss. It was slow, tentative at first, then, as they relaxed and hormones took over, things heated rapidly.

Kerry tickled at Adeline's lips with her tongue, coaxing them open and delving in immediately when they did. She sought Adeline's tongue, and they swept sensuously together, twining and fighting, then breaking away to explore the other's mouth.

With her free hand, Kerry enjoyed Adeline's body. Mentally, she'd already played with the blonde's perfect breasts and arse, but the reality was so much better. Eager tits jutted towards her, the nipples poking out further still, begging to be played with. Kerry was more than happy to oblige. She continued kissing Adeline as she pleasured her, stroking and pinching at the pert globes, figuring out what she liked, what made her moan. Quickly, she ascertained that the rougher she was, the more sounds she coaxed from Adeline's throat.

Shoving a thigh between the blonde's legs, she smiled as Adeline immediately began rubbing herself against it, covering Kerry's skin in hot pussy juice, and plenty of it. God, could this woman be any sexier?

Continuing to alternate between Adeline's breasts, Kerry was painfully aware of the increase in her own needs. It wasn't as though Adeline was just lying there and taking what she was given, but it was difficult to give and take pleasure without a crazy tangle of limbs. Instead, she'd cupped Kerry's face with one hand, and the other stroked the thigh and buttock she could reach, occasionally dipping into her crack when movement allowed. As a result, Kerry's own arousal had gone onto a slow burn while she put her energies into turning her lover on.

Now, though, she was ready for more. So much more. Pulling away from the kiss, she landed a sharp slap on Adeline's thigh. Then, with one short phrase, she indicated exactly what she wanted to happen next.

"Sixty-nine." It wasn't a question, either. And nor did Adeline answer it. Instead, she followed Kerry's lead and shuffled into the centre of the mattress as the brunette flipped around so she was facing the foot of the bed. Some quick manoeuvring later and they were ready.

Kerry pulled in a deep breath in advance of burying her face between Adeline's legs. Her nostrils were assaulted by the blonde's scent, so abundant, musky, mouth-watering, that she couldn't help herself. Resting her weight on her forearms, she nuzzled Adeline's thighs apart and began to feast on what was between them. Tart juices exploded over her taste buds, making her moan. God, she tasted even better than she smelled.

It wasn't easy to concentrate on what she was doing, given that for every lick, suck and nibble, she was being licked, sucked and nibbled right back. Her pussy was a mass of swollen heat, and with every passing second she felt her orgasm grow closer. Eager to ensure Adeline came first, or at the very least, at the same time as her, she upped her game.

Working her tongue, lips and jaw, she ate Adeline's perfect pussy as though her life depended on it. Gratifyingly, the blonde's clit and labia swelled further beneath her ministrations. Her wriggles and moans, and the copious liquid seeping from her core indicated she was perhaps closer to climax than Kerry had first thought. Damn, she so wanted Adeline to come all over her face.

She didn't have to wait long. The two girls teased and tormented each other, their grunts, gasps and moans filling the room, growing louder and more frequent. Kerry was teetering on the very edge, tingles radiating out from her clit and filling her entire body with a pleasant buzzing sensation.

Making sure Adeline's clit, massively swollen, was covered in plenty of girl juice and saliva for lubrication, she pulled it between her lips and began to suck, hard. There was a strangled yelp from the head of the bed, then Adeline mirrored her actions.

It became a race – each girl sucking on the other's distended bud, waiting to find out who would come apart first.

Whether it was because she'd had a head start with the masturbation and the filthy fantasy, or because she could still hardly believe she was having sex with the woman she'd lusted over for weeks, Kerry won the race. Bucking and rocking on Adeline's face, she tumbled into orgasm, her body overtaken by spasm, her cunt grasping wildly at nothing. Bliss radiated out of every pore, but she didn't stop sucking on Adeline's clit. Her moans had no doubt added extra frisson to what she was doing, and the blonde's climax followed soon after hers.

Hot liquid gushed from Adeline's pussy, and Kerry hurriedly released her clit and shifted down to gather it all up, or as much as she could, anyway. Her lips and tongue slurped and swiped happily at the come, delighting in the taste and the arousal that had caused it. She could stay between Adeline's thighs forever, she decided, worshipping at the altar of her cunt. Fucking perfection.

Just then, there came a series of bangs on the door.

Jerking apart, the girls looked at each other worriedly. Had someone heard them?

"Ladies, rendezvous in the yard in five! Looks like we're going on another exercise."

"Roger that!" Kerry yelled quickly in response. "We'll be there!"

"Shit!" Adeline said, scurrying off the bed and all but diving into the piles of clothes on the floor. "That was close. Good job he didn't turn up a few seconds before, he might have heard us."

Joining Adeline in the race to get dressed, Kerry couldn't help but grin. "Maybe he did. Maybe he's now got sexy Sapphic fantasies stored in his wank bank."

Adeline laughed. "Yeah, probably. Well, you know what I reckon?"

"What?"

Grabbing the lapel of the jacket Kerry now wore, Adeline tugged her in for a quick kiss. "I reckon we should continue this later. Never mind *his* Sapphic fantasies. Let's live out some of our own."

Driven To Distraction

Jamie Hiddler

Looking in the mirror, I saw a picture of crisp perfection. Peaked cap spotless and precisely level (no jaunty angles at Charmaine Chauffeurs). Make-up understated but feminine, without the slightest smudge. Sea-green suit jacket with polished brass buttons over a freshly pressed white blouse and loose black silk necktie. Even my normally unruly golden-brown hair was tamed into a short ponytail.

Stepping back, I ran my eyes down my matching skirt – knee length, with just enough side slit to aid getting into and out of the car. Not a single wrinkle or stray hair or speck of lint to mar the smooth green cloth. Stockings snag-free and demurely dark, too – what little of them could be seen between the hem of my skirt and the top of my sensible black chauffeur boots (themselves gleaming with half an hour's elbow grease).

God, how I loved this uniform. It had been a major part of the appeal when – after the taxi firm I worked for had gone bust – I had stumbled on this vacancy. Dressing smart made me feel sexy. And that was without the fact that today I was going without bra or panties, my stockings ending in laced garters and suspenders.

I opened a wooden jewellery box and took out a gold name badge with leather-gloved hands, clamping it over the slit of my chest pocket. "Kirsty" it read, above the company name Charmaine Chauffeurs and our logo of a winged wheel.

I stood smartly, with hands clasped behind my back, shoulders back, chin and chest out as I took a last look at myself in the mirror. Flawless. I'd truly outdone myself today. The picture of elegant service, imperturbable and professional. Though inside

I was shaking. After all, today I was driving Mr Gaitsbury. My pussy moistened at the thought of what he might do to me. Last time it had been all tease, with just a little "accidental" body contact. This time . . .

I hurriedly stamped down on the incipient daydream. It wouldn't do to break into a sweat and ruin my make-up. I left the drivers' changing room and headed out to the car, nodding to Gary the scheduler as I picked up my job pack on my way through the office. I'd given Mr Gaitsbury's Merc the once-over an hour ago, so of course it started first time, purring like a contented pussycat as I drove out towards the airport.

He was standing at the side exit of the airport hotel, exactly as noted in my job pack. I checked my reflection in the mirror as I pulled up. The tiny smudge of engine oil – which I'd applied to my cheek with a cotton bud at a motorway service station – was still there, as was the strand of blonde hair I'd placed so carefully on my chest. He did like to have something to fuss over. I opened the door and climbed carefully out, making sure not to show too much leg (yet), then stood smartly beside the rear door, opening it for him as he approached.

"Good morning, Mr Gaitsbury." My voice was level – pleasant without being obsequious. "I trust your flight was a smooth one?"

He halted in front of me as a hotel porter lifted his suitcase into the boot. He smiled. Then his smile turned to a frown as he spotted the smudge on my cheek.

"Oil, Kirsty?" he reprimanded me. "I am glad to see you've been taking care of my car while I've been away, but you really should clean yourself up better before you come out. What if you had got some on the upholstery?" As he spoke, he took out a monogrammed handkerchief and rubbed my cheek clean, pinching the skin hard. I gritted my teeth to stop myself from wincing.

Then his eyes fell to my chest, and the long blonde hair placed so prominently there. Making sure his back blocked his actions from anyone else entering or leaving the hotel, he ran the back of one finger down the slope of my chest, coming to rest on the offending filament.

"Whose is this?" he asked, mock-accusingly, holding up the hair for my inspection. "I hope you haven't been messing around with other people – other women no less – in my car?"

Of course I hadn't. The hair had been stolen from my flatmate's hairbrush. But I tried to sound contrite. "I'm sorry, sir," I said. "I'll have your car valeted if you wish."

"No need for that," he replied. "I shall check it over myself, though, and if I find a single stray hair . . ." His hand slipped round behind me to pat my behind with palm flat and firm, making it clear what my punishment would be. I silently cursed myself for not having thought to plant a few more hairs between the seat cushions to make sure I got it good and proper.

But first, work. Mr Gaitsbury stepped back and I ushered him into his seat, closing the door then turning to tip the porter.

Back in the driving seat, I tipped the rear-view mirror to catch his eye.

"Kingsdee Business Centre," he instructed me. "Building C."

"Yes, sir," I replied. I eased the handbrake down, and we were off.

Kingsdee Business Centre was forty miles away. He spent most of the time sorting through papers in his briefcase, though every now and then he looked up and caught my eye in the rear-view mirror.

Halfway into the journey he abruptly leaned forward and threw a glossy magazine onto the front passenger seat, so that it landed open there, right beside me. Even before I glanced down I knew what I would see – and I was right: the magazine had fallen open at a full-page photograph of a brunette in a maroon corset and nothing else, tied spreadeagled to a large X frame, her back to the camera. Her bottom was enticingly red and her head lolled forward as a man in a dark suit took another swing at her with a meaty-looking paddle.

I bit my lip and forced my eyes back to the traffic. Behind me, he said nothing, though I could feel his eyes boring into the back of my head through the leather headrest.

Five minutes of tense silence. Then he coughed. I looked up in the mirror. He was smiling – that "you're going to get it" smile I was so hoping for.

"Getting a bit warm, Kirsty?" he asked.

"A little, Mr Gaitsbury," I replied, flushing more.

"Then undo your jacket."

It was clearly an order, not a suggestion, so during the next lull in the traffic I popped open the top three buttons of my uniform jacket.

"Good. Now your blouse. Two buttons should suffice."

I complied, though the necktie made it damned difficult to do one-handed.

Then all of a sudden I felt him gripping the material of my jacket! As I drove, he tugged the garment wide open, folding it back and using the seat belt to keep it like that. Then with a brief caress across my silk-clad nipples he was sitting back in his seat again.

"It's still a little hot in here," he commented. "Turn on the air conditioning and crank up the blower."

I knew exactly what he was up to, and made sure the blast of icy air was directed straight at my chest. My nipples peaked in response, though to be fair they were already pretty hard. I looked in the mirror and saw him staring intently back, a small smile on his face as the tip of his tongue darted out to lick his lips.

For the remaining twenty miles he tortured me. Several times he made me reach up to adjust the sun visor, making the material of my blouse rub against my sensitized nipples. Several more times he reached forwards to stroke the outside of my thigh. Once he even reached through the gap between my seat and headrest to grip my ponytail and play with it. As you can imagine, I was in a right lather by the time we pulled into the road leading up to the Kingsdee Business Centre.

As we passed the first building, I slowed down to smarten my uniform back up, but he stopped me. "No, not yet," he kept saying as we got closer and closer to the car park for Building C. I became more and more frantic inside, and more and more aroused too. Charmaine would have my guts for garters if she heard that anyone else had seen me looking so dishevelled on the job. But if I disobeyed Mr Gaitsbury then I'd pay for it too, in a different way. And a certain part of me actually *wanted* some other businessman to see me like this, if just for one second. I imagined the knowing glance this imaginary man would give Mr Gaitsbury as I helped him out of the car.

Closer we got, and closer still, but then he surprised me by directing me on towards the far end of the car park, ignoring the knot of businessmen at the entrance. I breathed a sigh that was part relief and part disappointment.

I pulled up into a parking bay well away from any occupied vehicle, but before I could undo my seat belt he leaned forward and handed me a small package, along with an excessively large-screened smartphone.

"Clip this into the dashboard holder," he instructed me.

I complied, replacing my own phone with this one, twisting it to the horizontal and turning it on as instructed. Once the phone was displaying its normal wallpaper image, he had me open the package. Inside was a vibrator.

"Put it in," he commanded.

I hesitated. What if someone saw?

"Do it," he repeated. "I'll tell you if someone's coming this way."

This time I obeyed, spreading my legs just wide enough to get one hand between them. As I mentioned, I wasn't wearing any panties, so it was simple to ease the head of the vibrator between my swollen lips and push it home into my sodden sex.

"Hands at your sides," he told me. Then he reached forward to rummage around underneath the side of my seat, coming up with an elastic cord, the other end of which must have been attached to one of the struts under my seat.

Quickly and competently, he slipped the hook on the end of the cord through the buttonhole of the left cuff of my blouse, squeezing the metal hook to close it. Then he did the same to my other arm. I was effectively immobilized. No way would I be able to lift my arms up more than an inch or two without ripping the cuffs of my blouse (which I wouldn't do except in an emergency). Finally, he took my ponytail and tied it loosely around one of the struts of my headrest.

"See you in an hour or so," he said, patting me on the cheek then getting out of the car and walking away.

That next hour was the most intense I had yet experienced. First there was the waiting. For five whole minutes nothing happened. Then the vibrator suddenly burst into life, but at a very low setting, barely enough to tickle me. Every now and then it would speed up, but just for a moment before it returned to the relentless tease. Ten minutes of that had me squirming.

Then the phone pinged. Mr Gaitsbury's voice came over the speakers. I answered back but it was obviously a recording for he kept on talking over me.

"For the next twenty minutes I will show you a selection of images. Scenarios depicting what I would like to do with you. Pay attention, no matter how turned on you get, because when I get back to the car I will ask you to choose one – to choose what will happen to you tonight."

As soon as he had finished talking, the smartphone screen lit up with a photograph of a woman inside a garage, with her back to the camera, cleaning the side windows of a black limousine. She was wearing a chauffeur's uniform just like mine, except that she had removed her jacket and rolled up her sleeves. Her golden-brown hair – again just like mine – hung loose in ripples down her back. She could have been my double except that against the car she seemed to me to be a few inches shorter than I am.

In the next shot, a man in a smart business suit had walked into the frame. The next few photos showed him pointing out a tiny smudge on the car window and then whispering in the woman's ear. I was curious to see the face of this apparent double, but as she turned to face him, head bowed contritely, I saw she wore a mask, leaving me no better informed about her identity except that she had lips which were slightly fuller than mine.

The next image widened out to show my mystery double standing there motionless as the man took two sets of handcuffs from a bag in the trunk. She took them from him without even looking up. The view then zoomed in to show her leaning through the now-open side window of the car as he indicated to her to clip the handcuffs to the front and rear headrests.

By now I was beside myself. This was the perfect fantasy for me! To be made to prepare the setting for my own punishment . . . yes, I would like that very much indeed.

My pussy was fluttering as she clipped the other end of one

cuff to her left wrist. Then he reached around her to secure her other wrist. Finally I got a close-up view of him twisting the chains with rods, shortening them to pull her further into the car, until she was pinned hard against the car door, her legs outside, bent at the stomach over the lip of the open window, upper body completely inside the car with her arms out rigid in front of her. Now she was as helpless as I was!

The slow set-up had been wonderful, pacing the action so that I could imagine it happening, step by step, to me. However now I just wanted the man to haul her skirt up (or down – I didn't care!) and redden her arse before bringing her off!

It took five more shots before her skirt and panties were down around her ankles and she had stepped out of them. Five shots during which I admired her flawless, firm and so-far blemish-free cheeks, and wondered exactly what implement would be used to bring a blush to that fair skin.

The answer was satisfyingly in keeping with the setting: the very same chamois leather cloth she had failed in her duty with when she left a smear on the window. The man took it from the bucket, twisted it to wring it dry, then without further ado brought it down sharply across her bottom.

I was only seeing a series of still images, but still I jumped in sympathy for that poor woman. And the man had certainly not held back, for the next shot showed an angry red weal across her right buttock, a mark which was soon joined by others as the action stepped up a pace, each new shot showing a fresh blow landing, a fresh mark marring that once-perfect skin! And each whack was accompanied by a harsh buzz between my legs as the vibrator stepped up its stimulation in me. By the time both buttocks of the mystery woman were glowing red, I was squirming, knees pressed together in a desperate attempt to bring pressure to bear on my clit and get me off.

But it was in vain. The infernal toy had been programmed perfectly to keep me frustratingly on the brink. Even when the man dropped the vicious leather cloth and reached between the woman's legs to give her some relief, I gained none. Even as she arched into her climax, mine was tantalizingly just out of reach.

The vibrator in my pussy wound down to a low buzz, just

enough to keep me on a ready simmer. The screen went blank for a few moments before the next scenario started up.

Again, this new scene featured my double. This time the man was checking a car's oil level, making sure she had been looking after his car properly. When it was found to be too low, she inevitably took the blame and was bound face down over the engine compartment. Of course it was the (cleaned off) dip stick which was used this time to stripe her arse, and once she had been reduced to a quivering wreck the man used the hard, flesh and blood dipstick which nature had endowed him with to check her own intimate moisture levels. The reading must have been inconclusive, too, because he checked her time and time again to be sure. No doubt about mine, though. My thighs were sticky and I knew a damp patch must be seeping through my skirt into the upholstery of my seat, a faux pas the company staff manual would surely forbid.

Again the woman arched and came. And again I didn't. *Not fair*, I whimpered to myself. *Not bloody fair!*

More scenarios followed. My double was restrained on her knees in the boot of an estate car, her hands trapped underneath the headrests, her ankles tied to the luggage stay loops on the floor by lengths of elastic bungee cord, helpless as she was spanked and then fucked doggy. In the next image she was made to kneel and pick up the car key from the floor, then made to stay there and suck the man whilst he tugged her hair, stripped and slapped on the arse time and time again with the clipboard that bore the checklist for the valeting she had failed to perform correctly. Finally, she brought off with a vigorous use of a dildo as the man probed her arsehole with his finger. Tied to rear spoilers, over stacks of wheels, against racks of spare parts, whipped, spanked, beaten every which way imaginable, until my mind was a sea of overlapping images and crazy sensations, my body zinging with the need to come.

It was the last scenario that did it. The woman was tied – fully clothed in her chauffeur uniform – to an engine hoist, the arm of which had been raised to its maximum. With one ankle lashed to each leg of the base and her wrists tied together over the hoist arm above her head, she was then slowly stripped and teased, slapped and nibbled. Of course tied like that it was impossible to remove her clothing cleanly, and certain items had to be sliced open and cut away.

Soon she was standing suspended on the frame in nothing but her open blouse, leather chauffeur boots and peaked cap. She made a striking picture: helpless yet projecting erotic power, unable to move a limb yet able to move one to pity, and to envy. Yes, this might be the fantasy for me!

But what pain would she suffer? So far neither rod, cane, paddle nor bare hand had struck her, and anyway all these had been used in previous scenarios. What new was there to subject her to?

The answer came in the form of the two items of my uniform of which I am the most proud: my gleaming name badge and my five-year service badge. Both these are held on with clamping crocodile grips and, as I saw the man hold them out towards her, I knew exactly where *her* badges were going. Sure enough each one was opened wide then clamped over a sensitive, protruding nipple!

The woman on the screen grimaced. It was I who cried out, in sympathy and – frankly – in need. Of course I'd considered trying out nipple play on myself, but I'd always chickened out. Here, now, in front of me, was the image of what I would look like if I submitted to it, and I wanted to be that woman. I wanted to feel the bite of metal teeth on teats made already painfully rigid by what seemed an age of arousal without climax. And when the man took a slender chain and wrapped it around the two improvised clamps, making her breasts form downward-pointing cones under the weight, well, I wanted to feel that aching tug too.

The next image flicked up on the screen. Now the man was behind her, slapping her buttocks with open-palmed hands, making her body jerk forward and her breasts jiggle with each blow. I could well imagine the sharp stabs of pain as chain and nipples tried to move in different directions, unyielding metal yanking on sensitive flesh. Half a dozen images flashed by, showing her frozen in different attitudes of torment, before finally the man grabbed her shoulders and at last entered her.

Of course I couldn't see the details of how he penetrated her

– one picture showed him lining up with her, and the next showed him inside her to the hilt – but in my imagination it was a rough taking. My pussy clamped in on itself as I imagined being penetrated like that – no gentle easing in, but instead a hard shove, a grunt, and a sudden surrender as swollen lips gave way to hard, probing cock. Yes, I could almost feel it! I squeezed my legs tighter together, and finally managed to get that much-needed pressure on my clit.

And then I was away. No slow build-up of tightening muscles and aching belly, but rather a hard spasming, tumbling, crazy, out-of-control climax that hit me almost out of the blue and tore a cry from my lips.

I don't know how long it was before I came down from that high. All I know is that when things came back into focus the screen was blank and there was an insistent knocking on the window beside me. I looked round in sudden panic, but it was only Mr Gaitsbury.

For once he cut me some slack, letting himself into the back of the car – rather than expecting me to get out and hold the door for him – then sitting there quietly until I had composed myself. After a minute or two he released my wrists and unwound my hair from the legs of the headrest.

"So which will it be, Kristy?" he whispered in my ear. "Have you chosen? Or will it be a mix of them all?"

I nodded, but couldn't bring myself to speak. He seemed to understand my sudden reticence, for he instead took a notebook and pen from his briefcase and placed them in my shaking hands. I closed my eyes for a moment then scribbled down half a dozen words that together outlined my ideal initiation to this world.

I trusted him to flesh out the rest. After all it had been my boss – Charmaine of Charmaine Chauffeurs – who had first assigned me to drive Mr Gaitsbury, a week after a drunken works party at which I confided in her my fantasy to be dominated and caned. And when the man on the screen – who had actually been Mr Gaitsbury – had ripped away the woman's mask and brown wig in the last shot, it had been Charmaine's face I had seen, grimacing in the rictus of climax.

I smiled. She was loaning me her lover to initiate me, and if she trusted him that much then so did I. Though, as he whispered filthy promises in my ear and the car slipped into gear, I did wonder just how she would expect to be repaid.

Backdoorman

Michael Bracken

I never paid much attention to the doormen in front of my building, seeing only the uniform but never the men inside, until one afternoon when I hurried out of the building moments after a rainstorm had passed, trying to reach the cab standing at the curb, and slipped on the wet sidewalk. My feet went skidding out from under me and I fully expected to land on my ample derrière.

But I didn't.

The doorman working that morning somehow managed to catch me from behind, his muscular arms wrapping completely around my torso beneath my smallish breasts, and holding me aloft until I managed to get both feet beneath me. I extricated myself from him and turned to look up into his smoldering hazel eyes.

I said, "Thank you."

"Yes, ma'am," he said. "Is that all, ma'am?"

"You might hail me another cab," I suggested as I saw my cab pulling away. "Someone's taken mine."

"Yes, ma'am."

The doorman stepped to the curb and motioned for a cab while I straightened my skirt and adjusted my blouse. When the replacement cab arrived, he opened the door and held it for me. As I slid into the back seat, I asked, "What's your name?"

"Tony, ma'am."

"Thank you again, Tony. Maybe someday I'll return the favor."

"There's no need, ma'am," he said. "I was just doing my job."

Tony closed the door before I could respond, so I gave the cab driver my destination before turning my attention back to the uniformed man who had saved me from embarrassment. By then he had returned to his station at the entrance and was holding the door for one of my elderly neighbors. Over a crisp white shirt and dark-blue tie, he wore the same as all the other doormen employed by my co-op: a three-button charcoal-gray, double-breasted jacket with gold braid on the sleeves, the lapels and the outseam of the pants. A military hat with coordinated braid, highly polished black oxfords, and white gloves completed his uniform. If I had not just moments before stared into Tony's eyes, I would not have been able to distinguish him from the other men who attended residents at the building's entrance twenty-four hours a day.

I didn't see Tony the Doorman again for several days, but I certainly daydreamed about him, imagining what it might be like to have his arms wrapped around me once again, imagining what I might find beneath his custom-tailored uniform, and imagining his cock standing at attention before my personal entrance while wearing its own snug-fitting prophylactic uniform. I'm not certain why I fixated on Tony, though. Perhaps it was because his catching me in his arms was the closest thing to physical intimacy with a man I'd had in more than a year.

When I returned home from shopping the following Saturday, I realized the portly gentleman who had held the door for me when I left that morning had been replaced, and I had almost reached the entrance before I realized who had replaced him. When Tony opened the door, my gaze met his. I caught the twinkle in his hazel eyes and noticed the hint of a smile he fought to suppress.

I paused in the open doorway and asked Tony what time his shift ended. After he told me, I said, "Why don't you come up and see me after you clock out?"

"Ma'am, I—"

"I have something for you," I said. "Something I'd rather give you in private."

"Yes, ma'am," he said. "I'll see you after my shift ends."

"I'm in apartment—"

"I know which unit is yours, Ms Bottomly."

An ironic twist of fate, my name, because I'm built more like a pear than an hourglass, with every extra pound I've gained over the years—and there aren't too many pounds or too many years—having taken up permanent residence in my posterior. Surprised, I asked, "You know my name?"

"It's our job to recognize all of the residents, ma'am," the doorman said, "even if you don't recognize us."

Though I still couldn't name any of Tony's fellow doormen, I certainly recognized the man who had held me in his arms. "You won't forget me this evening, then."

"No, ma'am."

I stepped through the door and sashayed across the lobby to the bank of elevators, swinging my hips just a bit more than usual. I didn't know if the doorman watched because I didn't look back.

That evening I wore my uniform of seduction – a diaphanous black nightie, which hung to mid-thigh – and had just lit a pair of vanilla-scented candles in my bedroom when the doorbell rang. I took my time responding, but soon enough opened the apartment door.

Still in uniform, Tony stood in the hallway outside. He kept his gaze focused on my eyes, but I knew he had already taken in the entire view. "Ma'am, I—"

"Come in," I said, as I stepped aside. "I'll hold the door for *you*."

The doorman hesitated, glanced both ways, and then stepped into my apartment. I closed and locked the door behind him. Tony's uniform jacket blocked my view of his crotch so I couldn't tell if his cock had reacted to my near-nudity, but I didn't wait to find out. I reached up, wrapped one hand around the back of his neck, and pulled his face down to mine. As I kissed him, I slipped my free hand under the hem of his jacket and found the bulge at his crotch.

He pushed me away. "Ma'am—Ms Bottomly—"

"Sara," I insisted.

"You're going to get make-up on my uniform."

"Then take it off."

"But I—"

"You're off the clock," I told him, "and I promised you a little something in private."

I peeled myself away and crossed the living room, stopping only a few steps from my bedroom door before I looked over my shoulder. I caught Tony staring at my ass so I lifted the bottom of the nightie to give him a clear view. Then, without waiting to see if he followed, I stepped into my bedroom and perched on the side of my bed.

A moment later he joined me in the bedroom, just as I suspected he would.

"Why are you doing this?" he asked.

"Maybe it's because I like men in uniform," I said, though I suspect we both knew it wasn't the truth.

"You never noticed me before."

I decided to come clean. "I liked the way I felt when you had your arms wrapped around me the other day. Any man strong enough to hold me the way you did is a man I want more of." We stared at each other for a moment before I asked, "So why did you come up here?"

"If I may be blunt, ma'am—"

"Yes, do."

"Your ass, Ms Bottomly—"

"Sara," I insisted a second time.

"It turns me on," he said. "Watching the way your ass sways when you're walking away makes my day."

I'd never had a man compliment my derrière. "But it's so—"

I was about to say "big", but Tony interrupted me and completed my sentence, "—beautiful. When you opened your apartment door this evening my cock got so hard I could have used it to pound nails. Then when you flipped up your nightie a moment ago I almost came in my shorts."

"That would be quite a shame," I said as I spread my legs. I leaned back on the bed so that I was resting on my elbows. The hem of my nightie rose to my upper thighs and just barely covered the triangle of blonde hair at the juncture of my thighs. "Especially when I'm wet and waiting."

"Yes, ma'am—Ms Bottomly—Sara."

The doorman stepped toward me and then stopped, as if

confused about what to do. He turned and carefully removed his uniform, hanging each piece over the back of a wingback chair in the corner of my bedroom, until he wore nothing but lime-green boxer briefs, the one bit of sartorial self-expression not prescribed by his employment contract with the co-op. When he turned again to face me, his erect cock strained against the tight-fitting material and I wanted to free it from confinement and wrap my hand around it.

He didn't give me a chance. Without removing his last bit of clothing, Tony knelt on the carpet between my widespread legs and buried his face between my thighs. He grabbed my hips and pulled my crotch toward his face, causing me to fall upon my back as his warm breath tickled my carefully groomed pubic triangle. As he snaked his tongue along the length of my slit, I hooked my legs over his shoulders. He parted my lips with his tongue, sucked at my swollen labia, and then found the tightening bud of my clit. He lapped at it as he slid the fingers of his right hand beneath my ass cheeks and slipped his thumb into my female opening. As he pistoned his thumb in and out of my pussy, he drew my swollen clit between his teeth and teased it with the tip of his tongue.

My hips began to buck up and down on the bed, my pubic bone introducing itself to Tony's nose with increasing urgency. I wrapped my hands around the back of his head and tried to pull his face inside me. I knew I was about to come and I couldn't stop myself – didn't want to stop myself – and I ground my pussy against the doorman's face.

I cried out when I came, and I released a flood of sexual effluent over his thumb and fingers and down the crack of my ass, and I didn't let go of his head until my pussy quit clenching and unclenching. When I released my hold on his head, Tony drew away, stood, and finally peeled off his lime-green boxer briefs to reveal his straining erection.

Even though the orgasm had turned my entire body to jelly, I wanted more. I wanted his long, thick cock deep inside me. I had earlier that week restocked my supply of condoms, so I rolled over and retrieved one from my nightstand drawer. I tore open the square foil packet, removed the lubricated condom and slipped it over his erection.

The doorman spun me around and bent me over the bed, lifted my hips until I was on all fours, my knees just barely on the edge of the bed, and then stepped between my legs. He pressed the head of his cock against my slickened female opening, grabbed my hips, and then thrust forward. He buried his cock deep inside my pussy, drew back, did it again. And again.

As he fucked me, Tony moved his right hand from my hip to the small of my back. He slid his thumb down the crack of my ass until it pressed against the tight pucker of my asshole. His thumb and my ass crack were slickened with my juices, and my sphincter slowly opened to the pressure of Tony's thumb. No man had ever stuck a finger in my ass – not as foreplay and certainly never while fucking me – and I was surprised by how good it felt.

I was even more surprised a moment later when Tony pulled his cock out of my pussy and then pressed the head of his condom-covered cock against the pucker of my asshole where his thumb had just been. The pre-lubricated condom, now coated with additional lubrication from my pussy, made it easy for Tony to push his cock into my ass. He buried the entire length within me and then drew back until just the head of his cock remained captured by my sphincter muscles.

He fucked my ass hard and fast, slamming his hips against me again and again and again. If anyone had ever asked me if I'd like to have my ass reamed by a strong man with a thick cock, I would have said no, but Tony was proving me wrong with every powerful thrust.

As he fucked my ample ass, I reached between my thighs and stroked my clit with my two middle fingers. I matched Tony's rhythm stroke for stroke, and when I felt myself again approaching orgasm, I stroked myself faster, sliding my fingers forward and back over my engorged clit until there was no stopping the wave of orgasm that washed over me.

I came first and would have collapsed on the bed if Tony hadn't been holding my hips.

The doorman slammed into me three more times and then he came, emptying his spunk into the condom's reservoir tip. He held my ass tight to his hips until he caught his breath and his cock stopped spasming within me. Then he withdrew his cock from my ass, peeled off the condom, and tossed it in the wicker wastebasket on the far side of the nightstand.

My nightie was bunched up around my armpits and I pushed it down, covering myself again as I stood. Then I settled on the side of the bed again and examined Tony a bit more closely than I had in the heat of the moment. He had a broad chest, powerful arms, a tight abdomen and a narrow waist. His thick cock hung between his muscular thighs, nearly as long flaccid as it had been when erect, and it still throbbed from post-coital bliss.

"I've never done that before," I admitted. "Ever."

"You can't imagine how often I rubbed one out while thinking about your ass," Tony said. "I never thought I would ever have it."

"Really?" I'd never thought of my posterior as my best feature, but I'd somehow lucked into meeting a man who thought it was perfect, and who had taught me that it could play an important role in my erotic repertoire.

As the doorman stood before me, I realized I wanted him to fuck my ass again. I just didn't know if he could. I reached out and took his flaccid, come-covered cock in my hand and urged him to step closer. I stroked his cock a few times and then wrapped my lips around the spongy soft head. His cock tasted of come with a hint of latex, and I licked the head clean before drawing it into my mouth and hooking my teeth behind the glans. As I sucked and stroked, his cock slowly regained its former stature. When it was fully erect, I grabbed another condom, slid it into place, and made Tony fuck my ass a second time. This time I was ready for it and it felt even better than the first time.

When the doorman finished reaming my ass, leaving me nothing but a quivering mound of orgasm-induced jelly sprawled out on my bed with my nightie hanging from one arm, he stepped into the master bath to clean himself. When he returned, he dressed in his uniform, just as careful putting it on as he'd been when he took it off. Then he let himself out, leaving me with the realization that, beneath his employer-prescribed uniform, my doorman is really a backdoorman.

He's visited my apartment several times since that evening,

and each time anal play has been a major component of our erotic activity.

So these days Tony opens my front door in public and my backdoor in private.

A Right Royal Spanking

Nicole Gestalt

"Captain Mortimer Montague, please step forward." The caller's voice boomed out over the entire hall. Montague was sure he'd have been able to hear his name even had he been right at the back of the room. Not that that would have happened of course, the back of the room was where the people of lower rank than captain stood. It was an unspoken fact but clearly seen from a short glance over the occupants in the warm stuffy room.

"That's you, old boy, you can't leave the old girl waiting. It wouldn't be worth losing your commission over," Randolph Gatsby hissed into his ear, his elbow digging painfully into Montague's side. Montague glanced sideways getting an eyeful of the thick bushy moustache Gatsby favoured. So much so that Montague knew from conversations after hours in the club he would lose his airship before he lost his moustache.

"After all, old boy you can get another airship, but a moustache like this? Well that's an entirely different matter," he always said whenever the conversation was brought up.

Another dig in his side and this time so hard he was shoved a little way out of the aisle. Montague blinked and shifted uncomfortably. He hated all kinds of ceremonies, especially ones where he was the centre of attention.

After straightening out his dress uniform, he tucked his cap under his arm securely and began to march slowly down towards the Queen. She stood at the end dressed all in black with a cut that was traditional but fitted her body firmly, giving her if possible an even more regal look. As Montague moved forward, he was again surprised at how small she really was. Although he had met her a number of times, he always thought of her as very tall and imposing and yet when they met again in person he realized how slight and small her figure was. Nevertheless she was his Queen and the person he went into the air and battle for.

His footsteps were completely muffled by the thick carpet that Montague knew was more valuable than his own airship, let alone that of a few others in the hall. When his foot nudged the piece of wood carefully concealed in the carpet he came to a halt, straightened and saluted.

The Queen eyed him slowly with sparkling eyes filled with intelligence. When he had come back to report on the mission he hadn't felt this scrutinized, and was suddenly very thankful that it hadn't been the Queen questioning him as to how it was he had ended up with an extra passenger aboard. Images of the passenger lying over his knee as he brought his hand down on her bottom filled his mind, blocking everything else out. She had been found hiding in the engine room in oil-covered trousers and a shirt. He didn't realize at first who she was and it was only after he had punished her suitably that she had told him. Even then he hadn't believed it until they had come into land and the officers had been there to take her away. It had taken a lot of digging since to discover the paperwork that proved she was the Queen's eldest daughter, but he somehow wasn't surprised to discover she travelled around gathering information the Queen couldn't otherwise get. Not that many people knew she was the daughter of the monarch of course – that had been devilishly hidden on the records and Montague had half a suspicion who it was who had helped bury the facts.

"Captain Mortimer Montague." The sharp voice pulled him out of his thoughts and he focused instead on the Queen's face. "Five times you have now stood in front of oneself due to the deeds and services you have performed."

There was a pause and Montague wondered if she could guess quite what unspoken services had been performed on the last mission. He guessed not or he was sure he wouldn't be being knighted.

"Whilst one is happy at all you have accomplished in one's name, if you keep this up one will have to start creating new awards and titles." The Queen looked at him expectantly and he let out a practised laugh as was expected. The laughter quickly rippled through the hall before the place fell silent again.

"For your actions aboard the *Hanovers'Wings* and the gallant retrieval of the cargo that had been lost into the enemies' hands one awards upon you the Knighthood of the Golden Leaf." With that a steam-powered footman appeared at her side, holding in his hands a pillow with a sword resting on the top. The Queen turned slightly and took the sword up from the pillow. The automaton slid silently backward.

"Kneel," she battled out and Montague dropped down onto one knee, hoping his nerves weren't showing.

Out of the corner of his eyes, he saw the Queen lift up the blade high and desperately tried not to flinch. Tried not to think what she would do if she knew how close he had got to her daughter. The blade touched one shoulder and he lowered his eyes down, clenching his hand, his heart hammering.

I didn't know she was your daughter, he wanted to say, but bit his tongue, knowing death likely followed that conversation. Part of him knew that even if he had known it would likely not have made any difference.

The blade was lifted from his shoulder and he released the breath he discovered he'd been holding.

"You may now stand."

On shaky knees he did so and looked back up at the Queen.

"From now on, one will be following your career with great interest."

His heart skipped a beat as something in her eyes and the tone of voice betrayed that she knew a lot more than she had let on. He swallowed hard but his mouth had suddenly become dry.

"Thank you, my Queen," he said in a shaky voice.

The Queen leaned back and gave a half-smile, a rarity in itself.

"It is good to know that one's cargo is always in safe, secure hands, Sir Montague. I trust you to make sure that is always the case."

Montague blinked in amazement, wondering if she meant what she was saying or if there was another level to it.

"Of course, my Queen, I would guard it with my own life if that would be your wish."

That smile grew and she nodded her eyes sparkling. "One will rest better in the knowledge you will be there."

She took a step backward and Montague found himself being propelled away and down a smaller aisle, wondering what it was exactly he had just agreed to. The footman who led him away was silent but nonetheless Montague followed him, his mind in a whirl. He was led into an antechamber, beyond which he could hear general murmuring of people at a loss with themselves but glad to be out of the main hall. He looked questioningly at the footman who stood still, the lights that acted as his eyes glowing brighter.

There was a high-pitched noise and a card popped out of the footman's grid, which had been fashioned into a mouth. Leaning over, Montague pulled it out and read the message upon it: "Please help yourself to refreshments and refresh yourself for the next part of the ceremony."

Nodding to himself, Montague stepped back. "Thank you."

The footman rolled back, spun out of the room and moved away, leaving Montague alone. He breathed out deeply and then froze, someone or something was in the room with him. Moving slowly forward into the room, he ignored the noise from the chamber beyond and listened to the room. Unlike the other rooms this one wasn't lit as well, with only a few candles in the centre, leaving the corners dark. Tension coiled through him and his hand moved towards his ceremonial sword at his side. From a dark corner there was a rustle of fabric and a familiar giggle.

Montague groaned inwardly, although his body tensed in desire and anticipation. Moving into the darkness, he reached out and felt the silky fabric. The scent of jasmine and oranges wafted around him, allowing him to work out exactly where the person was. In one quick movement, he stepped forward and pinned the figure against the wall. The shadows concealed them but he knew it wasn't going be long before they were discovered.

"What exactly do you think you are doing?" he hissed into the soft curls of hair, breathing in deeply, his cock hardening at the memory of her.

"Waiting for you." She breathed out the words in an excited rush and his cock strained. It had been too long and now he had her in front of him. He tried to ignore the fact that the Queen was only a few feet away.

"Your timing hasn't improved," he growled, his hand running down her hair until it found her soft skin. He pressed himself against her, knowing she'd be able to feel his arousal and desperately trying to keep his hands away from her tightly corseted breasts.

"Well, I'm sure you could do something about that. After all—" He put his hand over her mouth silencing her as he heard the sharp clip of footsteps on a marble floor.

"We need to go somewhere else," he hissed and, feeling her nod, stepped away from her. Her hand grabbed his and suddenly they were out of the little side door and running down an empty corridor. A blur of doors and a set of stairs up and he found himself on the other side of a door in a more well-lit room. He gave the room only half a glance, long enough to confirm that they were in a small library, before he turned his attention to Alex.

Taking hold of her shoulders, he pulled her towards him, pressing his lips hungrily against hers. He could feel her breasts pressing against his chest and his cock hardened to a painful ache. Her arms wrapped around him and tugged at his uniform. He let go of her long enough to undo his sword, giving her easier access to his body. She wriggled provocatively against him and he hissed out a groan. This had gone far enough. Taking a firm grip of her, he pushed her back.

"What do you think is happening here?"

She looked at him her face flushed, eyes dark with desire. "What do you mean?" she said, looking him over. She bit her lip, trying to look coy.

"You know full well what I mean. Turning up like this when the last time I saw you was as the carriage pulled away. Why do you keep turning up when I'm least expecting it? And how much have you told your mother about us?"

She laughed and he ached to hold her, but he focused on the task at hand.

"The first time I found you, you had smuggled yourself aboard my ship. Do you remember what I did then?" He looked down at her, narrowing his eyes, remembering again that night she was found by his engineers and brought to his room, wriggling in a filthy pair of trousers and shirt.

She said nothing and he stepped forward to her, closing the distance he had put between them.

"Now, after no news from you, you turn up here and expect me to just fall into your arms? Especially with your mother not far from us? Are you just trying to get me into trouble?" He kept his voice level but inside the irritation he was feeling about the situation began to bubble over. Memories of their first meeting flooded through him and he felt his fingers itching He glanced around the room for something he could use. His eyes fell on a large book resting on a small table by the fire and he smiled. Without saying anything, he walked her to the fireplace and sat down on the chair facing the door so he could keep an eye on it. Glancing at Alex, he noticed with pleasure her face was even more flushed and her eyes darker though she smiled slightly at him and nodded a little. She knew what was coming and that was all he needed. He pulled her down onto his knee, lifted up her skirts and tugged down her drawers, pausing only to squeeze her smooth buttocks.

"You keep surprising me and turning up when I least expect it. That just isn't right. From now on you need to announce your presence in the correct way. I do not like surprises like that so you will conduct yourself in the correct manner when others are around."

As he spoke, he brought his hand down sharply on her, causing a short squeak to escape. He felt her take a deep breath every time he lifted his hand away from her but could tell from her ragged breathing how turned on she was becoming. As he had done the first time he'd met her, he spanked her until her cheeks flushed a bright red then ran his fingers over the abused skin.

"You look lovely," he whispered softly, running his fingers lower down between her legs, feeling how wet she was. "Hmm . . . delicious," he growled softly, his hunger for her growing by the minute. He knew she would be able to feel how hard he was and almost in response to his thoughts she started to sigh and wriggle upon him, pressing against his cock, causing it to harden further and his fingers to brush gently against her pussy.

"You are tempting me, you minx." He withdrew his fingers, ignoring the need that was growing in him. "I think a little more punishment is in order." As he spoke, he picked up the large book by the table and idly looked it over.

"Albert A. Alexandria's Atlas, Version Three," he read and smiled. It was large and flat, just perfect for teaching someone how to behave. Holding it carefully in his hand, he brought it down on her bottom, hitting both cheeks at once.

"Oh!" she gasped and jumped in reflex.

"That is for your simply wanton behaviour," he said, before bringing the book down again. There was another gasp but more lustful than the last.

"That is for your belief I will always be waiting for you."

The book was brought down again; the gasp became a groan.

"That is for being so delicious and delightful I really can't keep my hands off you." He paused to run his hand over her bottom then brought the book down again, so hard this time that a crack echoed throughout the room.

"And that is because I know how much you enjoy it."

He didn't tell her he was stopping, he just put the book back down on the table and nudged her a little. She took the hint and slipped off his knees. However she didn't stand up like he was expecting to. Instead, with her hair quite dishevelled and her clothing all in disarray, she turned to him, resting on her knees, and reached out for his lower placket. Her fingers nimbly undid the fabric and his cock was freed into her eagerly awaiting hands. He groaned and grabbed hold of the sides of the chair as she expertly began to move her hands up and down his shaft. He fought to stay still and let her enjoy herself, but he was completely undone as she wriggled between his legs and, looking directly at him, took him into her mouth. Hissing, he arched his hips and pushed himself deeper into her.

"This is how I expect you to behave when we're alone." He managed to speak the words in between her movements, which were driving his excitement. His hand let go of the chair and wound around the back of her neck, pushing her down to match his hips rising up.

She attempted to answer but it only came through as vibrations surrounding his cock. The pleasure he had felt before was nothing compared to what he was feeling now. The room spun and he closed his eyes, needing to concentrate solely on the wickedly delicious things she was now doing with his head and her tongue.

He couldn't say when she stopped or even removed her mouth, he was only fully aware of her suddenly being sat back on her legs speaking to him.

"What?" he muttered, trying to fight through the haze of desire.

"I said I completely agree. However, I also want you to behave similarly in private with me." With that she sat back and straightened out her legs, flicking her skirts up.

He grinned and didn't need to be asked twice. "That, my lady, would be my pleasure."

Nimbly moving to his knees, he wasted no time in running his tongue up her inner thighs, enjoying her soft gasps before he darted forward to spear her with his tongue. Her gasp became a yelp then melted into moans, as he pulled out and lapped at her clit hungrily. They hadn't been together for over three months but he remembered her body well and quickly got into a rhythm he knew she liked. Her hands gripped his hair, twisting and pulling him forward and back and, for the moment, he let her feel as if she had control.

He suckled down on her until her body pulsed and tensed under him then went limp. As her hand relaxed and let go of his head, he pulled up and pushed himself inside her. Revived, she wrapped her legs around him, her eyes filled with new desire. She clamped her muscles around him so tightly he knew he wasn't going to last long and after only a few thrusts he had to force himself to pull out, his hand tightening around his shaft. Alex wasn't just content to watch him spill his seed. She wriggled out from under him and had her mouth around his cock before he realized quite what was happening. Her tongue brushed over his head and he was undone, pulsing inside her as she happily swallowed him until every drop was gone.

As he slowly collapsed down onto the floor, wrapping his arms around her and pulling her close, he groaned and let out a deep breath.

"You still haven't told me what you told your mother. I think I've promised to take care of you always."

Alex pressed herself against him and laughed softly. "I can think of nothing better, but you will have to keep up with me," she said teasingly.

With a grunt, he kissed the top of her head and let himself relax in the afterglow of his orgasm wondering quite where they would end up.

Incentive Training

Theophilia St Claire

We signed up knowing the risk. But standing there on line, with drill instructors screaming in our faces, my platoon often wondered why they volunteered in the first place.

Not me.

I expected this sort of inhumane treatment long before I first visited my recruiter's office. My brother told me everything I could possibly need to know about Marine Corps boot camp. However, there was one tiny detail Tommy had left out.

He didn't tell me my drill instructors would be so fucking hot. And distracting.

I watch my senior drill instructor, Staff Sergeant Montgomery, stride across the squad bay, scrutinizing every recruit for even the smallest mistake. I admire the way his desert cammies and black leather duty belt fit the shape of his tall, muscled body. A body I would give my least favorite appendage to be under.

My cock stirs. I close my eyes, needing not to be aroused in this terrifying moment. The image of Staff Sergeant Montgomery's arrogant walk is burned into my retinas.

"What the hell are you doing, recruit?"

My eyes fly open. Montgomery is in my face. His handsome visage twisted in anger, his lips turned downwards, light blue eyes narrowed.

"This recruit is . . ." I stammer, unable to come up with a good lie while staring at his chest and the muscles in his tanned forearms.

"Did I say 'eyeballs'? Get your goddamned eyes to the front!" His Texas drawl is sexy.

"Aye, aye, sir." I force my gaze to the opposite bulkhead, away from him.

"OK, get louder, recruit."

"Sir?"

"Louder!" His body tenses like a coiled rattlesnake about to strike. With his face so close to mine, I can smell the roasted coffee on his warm breath.

"Aye, aye, sir."

Another drill instructor enters my peripheral. He's about six foot two, the same height as Montgomery. Sergeant Medina is our Kill Hat. With brown skin, a muscular body, and his campaign cover worn low over light brown eyes, he was also hot as fuck.

"Open your goddamned mouth!" he says, his Spanish accent prominent.

"Aye, aye, sir."

They frown, and my stomach drops. It's embarrassing. I never yell, not even when I'm angry.

Montgomery snaps his fingers in front of my face. I refrain from looking at him. "What's your name, maggot?"

"This recruit's name is Daniel Arrington, sir."

"Arrington, why did you join my corps?"

I hesitate. "This recruit liked the uniforms, sir."

The squad bay is quiet. Not a single body moves. If an ink stick dropped, everyone would hear it.

"Are you fucking with me right now?" Montgomery asks in a low voice.

"No, sir." My voice only a tiny bit louder.

Medina stands next to my ear. "Sound off, recruit, or I'm gonna PT you until you fucking drop!"

Shit.

"Aye, aye, sir."

My heart races in my chest as Montgomery walks down the main passageway. The sound of his boots on the concrete floor is ominous.

"Platoon 1811, ears," he commands.

"Open, sir," the entire platoon of sixty bodies responds in unison.

"Recruit Arrington is having problems sounding off. As a

result, you're all being quarter-decked right now. In my house, when one fucks up, everyone suffers. Every last one of you will be smoked until Recruit Arrington can scream loud enough for the company commander in the next building to hear. Do you understand?"

"Yes, sir!"

"Now get on your faces. Do push-ups until I tell you to stop."

We drop to the deck and exercise. Our limbs are already sore from yesterday's Initial Strength Test, and the earlier session of PT. No one looks at me, but I can feel the collective hatred coming my way.

Recruit Grant Thibodeaux is my new squad leader, and he's assigned the enviable task of helping me "find my voice". Lately, I've been unable to impress the drill instructors with my lack of volume.

"You've gotta start sounding off. You'll take a lot less shit if you do. And the entire damned platoon won't keep getting quarter-decked because of you."

We're sitting in the middle of the squad bay, wiping down our M16A2 rifles with rags. I glance over at Thibodeaux while he studiously scrubs the bolt. Thibodeaux's from Louisiana, and it's evident in his part-country, part-French accent. He's fucking handsome, too, with his dimples and emerald eyes.

His know-it-all attitude ticks me off.

Three days have passed since the first incident, and he's been saying the same shit on repeat, like a broken record. My volume's improved, but not nearly enough to please our DIs.

Thibodeaux wipes his hands on his rag. "I've gotta take a leak. Come on, Arrington, I want you to watch."

I arch an eyebrow at him. "You want me to watch you piss?"

"Ha ha, dumbass. No, I want you to learn how to please the drill instructors. Get them off your back a little."

I follow Thibodeaux to the front of the squad bay, towards the DI House. I wish to God he was talking about pleasing them in carnal ways. Especially Montgomery. He's my favorite.

Outside the doorway, Thibodeaux smacks his hand against the hatch and stands at attention. In a loud, clear voice, he says,

"Recruit Thibodeaux requests permission to speak with Senior Drill Instructor Staff Sergeant Montgomery."

Silence.

After a moment, Montgomery's calm voice responds, "What?"

"This recruit requests permission to make a head call, sir."

"Go."

Thibodeaux turns on his heel and strides toward the restroom. I want to wipe the smirk off his face. "Your turn, Arrington. Just do as I did, and you'll be fine."

Shit, my gut's churning.

Thibodeaux leans against the bulkhead, his gaze intense as he watches me. I approach the doorway. Montgomery is sitting at his desk, poring over paperwork. His campaign cover is off, revealing a blond High and Tight. His desert blouse is folded up in the chair behind him while he adorns only the olive-green undershirt that stretches tight over his thick chest.

My mouth salivates. I swallow. I smack the palm of my hand against the hatch. "Recruit Arrington requests permission to speak with Senior Drill Instructor Staff Sergeant Montgomery."

"Nope, try it again. How 'bout getting some freaking volume in your voice, recruit?"

"Aye, aye, sir."

I take a deep breath, willing myself to be as loud as they want. Thibodeaux told me they'd leave me alone if I did, but I don't think I want to be left alone. I attempt it again, but it still isn't good enough.

Montgomery approaches me. My heart pounds as he shoves his finger in my face. He's yelling, but I can barely make out a word. Meanwhile, my mouth is on automatic, saying "Aye, aye, sir," at random intervals to appease him.

It only makes him angrier.

He presses my back against the bulkhead and jabs a finger into my chest repeatedly. I shudder as the heat from his body engulfs mine.

Dear God, I want this man to fuck me.

Sergeant Miles, our Drill Hat, comes to stand at my other side. He's even taller than Montgomery, with dark skin, thick muscles and a piercing dark stare. Another fucking distraction.

"What the hell you looking at, fresh blood?" he drawls. His voice is deep and sexy.

I avert my eyes, staring at the American flag on the bulkhead in front of me. "The stars and stripes on the flag, sir," I respond.

This succeeds in even more yelling, even though I answered the question truthfully. The direct assault to my ears is unbearable.

By the time I reach the head, my ears are ringing. Thibodeaux is at the farthest urinal taking a piss. He shakes his head when he sees me.

"I told you, man. You want them in your grill, then you go ahead and keep squeaking like a mouse. Just don't get the rest of us in trouble."

I don't really hear what he's saying, mostly because my eyes are glued to his dick. It's pretty big, with a fat shiny crown. Briefly, I wonder what it would taste like.

Thibodeaux catches me looking. "You a fag?" he asks.

I meet his green eyes, and smile. "Don't Ask, Don't Tell has been repealed, man."

The look of disgust on his face as he tucks his junk is palpable. "I wish they didn't let fags into the service." He leaves without washing his hands.

I can't sleep. My mind keeps going back to hours ago, in the shower. When I caught Montgomery watching me while I bathed. He even licked his lips. I think he wanted me.

I think he wanted to force everyone out of that goddamned shower and fuck me against the tile.

My balls tighten at the thought.

As I lie in bed, I desperately want to touch myself. My cock has been like steel since hygiene time. If anyone noticed my raging erection, no one said anything, lest they be caught looking and accused of being a meatgazer.

I bury my face into my pillow, rubbing my crotch against the scratchy green blanket. I want to come so badly.

The thunderous sound of a steel garbage can being tossed down the concrete passageway snaps me out of my daze. It's zero-four-thirty. The loud banging is our cue to jump out of bed and get on line.

Our drill instructors stand at the front of the squad bay, examining us for even the slightest fuck-up. I haven't been fully asleep since I laid my head down hours ago. The slow one today isn't gonna be me.

"Ears," Montgomery commands.

"Open, sir," we reply, the tiredness evident in our voices.

"OK, ears."

"Open, sir!"

"Grab your trousers. Grab your blouse. Put it on right now. You have thirty seconds."

After the fuck-ups and routine game of Marine Corps Striptease, it takes fifteen minutes before we can finally remain dressed, boots and all.

"Starboard side, make a head call. Get cleaned up. You've got three minutes."

The thirty recruits on the right side of the squad bay grab their hygiene bags and rush into the head, trying to piss and brush their teeth in the allotted time. We, on the left, make our racks.

Three minutes are up and the other drill instructors go to harass the stragglers.

"Port side, head call. Three minutes."

I grab my hygiene bag. On my way to the head, I meet Montgomery's hard gaze. This time, he doesn't grill me for it.

Once we finish, all of us line up. Medina gets our attention. "Listen up. We're going to the pit, so you'd better stuff a clean shirt in your cargo pocket right now."

"Not you." Miles points at Thibodeaux. "You ain't going nowhere."

"Aye, aye, sir!"

"Arrington, too. He's staying behind," Montgomery says.

"This recruit, sir?" The words are out of my mouth before I can think.

Montgomery marches toward me. He stands in all of my personal space, and I can't help noticing how good he smells.

"Ask me another question, Arrington," he says in a low voice. "Ask me something else, and I swear to God."

"Aye, aye, sir."

His gaze is like hot lasers penetrating me. It's hard not to look up, to see if the expression on his face matches the one in his voice.

"You too, quarter-deck right now. Everyone else can leave."

Thibodeaux and I head to the front of the squad bay, passing brief, questioning looks, but choosing not to disobey. We'll only get it worse if we don't listen.

We do crunches, which is hard as fuck when you're hungry. I don't look up, but I hear the hatch close shut and the locking mechanism snap into place.

"Get up, recruits," Sergeant Miles orders.

We stand at attention.

The room is quiet, and I realize Thibodeaux and I are locked inside with Montgomery and Miles.

I swallow hard.

The two men stand in front of us, muscled arms folded across their thick chests, studying us with hard-to-read glares. They turn their attention to Thibodeaux, and I'm a little relieved.

"Recruit Thibodeaux," Montgomery says, "have you been working with Recruit Arrington on finding his voice?"

"Yes, sir."

"Let's see, then, because I think you're a bullshitter." They turn their attention to me and the relief melts away. "Recruit Arrington, what is your fifth general order? Loud and clear."

"Sir, this recruit's fifth general order is to quit my post only when properly relieved, sir."

I don't have to see Montgomery's face. The snort is sign enough.

"Recruit Thibodeaux, does that sound like freaking volume to you?" he yells. "You've been working with him for a week. Why does he still sound like a freaking house mouse?"

"Sir, this recruit has been working with Arrington, sir," Thibodeaux stammers.

"Bullshit," Miles says.

"No, sir. This recruit has tried his best with Arrington. This recruit can't understand why he's still not sounding off."

"Shut up," Montgomery says. "You know what you're gonna do, Thibodeaux? You're gonna show us."

"Aye, aye, sir!"

I hide my confusion, even though I'm curious to know. I'm

more afraid to ask them what they mean, however. I glance at Montgomery, and he's staring back at me, leering.

My heart sinks into the pit of my stomach at that look.

"Recruit Arrington, take that shit off right now," he says in a low voice.

My hands tremble as they find the buttons on my blouse. Since recruit training started, we've endured all kinds of debasement. Stripping down to my skivvies in front of the guy I like is by far the worst.

"Say 'Aye, aye, sir,'" he commands.

"Aye, aye, sir." I strip down to the olive-green undershirt and shorts we wear beneath our uniform. I glare at the deck, my cheeks hot.

"Skivvies off, Arrington."

I lick my lips. This time I gaze into those light blue eyes while I haphazardly pull them off. When I'm standing in the ill-fitting white underwear, Montgomery's gaze drops low, skimming over my body.

My cock swells, noticeable, I'm sure.

Montgomery closes the distance between us. His large hands drop to my waist, hooking into the waistband of my underwear. I suck in a deep breath as he slides the fabric down my legs, exposing me. His hand brushes my cock and I barely stifle a moan.

"Get on all fours, mouse," he whispers.

"Aye, aye, sir." My voice is a shaky whisper. He doesn't grill me for it.

Miles is checking me out, his dark gaze lecherous. "Damn, superstar. Looks like church mouse here's got a hard-on for you."

He has no fucking idea.

Montgomery glares at Thibodeaux. "Any day now, recruit. Show us."

Thibodeaux hesitates. His emerald eyes widen as he takes in the sight of me, bare ass naked and on all fours, waiting for him to stuff his cock inside of me. My own cock twitches.

How could Tommy not have told me about this sort of punishment?

Thibodeaux clears his throat. "This recruit isn't a fag, sir."

They're on him like vultures, shouting in his ears on either side. I want to tell him to just do it, to get them off his back a little, but I refrain.

Montgomery shoves him down onto his knees behind me. "Whip out your dick, recruit. Now!"

Thibodeaux's eyes darken as he gazes at me. He takes out his cock with trembling hands, hard and standing at attention.

Holy shit, he's gay.

Thibodeaux grabs my waist, lining his cock up with my entrance. My body tenses in anticipation.

"Hold on, numbnuts," Montgomery says. He digs into his pocket and retrieves a condom and small bottle of Vaseline.

That's going to be a bitch to clean out.

"I want to hear him screaming, recruit, otherwise that's your ass."

"Aye, aye, sir!"

Thibodeaux spreads my cheeks and shoves himself inside, deep and hard. I gasp, but I don't scream. The sharp pain accompanying his powerful thrust bows my spine.

"Fuck," I groan.

"Yeah, that's it. Take his ass," Miles cheers.

I focus on relaxing as Thibodeaux rocks against me. I can tell he's never fucked a guy before. He's clumsy, mindlessly shoving his prick inside me as hard and fast as he can. His deep groans fill the room. I gaze over my shoulder to see his expression. He looks like he's in heaven.

The concrete hurts my knees, but I ignore it while I thrust back against Thibodeaux's cock. I don't give him the satisfaction of hearing me scream. He's good, but not that good.

"Harder, recruit! He still isn't yelling," Montgomery bellows.

"Aye, aye, sir!" Thibodeaux pants. His fingers dig into my waist as he shoves inside me harder.

Shit, I'm close.

My cock weeps as Thibodeaux pounds inside me with abandon. But I still don't scream.

"Recruit Thibodeaux, you are a moron," Montgomery says.

"Aye, aye, sir!"

"On your feet right now."

I shudder as Thibodeaux slides out of me and stands at attention. He's still hard and glistening, his cock straining for release.

I ease off my knees onto the deck. Montgomery unbuckles his duty belt. He unbuttons his desert trousers and pulls them down. His cock springs out, hard and wet at the tip.

He has a monster of a dick, long and thick all around. My mouth waters for a taste.

"On your knees, recruit," Montgomery commands.

Thibodeaux drops to his knees, staring hard at the cock in his face.

Montgomery presses the tip of his erection to Thibodeaux's lips, smearing his wetness against them.

"How's it taste, recruit?" Miles asks.

Thibodeaux licks his lips slowly. "Good, sir."

"Open your mouth."

Thibodeaux obeys, and Montgomery shoves his dick between his lips. He growls as Thibodeaux swallows inch after inch.

Pre-come drips from the tip of my cock. I want to come so badly.

"Now touch yourself."

Thibodeaux doesn't hesitate. He takes his cock in hand and strokes it while he blows him.

"Don't think you're getting off scot-free, Arrington. Get over here right now," Miles says, ripping me from my thoughts.

I glance at him, surprised to find that he also has his large cock out, stroking the beast while smiling at me in anticipation. I stare at his cock. He's just as big and erect as Montgomery.

"Don't make me tell you twice, recruit."

"Aye, aye, sir."

I drop to my knees in front of him. My stomach tightens. Though I haven't been able to please my drill instructors in much of anything, I hope to get this right.

"Suck it."

I wrap my lips around the head of his dick, tasting the salty flavor on my tongue. I swirl it around the crown and lick the underside before I take him in deep.

"Yeah," he pants. "You like that, don't you, boy?"

I do.

Miles's head is thrown back in ecstasy, his hips slowly thrusting into my eager mouth. The rapture on his face makes me proud.

I stroke myself while I suck him. He swears and growls and

calls me "boy". His hips thrust faster and harder, and I almost gag as the tip of his dick touches the back of my throat. Even though I wasn't ordered to, I give his balls a squeeze.

"Goddamn," Miles hisses as his orgasm takes over.

We come together.

A strangled cry escapes him as he shoots a load of tasteless come down my throat. I swallow all of it.

Sergeant Miles removes his cock from my mouth and straightens up. I glance at Montgomery, who has a spent smile on his face as he pulls up his trousers. "You've got five minutes to swab the deck," he orders.

Once they enter the DI House, we silently grab our uniforms and make our way to the head.

I stare at Thibodeaux while he wipes come off his hand.

He glares at me. "What?"

"Guess this makes you a fag now."

"Don't you ever get angry?"

I look up from my notebook to glare at Thibodeaux. He's standing over me, his arms folded across his chest, though it looks like he's really hugging himself. The guy hasn't been the same since yesterday morning.

In a vain attempt at getting me to up the volume, Thibodeaux has been riding me hard since then, trying to antagonize me into yelling.

I don't.

I wonder if I continue to whisper, how will the drill instructors punish me this time? Being quarter-decked will be worth it for another session like yesterday.

"Yeah," I respond.

"So fucking get angry. Yell," Thibodeaux says through clenched teeth.

"I'm trying the best I can."

"That's bullshit," he barks. Most of the platoon looks our way.

I shrug. Thibodeaux huffs as he stomps off, approaching the elliptical in the back of the squad bay.

"Platoon 1811, ears," Medina commands. He'd just come from the DI House.

We stop what we're doing and face him. "Open, sir."

"Recruits Thibodeaux and Arrington will have last fire watch alone. Make sure the schedule's changed, Guide. Carry on."

"Carry on, aye, sir!" the entire platoon responds.

Not me and Thibodeaux. Our gazes meet across the room. His eyes darken with excitement and fear. Exactly what I feel.

At zero-two-thirty, Thibodeaux and I report for fire watch. We check footlockers and sea bags and make sure rifles are secured to their racks. We also fill everyone's canteens with water, and wash the last load of laundry that first fire watch started.

We don't talk, too busy wondering why we were singled out. Fire watch usually consisted of four recruits to divide up the tasks. The dryer machine in the backroom goes off. "I'll get it," Thibodeaux mumbles.

I grab his arm before he can leave.

"What?"

"I'm doing it on purpose," I admit. I hadn't meant to drag him into this. He's a damn good recruit.

Thibodeaux sighs. "I figured you were. Don't worry about it, man." He leaves me alone in the dark squad bay.

At zero-four-thirty, the drill instructors go through the same routine. The rude awakening, shuffling the other recruits in and out of the head, then out of the squad bay for morning chow.

This time, Thibodeaux and I are left alone with Medina, as well as Miles and Montgomery.

A surge of adrenalin shoots through me as Montgomery gives me a piercing glare. "Get over here, recruit," he demands. "Faster!"

"Aye, aye, sir." I move as fast as he wants until I stand within arm's length. He pulls me close, pressing me against his hard body. I moan into his mouth as he kisses me, hot and desperately. I taste his tongue against mine. It's sweet. My cock jumps as his hand snakes into my trousers and grabs a handful of my ass.

"Fuck!" Thibodeaux's groan grabs my attention. He's on all fours with Miles behind him, smacking his bare ass.

"Yeah, he likes it. Look how hard he is," Medina says.

Thibodeaux's cock is dripping.

"Get this goddamned uniform off now," Montgomery whispers into my ear.

I don't hesitate. In twenty seconds, I stand naked in front of him. My stomach churns as he stares at me.

"On the deck, recruit." He undoes the buttons on his trousers and whips out his monster cock. It's hard and straining.

I drop to my knees, but he pushes me onto my back. The cool concrete is uncomfortable, but I don't care.

Beside me, Thibodeaux curses as Miles shoves his prick deep inside of him. "That's what I like to hear," he breathes, smacking his ass again.

"Open wide, recruit." Medina thrusts inside Thibodeaux's mouth, stifling his sounds of pleasure.

Both men growl in ecstasy.

"Eyeballs, Arrington," Montgomery commands.

I face him. "Click, sir."

Montgomery is shirtless, his upper body more ripped than I'd imagined. I'm hard as fuck as he presses his heavy body against mine. I don't ever want him to move.

With little effort he tosses my legs over his shoulders, staring down at me with hungry eyes. "I'm gonna fuck you now, recruit."

I nod, licking my dry lips.

His dick prods my entrance. "Now say 'Aye, aye, sir,' if you want it."

"Aye, aye, sir," I respond, begging even to my own ears.

A bottle cap clicks open and something moist and cold slithers into my anus. I shudder.

Montgomery unwraps a condom and hands it to me. "Strap it on my dick, recruit. I'm sure even you can manage that."

"Yes, sir." I strap it on, giving his cock a squeeze as I roll it down. His groan is such a fucking turn-on.

He slides inside. My voice gets caught in my throat. His cock is so thick and hard, it stretches me painfully.

"Relax."

"Aye, aye, sir." I exhale a few times to steady myself. I've wanted this since the moment I laid eyes on him. The fact it's happening now doesn't even feel real.

Montgomery pushes deep, and I moan. With nothing to grasp on to, I stroke my dick, matching his slow and fluid rhythm. It's like he's massaging my insides with his cock.

I stare up into his hard blue gaze. It's bold, but he doesn't seem to mind my staring, and I can't miss his expression, the twinkle of confidence in his eyes, and the smirk on his lips.

Fuck, his lips . . .

"Sir, this recruit requests permission to kiss Senior Drill Instructor Staff Sergeant Montgomery."

He crushes his lips to mine, kissing me heatedly. I move mine against his, prepared to suck his tongue when he thrusts into me hard and quick, so deep that our lips separate and I throw my head back.

I cry out at the intensity of it.

"Holy shit, there it is," Medina pants from beside us. "Looks like you've got some volume after all!"

My face heats.

The embarrassment doesn't last long. Montgomery grabs my attention with another powerful thrust that bows my spine. I swallow the noises in my throat.

He slides out of me, and I shudder, already missing being filled up by him. He takes my place on his back on the concrete, and then pulls me on top of him. He positions my hips over his straining erection. "Ride my dick, Arrington. Face the other way."

"Aye, aye, sir." I slide onto his cock with a groan. He's so fucking deep inside me, I can't tell where our bodies separate. I don't even feel like myself. With both hands on my hips, he makes me ride him hard. The slew of cries and profanities leaving my mouth don't even sound like mine.

"Get over there, Thibodeaux." Miles's voice barely registers to my ears.

Until I feel a warm mouth sheathing my cock. My eyes fly open. It's Thibodeaux. His head bobs up and down as he sucks me from base to tip. My stomach tightens.

"Fuck," I groan, fisting Montgomery's trousers. The sight almost undoes me.

"He ain't a house mouse no more, are you, Arrington?" Miles asks with a grin.

"No, sir," I pant.

"What?"

"No, sir!" I cry out, as my body reaches its peak.

I ride Montgomery harder and faster, dizzy from the sensational overload. It makes things difficult for Thibodeaux, but I'm too lost to care. A hand pinches my nipple. I don't look to see if it's Miles or Medina.

All I know is I'm about to come and it's gonna be fucking amazing.

Montgomery's grip on my hips is bruising as he stills my entire lower body. This time, he thrusts his hips up, pounding into me like an animal in heat. The sound of his deep growls, and his flesh moving inside me so goddamn fast is too much.

"Oh shit, I'm coming."

Thibodeaux's mouth sucking my balls is the final push that sends me over the edge. I see stars as I cry out, spurting come into my squad leader's mouth. Medina and Miles are cheering.

Montgomery finally comes, releasing something close to an anguished cry as he shudders beneath me. I collapse onto his hard body, breathing in the scent of soap and clean sweat.

"You finally found your voice, huh? Took a lot of hard work to get there, but what kind of drill instructors would we be if we never pushed our recruits to their limits?" he says.

Despite how absurd the whole situation is, I smile. "Thank you, sir."

My throat hurts. Even though I proved I can get loud if necessary, I won't be quick to yell so soon. Only during last-ditch efforts to coax it out of me will my drill instructors ever hear my newly found voice again.

Speed Trap

Vivian Gwynn

It was a night that was made for driving. The stars were bright and the moon was full, and the air was that cool temperature that's perfect for cruising with your top down and the heater and seat warmers cranked up. The roads were empty, and it was an hour's drive from the party back to my house. A night like that, you could imagine that nothing in the world existed but the music in your car, so loud that it you felt it in your ribcage, the vibrations of the motor under you, the cones of light from your headlights, the flash of the yellow lines in the road and the bump-bump-bump of the reflectors if you drifted too far. It was a night that begged you to open up the throttle and let it go. You don't deny a night like that.

I'd had a few beers at the party, but nothing I wasn't used to driving on. And I needed to blow off a little steam – the blonde with the rack had teased me all night long, then ultimately refused to put out. As I drove back, I thought about just pulling it out and whacking off while I drove, but I didn't have any lotion or lube or anything, and I figured I'd just wait till I got home to take care of business. Besides, as far as blue balls cures go, you can do worse than doing 110 on a deserted road at 2 a.m., with the top down and U2 blasting at noise ordinance-breaking volumes.

The music was loud, so I didn't hear when the siren started up. I didn't know I was being pulled over until I happened to glance in my mirror and saw the lights. How long had he been there? Maybe I was drunker than I thought.

I looked in my rear-view mirror and put my hand up, pointing to myself questioningly, although I was the only person on the road. In answer, the policeman just gave me the finger. Guess he'd been there a long time. I laughed and put on my blinker.

I stopped at the side of the road, the police car's lights washing my car in blinding white. I was pretty sure he had his brights on. What a dick. I reached into the glove compartment and pulled out my driver's license and registration, then sat back to wait.

The cop took his sweet time, letting me stew in my worry at having been pulled over. I hunched down in my seat, out of the bright light reflected by my mirrors. Well, I wasn't too worried. This was hardly my first time being pulled over, and nine times out of ten, nothing came of it. When your dad's a judge on the state supreme court and your mom's company provides just short of fifty thousand jobs throughout California, you'd be surprised how many speeding tickets just sort of blow away.

A shadow approached, and I glanced up just as the policeman shined a blinding flashlight into the car. I blinked and got ready to put on my best "I'm-so-sorry-officer" smile.

"License and registration," the officer said, in a surprisingly high, feminine voice. I opened my eyes and squinted into the bright light. It was a woman, and actually a pretty attractive one. Nice face – angular and kind of mean in that sexy way, like Angelina Jolie. Good rack, flat stomach. Couldn't tell on the ass, unless she turned around. In my experience, police officers tended to frown on that request, though. Her uniform was clearly designed in that civil employee unisex-but-really-meant-for-men sort of way, and it fit her horribly. But it was the sort of horrible that pointed out all the wonderful ways that she wasn't shaped like a man, and that somehow crossed back over into sexy.

I smiled up into that bright light and handed over my identification. "I'm so sorry, officer," I said. "I was just trying to get home to Dad, and I must have lost track of how fast I was going."

"One hundred and twelve," the policewoman said sharply, finally dropping that awful light from my face. With it finally gone, I could see more of her. She had wavy black hair, which was tied severely back behind her, skin as white and smooth as eggshell, and full, red lips. She looked sexy and *angry*.

"Oh my goodness, was it that much?" I asked. "I'm so sorry.

Anyway, it's just that we've had a scare or two with Dad's health lately. So when he called and asked me to come to him, I did feel like I should hurry." I let my smile broaden. "I'm Oliver Blaine, by the way."

The policewoman looked slowly from my license to my face, her expression saying clearly that although she had seen stupider things in her life, I was making a strong campaign for the number-one spot. "I'm aware."

I rallied, looking at her badge for her name. "Officer Rawlins," I said. "I feel awful. I understand that you probably need to give me a ticket for going that fast, but if we could do it as quickly as possible, I really do want to get home to the Judge. And of course, I will be careful not to *ever* speed like this again." Sometimes reverse psychology was the best way to get out of things. Referring to my dad as "the Judge" might have been a bit much, but what if she thought I was just some other Oliver Blaine?

But Officer Rawlins just looked at me like I'd suggested, rather graphically, what she could do to herself. Or worse, what *I* would graphically like to do to her. Although I had to admit that I did want to do some of those things. Her big chest pushed out at the blue fabric of her tight uniform shirt, opening little windows between her straining buttons that I tried very hard not to look at.

Stupid blonde cocktease at the party. If she'd have put out, maybe I'd be able to think a little better here. I felt an erection begin, filling out against my tight pants, and I shifted, hoping that she didn't see it.

I opened my mouth to try again, but Officer Rawlins cut me off before I could even begin. "I'm aware that you are Oliver Blaine, yes, *that* Oliver Blaine, so you can stop the name-dropping. Your mom's company just laid off my brother, and some of your dad's decisions are making my work a lot more difficult, so things will go better if you just stop reminding me."

Rawlins gave me the whole bit. She pulled me out of my car for a breathalyser test and made me walk a line and recite the alphabet backward and forward. She glanced down at my crotch once while I was walking, and I think she could see my partial. Usually I don't mind when the ladies notice little Oliver, but this wasn't a sexy look; it was an angry one.

I was starting to get worried that I actually was going to get that ticket. Officer Rawlins wasn't warming up to me, and my parents were going to be mad when they found out. They didn't mind little things, but driving more than forty miles over the speed limit after a few drinks was going to steam them. Now, usually I care as little as any 22-year-old what his parents think, but when mom and dad got mad, they started taking away privileges. And when your parents are paying for your school, your cars and your trust fund, they actually have some sway over you.

Rawlins told me to sit by the side of the road and asked if she could search my car. I usually say no to requests like that, but I was hoping to get on her good side. Nothing I'd tried was working, and I thought that if I said yes, that might earn me some points with her. Besides, I had nothing to hide.

Or so I thought. Rawlins rummaged around the passenger side of my car, her ass sticking out into the night air – and it was in fact fine – and eventually came up with a bag of white powder.

Kenny. I was going to kill him. I *told* him not to bring his shit in my car. I'd given him a ride a week ago, and he must have left a bag in there. "That's not mine," I said lamely, sounding like every idiot on *Cops* ever. This was a nightmare. I should have just taken the speeding ticket. Now Mom and Dad really were going to kill me.

Officer Rawlins smiled for the first time, and it was not a nice smile. It was a smile that said that she had me by the balls, and she knew it. It was predatory and hungry, and for some reason that I couldn't fathom, it gave me a boner again.

"Look," I said, even as a voice inside me said to just quit, to stop digging myself deeper. "I was speeding, OK? And I was trying to get out of a ticket before, but I swear that this isn't mine. Some stupid friend of mine must have left it in here."

She didn't say anything, just smiled at me.

"If my parents find out, they'll freak out," I said. "Is there . . . is there any way that you could just give me a warning and I can try really, really hard to never do this again?"

Officer Rawlins looked at me for a long time before she spoke. "I don't like people like you," she said finally. I swallowed. "Driving your mommy's car, riding your daddy's coat-tails, trusting them to get you out of every mistake that you make. Spoiled. Soft. People like you never learn because you're always rescued from the consequences of your actions."

I was nervous now. She wasn't just being a hard ass, she actually had it in for me.

"I'd throw everything in the book at you," she said, "if I didn't know that it was going to just be your mommy's money paying the lawyers and the favors your daddy's owed getting you off the hook."

There was something in her eyes that frightened me, and I suddenly had images of my body, riddled with bullets, propped up in my car until some passer-by stopped and looked in the window.

"I'm sorry," I said for the millionth time, but I was actually starting to mean it. "There has to be some way we can deal with this. I'll do anything."

I was just about to start pointing out that mom and dad would actually be very upset, maybe even angry enough to refuse to give me legal help when Officer Rawlins looked at me.

"Shut up," she said. I shut up. There was something about her that just made you listen. "You need the experience of paying for your crimes yourself." She walked toward me where I was sitting on the ground. I stared up at her. Why was I so hard? I squirmed, trying to hide my erection and wondered how far I could get if I tried to run before she shot me down.

She came in front of me and crouched down. I tried very hard to keep my eyes on her face, instead of on the breasts that threatened to engulf my field of vision.

"I'll leave it up to you," she said, her voice like poisoned silk. "Option one: speeding ticket, DUI and possession. The state takes a run at you with everything we've got. Maybe Mom and Dad get you off, and maybe they don't. But even if they do, maybe they get a little tired of your bullshit and you lose a few rights."

I looked up, my heart beating. My throat felt dry. "Option two?" I asked in a whisper.

"Option two," she said. "I fuck you."

I *almost* laughed. I managed to disguise it as coughing. Oh God. Wait until the boys heard about this. It was like a damn porno.

Rawlins had almost fooled me with her whole angry cop shtick; she'd been *good*, but apparently all she wanted was a piece of old Oliver Blaine.

"Well," I said, "option two."

"You sure?" Rawlins asked, and I let my eyes finally go roving on her like they wanted. She was a hot piece of ass, that was for sure.

"Sure," I said.

"All right," she said. She pitched the bag of cocaine out into the bushes. "Strip and get in the patrol car."

I stood and took off my shirt, flexing my chest and abs just enough that I looked extra buff, but not so much that it *looked* like I was flexing. I wasn't one of those rich assholes who just trusted girls to fall for him because of the trust fund and family name. I put work into myself, and I looked good. I tossed it into my car, then pulled off my slacks and boxers and put them in too.

Rawlins looked me up and down, and I could tell that she liked what she saw. She sent her flashlight over me, illuminating my tanned chest, the definition in my abs and legs, aiming at my crotch so that my cock cast a shadow a hundred feet long behind me. She grunted and opened the car door for me.

I got in. I'd been in the back of cop cars before, but never naked. The seat was rough and hard, and the inside of the patrol car was colder than the outside air. Rawlins had been running the AC.

I grabbed at the bars and sat forward as Rawlins got in and started driving, taking us off the highway onto some small country road.

"So," I asked, trying to sound confident, like I turned traffic stops into booty calls all the time. "How are we going to do this? Missionary? Cowgirl? Doggy style?"

"Oh, doggy style," she said as she drove on the bumpy road. "Definitely doggy style."

Nice. I wouldn't mind getting a handful of that ass, watching her down on the ground in front of me, moving for me. I was getting hard again, and this time I'd finally be able to do something with it.

Rawlins stopped the car and got out, then opened the door

for me. The night air was cool and delicious, and once she turned off the car, it was dark all around. I couldn't see lights from the city or cars, couldn't even see light pollution. All there was were pinpricks of stars and the silvery light of the moon. The light illuminated the dust and brush, glinted off of the car – and washed over Rawlins's white skin as she began to undo the buttons of her shirt.

There wasn't any sound except the cooling of the car engine as I watched her shirt slowly come open. I stared in the darkness, willing my eyes to adapt. Her skin was nothing but shades of silver and gray, but what interesting shades of silver and gray they were. Here was a line of black in the middle of her chest – her bra. And here was a darker spot in the middle of her belly – her navel.

Her shirt open, she undid her pants and stepped out of them. She was wearing no panties, and I caught a glimpse of a dark triangle of hair between her legs. At the sight, I felt myself swell even harder, felt my heart pound like the recoil of a gun. She pulled her shirt off, unhooked her bra, released her breasts. They hung down in the night, large and heavy, the nipples only visible as small dark circles in the darkness.

She turned away from me, leaned into the car for something, and I saw her ass, pale and round in the moonlight. I moved forward and grabbed her, threading my cock between her legs and rubbing it against her pussy.

"I'm sorry," Rawlins said as she straightened and came out of the car. Moonlight glinted off the gun in her hand. Her voice was like ice. "You must have misunderstood me. I said, "*I'm* going to fuck *you*.""

I stepped slowly back, my hands in the air. OK, so she wanted to be in charge. That was cool with me. And again, I don't know why, but seeing that gun pointed at me, I was hornier than I could ever remember having been.

She reached down and tapped my cock with her gun. It was cold against me, and my cock didn't give an inch. It was so hard that it felt like it would burst.

"You like this?" Rawlins asked. "You like when a woman takes charge?"

It seemed like honesty was the best answer. I nodded.

"Put these on." Rawlins held out a pair of handcuffs. I slipped them on and clicked them shut. "Good boy."

Rawlins reached into the car again, and she came out with something that was hard to see in the night. It was dark, and it sort of looked like a nightstick, but there was also something that looked like fabric. I squinted at it.

Rawlins held it, stepped into it like it was a pair of panties. But that nightstick still stood out in front. And then I realized. It was a strap-on.

"Um," I said. "I'm actually not into anal stuff."

Rawlins moved toward me, a gun in one hand, a big black dildo protruding from her crotch. "Well, if you were," she said, "this wouldn't be much of a consequence, would it?"

She shot her hand forward, grabbed my balls and squeezed. I cried out. I wasn't sure whether it was pleasure or pain that I was feeling, but whatever it was, it was intense. She tugged downward, forcing me down onto my knees. I looked up at her, her breasts pale in the night, the stars dully reflecting on the matt surface of her strap-on.

"Tonight I'm going to fuck you," Officer Rawlins said. "You're so used to being the fucker. You're the one who does the girls, who breaks the laws – your perspective is the only one that matters, right? You're the one who acts, and if the world doesn't like it, then it can just fuck itself." She pressed the dildo up against my cheek. It was cold and hard and trailed smoothly over me. "But tonight you get to see what it's like to have someone else be the one in charge. You get to see what it's like to be just like the rest of us. Tonight I'm going to fuck you just like you fuck all of your little whores."

She was a piece of work. Ordinarily, I would have just told her to fuck herself and gotten on with my life. But ordinarily I wouldn't be naked and handcuffed in the middle of nowhere, with a gun-wielding policewoman who, at least at the moment, had a bigger dick than I did. I was terrified and strangely aroused. I couldn't see it in the darkness, but I could feel a droplet of pre-come ooze out of my cock and start to slowly drip down it.

Rawlins grabbed my hair in one hand and pressed the dildo against my lips. I tried to keep them closed, but she slapped me and whispered, "It goes in your ass next. I'd lick it if I were you."

I licked it. I ran my tongue all the way up and down it. I hadn't been able to see it in the dim light, but it was a realistic dildo, with veins and ridges and the swell of a head. I could feel all that detail now. Rawlins pushed into my mouth, deep enough that I gagged, and I tried to relax my throat around it.

"Yeah," she said, her voice loud in the silent night. "Suck it, bitch."

I sucked it. I'd never done anything like this before. I'd never been with a man, and whenever I'd been with a girl, I'd been in charge. Even if she was the one on top, I was still the one calling the shots. Now I was completely at this woman's mercy.

The ground was rocky and uncomfortable against my bare skin, and I shifted my weight to try and get more comfortable. Rawlins slapped me. "Don't stop, slut."

My face burned. She'd hit me hard, hard enough that I saw bright flashes in the darkness. This was humiliating. I knew that I should be taking notes, making plans to sue the bitch into oblivion as soon as this was over and I was home. But actually, this was the sexiest thing that had ever happened to me.

Rawlins pulled the strap-on out of my mouth and then twisted her hips, slapping my face lightly with it. She walked around behind me, then planted a hand between my shoulder blades and pushed. I came down, catching myself hard on my handcuffed hands.

She kicked my legs apart and came down between them. I stared straight ahead into the night. I couldn't believe this. I felt Rawlins's hand around my balls, grabbing and squeezing, tugging gently on them. I felt her run her fingernails along them, scratching lightly at the loose skin, and I suddenly and incongruously wondered if she'd painted her fingernails and what color they were. I'd seen them before, but I now couldn't remember.

Then I felt her fingers on me, pushing at my asshole, massaging it and pressing in. I tensed unconsciously.

"It'll be easier if you relax and let it happen," Rawlins said. "Fucking and being fucked are two different things. If you're fucking, you can just be a hard, stubborn dick. But when you're getting fucked, you'd better learn to accommodate another person's will. You'd better learn to be loose."

With that she pushed inward, probing into me with a finger that felt like it was the size of a mop handle. I whimpered, but relaxed. It was painful, but also strangely pleasurable. I felt strangely filled up, in a way that I hadn't known was possible.

I breathed and relaxed around the finger.

"Good, bitch," said Rawlins. "Now can you do two fingers?"

"No," I said before I could stop myself, and then she pulled her finger out and flicked my balls, hard. I winced and cried out, feeling a bloom of pain and tension in my loins. Rawlins reached out over my thigh and grabbed my cock. It was still hot and full and hard. She touched the tip, then wiped the wetness off on my ass cheek.

"You can't lie to me, you slut," she said. "You like this." She grasped my balls again, then squeezed gently, warningly. "Now can you do two fingers?"

"Yes," I whispered.

I moaned as she slid the second finger slowly in. The second finger was more painful coming in, but I did my best to relax and welcome it, and when it was in, I felt even fuller, even better.

I was panting, from pain and pleasure and excitement.

"Beg for my cock," Rawlins said. "Beg for it, you little whore."

I could imagine her fingers around my nut-sac again. "Please," I said, even as I winced, thinking about that big black dildo. "Please give me your cock."

"What do you want?" she asked.

"I want you to fuck me," I whispered. And suddenly I realized that I meant it. "Fuck me," I said again, louder.

I felt her place a hard, cold weight on my back, just under my shoulder blades – her gun. Then, slowly, she grasped my hips in her hands, twining her fingers into the hollow between my thigh and trunk. I panted, anticipating and fearing what was coming next. I gripped the dusty ground with my fingers and stared down at it, trying to make out the shapes of the rocks in the dim light. I'd taken a lot of women while they were in this position, but I'd never been in it myself. I felt more helpless than I'd ever felt before. I tried to listen, to feel revealing small movements, to notice anything that might give me a hint of when she was going to penetrate me.

Then, all at once I felt the tip of her strap-on pressing against me, and it felt enormous. I winced and cried out, my eyes wide and staring in the darkness. I bit my lip and tried to relax as it began to slowly slide into me.

"Mommy can't help you now," Rawlins said as she pushed in a fraction of an inch. "Daddy can't help you." Another thrust. I moaned, a strange high-pitched moan. "You get exactly what you deserve now, bitch." With the last word, she spat on my back, and I startled at the sudden splash of warm liquid.

And then, with that, she pushed up all the way inside. I cried out again, my mouth gaping wordlessly. I wanted more than anything to get away, to crawl away, but her weight was on me, holding me down, and her cock was in me, impaling me like I was a goddamn insect on a pin. And yet, at the same time, I was also ragingly hard, dripping, and I wanted to push back into her. I knew that if she pulled out, I'd be following her on my hands and knees, begging to be taken again.

Officer Rawlins came down on me, and I felt her against me, felt her belly smearing the pool of spittle around on me and pushing the hard outlines of her gun against my spine. I felt her breasts, warm and heavy, draping on me. She grabbed my arms in hers as she thrust into me. My arms began to shake, and I didn't know whether it was from the intensity of her thrusts or her weight on me.

And then her arm snaked down, trailing over my chest, brushing my nipple, tracing my ribcage and lower, until she grabbed my cock. I gasped when she touched it, then moaned as she began to rub it vigorously. I was dripping with my own pre-come, but it was still intense, almost unmercifully so.

Officer Rawlins thrust into me while she rubbed me, pumping me until I was crying out in the night, making sounds like weeping, every part of me shaking. I was about to come.

"Well then," she said. "If you can't last any longer than that, let's see what that little dick can do."

I felt embarrassed and ashamed and unmanned and *horny as hell*. I moaned and bit my lip and began to come, feeling my cock starting to clench and pump, feeling my ass tensing around her cock. And, as I came, she grabbed the back of my head, forcing it downward so my hot come spurted into my face. I startled – it was hot, like blood – then relaxed into it, surrendering.

My climax sapped my strength, and I sank slowly to the ground as Officer Rawlins pulled out of me and stood. I lay there, my come turning the dust below me to mud, which clung to my cock and belly and chest.

Officer Rawlins threw something to me in the dark. It bounced off my shoulder and landed beside me. It was the key to the handcuffs. "Follow this road back to the interstate, then head a half-mile south and you'll find your car," she said, as I stared up at her strange, confusing silhouette.

Then she blew a kiss at me, got back into her car and drove away.

Coming Clean

Angela Steele

Karen Delaney was lost, and everything she had relied on had let her down. Her GPS device and her mobile phone had failed her. Even her supposedly much-vaunted sense of direction had for once left her a long way from, well, anywhere.

Lost in the wilds with no one to help her get home.

The woman ran her fingers through her long auburn hair and sighed. She reached for the road map on the empty car seat next to her, but there was little point: there were no signposts and it was getting dark. The chance of being able to locate some feature she could translate into a meaningful direction was growing smaller by the second. She would have to ask for help, but even that seemed unavailable in the darkening landscape. Already the walls and hedges were fading into the blackness and the shapes of the trees were losing their definition against the late evening sky.

Briefly, Karen contemplated the prospect of spending the night in her car. She shuddered. Not because it was cold – it was summer and the day had been warm – but because she would be rushing to get to her appointment on time, assuming she could find out where she was when dawn broke. Karen would much rather be in the hotel her secretary had booked and thus able to arrive at her business meeting tomorrow fully refreshed and distinctly uncreased. That wasn't going to be possible, she thought, unless someone came along the twisting road and she could flag them down. The woman however hadn't seen a vehicle for ages, and she shivered again. While she didn't entirely believe in things that went bump in the night, she knew from childhood holidays spent in remote farms that the night was full of creatures that made unfamiliar noises. Even if she got comfortable on the back seat of the car and knew the doors were locked she wouldn't sleep much listening to various rustlings and scratchings and grunts in the darkness.

Still, Karen had no choice right now. She could drive aimlessly for a long time before she found a signpost she could read or locate an inn with a spare room. A meal would be good, too, as it was a long time since she'd grabbed a hasty sandwich on her way out of the office and told her secretary that she would be incommunicado for the rest of the day. Of course she wouldn't be if her phone battery hadn't died. The woman made a mental note to buy a better phone with a decent battery as soon as she got back to civilization. The social media manager of one of the country's brightest advertising agencies shouldn't be out here alone, she thought grimly, without some method of communication.

Feeling just a little sorry for herself, Karen was about to climb into the back of the car to make herself comfortable when she saw a light flicker through the darkened hedgerow ahead. For a moment she held her breath, listening for the sound of a car. But even with the window wound down there was no sound of an engine, and the light ahead of her wasn't moving. Oh well, she thought, a building, and if a light's on then maybe someone's at home. She started her car and moved off in the direction of the light, hoping that this twisting country road wouldn't in some devious way take her away from what she assumed must be a cottage or probably a farmhouse. They would surely have a phone or at least a decent idea of where she actually was.

Unlike her phone and her GPS, the road didn't let her down and despite numerous turns she was getting closer to the light. It was late but she felt better than she had for a while. A call to the hotel to tell them she was merely delayed, directions on how to get to a good road and then the prospect of a welcoming – and deserved – long soak in a bath wouldn't be out of the question. She would arrive on time at her meeting in the morning, uncrumpled, and in her usual confident way proceed to wow them. Life, she reflected as she turned her car into the long drive leading to the light, was good and she was too.

The light was the porch light of a small farmhouse. A small operation, she knew as she drew the car up on the gravel in front of the farm. Her many visits to farms as a child had told her all the signs to look for, whether they cultivated crops or raised animals (or worst of all, kept pigs too close to the house) and above all the size of the undertaking. But there was no sign of large machinery and the barn she could make out to one side of the house was old and not too large. It wouldn't, she concluded, be full of factory-bred chickens squawking furiously in their tiny cages. That would be a relief, almost as much as the absence of any pigsty smell.

Karen got out of her car and approached the farmhouse door, smoothing down her neat, knee-length dark skirt and flicking her hair back. She wanted to look presentable just in case the farmer – or more likely his wife who were often ill-disposed old bags – would send her on her way without any help. She knocked confidently and wondered if she ought to have spent a few moments applying her lipstick, but dismissed it. Most people in remote places like this wouldn't notice any subtleties of the latest fashionable shade. The door opened almost at once and an elderly man stared at her. His full head of white hair was a generous mop but his weathered face was creased and lined and he was probably about twice Karen's age, which would put him on the verge of retirement. But then farmers in small operations like this didn't retire; they just kept farming.

He was wearing blue dungarees in the way old farmers did, and that old familiar tingle swept through the woman.

"Good evening," said Karen with a smile, hiding her small gulp. "I'm afraid I'm lost and I was wondering if I might make a phone call? My mobile phone has died on me and my GPS seems to be offline and—" she shrugged helplessly "—it's late and I don't know where I am."

"Grove Farm," said the man, not moving and still staring at her.

"Yes, of course . . . but . . . I don't know where Grove Farm is." Karen smiled again and tried not to look at his blue boiler suit, tried not to imagine what was inside it. Ludicrous, the thought flashed through her mind. An old man, of course, with a podgy belly. But still, it was a podgy man in blue dungarees with a thick woollen shirt underneath the thin blue fabric, which always got her. That and the wellington boots he wore. She really tried hard not to look down at the shiny black rubber, wondering if they were splattered on the sole with animal muck and mud and God knows what else from rutting, fucking animals.

"It's here," said the old man, as if it was obvious. "Grove Farm's here."

Oh Lord, thought Karen, I have actually found the village idiot. A village idiot in the approved dungaree style.

"Is there a phone I could use? I'd pay you for the call, of course. Then I'll be on my way and you can, um, get a good night's sleep ready for—" Karen almost said harvest but it was still summer, so instead she said "Milking the cows."

"Haven't got any," said the man. He was looking Karen up and down and still hadn't moved.

"I see. Well, whatever. If you could point me in the direction of the nearest town I'd be grateful."

"You don't want to go there," the man said.

Karen felt weary. "No, probably not," she said, "but you see I have to be, you know . . . at my aunt's tomorrow. It's her birthday. Seventy she is and sadly not as healthy as she was." It was an unexpected lie but Karen had figured that this man would know nothing about meetings regarding the use of social media for advertising. Play the concerned relative, she had thought. Make him sympathetic.

The plan didn't seem to provoke a response, so Karen added, "Is your good lady wife in? Perhaps she can help me?"

"Cissy died five years ago," said the man. "Just me now."

"I'm sorry to hear that. Look, I know this is very strange at this hour but my appointment tomorrow—"

"Aunt's birthday," said the old man.

"Of course, yes. I always call it that, seeing family." She laughed nervously. "I need to get to her house."

"Which is where?"

"Oh, Bristol." The lie was out of Karen before she could stop herself, hoping the light from the porch wasn't good enough to reveal her blush.

The old man laughed with a deep unexpected rumble. "No it ain't. Bristol's miles away. You aren't that lost, girl."

Karen opened her mouth to say she wasn't a girl any more but the man stood aside. "You better come in and start telling me the truth. Maybe then I can help you."

"I don't—" began Karen, but she felt another wave of weariness come over her. It was stupid not telling the truth and she nodded. "Of course," she said, and stepped into the large stone-floored kitchen with its flickering log fire and polished copper pans hanging above the hearth and dominated by a large wooden table polished smooth by years of scrubbing. A big homely kitchen just like so many of the ones she had stayed in when she was a teenager. Places where men in their blue dungarees suits and muddy wellingtons would fascinate her and the sight of them would make that hot tremble in her sex grow and send her hurrying to bed early to masturbate. Times when she would gasp and imagine a man in such a uniform – because that was what it was, what they all wore – who would know about sex because they had seen animals do it. Seen it close up. Encouraged them to, maybe guided them. Sex mad, eager, powerful animals shagging and humping and making new life. God, she had come to that thought a thousand times. Not over the animals, but the thought of men watching them, talking about sex as if it was matter of fact, which to them it would be. Men watching in their rough blue dungarees and big, messy wellington boots. Walking in what the animals did.

"You're a strange one," said the man, shutting the door behind Karen. "You look at me like you want something."

"What? No, of course I don't! I mean, yes, well . . . just to use a phone. That's all. Some directions to, um, Tewkesbury, too."

"Not Bristol, then?" The man walked past Karen, leaving her standing. He settled into a large rocking chair in front of the fire, a chair with arms worn away at the front by years of rubbing the palms of his work-hardened hands on them. The only chair in the room, and he wasn't going to make way for Karen.

"Mr . . . Uh . . ." Karen hesitated, wishing she wasn't shaking the way she was. This, she told herself, was ludicrous. What she did as a teenage girl was a long time ago and shouldn't count now. She'd had proper relationships since then, even if she did think of rough men in dungarees and blue boiler suits and wellingtons whenever she climaxed. Every time. "I don't know your name. My name is Karen Delaney and I work in advertising and—"

"And you find yourself here." The man turned his gaze from the flickering flames to the flushed woman. "Telling lies."

"I wasn't really telling a lie," protested Karen. "Just trying to get some help."

The man in the blue dungarees lifted the sole of one his boots towards the fire, as if trying to warm his foot through the thick, ridged rubber sole. A sole streaked with muck and heaven knew what else. "My boots. You like 'em, Karen Delaney?"

"I-I d-don't know what you mean." Karen somehow stammered the words out. She fidgeted where she stood, unsure what to do. "Just . . . boots."

"Maybe. You know, girl, people from towns like to think they're cleverer than us country folk." The man put his raised foot down and offered the sole of his other muddy boot to the fire. "Seems to me though they come by places like Grove Farm looking for something. Something simpler. Bit more earthy, you know?"

"No, I don't," whispered Karen. Part of her was telling her to go and the rest of her refused to move.

"Well, let me say this. Gets lonely out here on the land at times. Makes you miss things, like that table. What it's good for." The man still was warming his foot but he nodded to the table. Worn and polished smooth and clear enough of cups and plates and pans. The right height, Karen told herself, which was ridiculous so she admonished her mind. Despite that, Karen blushed furiously. She clasped her hands in front of her. Nothing like the sort of thing she did in meetings when she used her hands to describe her power, her business prowess. Now they were holding themselves together the way a timid girl would, keeping herself in. Don't let me, a small voice in her said.

The old man in the blue dungarees got up and stretched. "It's late, woman, and I don't have time for games. All you have to do is get yourself over that table, face down, and I will see to you." He was undoing the buttons of the fly at the front of his dungarees. Karen watched mesmerized as he flipped his long, semi-hard cock out. "Skirt up, girl, and legs apart. I reckon you probably like it the way animals do it, from the back."

"It isn't like that," said Karen, eyes wide, but she wasn't moving. Not running away.

"Always like that when you get down to it," said the farmer. His cock was harder now, longer and shiny pink at the end. A stark contrast to the thin weave of his dungarees. The ones he wore when he made animals have sex, she was sure.

"I shouldn't," Karen said.

"But you will." The man took a step in his mud-splattered wellingtons towards Karen. Not threatening, but purposeful. A man who was used to things being done his way because you didn't waste time. Nature wouldn't wait, would it?

"What about after," said Karen. She was scared and aroused and desperate. The fire in her burned brighter than the flames on the logs.

"What about it?" Another step closer, his cock seemingly thrusting at her, its single eye open, weeping already.

"I mean, your clothes." Karen gasped as she finally said what she had never dared say to anyone before. The d-word, she called it privately. "Dungarees. Your dungarees. You don't want them to get soiled."

"Muck happens, girl. But you can wash 'em. By hand. Tomorrow morning, before I go to work. Clean my boots too, if you like." The old man laughed. Closer, harder. He knew, and they both knew. The dam in Karen broke and she didn't resist, ready to open her legs as much as her dammed skirt would allow.

"How many things do I have to wash and clean for you, sir?"

"Plenty," said the farmer. He chuckled at the word "sir". The old man was up to the woman now, taking her arm, helpfully guiding her into a bending position over the polished table so that Karen's breasts, with their hard nipples, pressed onto the smooth wood. Her skirt came up and the seam ripped under his strong hands and her pants were pulled roughly aside. His hard cock slammed into Karen's sex like it belonged there. She gasped, not at the invasion, but at the fact she could see now another pair of muddy wellingtons by the far wall, with a pair of blue dungarees by the side of them, thrown down carelessly on the dirty floor. His clothes, his boots. Waiting for her attention. What he wore, what she always loved.

Karen cried out as the man hammered into her, not from anger or resentment or fear, but the pleasure of knowing tomorrow she would be happy cleaning his dungarees, watching him wear them, watching him be appreciative of what she did, how willingly she took his thick cock without complaint at the back. His boots too. Polishing them, maybe kissing them. Possibly even using her tongue in those dirty hard rubber ridges, if the farmer wanted her to. And if he didn't then she would do it quietly when he was out with his animals and she waited in the farmhouse, ready to be fucked again the way he wanted. Any way he wanted if she was honest, which was how it should be, her tits sore from wearing a polished groove in the wood. Perhaps the way Cissy used to do for her husband.

But Karen wasn't a wife. She was little more than his faithful animal and animals had sex, didn't they? Willingly, from the back.

That was the thing she now understood. He was rough and ready, but the important thing was he was holding her down, using her his way and he was going to satisfy himself. She would tomorrow dress him in his spotless dungarees and ease his feet into the clean boots and then bend over without a sound and stare longingly at the dirty ones waiting for her attention. Ready for her tongue, her love.

The old stainless steel dog bowl lay next to them too, and she thought of eating from it with her arse in the air. Hungry and ready, some would say. Glad to come clean.

Karen Delaney knew she really wasn't lost any more.

Fenced

Sommer Marsden

I hear the sharp whistle. It cuts through the thick August air. I keep my window open if the night is bearable and tonight it is. I can picture him out there, having dropped his duffle bag somewhere. Having stripped off his uniform and taken a quick cold shower because things like hot water weren't important to men like him.

My pulse ratchets up and I suck in a shuddery breath.

I shove my legs into a short denim skirt and pull a V-neck T-shirt over my head. I know my nipples are visible through the over-washed fabric and I'm fine with that. I'm fine with everything about hearing that whistle.

I hurry down, past the living room where my brother and his goofy friends are camped out. Past the rat-a-tat-tat of some gangster movie. My parents are away for the weekend. The boys don't even know I'm here. I shouldn't be, after all. Twenty-six-year-old women should not be home, but between crappy pay and an apartment building that went and got itself condemned. Well . . . it happens.

None of that is important now because being home means access to him. When he's home and I'm home . . . magic happens.

I hurry, barefooted through the short dry crab grass. Past Daddy's vintage pickup he swears he'll get running one day. Past the chicken coop and its now-silent dwellers. They won't start making noise until the sun comes up. Past the wood-cutting stump where an ax sticks up from the beaten-up wood, an ever-present accent like something from a painting. Past the strawberry patch. I cover a lot of ground very fast, especially for being barefoot, because where I really want to be is at the fence.

The fence divides our neighbor's small plot of land from our much larger one. We have two-thirds of a working farm. They have a regular home with an acre and "play" at being country folks, as my father says. Which is fine with me. I have always played at *not* being country folk.

I bolt quickly through the dark, nothing but the stars and a piece of moon to light my way, duck beneath an ancient oak and then dart to the fence. It's hysterical, really. Not much of a fence if you own a farm. Fences like this are a joke – or, if you prefer, "ornamental". Chain-link of all things. It only runs from one copse of trees to another copse of trees to mark off what land belongs to them and what land belongs to us.

"There she is," Nick says softly. I can smell soap and aftershave and him on the barely there August breeze.

Cold water runs down my spine. Fire lights my face. I'm a mix of cold and warm and all of me is confused. But for the part of me that's wet and willing between my legs.

This ritual of ours started two years ago right after he joined the military. I'd come up to the farm for Fourth of July. He was home on leave, partying with friends and family. I remember seeing him pull up in a white Jeep, his camouflage on, his hat smashed down over his close-cropped hair. I hadn't really given him a second thought until we'd both stumbled back toward the fence drunk. Him on his side of the fence to pee, me to get away from my oversized, over-loud, over-inebriated family. I'd just wanted silence but what I'd gotten was a soft whistle and a "Well, look what just wandered up to my fence."

I'd thought he was a goof. A ham. A man who was more muscle than brain. I'd thought him a bit crude. But he was big and broad and God . . . just fuck-me-fast handsome and I had been tipsy and . . .

"Come over to the fence."

I went.

"Closer."

I went. Not knowing why. Just going. Maybe it was the command in his voice. You can't spend time in the military without picking up a commanding tone, now can you?

"Cloooooooser," he whispered in the dark. I could smell beer and cigarettes and the scent of woodchips and active man now that we were closer. I followed his voice the way the children followed the Pied Piper.

I drifted closer to him. The fence hit me above my waist. It hit him right at the hip bones. He was a tall one.

"Hi." He grinned down at me, his face predatory in the light from that slice of moon.

"Hi," I whispered.

"You're pretty. I've seen you. Marilee, right?"

I nodded.

"Off at school, right?"

Another nod.

He leaned in and smelled my neck. I figured I'd flinch but I didn't. If anything I'd found myself leaning forward as if to let him get a better whiff of my scent. I flashed briefly to the willing victims in vampire movies. The girls who swooned and offered up their pretty pale necks for the biting.

"I'm Nick."

"Nick," I repeated.

"Nick." He reached out and brushed a piece of my hair behind my ear. All that stood between us had been that fence. "Will you do something for me, Marilee?"

"Hmm?" I'd shut my eyes. For some reason, I was lulled by him.

"Shove your shorts down."

My eyes popped open.

"And your panties. And put your pussy right up to the fence."

It had stopped being a question.

A strangled little laugh had escaped me and I'd said, "You're joking, right?" There was no way. How could he even ask something like that. Maybe that worked with other girls. Maybe because he swaggered around in uniform all machismo and banter.

But he wasn't in uniform now and I was fighting the urge to obey him. "Right?" I whispered before he could answer.

He shook his head and made a tsking noise with his tongue.

To my surprise, but not his, it seemed, I found myself doing just as he'd asked. I'd pushed down my shorts and my panties and pressed myself to the fence links. I watched him, or more the shadow of him, drop to his knees on the other side. It had to be the most bizarre tableau I'd thought wildly. The fence was made of big, generous metal diamonds that allowed his tongue to snake through. To find my clit. It had some give, which allowed me to push against it even further so he could reach me better. He licked me with a nimble, generous tongue as I shoved my pussy against that stupid fence and clutched the top and sighed softly in the thick humidity of the July night.

I'd come just as the fireworks went off in the west field. His bowed head tie-dyed with red and white and blue.

He'd stood and turned and walked away without another word. I stumbled back to the party, stunned and flushed from more than summer heat. Since then, when I heard his whistle, I always went to see if he was there. Of course he always was.

We'd never breached the fence. But we'd gone further through those stupid diamonds than where we started.

I snap out of memory lane as he reaches over the fence and grabs my wrist, pulls me forward, my belly banging the fence top. He kisses me and pulls my hair and waits for me to whimper.

"Did you get home today?"

"Just an hour ago. I was . . . waiting." He cocks his head and looks at me.

"Waiting?"

"To see you. I've been counting the seconds until dark."

I can't help the rustle and thump of excitement in my belly. And something more too. But that I won't examine. Not now.

Are we ever going to hop the fence? I wonder. I think what keeps us from doing it is it will break the magical spell of this arrangement. It will suddenly be more than fucking and sucking and pleasure. It would sway into the territory of relationships and neither of us have much interest in being adults. At least we haven't up until now. He's stationed close to home at the moment and ever since I had to move back home the whistles have increased. So does the rate of my heart when I hear it.

"Where are you?" he says in my ear, fingers pinching my nipples hard enough to make my skin erupt in gooseflesh.

"Right here. Just remembering the first time you . . ."

"Hike up that skirt, pretty girl. Push it up and bend over. I want to fuck you tonight."

It's a challenge and a pleasure. Working around the fence. But we've found a million things can be done this way. And we're still trying. A blow job is so much more dangerous and alluring when done through the fence. His fingers in my pussy as I press my ass back against the links. And now . . . we've managed to master fence fucking.

I do as asked and push that skirt down. He makes a satisfied noise when he sees me bare beneath. I step free of the denim and push my ass to the fence. Bend over with my hands on my knees. My hair hangs down in my face, the cicadas screaming like banshees in the darkness.

The most challenging fence interludes are winter. Chain-links get cold. Very cold.

But not tonight. Tonight, his cock sliding through the fence to drag along slick split is intoxicating. There's not much room for play so within a breath he's inside me. Thrusting hard enough to get deep. I'm pressing back so that I feel the bite of the fence, the invasion of his cock. I push my hands back and weave my fingers into the metal, grip the links with trembling fingers, balancing myself in a squat so that I can be penetrated and taken. So that I can surrender to his will and the will that lives deep inside me.

This drive to fuck. This secret we share. The compulsion to put a barrier between us to keep this thing as it is and not let it progress any further. This is the pursuit of pleasure and nothing more. I tell myself that almost every day.

But he's started appearing in my dreams. And in them there is no fence between us.

He reaches over the top and winds a big hand in my hair. He tugs it just enough to send a hot, dark thrill shivering through me. I come. Just like that. Just like heat lightning when the full summer heat hits.

"There's my girl," he whispers and the words secretly elate me.

A few more thrusts and the fence is rattling. I stroke my tender clit as my thighs scream, and when he pants and then growls as he comes, I come again. A soft clenching pleasure deep inside.

Nick pulls free and I stand. I stoop to grab my skirt, start to walk away. I'm not sure I can look at him without him knowing that part of me wants to move past meeting at the fence. He reaches out, snags my shoulder and reels me in.

"Hey, there." He pulls me forward and kisses me on the

mouth. His tongue is warm and sweet. "I'm getting ready to run out with friends."

Something in my chest dips. I hate that thing. This odd dependency I've somehow grown inside myself. But then:

"Tomorrow . . ."

"Tomorrow?" I echo.

"I want to meet in the barn instead. The old one that's at the back of your property."

"The barn that used to be the barn before the new barn?" I laugh, because that's what my dad calls it.

He nods. "The old barn. I'm tired of the fence," he says.

I blink fast and hard and hope he can't truly see my face in the dark. "OK," I say, nonchalantly.

"Good. I'm tired of the fucking fence." Another kiss and he starts to walk away. "Listen for me tomorrow."

"I will."

"And then meet me at the barn."

"Yes," I say. And I smile at the foreign words. The new meeting place. We've moved beyond the fence. Another thrill worms through me and I'm smart enough to know it has nothing to do with location.

A Cock & Bull Story

Michael Bracken

Jeremy leaned against the worn wood of the bar one Friday night, nursing his beer and watching the other men crowded into the Cock & Bull. Whippet-thin – more runner than bodybuilder – he wore a short-sleeved blue-and-white-striped seersucker shirt tucked into khaki chinos, and I only knew his name because he had failed to remove the cheap "Hello My Name Is" tag stuck to his shirt front. He wore no jewelry save for a gold wristwatch, and his closely cropped, sun-bleached hair appeared more blond than brunette.

When I saw him tip his beer bottle up to drain the last of its contents, I opened a fresh one. As soon as Jeremy placed the empty on the bar I replaced it with the bottle I had just opened. He glanced at me, almost as if seeing me for the first time, and said, "Thanks."

The Cock & Bull is my place. With money from a loan shark and protection from a local made guy, I had opened the Cock & Bull thirty years earlier, when serving my clientele had been a high-risk venture, and I had kept the bar open during many lean times through sheer willpower. The Cock & Bull had grown increasingly popular in recent years thanks in part to society's increasing acceptance of my clientele and thanks in part to a retro feel that came more from inability to upgrade than from intentional decorating decisions. Though a part-time bartender helps on weekends, I still work the stick every night, and over the years I've seen my share of hook-ups, break-ups and make-ups. I'd even had a few flings of my own, but no relationship had ever lasted beyond my one-night-stands' morning-after sobriety.

Though the place was crowded, which meant both of us were

hustling behind the stick, I was able to keep an eye on Jeremy. He didn't approach anyone and, despite his obvious not-from-around-here vibe, no one approached him. Maybe that's because I had made it clear to some of the regulars that the new guy was clearly on my radar that night.

After a while, Jeremy slipped down the hall to the men's room. When he returned, the name badge was gone from his chest and his short hair had been freshly combed. He waved his empty bottle to catch my attention, and a moment later, as I placed a third beer in front of him, he asked, "Is it always like this?"

"Not always," I said.

Jeremy eyed me as we talked. Despite the lack of a mirror behind the bar, I knew exactly what he saw: a barrel of a man at least fifty pounds heavier, four inches taller and almost thirty years older than him whose broad shoulders and thick arms were squeezed into a too-tight black T-shirt with the bar's logo emblazoned on the front. A dirty, once-white apron tied around my hips covered my black button-fly jeans down to my knees, and I wore thick-soled black hiking boots more because they were comfortable than because they made any fashion statement. I'd been wearing the same thing every night for so long that it might was well have been a uniform. A graying flat-top and a face like a pug rounded out the package. In the dim light of the bar I might be ruggedly handsome; in the harsh light of day women and children moved to the other side of the street to avoid me.

"There's no place like this back home," he continued.

"Where you from?"

He mentioned a small town downstate, the kind of place you drive through without noticing.

"What brought you here?"

"A taxi."

I smiled. His joke wasn't worth a laugh.

He started to tell me about the teachers' conference that had brought him to the city, but I was called away to mix umbrella drinks for a couple of fey patrons before I caught all the details. I returned a few minutes later with a fresh beer.

Jeremy hadn't finished the previous one, but he thanked me and asked, "Are you trying to get me drunk?"

"On piss water?" I said. "If I wanted you drunk, I'd give you the hard stuff. What I want is you sober enough to fuck but drunk enough to fuck me."

"Blunt, aren't you?"

"Subtlety has never been my strong point," I said as I leaned on the bar and stared straight into his pale-blue eyes. "You came in here to get laid. Fresh meat like you shouldn't have any trouble hooking up but you're afraid to approach anyone and no one is approaching you." I didn't tell him why. "So, I'll make you a deal. If you're still here at last call, I'll take you upstairs and give you what you're looking for."

And then, except for replacing Jeremy's beer every time he emptied a bottle, I ignored him.

My customers are mostly well behaved because the long-time regulars keep the newbies under control. My older customers still remember the days when local cops would raid the Cock & Bull looking for any excuse to collect payoffs not to run them in and shut the place down. I tolerated some public displays of affection and a little groping under the tables, but cops with nightsticks were the only swinging dicks allowed in the bar. Customers were strongly encouraged to take their amorous activities off-site. That's why it pissed me off whenever I caught two men going at it in the restroom.

Shortly after midnight, Sammy Johnson tapped the edge of a quarter against the bar to catch my attention. When I looked his direction, he made an O with the thumb and forefinger of his left hand and pistoned his right forefinger in and out of it a few times before he pointed toward the back hall.

I wiped my hands on my apron, grabbed a bottle of seltzer water, and slipped out from behind the bar, conscious that several of the bar's regulars knew what was happening and were watching me. I stepped down the hall and pushed open the bathroom door, which hasn't had a working lock since I kicked the door open back in 1997. Inside the small room two unfamiliar young men were in flagrante delicto.

Both had their pants around their ankles and one was leaning forward, bracing himself on the sink. The other was standing behind him, holding the first man's hips and slamming his cock into the first man's ass with increasing speed and force. They both ignored me until I hosed them down with seltzer water.

As they sputtered, I slapped one meaty fist around the back of the second man's neck, grabbed his near arm with my free hand, and pulled him backward. His cock came free of the other man's ass just as he came, and he shot a thin stream of spunk on the back of the other man's shirt.

I pulled him from the bathroom and walked him down the hall toward the back door. He couldn't do anything more than shuffle because his pants were still wrapped around his ankles. After I pushed open the door and threw him into the alley, I returned for his companion.

By then the first man had managed to pull up his pants and had tried to escape by heading toward the bar. The hallway was blocked by several of my regulars who wouldn't let him pass. I grabbed him by the shirt collar and the back of his belt and walked him on tiptoes to the back door. I threw him into the alley with the other guy.

"This isn't that kind of place," I told them as they struggled to their feet and tried to pull their clothes into place, "and we don't tolerate that kind of behavior. You want to do that, get a room."

Then I slammed the door and turned. The show over, the bar's regulars returned to their previous activities and I returned to my place behind the stick.

"Pretty rough on those two, weren't you?" Jeremy asked when I replaced his empty beer bottle a few minutes later. "I was watching."

"I do what I have to," I said. "I don't plan to lose my license."

"Are you always so rough?"

I could tell that his face was flushed and that he was excited by what he'd seen. I winked. "I can be as rough as you want me to be."

For the next hour and a half, Jeremy seemed to watch my every move. He never made any attempt to hook up with any of the Cock & Bull's other customers, and he brushed off the one advance he received from someone who hadn't got my message.

When I announced last call, there was a run on drink orders. Then my part-time bartender and I started shutting things down and urging customers outside. After I locked the front door and there were only three of us left in the Cock & Bull, Jeremy asked, "Are you going to keep your promise?"

I told my part-time bartender that I would finish cleaning up and sent him home. As soon as I heard the back door close, I pulled Jeremy from the stool. I captured his face in one meaty fist and held it as I covered his lips with mine. I drove my tongue into his mouth, and I tasted the beer he'd been drinking all night and the peppermint he'd apparently been sucking on while I cleared out the bar. His tongue tried valiantly to battle mine for oral supremacy, but it was outmatched and overpowered.

"Jesus," he said when I finally pulled away. He wiped his mouth with the back of his hand.

I peeled off my apron, tossed it over the bar, and grabbed Jeremy's hand. I live in a small apartment above the bar because I don't like long commutes, and I led Jeremy up the back stairs through the living room, and into the bedroom. The place was decorated much like the bar – functional and so far out of style that it had a retro feel that was damn near back in style again. I didn't give him a chance to critique my housekeeping skills because I kissed him again – long, hard and deep.

Between kisses, we peeled off our shirts and tossed them aside. Jeremy was thin, not skinny, with a sparse patch of hair in the middle of his chest. I teased his nipples, stroking the turgid nubs with the balls of my thumbs.

He ran his fingers through my graying chest hair, seemingly fascinated by the abundance of it. As much as I enjoyed having my chest-pelt finger-combed, I was far more interested in having my cock fingered. I grabbed Jeremy's wrist and guided his hand lower. He took the hint. As I unbuttoned my jeans, the schoolteacher slid his hand under the waistband of my black low-rise briefs and found my rising cock. He wrapped his fingers around the stiffening shaft and tugged at the loose skin.

I pushed my tight jeans and my briefs down to mid-thigh, freeing my cock from confinement, and it rose up from a thick forest of graying crotch hair. I placed my meaty hands on Jeremy's shoulders and pushed him to his knees.

He leaned forward until his warm breath tickled my swollen cockhead. Then he snaked out his tongue and, using just the tip, licked the cleft on the underside of the glans. From there he drew a wet line down the underside of my thick shaft until he reached my ball sac. He paused a moment. Then he traced the wet line back to the tip and drew my cockhead between his lips, hooked his teeth behind the glans, and painted the spongy soft bulb with his tongue.

I'd had enough of Jeremy's teasing. I grabbed the back of his head and pushed the entire length of my cock into his mouth. He glanced up at me but didn't resist until my ball sac was pressed against his chin and he'd taken in the entire length, something I hadn't expected him to do because so few of my previous lovers had. He put his hands on my thighs and pushed until I drew back.

When just the head of my cock remained in his mouth, the schoolteacher grabbed my ball sac and squeezed, letting me know he could be a little rough himself. Still holding his head, I thrust my hips forward, sinking my length into his mouth again, and then drew back. I did it again and again. Faster each time.

And each time I did, Jeremy tugged on my ball sac until I was face-fucking him so hard and so fast that he had to release his grip on my balls. He wrapped his hands around the backs of my thighs and held on to my legs as I slammed my cock deep into his throat one last time and fired thick wads of warm spunk against the back of his throat.

I drew back so that he wouldn't choke, leaving just my cockhead in his mouth as he swallowed and swallowed again. When I finally released my grip on his head, Jeremy rocked back on his heels and looked up at me.

"Rough enough?" I asked.

He smiled and said, "It's a start."

"A start?" I snorted. I'm not as young as I used to be, and I've not yet resorted to chemical cock enhancements, so I knew I wouldn't rally to attention again for several minutes. I grabbed his hand, jerked him to his feet, spun him around, and pushed him forward so that he had to catch himself to keep from planting his face in the wall. I started after him.

Then my jeans, which had been caught mid-thigh, slipped to my ankles. I stopped, shuffled backward, and dropped onto the side of the bed to remove my hiking boots and peel off my jeans, briefs and socks. By then, Jeremy had turned from the wall. He saw me undressing, kicked off his loafers, and dropped his pants and boxers to the floor.

Finally naked, I rose from the bed, grabbed a deflated tube of lube from my nightstand, and squeezed a bit onto my fingers. I reached under his denuded ball sac and slickened his perineum, working my fingers backward until I could push a glob of lube into his tight little sphincter. I used another squeeze of lube to paint my cock shaft.

I pushed him back on the bed. Then I grabbed his ankles, spread his legs, and stepped between them. His cock stood at attention, rising up from his carefully groomed public triangle, but I wasn't interested in his erection. I grabbed his legs behind the knees and bent them up and toward his shoulders until his lube-slicked asshole was in just the right position. I pressed my cockhead against the glob of lube coating it and drove forward. His sphincter resisted at first, but soon opened to my pressure.

With my chest against the backs of his thighs, I rested my weight on him and stared into his eyes as I began fucking the schoolteacher. As I pistoned into Jeremy, his balls rubbed against my hairy abdomen and it must have turned him on because he reached between us and grabbed his own cock, wrapped a fist around it, and began pumping as I fucked him. He pumped his fist faster than I could piston in and out of him, and he came first, spewing spunk over his own chest.

As his cock repeatedly contracted, so did his sphincter, and it felt like his ass was trying to milk my cock. As my balls tightened, I sank one final thrust deep inside his ass and fired warm spunk deep inside him.

We didn't move until my cock deflated. Then I pulled away and sat on the bed beside him.

"You get what you came for?" I asked.

"More than I expected," Jeremy said.

"Then let me call you a cab."

He sat up. "You're kicking me out?"

"I'm not inviting you to spend the night."

"Blunt, aren't you?" he asked, repeating a question he had asked earlier in the evening.

"You came to my bar to get laid, and you've gotten laid," I said. "So what do you want now, a parting gift?"

Jeremy laughed. "You're a crusty old bastard, you know that?"

I shrugged. I'd been called worse.

He patted my arm. "I'm going to take a shower, then I'm going to fix us something to eat, and then you're going to tell me why you warned your customers away from me."

. I stared at the schoolteacher, realizing he might be more astute than I'd thought because of his obvious not-from-around-here vibe. I said, "You do that."

I didn't let him shower alone, though nothing more intimate than a good soaping happened because twice in one night is my limit. Afterward, I sat at my kitchen table with a towel wrapped around my waist while Jeremy brewed coffee, made toast, and fried eggs.

As we ate, he asked, "So why were you so eager for me to leave?"

"Better to boot you out now than wait for you to sneak out in the middle of the night." I told him how no relationship had ever lasted beyond my one-night-stands' morning-after sobriety.

"Tell you what," he said. "I'll come back tonight, just before closing time, and we'll see what happens."

I stared at him. The dim light of the bar made me appear ruggedly handsome, but the bright light of my kitchen told a different story, one that my companion apparently didn't mind rereading. Even so, I said, "I won't hold my breath."

I was wrong, though. Jeremy returned that night, and he's traveled from downstate one weekend each month ever since. Things are going so well that one of these weekends I might leave the bar in the hands of the weekend bartender and travel downstate to see what life is like outside the Cock & Bull.

The Clandestine Carabinieri

Zorba Tocks

Every Sunday after attending Mass at her local church and breakfasting on cappuccino and pastry, Donna Coletti would try to visit the National Gallery of Modern and Contemporary Art on the Viale delle Belle Arti road in Rome. On this particular day she was off duty sitting on a bench admiring *La Maja Vestida*, a painting of a busty woman in white underwear lazing on a chaise lounge by Francisco Goya, on loan from the Museo del Prado in Madrid.

Looking at her face no one could guess what she was thinking, but some would stare curiously at her curly black shoulder-length hair, rosy lips, bewitching dark eyes and the voluptuous figure oozing sexual promise that resembled the painting with astonishing similarity. Neither would anyone guess she held the rank of Sottotenente, a Sub-lieutenant in the Carabinieri Art Squad, sharing an office with her colleagues at Command Headquarters on Piazza Sant'Ignazio.

Although deep in thought looking at the picture, she was always alert and knew from the aroma of their different aftershave balms that Capitano Sergio Amadeo and Tenente Lanzone had crept up behind her and proved herself to be correct when one of them whispered:

"*Lei è* sexy," to which the other replied: "*Lei farebbe una buona moglie.*"

She turned around immediately with a pleased blush on her cheeks. "Tenente, I might be sexy in your eyes and, Capitano, you can keep wishing I'd make you a good wife, but what brings you sexist reprobates here disturbing my free time?"

"Oh and when did you get enough free time to pose for that painting?"

"*Vaffanculo* you guys! What's up?"

"She says fuck off sooo nicely, eh, Capitano?" Lanzone prodded.

They chuckled, loving the fact the banter didn't bother her and she gave back as good as she got. She also had their respect for her intelligent reputation, because she knew more about fraudulent paintings than they did. Their expertise was snooping out and catching the thieves based on her advice, which would, no doubt, lead her to supersede their ranks in the near future.

Nevertheless, both she and the Tenente were fully aware that given the opportunity Capitano Amadeo wanted to stuff her each time he saw her attractive, roundly protruding headlamp-knockers approaching or gloated at her deliberate swaying of hips and wholesome buttocks when she walked away, tantalizing his lustful desires. So far he hadn't dared to take a stab at her; not that she'd mind, because being a traditional Italian peahen taunting the peacock she desired, she wouldn't otherwise have bothered to tease him. However, she had her own ideas about a relationship and wasn't ready to submit to a foolish "love-you-hulk" flippancy yet with one who had a thirst for and reputation with women.

"The Colonel demands our illustrious presence," the Capitano said, resisting the urge to whip out his cock-carbine and have her in public, bending over the bench to the applause of his equally randy Tenente, while she wished he'd kidnap her and then break her cunt on a velvet chaise lounge.

"Have you any idea why?" she asked, aware of a sudden wetness in her pussy.

"None; you know how the arrogant man protects his secrets."

"Sure, like his mistress we're not supposed to know about." She winked as she followed the two men to the waiting police car, ready to take her home to change.

Many regard the Carabinieri uniforms as the smartest in the world and Donna felt proud driving with them to see the Colonel, who was as usual in a foul mood because his wife wanted to go to an opera and he wanted to have his rickety joints and feeble penis caressed and spoilt by his mistress, who was reportedly male if jokes in the ranks were to be believed, because no sane woman would bunk up with the grouchy sod.

They stood before his office nicknamed the "Grump Hole", and knocked on the door.

They heard his gruff response: "*Come!*"

"Sit," he said curtly. "A new case for you; another Alberto Burri stolen and from the same dealer, which seems more than a coincidence. I don't like that sniveling ponce Beppe Aquino; he's a distasteful, untrustworthy shit-head. In with the Mafia I should think. *You two* specialists – Capitano and Sottotenente – will watch your expenses because he resides in Milan and you'll need to stay over for a few days; and *you* Tenente will hold the fort here. Get onto it."

They knew the guy from before and didn't require reminders and with a typically scant file of information they departed from the Grump Hole. The Colonel was not incompetent, but when he had visions of alternative sex on his mind with a woman young enough to be his daughter and had to forebear the sound of his vocally overbearing wife for the evening instead, he became dithery and patently useless. He'd much prefer difficulty walking from his sore Bologna pony after his mistress got it up than anything else, even if she made it and his old bones creak.

It was the first case for the two Carabinieri officers in the field without the Tenente and Donna couldn't understand why.

"Because," Sergio explained, "a few weeks ago our boss got into his bully pulpit mode and Lanzone happened to be in the way, receiving the blame for something that didn't exist. Unfortunately, one never argues with the Colonel."

They packed their gear and set off on the 500 kilometer trip to Milan and phoned Lanzone to book a two-bedroomed business apartment near the city center, which they were obliged to take due to the budgetary restrictions and cuts in financial support in force for the Unit. Irrespective of the inconvenience the unwed male and female officers had sharing premises without appropriate privacy, the authorities obviously couldn't care less what their employees got up to, which was a wink-wink nudge-nudge situation to save money.

Recovering cultural goods in Italy is a tremendous task,

requiring constant vigilance to patrol thousands of kilometers with hundreds of churches, museums, archaeological sites and illegal diggings across the country, in addition to private collections and crooked dealers. According to reports, between 1970 and 2005, there were 845,838 objects reported stolen. Less than a third was recovered with only 4,159 arrests made. The Art Squad Unit has also confiscated over 228,000 counterfeit works since 1970. However, despite being overworked and understaffed, the Unit continued to do a good job.

Arriving at the hotel tired from their journey with a sticky feeling on their bodies from travelling in their blue and black uniforms, Donna felt uncomfortable while Sergio smiled at their predicament thinking that Fortuna, the old Roman goddess of good fortune, had finally turned his luck.

"The bloody Milan office could've handled this," she grumbled, eyeing him tentatively now they were alone.

"Not so, my dear Sottotenente, because *you* happen to have the skills," he answered. "Let's shower and eat; I'm thirsty and starving."

"Keep your distance while I'm in the bathroom and don't even try to peek or it'll be *arrivederci* for you and I'll shoot you on your way out!" she warned.

He nodded and mumbled agreement wishing he was permanently in her apartment, a place way above what he could afford. She lived on via della Bufalotta, an urban area of Rome, and the only way she could afford it on her salary was by winning the lottery or receiving subsidies from her doting parents so that: "*la nostra piccola bambina*," (our little baby), could enjoy the best in life. The latter was true, but she never indicated or took advantage of her privileged background.

While he was listening to the shower running, he stripped and laid down on the bed, his handsome, swarthy features and hairy body luxuriating in the coolness of the bedroom as his cock slowly rose from the thought of her naked body being over-lavishly smeared with slithering soap and water. *What a great job I'd make if I was in there with her,* he thought. It stiffened when he imagined her beautiful butt pressing against him as he held her delightful breasts and fucked her to delirium. He nodded off into a fretful nap.

"Hey!" he heard a voice say from the doorway. "Wake up, smelly – I'm hungry too!"

He opened his eyes and saw her head enshrouded in a turbaned towel with a robe covering up all that he'd imagined.

"Sottotenente Coletti," he jested in a serious tone, as he watched her drooling at his nakedness. "I thought you said no peeking. It would've been polite to knock."

"It's your fault," she countered. "I didn't think you'd be idling like that."

"Aha! Rules don't apply to you then?" he asked.

"Of course not!" she retorted cheekily. "You've got the *grande pene*, which makes you the dangerous one!"

"Well, thanks for the compliment. I'll ignore it and get ready."

Donna looked magnificent in a Marco Coretti dress from his "extreme white" collection while he was content with jeans and casual shirt. They found a small bistro offering fresh home-made minestrone soup, panzanella salad made with stale bread and ripe tomatoes followed by cannelloni and washed it down with a liter of chianti classico.

"That's a lovely dress," he remarked.

"Yes, one of my favorites designed by my hero. A few years out of date, but I don't care. I dress to feel good, not particularly to impress."

"It impresses me," he said.

"Carry on, Capitano; flirting might get you everywhere." She grinned.

He eased his back on the chair before answering. "We've been working together for three years now and all that time since your first day with the Unit, I've wanted us to be alone. For me, it was immediate attraction."

"I know, Sergio. I sensed it as well when I felt your eyes on me." Then she laughed, her wide smile covering a third of her face. "Ha ... and Lanzone bet me ten euro you'd court me within a month. What took you so long? You've been an itch on my back I couldn't scratch because you're my superior officer."

"Oh, he did, did he? The little rat!" he said. "Well, certainly it was my wish, but when I found out you're going to be a rich lady some day and considering my rank, I backed off. Anyway, your intelligence frightened me."

"*Idiota!*" she said as she reached his hand and squeezed it. "I never mention my parents' wealth and never will; and what's intelligence got to do with it? We're equals. So, will it be different tonight?"

"Yes, if your feelings are the same, Donna. It'd be an honor," he said, puffing his feathers inside because he'd answered as he thought a gentleman should.

"Humph! You really *are* an *idiota*, Sergio! Look at it this way: at work we keep it quietly clandestine and undercover for as long as possible, but privately in bed I don't want your honor or you to be honorable. I want a decadent life of excessive sex and love without a sense of responsibility between rights or wrongs because of our ranks or because I'm rich or anything else; and I yearn for your *grande pene* to make me happy."

"See what I mean? Too intelligent, that's your problem," he rebutted, arrogantly adding: "Unfortunately my *grande pene* has a mind of its own and—"

"*No, Capitano, it won't!*" she interrupted sharply. "There'll be no philandering, no waving your manhood like a flag, bragging in bars with your dirty-minded machos of how well you fucked me and positively no mistress – *capiche*? I know what goes on when you guys get together *and* I know your reputation. I'm a cop, remember?"

Sergio was astonished. His ego was bruised by the gorgeous Carabiniere who was plotting the map challenging all the tried and tested traditions of a healthy cock and balls Italian male before they'd even gone to bed. *What a presumption! I should either thank the angels for this gift or pray to God to save me*, he thought. *She's irresistible, though; so the angels will get the better of me.*

Normally, he'd have no intention of making promises and refuse to be intimidated by any conditions, but on this night he rather preferred to give her the benefit of his doubts.

"You're making it sound like a prenuptial contract," he murmured stubbornly.

"Well, it might surprise you to learn that in our oh-so-modern free sex society, I'm a virgin saving myself for the right man. Ah,

I see promises aren't your intention; that's what you were thinking, wasn't it, Sergio?"

He thought with slight consternation: Shit, *she can even read my mind!* Instead, he said: "No; now you've told me, your lecture makes sense."

"It wasn't meant to be a lecture. It was a statement, because right now you're a diabolical chauvinist male *porco* with your brains between your legs and with no thought of the future, whereas I want total commitment. So if you think you can be the twentieth-century Casanova with me, think again. I don't want to spend my life with a womanizer. I want a faithful husband, kids *and* to keep my job."

"All right," he replied meekly and then brightened up. "As your superior and a man of his word then, my last private order is to get your Goya ass to the apartment and make ready to get laid – *capiche?*"

She roared with laughter. "I *do* like a man in charge when he obeys me!"

Her heart was beating nervously fast when they got back to the rooms and he opened the door, because whereas she hadn't been at all coy seeing him naked, she hadn't told him about her own shyness. He made to embrace her but she gently pressed his chest away. "Not yet; why don't you get on your bed and wait for me like when I caught you before?"

She took only a few minutes and returned wearing long, flowing lingerie.

"Very becoming," he remarked; "but that's a lot of fabric to fight with. Won't you strip for me?"

"I'm shy," she said in an unsteady voice, praying he wouldn't reject her, yet oddly bold enough to stroke his magnificent *grande pene*. "Do you mind if I turn the lights off?"

"Donna, if I'm going to be your partner I'm not going to spend my life wondering what you look like," he replied. "What's good for the goose is good for the gander. Yes, I mind."

"It's only until I get into bed; I'll be OK under the covers. Please, only for the first night."

He sighed with disappointment, wanting desperately to feast his eyes upon her body, but settled his mind to only feeling and ravishing it in the dark. She climbed into bed and cuddled him.

For all her brave talk and enticement she seemed to be sexually naive, which only magnified her reticence to show herself. Practise makes perfect, her parents had told her; but neither had prepared her for intimacy, although she was sure her peahen instincts would overcome all obstacles naturally.

While Sergio didn't understand shyness between lovers, he sensed hers was real and was content with the opportunity to tenderize her to his own liking and decided to be patient. There was no point hurriedly burning her fleshy, juicy tissues to dread the fire, but he would soon learn that the fire was not something she feared.

Gently lifting up her garments out of the way, he began to kiss her lips and fondle her warm bush, her liquids flowing freely as her body responded eagerly. He was surprised when she shed the troublesome lingerie and threw it on the floor and then yanked him on top to attack her like a ravenous beast, stimulating his reflexes to involuntarily raise his cock to a remarkable rigidity, which immediately made her pounce and engorge it into her sweet cunt.

"*Mamma mia!*" she screamed, arching her back as it penetrated her deeply, writhing and grinding herself against its hard shaft and gripping him tightly with her arms and legs. "Sergio! My Sergio . . . oh, God . . . faster . . . faster!"

Donna pushed against him relentlessly as they sped, heaving and breathless, to orgasmic waves of ecstatic satisfaction. The Capitano, sexually competent and full of experience, had met his match.

The two lovers were lying together quietly exhausted while she held his lovable spent *grande pene* and he caressed her dauntless, fruity chasm when suddenly he turned his body above her.

"Unit regulation sixty-nine," he grunted before licking her clit and making a meal out of her dripping cunt still weeping for more.

"Hmm, and for my dessert I'll have the rest of your hot milk," she panted, slurping his cock as if there'd be no tomorrow and nearly biting its tip when another orgasm overcame her.

In the morning, after awaking to a bright sun shining through the window shutters, the Capitano and Sottotenente showered together, he at last experiencing the delights of her incredible body and her no longer shy. They soaped and teased each other all over and it didn't take her long to get him up again.

After three days of blissful lovemaking during breakfast in the same bistro she asked: "What do we say to the Colonel and our investigation of his crook, the sniveling ponce Beppe Aquino?"

"Fuck them both," he said.

New Year's Resolution

Richard Hiscock

It was the third week in the New Year and I was feeling pretty flat. I'd ended my relationship with Sophie, my long-time girlfriend, thinking I was being suffocated and thought I needed a change. The problem I found pretty quickly was most good-looking chicks are taken. I'm not a bad-looking guy; I've got a good body, work out a bit and am a concreter by trade so am always tanned and muscular.

Women usually flock to me, well they did when I was with Sophie but now they all seemed to be paired up and the pickings were grim. I was alone, drinking at a bar, watching young chicks dancing under strobe lighting. I wondered how they managed to drink so much and keep bopping about. They didn't hold my attention too long as they were too young for me and the last thing I needed was to be tricked by a seventeen-year-old that she was over twenty.

I noticed a woman, not quite a cougar, looking my way. I'm not into older chicks but this one had something special about her, the way she scanned the room, almost like a lioness searching for prey. Her eyes flickered over me, then came back for a second look. I puffed out my chest and pretended not to notice.

I was intrigued as to what she wanted. She was, as I said, a bit older, but she did have a great body. Her make-up was perfect and her long hair caressed her shoulders as she swayed to the music, continuing on her search for who knew what.

Finally, she made her way over.

"Alone?" she asked.

"For the moment," I said, as casually as I could muster, pretending not to be interested in her.

"Meaning?"

"What's it to you?"

"I have a proposition for you."

Immediately I thought undercover cop. My senses became alert; adrenalin surged through me as I weighed up how to answer without incriminating myself.

"How so?"

"Well, it's not sex I'm after," she said, her eyes sparkling mischievously

"That's good; I'm not after it either."

She giggled. "Sure you're not."

"Look, I don't know you and I certainly don't want to offend you, but I'm not into playing games."

"Neither am I, that's why I'm being honest up front."

"So what is it you're after?"

"I need someone . . . someone to help me out in a . . . a situation."

"What sort of situation?"

"I want to take a movie of myself for my boyfriend. I've got tripods, but want to make sure some parts are zoomed in on—" she giggled "—if you know what I mean. I want photos too so I need you to hold the camera, take the sort of shots you'd like to see your own girlfriend doing and I need to know I can trust you not to take advantage of me . . . you know . . . being naked and all."

I laughed.

She eyed me.

"You're not serious."

"Yes, I am. I told you I don't play games. I can't afford to pay you much but figured you'd get a bit of a kick out of it for yourself, if you know what I mean."

She was serious. The thought of seeing her naked appealed to me and filming her doing what would please me would certainly be something that would turn me on in the future. Not having sex with her, well, we'd see how things progressed. Her face flushed under my scrutiny.

"Sure, why not."

"Fantastic. I have my car out back. Let's go."

I followed her out, hoping she wasn't some crazy satanic

follower or anything and was pleased when she pulled up at a
ritzy apartment block thirty-five minutes later. All seemed well
and, as we climbed the stairs, I felt the stirring of my cock. This
really was too good to believe.

"So, you can see how I've set tripods everywhere. I want the
filming to be as realistic as possible so I don't want you to hold
the camera too much, just get me in focus and then put it on
the tripod. We'll start with me coming home and you following
me, OK?"

I nodded.

"But first I need to change. He's rich and loves me to wear
different outfits to turn him on, you know, like a sexy nun's
outfit, a barmaid, a playboy bunny, stuff like that. Today I'm
wearing a maid's uniform. Go and pour yourself a drink while I
change."

I moved about her apartment. It was quite classy. She had
good taste. I wondered if the guy she was talking about was her
lover or if she was a prostitute and got paid for this sort of stuff.
Either way I didn't really care, being the cameraman was
something new to me and, if she wanted more of this sort of
stuff, I would be happy to oblige.

"Oh, by the way," she said popping her head out of the
doorway, "I'm Carmen."

"Adam," I said and she disappeared.

I found the bottle of Scotch and poured myself a drink. This
was certainly an unusual situation. As the Scotch coursed
through my veins there was a knock on the door.

"Can you get that, please," she yelled from the bedroom. "It
should be Sam."

Who the fuck was Sam? She didn't mention anyone else in
this film. A flicker of anxiety caught me off guard and I shook
my head, took a deep breath and opened the door.

"Hello, I'm Samantha," she purred.

Fuck, she was gorgeous. She was dressed in a business suit,
her dark hair pulled back and in a bun. She was wearing horn-
rimmed glasses and carried a briefcase. I was surprised. I'd
expected someone dressed more outrageous.

"Adam," I said, allowing her to pass.

She made her way to the bedroom and I heard them talking

quickly. Samantha came back out, poured herself a drink and sat on the couch. She eyed me as I waited for Carmen to reappear.

I didn't have to wait long. She came out with a little maid's uniform on, if you could call it a uniform. It was so short that when she walked it flicked up and I could see her plump cheeks peeking out. The bust area was a frilled white type of shirt, open so her boobs popped up, almost spilling out. She had a little cap on and her blonde hair was pinned back into a bun. She didn't look at me. She had a feather duster with her and began to clean the apartment.

I hit the record button and stayed quiet. She stopped for a moment, glanced over her shoulder and gave the camera a sultry look. "Sam's here. She's paying me to clean her apartment. I can't wait to see you, big boy."

She didn't look at me again and I watched her through the lens, making sure she was in focus as I picked up another camera in case something caught my eye. As she began to dust, Sam opened her briefcase and placed some paperwork on the couch.

Carmen focused on wall unit. She stretched upwards, causing her breasts to almost fall from their cups, and flicked the duster about. Then she began to dust the shelves between some glass objects, one of which she knocked and it shattered on the floor.

Her hand went to her open mouth.

"What the fuck!" it was Sam.

I got a shock as I hadn't expected her to speak.

"I'm sorry, miss," Carmen said.

"You're sorry. Big fucking deal. That piece of crystal cost me a fortune."

"I'll pay you back." Carmen seemed to cower as Sam rose.

"You don't earn enough money to ever pay me back. You know you'll have to be punished. My husband insists upon it."

"Yes, ma'am," Carmen said.

"Over the desk, bend over and spread your legs."

As Carmen made her way over, Sam retrieved a ruler from the desk. She came back and stood behind Carmen, slapping the ruler in the palm of her hand as she watched her. She lifted the flimsy uniform up over her backside and ran her hand over Carmen's smooth cheeks, taking care to run a finger lightly down the crack of her bum. Carmen gasped and my cock stirred. We all knew what was coming.

"If you want to be a maid and work here you'll have to learn to be more careful," Sam said.

"Yes, miss," Carmen whimpered. "Please don't hurt me."

"Why shouldn't I? You've taken something from me which I can't replace and for that you must be punished. I'd say ten administrations with this ruler may suffice for this first offence."

I moved around and took a couple of shots of Carmen's butt and the first slap. Carmen was facing the camera and tripod and her face contorted with the hard slap from Sam. I was surprised to see a welt form instantly and zoomed in with the camera as Sam continued.

"Ow, please, miss, no more," Carmen screamed as her backside became a criss-cross of red and blue markings.

Sam continued as though not hearing. She was clearly enjoying herself. The tenth slap was by far the hardest. Carmen screamed as she lay face down her arms outstretched. Sam stood behind her, unperturbed by her whimpering.

"Spread your legs further," she said.

Carmen did and Sam plucked the G-string from between her cheeks and ripped them clean off her.

"You don't need those," she said, as she ran her finger down the crack of her arse and then further to her slit.

I held my breath eager to see where this was going.

She sunk her fingers into her cunt. "You're wet," she stated. "You're not going to tell me you enjoyed that, are you?"

"Sorry, miss."

"You little slut. I'll have to teach you a further lesson, one you might not be so interested in."

"Yes, miss," Carmen said, rising and smoothing down her uniform.

She glanced quickly at me and I hoped she didn't notice the bulge in my trousers. Seeing her like that really turned me on.

"What can I do to you to punish you further?" Sam said. She walked around Carmen slapping the ruler in her hand. "Go in the kitchen and fill up the jug with water and then come back."

As Carmen left the room, Sam returned to the couch to read through some papers.

Carmen returned with the jug.

"Drink it," Sam said. "I want you to drink the whole jug of water and stay in that spot."

Carmen struggled but eventually finished. Sam said nothing for the next half-hour or so and I noticed Carmen fidgeting. More time ticked by before Carmen asked, "Please, miss, can I go to the toilet?"

"No, you may not."

"But I'm bursting," she insisted.

"Really? Is your bladder so full it's hurting you?"

"Yes," Carmen said, jigging around on the one spot.

"Then open your legs and piss," Sam commanded.

"Here, on the floor? No, miss I can't do that."

"You can and you will. Now piss."

Carmen stared at the camera for a few moments. Her face flushed with embarrassment as I zoomed in on the bottom of her uniform.

"Lift your skirt so I may watch," Sam said.

Carmen's face shone with perspiration. Clearly her bladder was giving her quite an amount of discomfort.

First I heard a trickle hit the tile floor, then more, until she pissed like a horse; the amount of urine spilling from her made up quite a puddle. I snapped away with the camera then I zoomed right in on her pussy. I could see the flaps open slightly and when she finished peeing droplets hung on to her pubic hair before dripping to the floor.

"You filthy pig," Sam said. "Clean up that mess and hurry up."

Carmen scurried from the room to return with a mop, almost slipping as she did.

Sam watched her carefully and when she was finished she told her to continue with her cleaning. Carmen picked up the small pieces of crystal and threw them in the bin. Then she began to fluff up the cushions on the couch. As she bent over, I got some great shots of her arse. With her bum bare and her pussy flaps hanging down I could only think about sticking my cock in her cunt. It took all my willpower to stay where I was.

"That cushion is crooked," Sam said, coming over to the couch.

Carmen straightened it.

"You need to do a good job without me having to constantly remind you. Stand and face me."

As Carmen turned, Sam pulled down the white shirt of her uniform, flipped her breasts out of the bra and exposed them. From her pocket, she retrieved some clamps, which she opened and closed right in Carmen's face.

"These will remind you to do a good job," she said.

She pinched Carmen's nipples until they stood to attention then attached the clamps firmly. Carmen let out a yelp and Sam hissed at her to be quiet.

As Sam sat back on the couch, Carmen picked up a cleaning cloth to wipe down the coffee table. The cloth made streak marks all over it.

"You fucking useless idiot!" Sam shrieked. "It's worse than before. Can't you do anything right?"

"No, miss," Carmen said.

"Then why take on a job you're clearly not any good at."

"I'm good at cleaning some things," she whispered.

"What?"

"I'm very good at cleaning pussies."

"What? What did you say?" Sam appeared shocked.

"I can lick your pussy cleaner than anyone you've ever been with." Carmen stood up straight for the first time and stared hard at Sam as though challenging her.

"Well, let's see if you're as good as you think you are. Undress me."

Carmen stood before Sam and held out her hand. She pulled Sam up and removed her jacket, discarding it on the floor. I was surprised that Sam didn't tell her off but I kept filming, eager to see Sam naked.

She undid the buttons on her blouse and discarded that as well. Her bra was next, allowing Sam's full breasts to hang, the nipples slightly rigid as Carmen's hands gently touched them. Then the skirt fell to the floor with Sam stepping out of it. Carmen peeled down her panties and Sam stepped out of them, leaving her in her high-heeled stilettos and glasses.

"Lay back on the couch, miss," Carmen said.

Sam lay back and Carmen slowly opened her thighs wide. Carmen climbed up on the couch and kneeled into her, sniffing her snatch to comment, "Beautiful. As I knew it would be."

Sam smiled as Carmen tentatively licked at her pussy, opening her flaps and teasing her with her tongue. I moved quietly to another spot to get a better shot. Sam looked amazing laying back against the brown couch. Her pearly white skin and blonde hair made her stand out against the dark background.

Sam pulled her flaps out wider, exposing herself completely; her pussy gaped at me. Sam began to caress her own breasts and Carmen leaned in to lick her long and hard, starting from her puckered hole, her tongue flicking about maddeningly to make Sam squirm before zoning in on her cunt.

Sam's eyes glazed over as Carmen continued with her cunnilingus, slurping and licking, barely stopping for a breath while Sam squirmed beneath her. I took some shots of Carmen's welts, some of which had now turned a dark purple. After about fifteen minutes, Sam was writhing with orgasm on the couch.

When she regained her composure, Carmen brought over a mirror so Sam could inspect herself.

"Not bad," she said. "But I've had better."

"Of course," Carmen said.

"I'm willing to give you another chance. I have in the top drawer a big black strap-on dildo. I'd like you to fuck me with it if you think you can manage it."

"I'm sure I can but my boyfriend wouldn't like it."

"I don't give a shit what he likes. You work for me and while I'm paying you, you'll do as I ask, is that understood?"

"Yes, miss," Carmen said, as a wicked look crossed her face.

Carmen made her way to the drawer. She fitted the strap-on around her hips and sauntered back to Sam who was now reclining on the couch smoking a cigarette. Sam stubbed it in the ashtray as her eyes raked over Carmen, honing in on the large thick rubber cock.

Carmen climbed up on the couch and positioned herself between Sam's thighs, hesitating for only a second before opening up her flaps to spear straight in to her saturated cunt. Sam squealed as Carmen pummeled her, screaming out further when she pushed into her open thighs and fucked her mercilessly.

She was on a mission to prove she could fuck as good as anyone and withdrew the cock, pulled Sam up and had her turn over doggy style, her perky butt up high as Carmen pulled her cheeks apart and slapped her with the cock before impaling her.

Sam flung her head back and forth, her bun coming undone in the process. Carmen pulled at Sam's hair, causing her neck to arch back then she leaned forward to grab at a breast and squeezed hard. She pushed Sam down onto the couch causing Sam's butt to rise further, while she spread her butt cheeks.

I wondered if she was going to fuck her puckered hole and sure enough she pulled out of her cunt and slathered the wet strap-on over her arsehole, prying it further open and pushing the cock in. Sam was really getting into it and before long she was coming again.

Carmen withdrew and Sam collapsed on the couch totally sated. She was one hot chick I can tell you and my cock was by this time so constricted in my jocks I thought my zipper might break.

Sam rose and began to get dressed. She quickly pulled on her clothes and began to make her way to the door.

"Not bad," she said, peering at Carmen over her shoulder as she opened the door, "and by the way, you stink of piss, go and clean yourself up and see if you can get that right."

With that she was gone.

Carmen sat on the couch staring at me. She was half dressed, her breasts hanging out with the clamps still attached. She must have been exhausted and when I looked at my watch I noted two hours had passed.

"So, what do you think?" she asked me.

"About what?" I said.

"The filming and the photos . . . you think he'll like them?"

"Shit yeah, who wouldn't?"

"Thanks. Listen, this episode with Sam was a spur of the moment thing. Do you think you could come back again tomorrow and give me another hand?"

"Filming?" I asked.

"Yeah, this time it will just be me."

"Sure."

"Thanks, so how about ten tomorrow night?"

"I'll be here."

"I'll try to get some photos done by then, see if we can improve them."

When I left it almost felt as though it had been a dream. I wanted to tell someone, but who? Most of my mates were in relationships and they'd probably think I was making it up. If she got some photos done I'd see if I could get to keep at least one copy and then I'd have some proof to my story.

I was missing Sophie and was desperate for some form of release. I guess masturbation was on the agenda again tonight.

The next night I arrived promptly at ten. Carmen looked very normal and demure, dressed in a skirt and cardigan. I hoped we were alone and was slightly fearful of her boyfriend perhaps showing up and me being coerced into a threesome. Not that I was averse to a threesome but I would have preferred two women.

"Do you want to grab the camera and start filming?" she asked.

"Sure," I said, taking it with the tripod and turning it on.

"Hey, honey," she purred to the lens. "I've had such a hard day and can't wait to see you. Thought I'd give you a special treat. Keep watching and you'll see what I mean."

She began to unbutton her cardigan, staring at the camera as she did so with a slight pout on her lips. Then she unzipped the skirt, turned and walked away, the skirt falling to the floor as she stepped out of it.

By the time she entered her bedroom she was clad in only bra and panties. I scanned the room, still nervous of some sort of ambush but all was well. She opened a door, which led to her bathroom. Now she peeled her underwear off. She raised her arms, stretching them upwards, which gave her abdomen a sunken look and pushed out her pelvis. Her bush was dark and wiry, which surprised me as most women took care of that area and I realized I hadn't noticed it yesterday.

I wondered if there were any welts on her bum, if she'd covered them with make-up or left them as they were. I also wondered if this film was really for a boyfriend or if she just acted out her own fantasies and was using me to help her fulfill them. Either way, I didn't care. I was happy to oblige.

She ran the water into the bath, threw in a bath bomb and, when it was a third full, sat on the edge. She spread her legs and massaged her pussy, fingering herself as she did. A sigh escaped her lips and she closed her eyes, enjoying the moment. I must say I was enjoying it as well.

She turned off the water and slipped into the bath. Water cascaded over her breasts, the soapy residue of the bomb leaving swirls of foam in her cleavage. She massaged her tits clearly enjoying her hands on herself.

She slipped further down, rolled over and leaned up on her elbows. Her gorgeous rump stuck up out of the water and was surrounded by bubbles. I took some shots as well as she peered at me coquettishly over her shoulder.

Yesterday had been great although slightly intimidating with someone else there, considering I didn't know either of them, but today was so much better. Having her to myself would have been every guy's dream.

Even though Carmen was slightly older than I was she was in great shape. She obviously took care of herself and I began to wonder about her and her life. I contemplated what would make a woman bring home a man she didn't know and parade herself around him without a care in the world. She must have lots of confidence and probably a black belt in judo . . .

She began to stand and water washed over the side of the bath. Her body shone with the effects of the water. She didn't ask for a towel and I didn't offer. She sat back on the edge of the bath and opened her legs wide. Then, she reached down and retrieved a can of shaving cream. She sprayed it all over her mound and pussy; it looked like a Santa beard by the time she finished. Then she ran her fingers through it and, as I was so focused on her pussy, I didn't notice she had a razor in her hand until she slowly began to shave.

She dropped the dollops into the water and every now and then she'd rinse the blade.

"You know I did promise you I'd do this for you and now you'll have it to watch forever won't you, baby?"

I almost answered yes.

As she carefully shaved her flaps, I zoomed the lens in for a closer shot. I wondered at times if she was looking at me or the camera. My cock was rock hard again and by the time she finished all I could think about was fucking her.

Sophie's face flashed before my eyes but I quickly blinked her away. This was too good to give up or even feel guilty about.

Releasing the plug, she stepped into the bath and turned on the shower taps. Water washed over her as she soaped herself and allowed the suds to swirl over her. She massaged her tits and ran her hand down to her hairless mound. She turned off the taps and dried herself then motioned to the camera.

"Come on, I have another surprise for you, baby," she purred.

I carefully followed her, keeping the camera as still as possible, yet focusing in on her gorgeous rump, which did indeed display some bruising. She lay on the bed, squirming around a bit, making herself comfortable, opened up her legs, lifting her knees to place her soles flat on the bed. She dropped open her knees and her cunt opened up like a flower that had just bloomed. I could almost smell her scent from where I was filming.

"I know you love to watch me masturbate and I'm feeling really horny after shaving. You like my naked snatch, you like seeing it hairless don't you, baby? Remember I did it just for you."

She began moaning as her fingers slipped about, then she was pulling up the hood of her clit and rubbing like crazy. I almost came as she bucked against her hand; sweat covered her body as her orgasm consumed her. I could see her juices pooling out, dribbling onto the bed.

Fuck, I didn't know if I could keep doing this. I wanted nothing more than to jump on her and fuck her senseless.

"Oh, God, that's good, so good, baby. Now for your other surprise," she laughed.

She beckoned me with her finger. I stared at her unsure of what she really wanted. Was she still doing this for the camera or did she really want me to join in?

"Come on, don't be shy. I've brought someone here. A stranger, a guy I picked up at a bar. A guy I'd like to fuck me. You remember how you've always said you'd love to see a guy fucking me, well, now you can. Come on," she said again. "Don't tell me you don't want to with a hard-on like that." She pointed to my cock.

I shucked off my clothes and jumped onto the bed, not caring if the camera was still rolling. This was too good to believe. She opened her legs wider and I made my way in, my knob leading the way. Her pussy was glistening and my cock was almost purple it was so engorged with blood.

I sunk straight in and she kicked me in the back, her heels spurring me on, not that I needed it. I was raring to go. I fucked her like crazy and she writhed around the bed, screaming out what a great fuck I was, how she wanted it harder, faster. Then she pushed me away, turned and got up on all fours.

"Fuck me doggy style," she said.

I grabbed on to her hips, pinching her skin cruelly. She screamed in pain but didn't ask me to stop. I thrust myself into her saturated pussy and rode her like a madman. Now sweat was pouring off me too. Her hair was plastered to her face as she glanced over her shoulder and mouthed to me, *Fuck me up the arse*.

I didn't need to be asked twice. I pulled my cock, dripping with her juices from her cunt, pried open her hole and slipped the knob in. She tensed for a second and then relaxed. It was as though she had a device inserted as her hole sucked me in. Oh, God, it was magical. Most women I've been with have never wanted it up the arse and now here she was offering herself to me, but, before I knew it, it all became too much and I felt my balls tighten and involuntarily I spewed my spunk before collapsing on her.

She sagged beneath me and I rolled off her. We lay together on the bed trying to regain our composure.

"That was awesome," she said.

I said nothing.

She rose and kneeled up on the bed. "So, you see, baby, now I've done all the things you wanted me to and you were right. It was amazing shaving myself . . . and fucking a stranger, well, who would have thought I'd be so bold. I'm so glad you suggested those things. It's a shame I'll never know if you enjoyed watching, but, knowing you, I'm sure you will. After tonight's success I think I might go out every week and bring home a different guy. Won't that be interesting? I'll tape them too, not for you but for my own private collection. See what you're missing."

She switched off the camera and lay back down.

"I don't get it," I said.

"Just want him to see what a mistake he's made. Caught him having a bit of a fling with a waitress at a party. Payback," she laughed.

"And the photos. Did you get them developed?" I asked hopefully.

"Yes, you did a great job," she gushed.

It turned out Carmen has a lot of friends who are into the same sort of thing and she's offered my services if I'm interested. She's also moneyed and ended up paying me quite handsomely, which at first I rejected but she insisted so who was I to argue?

I've now decided this is my New Year's Resolution and I'm going to stick to it.

No more going steady. If older chicks want to show their exes that they're having the time of their life without them then I'm more than happy to help them out. Making extra money on the side is a bonus and this way I never have to worry about being suffocated by a chick as all the women I will be servicing are after the same thing.

Showing themselves having great sex means they work even harder to please me and I am more than happy with that so all in all it's a great way to begin this year. Oh, and by the way, the photos are a bonus; I just can't believe my luck.

The Cops' Whore

Serena Akeroyd

The bar stank of smoke from cheap cigarettes and made Haley Downton wish she were eight feet tall. Tall enough to have her head peeking through the smoke, like a mountain summit did a layer of clouds, so she could breathe freely.

Each breath was hard won. She wanted to cough every time she sucked in air and considering she was there on business, hacking splutters weren't exactly doing anything for her image.

How could she sell her product if she portrayed a picture of ill health?

That's just what every "john" fantasized about. Catching a cold from their hooker!

Grimacing at the thought, Haley was on the brink of leaping from her seat and getting the hell out of Dodge. Anything to be able to breathe again. She didn't care if Tony, her pimp, beat her to the curb. She'd survive yet another round with his fists. Lung cancer . . . yeah, her odds weren't all that great. With no health insurance, she was fucked.

And considering she made her living getting fucked, she knew how shitty that could be.

When a patron of the illustrious "Dirty Dayna" Dive – so named for the owner's beloved motorbike – shot her a wink, she nearly gasped in shock, because between the splutters, coughs and sneezes she hardly looked like sex on legs. Only realizing that a gasp would make her hack her guts up and turn the potential customer off, she managed to counteract the smoke rumbling through her lungs with gentle, unnoticeable coughs.

Working it for all she could, she slid down from her barstool and left her perspiring glass of warm soda to its own fate.

Striding across the bar, she passed hardened bikers, tattooed up to their eyeballs – literally – muscles larger than her head, but they paid her no mind. She was one of their own. Of no interest.

A few catcalls hollered her way as she rolled her hips and strutted her stuff, but she spun around artlessly on her five-inch heels, grinned at whoever was doing the whistling, and received a round of applause for her guts.

As she neared the shadowed corner where her potential john awaited, she realized she could actually breathe here without choking. She supped up air like some of her sisters did coke, reveling in the burn-free breath as she took a seat at the scarred wooden table. Patrons, over the years, had done their own decorating on the scratched surface. This particular one sported a picture of a woman astride an anaconda. A definite what-the-fuck kind of image, but Haley ignored it to smile at her client.

He was young. Younger than her usual clientele; in his early thirties? Clean cut, shaved. No tats. That alone should have had a red warning sign popping up in front of her eyes, but he was handsome and Haley rarely managed to fuck a man that didn't make her feel nauseous on her beat.

The very idea was novel and she shot him a winning smile, forgetting to be coy, just grateful this man wanted her and that he wouldn't make her want to vomit as he rutted on top of her.

Of course, all men looked the same as they came. She'd learned that shortly after becoming a hooker. None of them gave a shit for her pleasure. She was just a willing hole. They didn't even care if she was wet. The bastards.

Someone, a long time ago, had told her that hookers became hookers either because they were poor and desperate, or because they were addicted to sex and thought they might as well get paid for it.

As far as Haley was concerned, neither reason fit. She was as poor as she'd ever been and there was no pleasure to be had with strangers, whose only thought was to get themselves off.

She reminded herself that as good-looking as this guy might be, he was too clean cut for this bar. "You're not a cop, are you?" she blurted out.

The stranger smiled, shooting a white-toothed grin her way. That dentist job alone must have cost a pretty penny and Haley wistfully dragged her tongue along her own crooked front teeth. "Do I look like a cop?"

"I don't know what you look like, but I'll tell you one thing for certain: you don't fit in here."

"How do you know? I might have a bike outside."

She narrowed her eyes at his blithe response. "Do you?"

He nodded.

If she had a clue about bikes, she'd have asked him which one and what brand of bike it was. She'd have no idea if he lied to her though. "What are you doing in this dive?"

"I just wanted a drink, baby."

Ugh. She hated it when they called her that. His use of the endearment was a reminder as to why she was here and she leaned back, arching her spine so her breasts nearly spilled out of the garish red latex bandeau she wore. Her stomach muscles tugged a little as she tightened them. Being skinny was a natural by-product of poverty; in her line of work, it was the only advantage.

"And now you want something else, do you, shug?"

His smile returned. He sat forward. As he moved, his white shirt parted to display bronzed muscular flesh.

What the hell did a man like this need a woman like her for?

This did not bode well.

He was either a cop or a serial killer. They were always good-looking, weren't they? It was how they lured their victims away.

Trembling at the thought, she almost missed his next words. "How much for you to come back to mine?"

If Tony found out she'd refused a john, even if he was potentially a cop or a murderer, then the beating would be worse than her leaving her post. The last girl to turn down a client had ended up in a charity hospital having her jaw wired shut. If it turned out he was a cop, then Tony would beat her for being dumb enough not to spot the guy was with Vice.

Yeah, it was a damned if you do and dead if you don't moment.

Her life really sucked.

The only thing she could do to protect herself was say, "Sorry, shug, no can do. It's a place of my choice or not at all."

He narrowed his eyes, then smiled. "I get it. You're trying to protect yourself. But there's no need. I'm staying in a hotel. I can't do anything to you there without someone hearing. Even if it is only to listen in on us fucking."

Haley pondered his words and deciding he was right, nodded. "OK, your hotel. What kind of services do you want?"

This time, his grin was dirty. "I want it all, baby. Every little bit."

"That costs a lot," she warned him.

"I can afford it."

She frowned at that and deciding he could, if the $300 shirt he was wearing was any indication, she added an extra $150 on to Tony's price for herself. "Three-fifty, for *everything*. All night, until dawn," she told him, bricking it and hoping he wouldn't walk out the door. She brazened it out by saying, "And I'm worth every cent, darling." She rimmed her top lip with her tongue and waited for his reply.

Haley nearly cried when he stood up and walked away. Then, he turned round and spotting she wasn't with him, asked, "Is something wrong?"

The thought of that extra $150 nearly had her jumping out of her seat, but she contained her exuberance and coolly – sexily, she hoped – stood and strode toward him.

As they walked out of the bar, she knew the scents of matured tobacco would linger in her hair and her clothes, the pair of them would reek of old cigarettes for ages. The grease from a dive that prided itself on nothing ever being cleaned but the glasses and the beer pumps, would stay with them all night as well.

She longed for a shower. She longed to be anywhere but where she was and only the thought of that extra money, those notes that she could keep for herself to eventually run away from this hell of a life made her put one foot in front of the other and maintain this john's pace.

Haley had always been a thinker and from a young age, everyone from her ma to her teachers had told her her lack of concentration and focus would be the devil of her.

They weren't wrong.

So deep was she in her thoughts, her pit of self-pity, she didn't realize when the damp heat of the bar gave way to the cooler night air, she didn't take note when a man pressed against her from the other side, she failed to spot the unmarked cop car that nevertheless screamed "Police", and she only started to realize what was going on when the new guy pushed her roughly around and pressed her into a wall.

Such behavior wasn't entirely unexpected from her clients, but the man's next words froze her eardrums. "You're under arrest for soliciting . . . for . . ."

As the offences she'd committed dripped off the guy's tongue, she turned her head to the undercover cop and stared at him, sadly. Most in her position would scream acid at him, rip at him with her words. Haley just saw that extra $150 slipping down the drain. Plus, there was the beating from Tony to look forward to.

Who said a hooker didn't have a fun life?

When she was read her Miranda rights and led over to the car, the "john" shoved her into the back seat and got in beside her, while the new guy sat behind the wheel.

Silence brimmed in the car until the ignition was fired and they set off. The purr of the engine and the sound of their radio rumbled along with them as they rode out of Dirty Dayna's parking lot. She turned her head to the side to look out of the window as apathy settled in her gut.

This was it.

For nearly eighteen months, she'd managed to cast herself under the net, stayed in joints like the Dirty Dayna where the police rarely ventured, unless they wanted six weeks' break for rehab and a broken jaw. She'd never been arrested before, never been in jail.

How had it come to this?

She thought back, pondering the childhood where things had seemed promising, only as her adolescence reared its ugly head did things start to go wrong. Her situation had spiraled and had resulted in her becoming someone she couldn't recognize.

Misery, self-pity and anger were her travel companions and they were louder than the two cops. She tried to push her feelings to the side, watch the world go by in a swirl of night lights and city glow, but failed.

When the car came to a halt, she frowned. Ahead, and all around them, was darkness disturbed only by a few, weak streetlamps. The area was no better or worse than the one they'd just left, but it was deadly quiet.

Like a ghost town.

"W-What are we doing here?" she asked, voice quivering. "This isn't a precinct."

"Well spotted, blue eyes," the "john" from earlier commented.

The driver turned around and peered into the caged cab. "We have a deal to make with you. And if you play your cards right, you won't be seeing the inside of a cell tonight. We won't take you anywhere but home."

"What do you mean?" she asked, even though she had a feeling she knew where this was going. Christ, she'd have to be dumb as hell to not be able to predict where this was leading.

"I think you know very well what we're suggesting," the "john" said.

She tilted toward them, sitting up rather than slumping against the door as she had been. "Take off my cuffs and let's discuss this proposition you have for me."

The "john" grinned and said, "It's in my pocket. If you want it, you'll have to come get it."

The despair she'd felt at being locked away dissipated with his words. She could handle this. She knew the score here. She was paying her way, as she usually did, but the end result was different. Instead of cash, she had freedom and nothing on her record that would forever label her a whore.

She turned around and shuffled on her butt toward him, stopping only when her back caressed his front. She tilted her head to the side to stare at him and in the shadowed lights of the distant streetlamps managed to catch a glimpse of his glittering eyes; he was excited by what he was doing. The power play turned him on.

She reached for his lap with her cuffed hands; ignoring the strain in her shoulders and elbows as she twisted and turned her hands to reach for his groin. She finally managed to work her fingers deep into one of his pockets. Digging, she found nothing, aside from a hardness that started to butt the tips of her fingers.

Taking the man's arousal as a good sign, she pulled out, caressing his hardening cock through the thinner fabric of the lining, then attempted to find the key in the second pocket. She made more of a show with this one. She slid her fingers purposely down his shaft, hid her smiles as his hips jerked when she teased the tip that butted through the heavy fabric of his jeans. A part of her was surprised he was a cop, because she hadn't underestimated the quality of his clothes. They even felt expensive.

After a good two minutes of digging, she found the key and dragged it along his shaft as she pulled it out into the open.

By that time, the "john" was panting. He gritted out, "Hot stuff, baby. We've got ourselves a sizzling little thing here, K."

K. chuckled. "I think you're right, D. She looks like she has you primed and ready to go."

"Can you unlock the cuffs now, guys?" Haley asked, her voice low.

"What if we want to fuck you with the cuffs on?" D., formerly the "john", asked.

"Feel free," she retorted, even though inside, she winced. She hated being tied up. It was one of her pet hates.

Around a grin, he said, "Good, I think we'll keep those cuffs on then. Get on your knees and suck me off."

His order and his desire to keep the cuffs on had her stiffening, but she awkwardly maneuvered herself onto her knees and crawled closer to him. As she bent over his lap, he didn't help her pull his zipper down. She had to grab it with her teeth. She made sure her hot breath worked down the line of his cock and, within seconds, he'd started to pant again.

"No rubber?" she asked.

"No rubber," he confirmed. "Where would be the fun in that?"

She shrugged and nuzzled her face into his now open fly. His cock popped out with little urging and she immediately started to work on it. Swirling her tongue around the head, suckling and nibbling it. Every time she bit down gently, he tensed and his hands came up to grip her by the head in a silent warning. But she meant no harm. Christ, if anything, she knew her clients got off on that tender bite. It made them come all the quicker, which in her line of business was a very good thing.

She slithered her tongue up and down the bobbing shaft, then nearly gagged when his hand began to force her down. He used her mouth, shoving his cock deep and enjoying her ability to take his cock down her throat with little more than a gasp of air.

He fucked her tongue, her lips. Forced his shaft back and forth, back and forth. Just as she began to pray he'd come, as her jaw began to ache and her eyes were wet with tears, she felt a hand on her ass. Seconds later, another hand appeared. One moved between her thighs, sliding the flirty miniskirt away and tugging at the thong that covered her cunt. A finger slid up and down between her pussy lips, nudging her clit every time D. nudged her gag reflex.

Somehow, that slight caress had her creaming, even in spite of the discomfort of being face-fucked. She felt that finger drop down to rim her hole and tensed as he began to thrust it into her cunt. Haley hummed around D.'s shaft, making him laugh and bite out, "Whatever the fuck you're doing, K., don't stop! She fucking loves it."

And God help her, she did!

K.'s finger began to thrust in earnest as his thumb rode her clit and triggered more pussy juice to flood her hole. She moaned around D.'s cock, then grunted as the second hand slapped her ass every time she swallowed D.'s dick. When come pelted the back of her throat, she gagged and coughed, but he wouldn't let her up. He continued to ride her face until he was satisfied and only then, did he let go. His hips still twitching with remembered pleasure.

She pressed her face against his thigh, coughing as she fought the choking sensation. It was strange to feel the agony of burning lungs and yet, at her cunt, feel on the brink of an orgasm. Suddenly, K.'s hands disappeared. She made a mewl of disappointment that had both men laughing, but she was otherwise ignored. The car door opened then shut, and the one at her back did as well, prodding a draft to slide along her most private parts.

D.'s face-fucking had tired her out, she was too exhausted to even move. She just wanted to get her breath back and get this nightmare over and done with.

She noticed the draft didn't disappear, it intensified when a brush of hot air slid down the crack of her ass and then centered itself on her cunt. She had two seconds to suck in a breath before lips captured her clit and sucked down, hard, on the little nub. Haley cried out as immediately, sensation throbbed from her cunt down her veins. She whimpered when K. nibbled her pussy lips, slurped up her juices. His sounds of enjoyment fed her own and within a minute, she was on the brink of coming.

He pulled away, to the very millisecond, as though fully aware she could come. A sound of a zipper filled the night and his cock was there, where she needed it. He pressed the blunt tip of his dick against her cunt hole and thrust deep. She screamed as he filled her to the brim and immediately began to fuck her. His hips rammed him deep as he used her cunt for his pleasure. She was wet, horny and ready to come, but he was too fast. A few slow thrusts and he'd have driven her to the top as well, instead, he seemed intent on coming as quickly as possible.

A few minutes of his hard ramming and she was whimpering, that need to come hadn't dissipated and every thrust was torture, because it kept her on the edge but wouldn't knock her over. Her tears dampened D.'s jeans and it was only then she realized his hand was on her head and he was stroking her hair. The thought passed through her mind only to be batted away when, impossibly, K.'s hips moved faster and faster until he suddenly pulled out. She heard the wet sounds of his hand against his cock as he jerked himself off. His grunts of pleasure had her pussy clenching down, wishing for more of his earlier attention.

When his come splashed her ass, pelting her with creamy seed, she rolled her hips and let him decorate her behind with his very own paint. Even as his harsh breaths filled the air, his fingers went to work as soon as he'd finished. He swirled through his come and started to ply her asshole with the liquid. Her hip rolls weren't to entice now, but an honest reaction to his touch. His work-roughened fingers did things to her insides as he rimmed the delicate, sensitive area, taking her as high as he had done with his digits working her pussy.

Her own breathing was rough now. She panted against D.'s thighs, wishing they'd fuck her and wondering if they cared enough to let her come. She hoped to God they would, but knowing how selfish men could be, wouldn't be surprised if they dumped her out here in this deathly silent neighborhood and let her walk back to her digs.

The thought had her pleasure dimming a little, only for it to be rammed up into the stratosphere as K.'s fingers continued their magic play. With one of his hands busy at her ass, he pushed his free one against her butt cheek and urged her deeper into the cab. She had nowhere to go but forward and as D. helped her, K. removed his fingers and left her to suffer with the unquenched hunger throttling her body.

She was limp, borderline lax with the need rushing through her and D. had to maneuver her around so that she sat in his lap, her back to his chest – the move hurt her shoulders, strained them as her hands were still cuffed, but she remained silent, knowing to complain was of no use.

With her so seated, he moved and tilted himself so that he rested against the door. As soon as he was positioned like that, he grabbed her legs, spread them and cocked them over each of his knees. Letting his own thighs fall apart, she was as spreadeagled as could be, her cunt bared to K. and to the world visible through the open doorway.

Immediately, D. buried his hand between her legs. He sought his cock and rubbed it along the seeping flesh of her cunt. He was already hard and K. was slowly getting stiffer; she could see his reaction to her new position in the dim illumination from the streetlamps. D.'s cock slid through the sloppy mess K. had made of her ass and she felt his cock begin to butt at the tiny pucker, demanding entrance. His own pre-come helped him as he worked the thick tip into the tight hole, spreading the tissues, demanding they open to him with his insistent and tireless thrust.

She cried out when his cock sank home, branded quivering tissues with his molten heat and lodged himself deep inside her ass. Her cry was the catalyst. K. moved into the cab and sank between her thighs again. He rubbed the hard tip of his dick against her pussy, jerking himself off against her wet flesh. Each thrust nudged her clit and she began to roll around on D.'s lap, working his cock without meaning to, simply needing to move to burn off some of the heat K. ignited with his moves.

D.'s fingers slid upward and the two of them, D. with his hand and K. with his cock, began to massage her clit. Her mewls and whimpers filled the cab and she nearly screamed with frustration as K. rammed his cock deep inside her cunt and, still, that need didn't explode into satisfaction.

Tears leaked from her eyes and gushed down her cheeks. They'd taken her so high, so fast, she was floundering. Her head rolled from side to side against D.'s chest as their cocks, deep inside her pussy and ass, began to rub against each other, the thin sliver of membrane keeping them apart.

"Dave, oh, Dave!" she cried out. "Please. Fuck me! Fuck me!" Her urgent screams urged them from their cautious thrusts into earnestly ramming their cocks deep inside. They worked to a pace they'd established years before. Dave pushing into the trembling walls of her ass, as K. freed himself from the clinging tissues of Haley's cunt.

Inside, she felt like a rumbling volcano. The molten lava surging upward as pressure rent her insides in two. She screamed with fury as their thrusts merely ratcheted up her need and didn't quench it. She needed to come. Now!

"Fuck me, Kevin. Fuck me, *harder*, damn you!" she screeched.

Only when they complied and their fingers returned to rub her clit did release finally come.

Her shrieks filled the cab as pleasure bombarded her. Throttled her, choked her with its power. She cried, her tears this time of joy, as her climax rattled through her veins. As Dave's and Kevin's come shot deep into her body, she rode the crest of that particular wave like a woman born to surf the pleasure of two men. And she was that.

A two-man woman.

She groaned as their hips ceased their ramming, as Kevin's heavy weight settled atop the pair of them. She didn't even care that her shoulders had stopped protesting and were now on the brink of outright revolution as his weight added to their strain. She sank against Dave's chest, relieved to have come, to have that delicious buzz sizzling along her nerve endings.

She'd needed this all day.

Christ, had needed it since they'd worked out this plan two weeks ago.

As they'd come up with the discrepancies, worked out what she'd wear, she'd found herself getting hotter and hotter. Needing to come at the very prospect of what they would do to her in her role as Haley, the hooker, instead of Haley, their girlfriend.

The fact they hadn't touched her in a fortnight, hadn't helped. That was the rule of their games. When one of them came up with the fantasy, they had to suffer the torments of the damned until it was all arranged. It was why both men had had two erections within the space of five minutes.

Accustomed to sex twice or three times a day, minimum, all of them had been on edge. Two weeks had started to feel like two years. Only when they'd managed to confirm that all three of them could have the night off from the precinct had they known release was in sight.

In reality, this car was Kevin's and her squad car. Dave had his own partner over at Homicide. Nobody on the Force knew about the three of them. Nobody knew they all lived together. That Dave and Kevin shared her, that she shared them both and that was just how they liked it.

Sure, it was living a little dangerously role-playing in this way. But fuck, sometimes, after working the beat all day, after catching scum and upholding the laws of the land, the only way to relax was in a way that broke all the rules.

And, boy, was the orgasm worth it or what?

She grinned into the night, her smile invisible in the shadows and whispered, "You better wash that come out of my ass, David."

"What with? A sponge or my tongue?" he asked, the mocking question also deadly serious. He would rim her butt if she wanted.

"I think I'd die if you touched me again tonight," she replied, just as serious. "My nerves are fried. You both fucked me to death."

"You're breathing, so technically, we didn't do our job right." Kevin's retort was followed by a thrust of his hips that had all three of them groaning. Her legs curled up against her chest, moving free from Dave's knees in a self-protective gesture.

"No!" she cried as her body, from the ashes of her pleasure, started to respond even though everything inside her was on shutdown. She panted as Kevin, obviously in agreement and regretting his earlier move, pulled out. The three of them sighed in relief and, soon after, Dave's shaft slipped out of her ass, leaving her cock free.

She was too tired to even ask them to remove the cuffs and Dave only remembered when the hinge caught on one of his pubes. Kev laughed as he borderline squealed and dopily, Haley told him, "If you think that's bad then come with me the next time I'm booked in for a full Brazilian."

Dave shuddered as he unlocked her cuffs and said, "No. Fucking. Way."

Her laughter turned into a groan as he began to massage the balls of her shoulders and work her biceps to dispel the faint numbness that had gathered there. As he manipulated her sore flesh, he pressed a kiss to her cheek.

"Thank you for tonight," he murmured when Kev fastened himself up and moved out of the back seat and toward the front.

As he started the engine, Haley whispered, "You're more than welcome."

It had been Dave's fantasy to pick her up in a bar, to arrest her and then take her as though she were a whore and to make her come as both of the corrupt cops fucked her hard and fast.

It had taken her nearly six months to manipulate this particular fantasy out of him. He'd been ashamed at his desire to use her and only after telling him, repeatedly, that she loved him and that no matter what she'd continue to do so, had he divulged his particular kink.

After months of umming and aahing, she'd started to wonder if he had some particularly gross or worrying kink. It had come as a relief to only have to dress up and play the part of hooker.

Some might say that she was greedy. To need, want and love two men. She just thought she was lucky. And that they shared her love of role-play, well, that just made her the happiest woman on the Force . . . make that, the city.

Undercover Lover

Landon Dixon

The bum charged at me with a knife. I jumped to one side, chopped his wrist with my hand. The knife went skittering out onto the concrete. The bum met my upthrust knee with his gut. He blew 100-proof chunks all over the sidewalk. I slammed my foot into his dirty ass and sent him sprawling into the street.

All because he'd asked for a handout and I'd asked back, "Got change for a quarter?"

That's the mean streets for you, right here outside the downtown office building where I hang out my shingle: John Doo, Private Detective.

The elevator was like Marlene Dietrich riding one of her Teutonic lovers: on the Fritz. So, I hiked up the stairs to my fifth-floor office, keyed the door open, and trundled inside. It wasn't much of an office, at that – a desk, a few chairs, water cooler and a couple of filing cabinets – and it wasn't really even mine; it was a rental.

I kicked the door shut and dropped down behind my desk, pulled my camera out of my coat pocket and fired up the laptop. I was soon transferring the dirty digital pics I'd taken from my shooter to my hard drive. As I viewed the pornographic slideshow for a second time, my flesh-shooter got a hard drive going of its own.

The sexy pixels portrayed local power broker Sid Tumkins's wife, Enid, making merry with a jane making with a strap-on dildo up the elderly society lady's ass. They were up on the politico's marital bed, the teenage whore giving the sixty-year-old matron the dirty business end of the long, black dong strapped to her loins, right where the sun don't shine but the camera do.

I'd been hired by a rival city councillor to dig up some dirt on Hizzoner. And I'd found it, in steaming spade-loads. I'd posed as a meter man (one of the many "uniforms" I don as professional disguises) a day prior at the Tumkins's mansion out on Grove Road, surreptitiously cracking a sliding patio door an inch open to allow for easy re-entry later that evening. And then I'd re-entered last evening, and discovered that while Hizzoner's away, the pussies do play. Enid Tumkins had a serious case of butt itch that could, apparently, only be scratched by a pretty, teenaged girl wielding a foot-long.

I'd struck paydirt, and now, re-watching the filthy action, I was getting a "payload" building up in the crotch of my pants. I leaned back in my chair and loosened my zipper, pulled out my cock, started stroking to the butt-reaming beat of that teenybopper's dildo donging the handsome GILF's glory hole.

"John? Hello?"

Somebody was knocking on my door, then knocking it open.

I jumped to my feet and stuffed and zipped all in one motion. You've got to be quick to react in this sleazy biz.

My next-door neighbour from the apartment house I call home, Kitty Furr, pushed through the door and stepped into my office. "Hi, John," she said. "I've got a case for you."

She scoped out the bulge in the front of my pants right off the bat, as eagle-eyed as her hawkshaw neighbour.

"A case?" I cracked dubious. "I don't give handouts, even for friends." There was a bum with a size-twelve tattoo on his heinie who could testify to that. Kitty was usually as broke as an Edsel, I knew from experience.

"This is serious, John," she said, walking around my desk and up to my side. "Patty is missing. I want you to find her."

Patty was Kitty's daughter. A quiet, skinny, dark-haired girl with braces, glasses and pimples. I'd met her a number of times in the apartment building where she'd dwelt with her mother until she'd turned twenty-one and struck out on her own. Kitty pulled out a recent pic and handed it to me. It portrayed a skinny, pink-haired girl with piercings and tats, and no braces and no glasses.

"What the hell happened to her?" I yammered.

Kitty sighed. "That's what I want you to find out. Patty's

lifestyle totally changed once she turned twenty-one. She got wilder and wilder, hanging out with a bad crowd, skipping her college classes and quitting her part-time job." Kitty gripped my arm, her big, brown eyes brimming with brine. "And now I can't find her!" she bleated. "She's gone missing, John!"

Runaway daughters weren't my bread and butter. But I'd take almost any job, so long as I got the bread. "You have any money to pay me for looking for Patty?" I grilled my neighbour.

Her eyes dropped like my chances of collecting a pension in twenty years. "Well, no," she murmured. She glanced at the sex-stoked slideshow I'd forgotten to shut down, still playing X-rated on my laptop.

Kitty looked up at me, her full red lips curving into a sultry smile, her slender fingers stroking my arm. "But I could . . . trade you services."

I grunted; then gulped, as the woman moved in behind me and wrapped her arms around my rigid form, one of her hands catching onto my stiffened member.

"Just like when you were baking that cake that one time," she breathed in my ear, her lush body moulding warm and soft to my tense frame. "And *you* needed a helping hand."

I'd forgotten about her assistance with that stag party I'd been roped into organizing. She'd built a cake sizable and sugary enough for two strippers to pop out of (and they did). Now, she grasped my burgeoning boner through my pants and briefs and stroked. I flooded with heat, my head spinning from the triple combination of her rubbing hand, pressing body and intoxicating perfume. I groaned, as Kitty gripped tighter and stroked faster, her palm warm and smooth, her fingers adept and squeezing.

I ripped down my zipper. She drew out my dong and grasped me barehanded. I bucked and howled, getting jacked skin on skin. The dirty slideshow blurred before my eyes, my forehead bleeding sweat, my slit tearing up down below. Getting pumped faster and faster, with an exquisite flick of the wrist at the bloated tip.

I spasmed and shot, blinding white-hot joy basting my body and soul, sperm leaping out of my hand-cranked tool and splattering my laptop.

Kitty provided me with the name and known hangout of Patty's latest boyfriend, as well.

His name was Jack Oft, and he looked it. A hairy runt of a rat with buck teeth and a layer of skin grease. I found him gripping a pole-side seat at a local strip club with his buttocks. We took our confab out into the alley, when I hooked a hand into his collar and made him dance my way on the end of my arm.

"OK, OK, dude! Chill! Chill!"

"Where's Patty?" I growled, pinning the perv up against the grimy alley wall, mixing dirt with dirt.

"Hey, man! I-I don't know, dude! She took off on me, too, dog! She was supposed to shake it at the Pussy Palace, like, a week ago, but she was a no-show!"

I gave his heroin-thin body another jolt, bouncing his bony skull off the back brick. "What else did you get her into, besides stripping?"

"Hey, bro, nothin' she didn't want to get into! She's wild, dog, wild!"

"What – in particular!?" His chicken-brain rattled inside his rat-head as I rocked him again.

"She was turnin' tricks, man! Then she got me to send out her nude pictures – to skin traders, dude! I think, yeah, I think she was gettin' into porn, homeboy! She wanted to be a porn star!"

I persuaded him to show me the pics on his cellphone, the names and addresses of the meat-men he'd sent them to. I hardly recognized my ex-neighbour naked. She'd obviously gotten a pair of implants, shaved her quim bald as the King of Siam's head. It played out as the same old sad story – from rebellion to runaway to stripping to hooking to spreadin' 'em wide for the camera and comers, fresh meat for the smut-mongers.

I tossed Oft into a garbage bin and made rubber tracks for Porn Valley.

Meter man is only one of my many uniforms/disguises. For this investigative performance, I was Chuck Jissum, talent scout for a Las Vegas-area brothel, out on the West Coast running a recruitment drive. Straw boater and spiky yellow wig, wrap-around shades and charcoaled-on soul patch, florid shirt and flaccid pants, stick-on tats and clip-on nose ring. You get the flamboyant picture.

What stays in Vegas should've been me, if there were any decent health regulations. But I was on the prowl for poontang to feed the tourists and regulars. So, I made the rounds of the sex-shooters, showing my pictures of Patty around.

And after trekking through twenty or so sperm-scented offices, trailers, vans and motel rooms, the only decent response I got was a request to play "dick #3" in a glory-hole group scene being shot on location – in a grungy park restroom.

"One of our guys dropped out," Lemmy Choad told me, appealing to my sense of adventure and greed with his come-on and fifty dollars cash. "All you gotta do is stick your cock through a hole and get blown. Easy money and a good time, right. What d' you say? We won't even film your face."

I *was* low on dough. And who doesn't want to get their cock sucked – and paid for the privilege, to boot. I took my place in the six-man line-up in the dilapidated restroom.

All us "dicks" could see was a sheetrock wall, with a hole crudely drilled into it at waist level. I watched the two guys in front of me spear their erections through the opening, grunt and pump their hips, then convulse with the telltale spasms of orgasm. And then it was my turn to fill the dripping void.

I suddenly got stage-fright, and real fright. I didn't know what the fuck was on the other side of that sheetrock. For all I knew it could be a guy, the whole shooting match a gay play. Choad had been a little vague about the theme of the flick, the backstory and motivation of my character, dick #3. My cock drooped limp as Liberace's wrist, as I pondered the unpalatable possibilities.

"Action!" Choad screamed at me from six feet away.

I shovelled my soft-on through the greasy hole. It was met by a warm embrace and a hard stroke.

I was jerked up against the sheetrock. It *felt* like a feminine tug, soft and smooth and anxious. With an exquisite flick at the tip that I seemed to recognize from somewhere. My rigid body relaxed, and my relaxed cock went rigid.

The lady (I hoped) on the other side wasn't risking herself a case of carpal tunnel syndrome. Because once she had me poled out long and hard, she quickly engulfed my straining member with her mouth. I bucked into the board, flattening my hands and face and body against the barrier, sticking my cock as far out onto the other side as I could – into that hot, wet, sucking mouth.

The vaccing was pure moistened velvet, feeling like a woman's mouth, for sure; a real pro, judging by the depths the doll went without so much as a gag. I pumped my hips into the sheetrock, my cock into the mouth and throat, fucking that tight, sucking, satiny sexhole through the gruesome glory hole. And in even less time than it took Choad to produce and package a skin flick, I was spasming and shooting, busting a nut and blowing a load.

I pounded on the wall, fists and groin, blazing with heat and blasting my juice. The seasoned performer on the other side of the curtain drawing the best and stickiest out of this amateur thespian. She jerked my jumping, jizzing cock out of her mouth and jacked me all over what I could only hope were her big, juicy tits.

I was left as drained as Brando after a session of method-acting madness.

And when the last guy in line had emoted through the hole, and Choad hollered, "Cut!", I stumbled around the side of the sheetrock and spotted: my quarry, Patty, down on her knees, her pretty face and jutting tits covered with come.

It was a shot below the belt I hadn't seen coming. So when Choad ambled up to me and offered me a follow-up role in a thirty-man gang-bang he was piecing together for the following day, I almost slammed the guy in the gut. Like I'd been knocked back on my hocks.

But as I turned my head away from Patty towelling off her pretty young face and protruding fake tits, I nodded at Choad. Hell, it seemed the best way to keep tabs on the girl. Until I hatched a plan to bundle her away from this hedonists' playground and back to her mom.

I added a pair of green-tinted contact lenses and a couple of stencilled-on facial scars to my disguise for the follow-up shoot. It took place in an abandoned warehouse, just a ragged mattress right in the middle of the concrete floor to cushion Patty's knees, and hands, and back.

I mingled into the crowd of twenty-nine hard-ons (the same one – dick#3 was a no-show again), but it was still slightly uncomfortable hiding out from my client's daughter, seeing her naked in living colour. But I had a job to do. I'd found the missing girl, and if I had to fuck her to save her, so be it. To be honest, I'd done worse, to better people.

And I had to admit that Patty looked mighty appetizing there in her all-together; big, creamy-white tits thrusting off her slim body, cherry-red nipples jutting off the succulent melons, coral-pink pussy lips glistening with lubed-on moisture. I'm not normally a fan of tats and piercings on the twats I bang, but in this case, it really suited the whole nasty situation. My wood was as hard and as real as any stiff's there.

I eyeballed "Sweety Sinsation" (her porn nom) eagerly grab on to the first two guys with her hands, suck the third into her mouth. Her glims were a little glazed, her movements a tad too jerky – like maybe she was *on* something more than an oestrogen high from meeting and greeting all of that meat.

We moved in a circular rotation, Choad keeping the action flowing. It was soon my turn up to bat.

I stood alongside my kneeling ex-neighbour. She jacked the cock on her right, sucked the prick in front of her, then reached out her groping left hand for my rigidly twitching erection. I gulped heated air and gripped her thin wrist and guided her slender hand onto my raging dick. She instantly laced and tugged, making me and my cock jump.

The girl was a wet dream with either hand. And when I shuffled into position in front of her face, her mouth consumed me with a practised passion and precision that boggled my mind and buckled my knees – all over again. Patty excitedly sucked on my cannon, blowing hard and tight and deep, pumping the two other dicks off to her sides. I shot my fingers through her soft, pink-tinted hair and hung on, thrusting my cock into her face to keep pace with her blow job.

Patty's eyes flickered wide open and she looked up at me, her nostrils flared wild. I looked directly down at the girl, staring into her big violet eyes, as she sucked and sucked and sucked on my cock. I almost came wad and all right there and then, getting wickedly hummed.

But I held on, fucking her pretty face. She obviously didn't recognize me in my slum-uniform – I was just another throat-plunging prick. It was immensely erotic, tiptoeingly sensational. Choad had to bodily yank me back to get the gang-bang on keel again.

Men fucked Patty – pussy and ass – as she sucked on more slapping cocks. White and black men, Hispanics and Asians, old and young guys, a midget and his tiny todger thrown in for a small measure of comic and sexhole relief. By the time I spraddled up to Patty's spread pussy, my cock was a throbbing numb length of beef, up for anything.

She was laid out on top of a black dude, his chocolate cock lodged up her chute. She had two pricks at her dewy head, sucking and stroking them in turn. I stared into her slick, gaping, gasping pink slit, gripping my hard-on with whitened knuckles. Choad bellowed in my ear, and I took the plunge, donging Patty in the pussy full-length.

I grasped her splayed thighs and rocked back and forth, churning my cock to and fro in her cunt. Her pussy was as wet and juicy as her mouth had been, even hotter and tighter, and just as talented. I felt her inner walls clasp on to me, as I pistoned her poon. My teeth ground together and my fingernails bit into her flesh, my hips flying and cock drilling; brutally fucking my neighbour and client's daughter.

It took every ounce of willpower I possessed to pull out before I ruined the popshot.

I never got a go at her ass, unfortunately. Only three or four guys, with extra-huge horse-cocks, of course, were ladled out that "members'" privilege. But it didn't matter. Because only a minute or so after I'd banged Patty, Choad directed us to get into lines for the come-splattering finale to his fucking spectacular.

We formed two lines, on either side of Patty, who was sitting up on her knees on the sweaty mattress. There was no sheetrock barrier between my quarry and my nude self this time, no wall to shield my professional and personal lust. Patty jacked two spraying cocks against her cheeks at the same time, and then it was my turn.

I was fit to explode, my prick wound even tighter. Patty grasped my erection and pumped, smiling up at me, her face creamed with come. She stuck out her tongue and swabbed the straining, leaking tip of my pressurized hose. And I howled, "Patty!", bucking in her hand, blasting against her face.

I was like a fucking puppet on a twisted string, jetting rope after rope of sizzling sperm out of my ruptured pipe, splashing Patty's tongue and her tonsils with my ball-batter. If she'd heard me call out her non-porn name, she gave no indication. She sucked my spouting cock into her wanton mouth and vacced every last dissipating drop of super-heated come out of my boiling balls.

I was barely conscious, myself, when she popped me out, drained, and Choad dragged me away.

I quickly changed in the makeshift dressing room. Out of my pussy talent scout disguise and into a snap-brim hat and a two-piece suit, a one-piece trench coat, a pair of no-nonsense shades and a cop moustache, an earpiece on a wire that went nowhere. My law enforcement uniform was so convincing the other studs in the room started to get antsy, wondering if their cocks had gone too far.

But I wasn't working local vice (in a legal sense, anyway). I had a federal warrant – for runaway Patty. I hustled out to the parking lot just in time to catch the girl sliding into a taxi. She was dressed rather demurely now in a red tube-top and a pair of black shorty-shorts, six-inch cork wedgies.

"Federal marshal, ma'am!" I intervened, grabbing onto her arm. "I have a warrant."

She was still dazed from her recent glazing. She didn't put up a fight, as I led her away from the cab and over to my car. My guess was she'd broken so many laws, drug- and prostitution-related (and laws of nature), that she just figured something she'd illicitly done had finally caught up with her.

It wasn't until we were out on the Interstate, heading north, that Patty made her play for freedom.

She slid her hand onto my crotch and ducked her head down into my lap. "Are you sure there's no way I can beat this rap, officer?" she breathed, warm and wet over my groin, grasping my dick through my pants.

The talented trick had me unclothed and unsheathed in

seconds, her fingers winding around my shaft and lips sliding over my hood. Making me jump lanes, send some poor sap off into the ditch. I gripped the steering wheel and stared straight ahead, my cock swelling up like a Macy's parade float in Patty's hot, damp hand and mouth.

"Hey, I recognize this prick!" she yelped, jerking her head up. Her pink-painted fingernails bit into my shaft. "You were at the glory hole and the gang-bang! I sucked and jerked you off!"

I guess when you get immersed in the jizz biz, you get good at identifying dicks. She'd blown my cover, no doubt about it, and I'd blown my chances for a seventy-mile-an-hour farewell front-seat blow job. Before I could stop her, and still steer, she'd smacked off my snap-brim and ripped off my shades, torn away my fake moustache.

"John Doo!" she gasped.

I was no longer just *another* "john" to the girl.

I came clean, forced to by the sudden shift in circumstances. "I'm taking you back to your mother," I explained. "She's worried about you."

Patty threw herself back over into her seat and pouted for a moment. Then she shrugged, sort of grinned at me. "OK. I've got the wild out of my system, anyway."

Women! They're about as unpredictable as tropical storms, and sometimes just as wet.

"But *you're* going to have to pay me some money – to make up for my lost income. And to make sure I don't tell my mom that you fucked me – a poor, vulnerable, misguided, young girl."

She added, seriously tongue in cheek, "I'm worth it after all, wasn't I?"

She gave me a pretty smile and an outstretched hand. Grabbed me by the short hairs where it really hurts the most – my billfold.

I grunted. Not only was I *not* getting paid for all of my "hard" work; now, *I* was paying out. See why I don't like freebies for friends? They're nothing but headache and bank pain.

The Forest Ranger

Peter O. Savage

It was a chilly day that October 2012 in British Columbia's Fraser Valley region, because the temperature was 10 °C – about 50 °F – with a timid sun and slight breeze wafting in off Cultus Lake. Nothing much was happening as a few campers were preparing for their last hikes of the autumn season with the busiest period long gone before the winter set in.

Sergeant Kyle Roy wasn't too concerned that an over-busy day would occur after he'd driven down from the scenic clad mountains surrounding the lake, stopping briefly along the way to eat two cold bran muffins and sip tepid coffee directly out of a Thermos flask. His breakfasts were always hearty and he wasn't bothered with what he ate at noon as long as his hungry stomach was temporarily satiated. As a bachelor, his habits were regulated with a monotony that would bore the bellies of most folk and he looked forward to grilling a tasty T-bone steak or any other kind of steak, which he consumed every evening with mashed potatoes and a tin of veggies.

After his short bite, he fired up his truck and headed towards Cultus Lake Provincial Park with one thing on his mind, to warn campers that he and his colleagues had to shoot an aggressive cougar – a beast common to the area because of the abundance of edible animals – that had persistently approached snarling at and pestering some of the people on the Teapot Hill trail the previous day. Apparently it was an underweight young male obviously trying to find its way in the world and hungrily searching for a source of food; but when a dangerous cougar nags humans too close for comfort it had to be killed, because capturing them for relocation doesn't work.

Kyle saw a group of hikers studying a map deciding where to walk and noticed another standing apart from them looking at the mountains through binoculars. After he'd warned them to be careful should another cougar be around, he approached the single person, unable to resist admiring the possibilities of a shapely figure hidden beneath a knee-length red anorak with its hood covering half of her head because, much to his surprise, she wore printed tights and ankle-length leather boots, which were oddly fashionable and entirely unsuitable for hiking.

Camille Côté was a fine-looking woman, out for fun, the kinkier the better, who was only interested in the *idea* of camping and hiking. Anything real, like the prescribed unattractive clothing, sleeping outside in a tent with snakes, flea-infested creatures, gnats, mosquitoes and the like, gave her the heebie-jeebies. She'd come to the area in search of a man; not just any man, but one in the navy uniform of a forest ranger, or warden as they're often called. The thought of a big guy with a big dong to fulfill her fantasies, to stick it in her any-which-way and make her wetness ooze with passion and wanting. And if she could find a dong as intrepid as her trusted dildo, the happier she would be, for her dildo had become a tiresome friend that no longer brought her the pleasures she craved. She wanted a special man who could understand her; one she could bait and rile up enough to make him angry then manipulate him to do to her what she needed. And she chose the handsome sergeant, taking the risk that he would be the one for her.

"Excuse me, ma'am," he said politely. "I'm not sure if you could hear my warning, but if you're thinking of going up there alone, don't."

She turned to look at him and smiled. Her dark eyes and full lips convinced Kyle that she wouldn't have to do too much to entice him to a bout of phallus flinging, as he felt a stirring in his regulation pants pushing against the zipper. Although he was often on the alert for a shagable woman, his sexual escapades had been unremarkable to date and he was struck by her mysterious beauty. No woman had got him feeling that way so instantly before.

A head shorter than him, she lifted her face and said: "*Non, monsieur,*" in a lilting, sexy accent that gave him a lustful urge to fling her over a seat in his truck and fuck her faster and better than a young male cougar could do.

Technically, Kyle was a trained conservation officer among many other duties – a lonely job at times – and as a professional knew he shouldn't push his luck. So he controlled himself and swallowed his courage, his spittle nevertheless leaving his throat dry.

"Well, ma'am," he continued, explaining why she shouldn't venture that far, "it's not only the cougars. There're also other dangers – the weather, coyotes, bears and wolves to name a few – and it just wouldn't be safe in the mountains alone. In any case, you could easily get lost, and with no means to protect yourself or a tent to shield you from an unfavorable climate, you'd probably not survive."

"I'm not afraid," she replied, unable to resist a glance at his bulge, feeling wet already.

"Afraid or not, you can't go there," he stated.

"Oh, really, officer, and who is he that'll stop me?"

"Well, I do have the authority to order you. That means if you disobey me, I could arrest you."

"Oh, dear—" she pouted "—that would be frightening for me, a poor little Québecer who doesn't mean any harm, eh."

Like a peacock, he seemed to ruffle his feathers, inflating his wide chest and letting out an almost impatient blast of air. "It's not a funny matter," he insisted.

"I never said it was," she said and boldly added: "But your uniform does something to me. How should I say it . . . turns me on? Maybe you want to show me how strong you are after the arrest and protect me, hmm, *mon cher*? Will you put your cuffs on me . . . strip me naked . . . give me a severe hand spanking over your knees . . . or will you use a nasty rubber paddle to tame me . . . then fuck me hard, like how a vicious cougar would do?"

He knew he was going to lose this battle, yet still controlled himself. She'd said it all and what he really wanted was to tackle her impertinent challenge, then stuff his rigid cock into her until she screamed loud enough to frighten the wildlife.

"Please, ma'am," he said with reluctance walking away from her. "I'm forbidding you to go it alone. Be safe and join that group over there."

She laughed, but it wasn't scornful. "Running away are you?" she teased. "I was told you rugged officers were tough, but you're like one of your frightened black-tail deer. Run, run, run then, you timid man officer."

He blushed with embarrassment, turned and went to his truck saying nothing. *How*, he thought, *can a man handle something like that? But, Jeez, what a woman!*

He decided to drive straight home for a cold beer rather than stopping at the local bar frequented by most of the other officers. He wasn't in the mood for conversation. He wasn't even looking forward to a steak. All he could do was think about the brazen woman with a French accent and silly clothing who must have an ass worth the effort to kiss and fondle and maybe slap lightly a couple of times, who probably had full boobs with nipples sharper than the spires of Notre-Dame Basilica in Montreal, which he would suck to make her squirm before leaping down upon her sweet beaver and rummaging with his tongue prior to his dick plunging into her. "Aah, the effort!" he mused. "Why do women require such effort?"

But he knew in his heart that if he met her again he'd make a bloody good effort and have her in his truck or in the forest or his bed, whichever came first. He had no intention of letting her get away, which was as great as his intention to say goodbye after the deed was done. No lasting romantic stuff for him, no-way-no-sir! Not ever! Survey, entice, pounce and be gone was his usual motto.

Meanwhile, in a small hotel near the lake, Camille relaxed on a bed staring at the ceiling, tickling her clit with one hand while thinking of the conservation officer and what lay behind the zipper she'd spied that offered an irresistible invitation. She giggled quietly as she remembered how she'd teased him and made him blush. In her other hand she held a round black rubber paddle that she caressed along her slim thighs, its cool surface making her imagine it landing on her round, wholesome bottom, which would wobble with each smack.

Frustrated, she got up, twisting her body to examine her butt in a mirror, and pouted.

That's a difficult one to persuade him to do, she thought. *No one has ever had the guts to spank me except for a lesbian acquaintance once in my late teenage years, but only because we'd had a slight tiff and she threatened me. I said she wouldn't dare. Pity I wasn't a lesbian, because it was a delight, with her holding me over her knees reddening my butt until I screamed, then licking my clit and cunt to oblivion. It was the only same-sex fling I've ever had. But it didn't feel right afterwards and I didn't pursue the relationship – not that she didn't try – I just decided it wasn't my thing.*

Thinking like that had always conjured up the image of a guy in uniform and it wasn't until she flipped through a *National Geographic* magazine about a male forest ranger in BC, while waiting for the dental hygienist to finish with a client, that she realized what she desired was exactly him, or one very similar.

She couldn't wait any longer and began to prepare what she normally did, first to run a hot bath, sit in it until she turned pink and then whack herself with the paddle while her buttocks were wet. She would do that until the stings made her randy, then grab her dildo and play with it until her cunt became hotter than the water and produce a yelping orgasm.

But those fun times always ended without fulfillment of her inner self. She yearned to be played with, to be overwhelmed and then played with again and again, with a guy who was like a wind-up mechanical toy that could wind down and be wound up continually.

She plugged in her mobile to the battery charger and closed her eyes with a determination to disobey the officer and venture into the forbidden mountains the next day far enough away to perhaps cause concern.

She was the last to leave after breakfast. The hotel manager had provided a packed lunch and bottled water and gave her the same warning that Kyle had given. But there was evilness on her mind that somehow she could lure her prey to rescue her; and if then arrested, perhaps he'd take her to a police station or lock her up in a hotel room, gated like a naughty girl.

She had taken no precautions – not even a basic map of the trails – and without a firm idea of where she was going, began walking in the direction she'd been told not to go. With luck, the officer would be concerned. On the way, following the shoreline, she passed a few anglers hoping to land steel-head and cutthroat trout who greeted her with a casual wave of their hands, one of them holding a live silver thing by its fin tail. She huffed in disgust; the only suitable fish for her were headless dead ones in a supermarket.

As it happened, Kyle had to return to Cultus Lake on the same day and it wasn't too long before he heard that the French lady had taken off and where she seemed to be headed. News travels fast in those areas and all the locals kept an eye on their guests to avoid mishaps. It was the hotel manager who gave him the tip.

"Thanks, Jim," he said. "My God, why is it that some tourists don't listen? I'll tell you, I've got enough to do without traipsing after an idiot and, well, this one is a particular idiot, if you get my drift."

"Yep; city dwellers don't believe there's anything to worry about, do they? And after you got that cougar recently, in my opinion it's their own faults."

"Too right," Kyle sighed. "But I still have to waste my time tracking her down and I've a mind to kick butt when I do!"

"Even so, I hope she's safe," Jim said.

"Safe or not, she's going to get it real good!"

After two hours of wandering, true to form going off the beaten tracks, the careless hiker went into the bushes and lost her way. Fortunately, she managed to retread her steps to the muddy track she should've stayed on and slumped down onto a fallen tree trunk in despair.

"*Tabarnac!*" she wailed. "All I intended was a little walk to maybe get the officer to follow me. But what if there's no search? What if a different person comes? *Moi stupide*! *A real fucking you mess!*"

At that moment, she heard a faint rustling in the damp bushes, leapt up and screamed, only to watch a small rodent look at her and scuttle away as fast as it had arrived. She shuddered in a cold panic. To her, the diminutive rodent appeared to be a dinosaur.

Kyle parked his truck. Although it took him over an hour, he was an experienced tracker and quickly saw fresh footprints. Within five minutes, he heard her scream and rushed towards the sound.

She ran into his arms when she saw him and, hugging him tightly, began to kiss him.

"Thank you, thank you, mister! You saved my life!"

He pushed her away angrily and then shoved her down onto the tree trunk. "Name?" he asked brusquely. "And identification."

"Camille Côté," she responded demurely, taking out a purse and handing him her driving license, thinking at the same time that she'd succeeded with phase one – rescue and anger – and couldn't help herself from smirking.

"You think it's funny, Miss Côté?" he said. "You wasted my time and you *could* have gotten yourself into serious trouble out here, as I warned you. Aha, I also see that you're thirty-six years old and live in Montreal. That's a long way to come to play silly games for a woman your age, don't you think?"

"Yes, sir," she replied, pretending to be contrite and respectful. "And it *was* only a game. I was honest, wasn't I? I did tell you that you turned me on, didn't I?"

"No." He smiled. "You said my *uniform* turned you on with a lot of exceedingly direct and promiscuous insinuations too, I might add!"

"Oh, yes, I forgot." She grinned.

"A short memory, hmm," he jibed, taking out his cuffs. "Well, disobeying my caution, wasting an official's time and verbally accosting an officer with intent to entice him, are all violations that deserve punishment. Hold out your hands!"

She did so and a trickle of anticipation crept down her spine. He led her to his vehicle and put her on the back seat. Then he picked up his phone to call in a report, thinking if she wanted to play games he would accommodate her. "Culprit retrieved," he said curtly, then turned towards her and added: "I'm Kyle."

Camille was curious as to what would happen next, because before long she realized he might've cottoned on. *He* must *have*, she thought. *I'm not* that *stupid. What officer would phone in a report without the phone on and why bother to give only his Christian name?*

He drove towards Cultus Lake and turned right at a crossroad instead of going into the town. She wondered where he was taking her. After a while they were passing through a pretty wooded region along a river. "This is the Sweltzer River," he explained. "My grandparents built a house here ages ago and it belongs to me now, otherwise I couldn't afford to live here on my salary."

He turned onto a bumpy entry to a small cottage hidden from the road by a shield of tall trees and bushes. It was a quaint-looking house and she could see he was a fisherman from a canoe and rods and a fish basket that were stacked under a lean-to.

"Out," he said.

He led her into a pleasant lounge/dining room with a galley kitchen to the side. She noticed three doors and later discovered they were two bedrooms and a bathroom. In the dining area was an old wood table encrusted with age with matching chairs, which he told her his grandfather had carved by hand.

He opened one of the doors to reveal twin beds with a single chair. He sat her on the chair, then pulled out his mobile and phoned his friend at the hotel who he'd known since they were kids.

"Hi, Jim," he said. "I'll be coming to collect Miss Côté's gear. She's feeling a bit tired and decided to rent my bedroom for a week."

"Uh-uh, is that so?" Jim answered, chuckling; and said what he always said when he knew Kyle had had a bit on the side or intended to: "Randy bastard!"

Camille stared at Kyle quizzically, her thighs beginning to tingle. "I am?"

"Yes." He grinned. "You're under arrest by free consent, right? Now, I have to finish my shift and *you*, young lady, will be cuffed to this chair until I get back."

"Oh, you're so cruel, *mon cher*! How long will you be?"

He looked at his watch. "Two hours; can you last that long?"

"It depends what you're going to do. Maybe I can; maybe longer if I know."

"I'll do what you want," he answered, "perhaps what you invited me to do . . . or questioned if I might . . . when we first met. On the other hand, I might do what I want. How will you like that?"

She sighed deeply. "I have fantasies," she stated simply. "You can do what you like."

"In that case, I'll leave you to ponder your delinquent behavior." He unlocked one of her wrists and fastened it again with her arms around the chair back. She looked pitiful, still in her anorak and boots mucky with dirt.

After he left, she realized she wasn't tethered to the chair at all and could easily stand up and wander about if she chose to do so. Instead, to prolong her excitement, she stayed put.

The two hours passed quickly and she heard his truck crunch to a halt. He took his time before going to the bedroom. She soon found out why. He entered completely naked and sauntered towards her, his dick flapping between his muscular legs, purposefully taunting her. She gulped and it was her turn to blush.

He hauled her up and took off the cuffs. She ripped off her clothes, allowing him to undo her bra – an expensive embroidered Lise Charmel and then slid down her lacy panties to reveal a bushy, unshaved beaver very much to his liking. Her body was just as he'd imagined. Even better for his taste was her comparatively slim waist and ample buttocks, which sagged slightly at the plump, and her boobs were exactly as he'd imagined, too, yet her nipples naturally more thrilling than his allusion to church spires.

"You're extremely attractive," he breathed. "Far more beautiful than all the natural wonders surrounding us; I see the mountains and valleys every day, but none are as special and precious as yours."

"And you're superb," she parried, reaching out with her hand to squeeze his dick and kissing his lips. "It looks like I won't be disappointed, but first . . . would you?"

"Ah, yes, the punishment." He winked. "I'll do it my way first. If later on this week you want it your way it'll be OK by me. The problem is I'm not angry with you any more. Do I have to be?"

"Yes, I want to feel it," she said and slapped his face several times. "That's for cuffing me!" she yelled, then kicked his legs. "And that's because I hate you!" Then she yanked his dick hard, making him wince. "And that's for taking so long!"

He was taken aback sure enough, but far from angry. But he got the drift of her game and complied by grabbing her by the waist and carrying her butt-forward to the chair. He plunked himself heavily upon it and threw her unceremoniously over his knees, the warmth of her skin against his making him impatient to fuck her.

He raised his hand high up and slammed it down forcefully on her white fleshy orbs. Whack*!* "Ouch!" Whack! "Ow-ooh-ouch! I hate you – you beast!"

She giggled, urging him on. Whack! "You think that hurt, *mon cher*, humph!"

Then he got the hang of it and pounded her relentlessly with an enthusiasm that was formerly beyond his experience.

Slap! Whack! Slap! Whack! Slap! "OOOH! OW! OUCH! OW! OOOWOW!"

She yelled and swore at him as he disciplined her rapidly from side to side, the plump of her red butt flapping up and down as she wriggled from the stinging slaps, trying to get out of his grasp yet wanting him to grasp her forever; complaining from the hurt yet complaining it wasn't hard enough. She didn't know how much she wanted but thought too much wouldn't be enough, yet his heavy hand soon became unbearable and she realized, without regret, that her appetite had been overzealous.

By now her slippery cunt was pining for his dick and after a good fifteen minutes of relentless spanking, her butt couldn't take any more. She begged him to release her, but he didn't comply.

"No! No, Kyle, please! OUCH! Enough! No, OW! I really mean it! STOP! AAAH!"

Finally, he let her go. She stood up and refused to rub her sore butt, still enjoying the stinging bruises and the thrill of a masterfully administered spanking that'd set off her loins. She spread over him and clasped him behind his neck and, as her legs dangled towards the floor, he cupped her soft buttocks with his large hands. She eased herself onto his stiff cock and slid down on it urgently. He gasped from the pleasure of her hotness, helpless to move as she rode him furiously.

Her movements were energetic and soon became cramped. She got off and dragged him to the bed, immediately throwing herself onto her back, legs akimbo and her cunt aching for more. He linked his arms around her knees, bending them backwards, kissing her wildly as he drove into her with a mighty sigh, while she heaved from the impact of his deep thrusts and clung on to him.

"OOOH! OW! OW! OOOWOOW!" Her cries a different kind of pain – the pain of utter joy and satisfaction as an orgasm burst, followed by another after he'd spurted into her.

They rested peacefully cuddling each other. Yet after half an hour, Kyle murmured: "Are you hungry?"

"No," she replied.

"I am." He laughed as he swiveled around head first and ate her ravenously, quickly bringing her to another *magnifique-mon-cher* orgasm.

She didn't stay only for a week. She moved in, eagerly waiting for him to come home each day, hoping and praying that he'd be in the mood; and she didn't mind doing all the cleaning, because that became their new game when she didn't do it perfectly.

Kyle became a happily proud protector and excellent provider for his naughty little Québecoise companion and he did whatever she wanted, including the use of a black rubber paddle on her alluring wet bottom while bathing together in a hot bath, then mounting her from the back like a fierce cougar. And he didn't mind at all that she refused to cook steaks every day and soon appreciated her flavorful cooking. His life changed completely.

So did hers. She learnt willingly how to catch and gut fish and came to enjoy camping and hiking, wearing the prescribed unattractive clothing, sleeping outside in a tent with snakes, flea-infested creatures, gnats, mosquitoes and the like, from which she no longer got the heebie-jeebies.

And Jim never called Kyle a randy bastard again

Number One

Jacob Louder

It's not like it was written in our vows, but Jack and I each had a list. His, if you ask me, was filled with five of *the* most improbable women: Kim Kardashian was his number one, Khloe Kardashian his number two.

"I'd really like them together," he had told me one night as we ate Chinese takeout in bed, my pussy still wide and wet from the hard, deep fucking we'd shared not a half-hour before. This admission brought a smile to my lips, the kind that only Jack could bring, and I watched as his eyes grew bigger, much like his bulge beneath our sheets, from just thinking about it. "Kim licking my tip, Khloe licking my balls," Jack said. "*Imagine*, sweetheart!"

Jack filled out the rest of his list with Jennifer Gardner, *Miley Cyrus*, for Chrissakes, and Kate Middleton.

My top five celebrities that I could sleep with – no questions asked, no ifs, ands, or buts – were much more reasonable, and, that night, number one was sitting right in front of me at the Four Seasons hotel bar. Hunter Caldwell – Portsmouth United's best midfield weapon – was by himself, drinking whiskey from a snifter. I had studied this man for years on the television, thanks to Jack's subscription to some sports package through our TV cable company, and thanks to my niece Amelia, who showed me Hunter's picture in a teen magazine in a spread entitled "Cuties From Other Countries". I was astonished not only because Amelia, so enthused about Hunter, had that electric, pre-pubescent sexual energy she typically saved for Justin Bieber, but because, in the case of Hunter Caldwell, "cutie" was an understatement even for the under-fourteen crowd.

I had watched Portsmouth's matches whenever they were scheduled for broadcast, but I almost didn't recognize him, his dark head low as he sat at the bar. I had never seen him off the pitch, without his blue and white uniform, without an ounce of sweat to be found on him, not his face or clothes or anywhere. But I was keenly aware of – and had studied for months now – the body that rested beneath those business-appropriate clothes of his: the tantalizing hard muscles that ran from thigh to calf, but especially around his knees; the strong and sinewed shape of his arms; and even the V-cut at his lower abdomen, which he'd flash whenever he raised his jersey to wipe the sweat from his face.

Because of that V, I would pray for the hottest of hot weather at Fratton Park, Turf Moor, Liberty Stadium.

But with Hunter alone in his seat, and with me alone at a tiny table for two, and with the strange quiet of the bar surrounding the few us of who were present, even on this Thursday night in the city of Boston, the only thing left to do was weigh my options: I could admire him from afar and let him drink himself into impotency, or I could do my best to catch his eye, to strike up a conversation, to make him smile – just once, if I could. His smile was something I'd seen so few times on television (Portsmouth FC – well, it had room for *growth*), but when I had, his face had lit up the screen and sent a pulse right to my pussy.

Lucky for me, I was already in my tight, black evening dress, revealing in its high cut at the leg and low dip at my breasts. I had taken my time dressing, attaching my stockings to their garter with patient, steady fingers; caressing the silkiness of my black panties with their lacy trim at the thigh; and cupping my breasts over my matching black bra, teasing my nipples through the fabric until they were hard against the thin lace. Tonight, I had wanted to wine and dine myself, and planned to take me to bed and fuck my pussy silly with the new vibrating seven-inch silicon cock Jack had bought me for my business trips away. But these plans of mine? I now hoped they'd change just slightly.

I grabbed my purse and crossed the plush red carpet, moving my legs and hips slowly, rhythmically, the way I knew Jack liked. ("When you walk like that, baby," he had said to me once, "you make dirty sex look dainty.") When I reached Hunter, I stretched an arm out to grab a napkin that I didn't really need – I had finished my martini long ago – from the small stack in front of him. It was a long, exaggerated movement, and I was certain to brush against him, to connect my heat with his: that gentle pressure of my breasts against his upper arm. He turned in his seat in response, took a look at my tits first (which, in that dress of mine, was really the point), and then my face.

Hunter smiled and, just like that, I felt the growing heat of my wet cunt.

He was beautiful, with his chiseled good looks, his brown eyes intense, nearly predatory on me now. His haircut was expensive I'm sure, with its perfect part and those sculptured sideburns, and he needed a shave—oh, I *loved* that he needed to shave!

Hunter said, "Hello there."

I was hovering – I knew this – but I couldn't take my eyes off his. I was enraptured. That, and I was finding it difficult to move my tits – the whole front of my body, really – away from him.

A soft chuckle came from Hunter's throat. "Well," he said confidently, and then suggestively, "can I give you something else, then?"

Not long after, I knew I needed to call Jack.

At first, on the line, there was silence, and then, "No – he's right there right now?"

"Yes," I said. "He just bought me a drink. He is *stunning*, Jack. You should see him."

My husband had experimented when he was in college ("I was quite the cocksucker!"), so, really, I knew he'd understand. "I bet he is," he said in a pensive tone, like he was crunching numbers in his starched white shirt and tie at the office, when I knew he was at home on the sofa watching television, and likely not in a shirt at all – his chest and big, beautiful belly exposed. "So are you going to do it?"

"I'm going to try."

"Baby, it's a done deal. If he passes you up, he's queerer than I am." I heard Jack shift against our sofa's cushions, and then the quick zip of his fly.

"What are you doing right now?" I asked, but I knew. I totally knew.

"I'm playing with my cock," he said, his voice suddenly

playful. "I'm imagining you seducing this British soccer dude, and I'm getting nice and hard."

Before we hung up, Jack said, "I hope he's hung like a horse, baby. I hope he fills that gorgeous pussy of yours to the brim with his big, hard cock, and that it's nothing but the best thing ever."

That was all the encouragement I needed.

When Hunter and I moved to a booth toward the back of the bar, I told him no lies – not one. I told him that my name was Amy Stuart, that I was forty-three, married, a natural blonde, and had no children. I told him that I was traveling on business, that the Four Seasons was a hotel I frequented, but had no idea his team, which was visiting the States for friendly matches against clubs from our domestic league, was staying here as well. I told him about Jack and our lists. I told him that he was my number one.

This made him cock an eyebrow as he took a gentle sip of his whiskey. There was a flash in his eyes that made my nipples harden. I could have run my hands over the short, dark stubble on his cheeks and chin right then, bringing his plump, pink lips to mine for a kiss that I was sure would be sweet and heavy from his liquor. I shifted in my seat instead, feeling the dampness of my panties.

"I don't know what to say." Hunter leaned his head back against the tall booth. He smiled again, that sexy, confident smile, one that looked practiced, and probably for reasons like the one I was giving him. How many propositions did he receive from women like me, or from men like me, on a monthly, maybe weekly, basis? "I'm flattered," he said. "Truly flattered. And a little intrigued." That's when I felt it – his dry, warm hand on my thigh. "I've never been with a woman like you before."

I figured he was being a gentleman, that someone had raised him well. "Someone older, you mean?" If I was remembering correctly, I nearly had two decades on him.

His smile grew bigger. "Yes, *that*," he said, then shook his head and looked down into my lap, like he was suddenly feeling shy, although he didn't move his hand away. "It's more than that, though. I've never been with a woman so forward, so honest. It's kind of refreshing."

"There must be plenty," I said. "Girls from all over the world."

He scratched at the stubble of his chin and raised his eyes to mine. "Yes, but they all want to be girlfriends or wives, like, *instantly*."

"Some women, I'm sure, are simply taken by you – your beauty, your athleticism – regardless of intent," I said. "I won't ask of you what they have, though. I certainly don't want your commitment."

In this time, Hunter had worked his hand all the way up to my hemline. He held my gaze. "I know," he said. "It's perfect."

I felt that pull in my pussy, the one that signaled how much I wanted his fingers, his tongue, his cock deep inside me. I felt nearly desperate for it. I wanted all of him.

I said, "Let me show you how perfect."

Apparently, that was all he needed. Hunter pressed his lips against mine, and I pressed harder into him, demanding more – there was, after all, no need for convincing. His tongue was swift, experienced for someone so young, although he tasted like a much older man, like my Jack would on some nights, of the finest of fine liquors.

I felt one of Hunter's firm hands on my breasts, the other beneath my dress as he ran his fingers over the wet spots along the crotch of my panties. "You feel amazing," he said. "I can feel how ready you are for me."

I pressed my lips against his ear, gently brushing my hand over the bulge in his pants. "I can see how hard you are for me."

His soft laugh, I could feel it against my neck, but his voice came low and serious. "Will you rub me?"

It was my turn to laugh. I pushed him back against the booth, looking into his dark brown eyes – what I found: a fiery, urgent desire. He sat still, waiting for my response, the top button of his shirt undone and black tie loose at this neck, his sleeves pushed up over his elbows. I asked, "What about discretion?" but, hell, my fingers were already on Hunter's zipper, feeling beneath his pants the hardness, the considerable size, of his youthful cock, which sprang out at me through his fly when I went in for a little exploration. Hunter's dick was hot and heavy in my hand. I could feel my body react to the sight of him, to his heat, the way his hands were gripping the leather seat of our booth.

"Fuck discretion," he said, his smile lazy now. He looked down at my hand on his cock, then back up at me. "So, what do you say?"

I scooted closer, enjoying his warmth. I pulled my dress up my thighs and spread my knees slightly into the darkness beneath our table. I moved my hand from his cock – so long and thick, it dipped forward when I released him, resting on his leg – pulled the crotch of my panties to one side, and rubbed my fingers along the hot, wet folds of my pussy.

Even I was surprised, if not impressed, with how ready, how excited I was, and a tiny laugh slipped from my lips. Hunter's eyes watched my hand move slowly up and down along my cunt, taking some time to tease my hardened clit. I watched Hunter lift his head slightly as he inhaled through his nose, and I wondered if he was trying to smell me. I dipped one finger inside my pussy, and then a second. Hunter moaned loudly, shifting his body, impatient.

"Feel this," I said, rubbing my two fingers, still hot and wet from my pussy, along the length of his cock. It twitched in response, so I teased the head, massaging it with gentle circles.

Hunter brought his face close to mine. He said, "Your husband is a lucky man."

I grabbed his cock, and he gasped. "My husband is a *very* lucky man," I said.

The bar had grown louder around us, thanks to the arrival of a bachelorette party with at least twenty already tipsy young women, and the stragglers from the baseball game that had ended only a few blocks away. Hunter kept his eyes on me and did his best to keep his face straight. I teased the length of him, varying my pressure and speed until I found the ones he liked. He thrust up his hips and hissed, "Yes."

Hunter lowered his eyes, stopping to watch my tits shake just slightly on my chest while I jerked him off. His lips only parted slightly when he squeezed his eyes shut – anyone else would have thought that he had experienced a quick, surging pain – and then I felt the warmth of his come on my hand and wrist.

"Oh my God," he said, exhaling deeply. He moved his hand to my pussy, deftly working his fingers into my panties and sighing when he felt what awaited him: me – hot, slick, beyond ready. Hunter leaned his forehead against my ear, his hot breath again on my neck. "Your room, please," he said. "Your room right now."

Alone in the elevator, Hunter tore at my panties until I finally stepped out of them. It's times like these I'm thankful for wearing the skimpiest of underwear over my garter belt. I tucked the damp, silky fabric into my purse, while Hunter lifted the front of my dress to observe my naked pussy.

"I've never seen a cunt like yours – so hairless. What, do you wax?"

It was hard to believe that, up until this moment is his life, he had only bedded women who trimmed.

Hunter pressed his tall body against me, rubbing the soft skin of my pussy until he parted the lips and plunged two fingers so deep inside, I dug my nails into his hard shoulders and gasped. "Just making sure," he said, practically a whisper, "that there's enough room in there for what I've got."

"You talk a big game, don't you?" I said, running my hand along that cock of his, which strained against the fabric of his pants, ready again. I pushed my hips down as he fucked me, the palm of his hand tapping my clit with his quick thrusts.

He looked at me with his dark eyes. "Don't come yet," he said. "Don't come."

Over Hunter's shoulder, I watched the numbers of the hotel floors light up above the elevator doors. It progressed at a snail's pace – *six ... seven ... eight.* I swear the elevator hadn't moved *this* slowly on the way down to the lobby. I let him fuck me, listened as his breath grew heavy, and somehow held back what I knew would be a crushing orgasm. When the elevator sounded, having reached the tenth floor, I pushed him away as the doors opened, revealing a white-haired, blank-faced elderly couple who were dressed, I could only guess, for a ball.

In my hotel room, it started – to my complete and utter delight – with much of the same, except Hunter fucked me with his fingers after I had taken my place on the mattress, the flower-patterned bedspread without a wrinkle beneath my hands and knees. I had thrown my purse down on the bed, lifting my dress over my hips so he could see my stocking tops, my naked ass, my hairless cunt he seemed to like so much.

"This pussy," he said, moving his free hand, the one not being clenched at and sucked in by my eager hole, to my clit, teasing it lightly with the tip of his finger. "This pussy needs cock."

His words, his hands – together, they were too much, so I squirmed away from him, resting my ass on the mattress. "O°," I said, taking a long, deep breath, trying not to feel so high so soon. "I don't want to come yet, and you need to get naked."

Hunter sucked his two fingers, which had been glistening with me, and then made quick work of his button-down shirt and pants. His chest was thin, but muscled like the rest of him, and across his pecs, positioned expertly around his two pink nipples (*I will suck and bite them*, I thought, *I will suck and bite them until he screams*), was a tattoo done in black ink of angel's wings. He was hairless until he dropped his trousers and pulled down his black boxer briefs, revealing not only that monster of a cock and beautiful V-cut, but a neatly groomed patch of dark pubic hair.

I must have been gawking, must have been *something*. Hunter raised his arms at his side, giving me a little shrug. "So?" he said, the expression on his face open, innocent.

"Turn around," I said. "Show me your ass."

"Oh, no," he said, putting his hands over his face, but turning for me anyway. "It's kind of flat."

OK, he was right. But the smooth skin of Hunter's young white ass on top of those long, tanned legs of his – what a shame this man had to wear shorts so long on the pitch! It was breathtaking, having those muscled thighs and knees and calves in front of me, seeing them flex as he moved in a circle. No TV camera could do them justice. That ass of his, though – it needed my nails gripping him firmly as he fucked my pussy with the quick, deep thrusts of his long, thick cock. I wanted us frenzied on this bed.

"Help me out of this dress," I said. He did, carefully raising it over my head, and then laying it on the recliner in the corner of the room while I emptied the contents of my purse. I always had a condom or two because Jack and I were the *definition* of spontaneous, and I couldn't say how many times they were necessary in the women's room of our favorite Italian restaurant, or in the alley behind our local movie theater after watching – yes – the new Jennifer Gardner film. And I was not disappointed because beneath my cell phone, right next to my sunglasses, were two condoms.

"Oh good," he said, looking at the packets in my hand. "I'm so happy I don't have to go down to the gift shop in the lobby."

"Sit," I said, patting the mattress at my side.

Hunter leaned back on his hands and spread his legs for me as I moved to the floor, the plush, green carpet soft against my knees. I kissed his balls, pressed the tip of my wet tongue against them, and reveled in the sound of his tiny hiss. "Please," he said. "Don't tease me."

I appreciated his honesty, and I love men who say "please", so I licked the palm of my hand and jerked his cock just like I had in the bar, the way I knew he liked, while I licked and sucked his balls, my lips pulling at and smacking against his soft, tender skin.

"Fuck," he said. "Give me that mouth of yours."

I repositioned my body so that I could take him easily into my mouth, loosening the muscles in my throat to accommodate as much of him as I could. He tasted only a little sour, thanks to any remnants of his dried come courtesy of my handjob earlier in the bar, but this was in no way a distraction. As far as I was concerned, Hunter Caldwell's cock was the sweetest and slickest of candy canes, something to crave, to be eaten with gusto. I worked that cock of his with my lips, teeth and tongue until I felt him pull at my hair. "Stop," he said, his breaths quick and heavy. "Where are those condoms?"

I crawled back on the bed beside him and located a condom, now on top of the pile left by my emptied purse. I handed it to him, and he ripped at the package, but I was suddenly taken by the presence of my cell phone. The idea came quickly, and I didn't even think it over before I asked.

"How do you feel about letting my husband listen to you fuck me?"

Hunter stood at the end of the bed, his long cock wrapped in latex, with a look on his face that I couldn't decipher at first. "How do you mean?" he asked.

I snapped the hook of my bra and out poured my tits. Hunter smiled then, instantly relaxed, distracted. He started to rub his hand slowly over his cock.

"Fuck me," I said, positioning myself again on all fours. "Fuck me from behind while my husband listens in on the phone."

When Hunter joined me on the bed, I touched the screen on my cell until I found the number to our house line. Hunter pressed the tip of his cock against my hot pussy, then moved inside with ease, filling my cunt, making it stretch, just as I had pressed the call button.

The phone lay on the mattress, and by the time I heard Jack's "Hello?" Hunter was already thrusting his hips hard against my ass, his cock moving in a perfect rhythm, the sound of our fucking loud from the urgent smack of skin. I heard Jack speak again, so I let out a moan, one that I knew he'd recognize, and Hunter said in his beautiful British accent, whether he had heard Jack or not, "What a lucky man, the one who gets to fuck this hot, wet pussy of yours. Damn, I could fuck this hole all night. Does my cock hurt, honey?"

I turned my head and caught his eye. He smiled at me, lips parted, loving this.

"I love your cock," I said, turning my head again so that my voice carried in the direction of the phone. "So big and thick. Don't stop fucking me."

I wasn't completely sure, but the words that I *think* I heard come from my cell were, "Oh my God."

"Come here," Hunter said, leaning forward to wrap my body in his arms. I turned into his embrace, and he kissed my cheek quickly before he lifted me from the mattress and up into the air, secure in his arms. I let out a playful squeal, loud enough, of course, for my husband at home to hear – my husband, who was very likely jerking off like a madman. I loved this thought of Jack, cock hard in his hand, just as much as I loved the feeling of Hunter positioning his cock against my slit as he held me like a little girl, my tits pressed hard against his chest.

When he let my body slip – slowly and firmly – in his arms, I felt once again the fullness of his cock deep inside my pussy.

The acrobatics! So *this* was what it was like to fuck a professional athlete!

With my legs wrapped around Hunter's waist and my ass in his hands, this was how I fucked my number one or, more accurately, how my number one fucked me: deeply, intensely. He stood, thrusting that thick cock deep into my cunt, and I bobbed up and down, watching the veins in his throat pulse with every effort he made to ensure that my pussy was positioned for both of our pleasure, that he wouldn't lose his grip on me. He watched me as we fucked, his brown eyes slightly squinted, his beautiful bottom lip in what could be easily mistaken as a perfect, unforgettable pout, and this made my orgasm all the better – that determined look of his, as if he was entirely committed to making sure that both of us in this room and everyone else on the line ended the evening in a sweaty, sticky mess.

It was amazing the way I came, how that cock of Hunter's hit all the right places that, up until now, only Jack had. I wanted to feel it forever: the pulsing pleasure that came from somewhere deep inside my pussy, traveling all the way up to my clit, to my nipples, and to my throat, where my moaning had grown dark and serious, and, before I knew it, I was roaring, my head back, something wild in his arms.

"Fuck, girl, you are so hot," Hunter said loudly, and I knew why – the phone, my husband, our show. "You went off like nothing I've ever seen before."

I had never, ever been so relaxed in a stranger's arms, especially not one who held me, what – three, four feet up in the air? I kissed the spot between Hunter's pecs where his angel's wings met. "How close are you?" I asked, but with so little energy, I'm sure Jack hadn't heard me.

"Just tell me where to blow my load," he said, and just as loudly as before. I loved him for this, how easily he had embrace my fantasy – my *two* fantasies – without asking, not even hinting at, what it was that *he'd* get out of it.

I ran my fingers down his cheeks, along his jawline, while he walked us to the bed, lifting me so that he could slip his cock from my cunt. I gasped again, this time from the sensation of him leaving my pussy so suddenly, instead of filling it so completely with his fingers, as he had in the elevator. Hunter placed me on the bed, and, when I could, I grabbed his cock and slowly rolled off the condom.

I tossed the sticky latex on the floor. Hunter grabbed the hand that held his cock. "I want to do this," he said.

I didn't fight. "Where are you going to come on me?"

He smiled, his face relaxed, like he hadn't a care in the world, even as he fucked somebody's wife while that somebody listened in on the phone. "On your face," he said, "and your tits."

We both heard it then – Jack's obvious groan.

Hunter held back his giggle, but I wasn't so lucky with mine. "Quiet," he said, just a little more seriously, and grabbed the hair at the back of my head, holding me perfectly still, the tip of his cock only inches from my mouth. He worked it slowly, purposefully, with his hand. I loved the sound of his breathing, quick and heavy, and the look in his eyes that showed me he wouldn't last long.

Then Hunter said, "All over your face – take it all over your face," and that's when I closed my eyes, but his hot come only hit my lips and chin. I was more interested in the noises Hunter made – quick bursts of *unh, unh, unh* – which were in unison with Jack's more high-pitched wails, a desperate, more vulnerable sound he always made when he came, and one I loved so much. The way I saw it, my two favorite guys were coming on my face – no, my tits now – coming all over my tits, as promised, huge loads of it, Hunter Caldwell's hot, white come dripping down my breasts to the bedspread, his eyes closed, hand moving quickly on his big, young cock.

What *exactly* do you say after all that? Hunter wiped some of his come from my chin, and then fell on his back next to me on the bed. He picked up my cell phone, stared at the screen for a little while, watched as the seconds ticked up and up – it had been over fifteen minutes now since I had called home – and then looked at me again. He raised his eyebrows. "Jack?" he said, holding the phone close to his mouth.

"Yes," Jack said, sounding breathless and exhausted.

I stretched out next to Hunter, smiling.

"You've got a great lady here, Jack," Hunter said, his grin big.

"Yes," Jack said, and I heard him swallow, still trying to catch his breath. "Yeah, I know."

"You've got to change your top five, though, mate. You've got to really strategize on that one." I loved the way Hunter gestured, his arm up and finger pointed, as if he were poking Jack emphatically, but supportively, in the chest. "You need a new number one."

"You're right," Jack said, louder, more confidently. It surprised me, but I sighed audibly, dreamily, at this new sound in my husband's voice, especially when he said, "I need a new number one like you."

Home Delivery

Jean Roberta

"Door-to-door delivery will continue until the end of the calendar year, but plans are in place to phase it out. The Corporation can no longer justify the expense of this service, especially in rural areas." The television newscaster looked like a mannequin in a display window, and she read her lines without a trace of feeling. I wanted to shoot her.

I could hardly imagine not seeing Bernard, my favourite mail carrier, striding up my front walk every weekday morning at eleven o'clock precisely. In winter, he wore his regulation black parka and the black balaclava, which covered his whole face except for his sky-blue eyes. In summer, he wore his summer uniform: a short-sleeved khaki shirt and shorts, which revealed his muscular, sun-tanned legs. In all seasons, he proudly wore the symbol of the Canada Post Corporation, a red chevron or a partly opened envelope speeding towards its destination. Just seeing it made my heart beat faster.

What gross timing, I thought, *for the phase out of home mail delivery to be announced on 1 July, our national holiday*. But there was Bernard, coming up my walk in his uniform on his day off! The only difference between his workaday look and his holiday look was the absence of his mailbag.

He approached my front door empty-handed, turned the knob, and walked in. He knew he was welcome. "Bella!"

"What have you brought me today, man?" I laughed.

He picked me up with both arms as though I were made of feathers. He pressed his lips to mine, and I could taste the salt in his sweat.

I caught a glimpse of us in my hall mirror: Bernard's solid body, topped by shiny brown hair, my flushed pink face, reddish curls, and bikini top that showed cleavage. He had told me he would come over, but he hadn't said when. I knew he liked my "brave little titties", as he called them, and the rest of my slim body.

Before I could guess his intentions, Bernard was holding me around the waist with one arm, and using the other to cup one of my breasts under the fabric. He pinched my nipple, and I squeaked.

"Are you ready for me, girl?" *Oh yes*, I thought.

I couldn't help wondering, once again, what Bernard's supervisor would say about all this. I had seduced him in November by inviting him in to ask him about temporary sorting jobs in the Post Office over the winter holidays. Almost everyone from my old neighbourhood, where money was precious and rare, had relied on one of those jobs to pay for Christmas. Bernard had answered my questions, then continued on his rounds. That evening, he had called me for a date.

Sunlight and the sound of an uncoordinated local rock band poured in through my windows. "Would you like to go to the park?" I teased.

"We can make our own entertainment." He set me down gently. "You can unwrap the parcel I brought you." Bernard unbuckled his belt.

I loved this part of our usual routine. I knelt on the floor and pulled down the zipper of his shorts. His cock was stretching his briefs, and it jumped as soon as I pulled them down. "Just what I ordered," I told him.

I knew that Bernard was proud of his trouser-snake, even though he was too modest to say so. Without a word, he stepped out of his clothing, unbuttoned his shirt and tossed it on the floor. He stood naked in my hallway, as if for inspection. I caressed his cock, and it grew long and thick, with one visibly pulsing vein on its shy underside. The head was purplish-red, with a drop of dew in its eye.

After trips to the doctor for testing, and several months of monogamy, we had progressed to the next level in our relationship: naked tongues on sensitive skin. I guided Bernard's rock-hard cock into my mouth, and licked the shaft. A heartfelt groan rewarded my efforts.

My man stroked my hair, then gripped my shoulders as I swirled my tongue around the hot, smooth head of his cock. I gave it a few careful nibbles with my teeth, and reached underneath to cradle his heavy balls.

"Bella!" he moaned, and a liquid tribute flowed over my tongue. I had never swallowed a man's jism before Bernard, but in his case, I felt it was worthwhile to acquire a taste for it. "Sorry," he muttered self-consciously, as his cock jerked and shrank.

I stood up and wrapped my arms around his back. "No need to apologize," I told him. "I love taking care of him."

We stood entwined for a golden moment, then Bernard picked me up and carried me into my front room. He laid me down on my comfortable chesterfield. "Oh, girl." He grinned wickedly, and his eyes sparkled. "I want the taste of your sweet cunt." At such times, his quaint Newfoundland accent was noticeable, even though he had left his native island as a teenager to attend school while living with his aunt and uncle.

I pushed my own shorts down my legs, and spread them apart to let him in. The air on my bush felt cool, and I realized how wet I was. The smell of my arousal wafted to my nose, and I was grateful that Bernard never seemed put off by it. I untied my bikini top, and exposed my hardening nipples to the air.

"Ahh," he sighed. He crouched beside me, and arranged me so that my fragrant cleft was at a convenient angle for him. He poked his tongue out at me, rolled it up and down, and wiggled it.

When I felt the tip of that devilish tongue on my quivering clit, I jerked. I suppressed a scream, but when Bernard licked me with broad strokes, I felt as if I could melt. Two strong fingers plunged into me, investigating my slippery folds. His warm mouth continued to suck on my swollen nubbin as his tongue and his teeth took turns getting into the act. Before long, I felt the first spasm, and then I was coming as though I could never stop.

Bernard stood up, his face wet and grinning. He pushed me over so that he could lie beside me, but somehow I ended up lying atop him, while he held me on with both arms. He pulled me close so he could kiss me, and I tasted my own juice on his lips. I could have explored his mouth forever, but he was impatient.

"Aw, girl, I need to feel you." I knew what that meant. I hopped up, found his shorts on the floor, and reached into both pockets. In one, I found the prize: a packet with a rubber in it. I came back to Bernard, and almost laughed aloud to see his cock sticking straight up like a flagpole. I unrolled the rubber on the head of his cock, and smoothed it down the shaft. Then I guided it to my opening, and slid down until I was sitting on him.

I enjoyed feeling full for a while, then we moved together. Bernard pushed up and I pushed down until we were galloping towards the finish line. He groaned and closed his eyes when he came. I didn't think I could come again so soon after the last time, but my cunt wasn't finished, and it was shaken by tremors like submerged explosions.

Bernard and I lay together as our sweat cooled in the breeze from my electric fan and an open window. "Fireworks for Canada Day," I snickered, looking him in the eyes.

"For sure." He laughed with me. "Do you want to watch them in the park later?"

"We can see them from here," I told him. "We don't need to go outdoors." Hot summer days were usually followed by rainy evenings, and I didn't want to be exposed to bugs and weather. I knew that Bernard probably wouldn't notice, since he spent most of his time outdoors. I knew we couldn't avoid talking about the future of his job.

"Bernard, did you watch the news today?"

He shifted into a sitting position, but kept a comforting hand on my back. "Girl, I've known what the board was planning for months. Do you think it's really a surprise that they're planning to phase out home delivery? They've been closing post offices in small towns for years. This comes from the feds, did you know that? They say the culture has changed with the technology, and emails have cut into our business. They say we're not sustainable."

My heart sank, but Bernard seemed strangely calm. "What will you do?" I sat up beside him, and he pulled me onto his lap.

"I won't give up unless I have to," he told me. "There's a way to fight this." I had never thought of Bernard as a militant union man, or as a clever strategist. I realized that I had underestimated him.

He looked at me thoughtfully. "You know what turns people against the government, babe? A good scandal."

I considered this. "You mean, like politicians spending taxpayers' money on themselves?"

Bernard laughed bitterly. "Nah, they do that all the time. I'm thinking sex. They say delivering mail is outdated because of technology. I wonder what they'd say if someone secretly recorded them in the act, and threatened to post it online? Do you think that would be news?"

I was curious. "Bernard, are you thinking of someone in particular?"

He was three jumps ahead of me. "You know the head of the corporation is the Minister of Transport, eh? That's Madame Avion. She appoints most members of the board, so they're all her friends and everyone gets along. They make the rules, then they all go drink cocktails and screw around."

I was trying to see where this explanation was going. "So we need to get ourselves onto their guest list? How could we do that?"

Bernard kissed me. "You're a trendy designer."

"I am?" I liked to think I had a lot of talent for making my own clothes, but I had no customers outside a small circle of family and close friends.

"Stacy Lovat is on the board, and her husband Morris Fois-Gras runs a restaurant in Ottawa. All their friends in the government go there, and they entertain a lot. Stacy likes clothes, and she likes them to be one of a kind so she doesn't see herself coming and going. She likes to make a statement with what she wears." Bernard waved one hand in the air like a socialite.

I had the impression that my Bernard was planning some kind of class warfare against the People to Know, but I still didn't see how he could create a scandal that would save his job.

"Bella," he continued, "you know how those people are. She swings both ways, and he likes all the women on the planet. They always have a little party in their hotel room after a meeting of the board. We can be there."

"Why would they let us in?"

"Oh, my love, use your head. After a few drinks and something stronger, they won't be that choosy, and we'll drop some names.

And they'll remember you because they'll have cards in the mail, announcing your new mail-order fashion boutique."

"You're insane, man."

"You love me for it. It's part of my charm."

He was right. We kissed to seal the deal. "Oh my God, Bernard." The possibilities were starting to seem real to me. "Do you think I could sell some of my designs?"

"And make the board think twice about cancelling home delivery by next year."

"That too. How long do we have?"

"The board meeting is in two months, my girl. You've got some work to do."

That evening, we watched the fireworks making multicoloured patterns in the sky. We clinked our bottles of beer to toast our future together.

At the end of July, Bernard's friend and fellow postie, Ralph, helped him move all his belongings from his apartment into the little house I inherited from my parents. We did the move after dark, and the Canada Post van was roomy enough for all Bernard's furniture.

Over the next few weeks, things fell into place. Gail, the woman who designed the website of Awesome Accessories, the store where I worked, designed my new site for less than the going rate. I realized how important it is to have friends.

At last, the day of the board meeting arrived. Bernard and I took the train to Ottawa, the capital city, and had supper at a cheaper restaurant than Fois-Gras. We were going to meet its owner soon anyway, and we were dressed well enough to impress the servers. Bernard looked suave in his best suit, and I was wearing an evening dress of clingy black silk, cut on the bias. A row of embroidered red envelopes, the logo of Canada Post, decorated the low neckline of my dress. My push-up bra enhanced my décolletage. Aside from my garter-belt and black stockings, I was naked under silk below the waist. It was the best way to dress for a warm evening.

Bernard and I took a taxi to the Chateau Feuille d'Erable, and took the elevator up to the tenth floor. Luckily, the couple ahead of us were going to the same room, where the sound of laughter

and tinkling glass could be heard from the carpeted hallway. I
saw Bernard's jaw muscles tighten, and I squeezed his arm.
Whatever might happen, we were together.

"Margaret and Frank! Bella Couture!" warbled Ms Lovat,
swaying on her spindly heels. She gave each of the people she
knew a quick hug, but her eyes never left my face. "I recognize
you from your card," she told me. Her dark hair was in a smooth
upsweep, and her face was beautiful; I was sure I had seen her
on television, being interviewed for some reason. Her breasts
were disproportionately large, and spilling out of her
asymmetrical blouse that had a sleeve for one arm only. When
she noticed Bernard, she seemed to push her bust forward.

I smiled, and refrained from telling her that she could thank
her local mail carrier for delivering my card to her mailbox.

Bernard introduced himself as Billy McLaren, singer-
songwriter from Newfoundland. He was a man of many talents,
and I had no doubt that he would burst into "I'se the B'y" if
anyone asked him. He had grown up in a musical family. I could
see Ms Lovat drooling.

Morris came to join his wife in checking out the guests. He
was a balding, paunchy man with a lot of energy – or maybe it
was just a sense of entitlement. He looked at me as though I
were a tray of interesting hors d'oeuvres. The possibility of being
his little tidbit for the evening was strangely exciting.

"Billy," cooed Ms Lovat, "call me Stacy. Do you have an
album out?"

"Not yet." *When he starts recording songs about the things that
piss him off,* I thought, *you won't want to hear them.*

Morris sidled up to his wife in a way that looked both intimate
and threatening, and he wrapped an arm around her waist. I
suspected that they had an agreement: threesomes were fine
with him as long as the third person was female. So if Stacy
wanted a hunk of something male, she would have to get that
when her husband wasn't watching.

Morris casually ran a hand down my back, watching Bernard.
"Let's get you both some drinks," he said. "The bar is over
here." He led us to a small bar stocked with bottles of every kind
of booze I had ever seen.

Bernard considered his choices. "Scotch and soda," he

ordered, as though he never drank anything else, and only the best brands. I was impressed.

Margaret and Frank, the couple that had come in with us, crowded up behind us. "Look, Frank, how clever!" Margaret pointed to the neckline of my dress, as though she admired my cleavage.

He laughed, obviously noticing the logo of Canada Post. "You're the fashion designer, aren't you? Do you make that dress in her size?" He gestured towards Margaret, who was as tall as he was, a good six feet, and built in proportion to her height.

"I can make it in any size," I bragged.

Morris glanced at Frank. "Bella, what will you have to drink?"

For the occasion, I thought I should drink wine, but I didn't know anything about brands. "Do you have a merlot?" I tried to sound confident; my last boyfriend before Bernard had introduced me to it.

Morris put a glass of something red in my hand. It suddenly came to me: these people thought we were the entertainment.

I looked at Bernard, but he was already in a conversation with Margaret, who seemed to admire his chest even more than she admired mine. He was standing with a Scotch in his hand and a mischievous smile on his face, as though he were the master of his fate. I certainly hoped so.

Morris and Stacy never left me alone. I saw her looking towards a small table where a man was using a straw to inhale some white powder. "Do you . . . ?" she asked.

Cocaine. Oh my God. "No," I blurted quickly. I needed to keep my wits about me. "Not tonight." She and Morris nodded calmly.

"You're such a cute little thing," he told me. "I bet I could lift you with one hand." He actually did it with two hands, and one of them got a good feel of my behind as he lifted me off the floor. "We can go someplace more private." Stacy leaned forward to kiss me on the lips like a lover. She seemed to have had a lot of practice.

"Billy," I said, loudly enough for him to hear me.

Morris seemed resigned to accepting him as excess baggage, so he put me down, and the four of us adjourned to a bedroom with a door.

As soon as we were all in the room, which was dominated by a queen-sized bed with a white comforter, reflected by a mirror on the ceiling, Stacy wrapped me in her arms. "I wish I could sew," she told me. "It's something I never learned, even though I love clothes. I'd like you to make me something." I could guess her style: dramatic, even over the top, but not really much different from whatever was being flogged this season in Holt Renfrew. *Everyone wears some kind of uniform,* I thought.

Stacy helped me out of my dress, which didn't take much effort. Then I helped her out of her blouse and clingy skirt. I took off my own underthings, and Morris licked his lips. "I'd like to tie you to the bed," he told me. "You'd look so adorable in padded handcuffs. Do you . . . ?"

"No," I said.

"Morris," scolded Stacy, almost laughing. "You need to . . . use some common sense. We won't hurt you, honey," she told me. She turned me around, and ran her hands down my hips. It was humiliating, but I couldn't help shivering with pleasure.

Bernard approached Stacy from behind, then Morris pushed his substantial body in between them. His cock was already making a visible bulge in his pants, and he pushed it against Stacy's firm bottom. So that's how it was. Apparently Bernard was to be a witness only.

Stacy shimmied and rotated her hips against Morris, then he pushed us both towards the bed. I climbed up, and spread myself out on my back, posing like a centrefold. "Do you like girls?" she asked me coyly.

I stared at my reflection in the overhead mirror, then I focused on her pink curves. "Um," I said. "I do now." I hadn't had a girlfriend in that sense since I was in high school, but I didn't want to turn Stacy down. Her breasts were surprisingly firm, and I wondered if they were natural. If they weren't, someone had done a good job, since they were nicely shaped, and crowned with big dark-pink nipples; one was already pebbly-hard, and the other was hardening by the second. Stacy's breasts bounced when she climbed onto the bed and spread herself over me.

Stacy's weight on me felt just right: heavy enough to pin me to the bed without pressing the air out of my lungs. I liked the feeling more than I expected to. She kissed me and slid her tongue into my mouth as she stroked my hair.

I wondered if I could turn into a lesbian, but then I remembered that Bernard was right there, waiting his turn. I couldn't imagine giving him up.

Bernard was watching when Stacy slid down to suck each of my nipples, gently licking and tugging them with her teeth until they felt as huge as hers looked.

She kissed her way down my midriff to my bush, and used her fingers to expose my swollen clit. She took it into her mouth, and then I noticed that her head was already bobbing up and down. I looked up at the ceiling, and saw Morris doing something to her from behind.

Stacy's lips and tongue on my bursting little button of flesh were very distracting, but I managed to raise my head and look directly at her. I saw her rump in the air, while Morris stood at the foot of the bed, pumping into her.

I had heard of kinky scenes before, but I had never expected to be in one! There was nothing to do but surrender to the feeling of being well and truly sucked off by a woman who was channelling her husband's energy – along with her own – into me.

Somehow, Bernard was involved. I wouldn't have been able to come if I'd thought he was upset by what he was seeing, but I heard him chuckling, and I felt his encouragement like fingers on my skin.

Stacy almost bit me when Morris reached his climax, and I came a second later. I suspected that we all went off like a string of firecrackers, one after the other.

"Ahh!" was the sound coming from Morris, something between a moan and a growl. Stacy withdrew from me as though to let Morris take his turn with me, or as though to claim him for herself. I couldn't be sure who was planning to do what, and I felt like an awkward novice in a complicated ballroom dance.

She murmured something to him that I couldn't hear, and then he was holding her in his arms while she wrapped her legs around him. So that's how it was. Morris gave me a look over Stacy's shoulder that seemed part hungry, part wistful, but his wife was obviously his first choice, and I preferred it that way.

Much as I wanted Bernard to keep his job, I didn't want to complicate our relationship.

Morris showed off his strength by staying on his feet while he fucked Stacy against the wall. She held on to him so well that he was able to knead one of her breasts with one hand. Watching them and their reflection from several angles was almost unbearably arousing, and they seemed to love putting on a show for us. I was fairly sure this was not the first time they had done it.

My whole cunt was tingling when Bernard crawled on top of me. Like the gentleman he was, he had already dressed his rock-hard cock in its tight suit. He guided it into me, then used his elbows on the bed for leverage. He managed to kiss me while plunging as deeply into me as he could, and the feel of his hot tongue in my mouth echoed his thrusts lower down. I felt as if I could explode.

After all of us had clearly reached our second or third climaxes, I felt as if we all looked different, as though all our cells had been rearranged. Stacy was standing, then sitting on the bed beside us. I could see Morris looking at us hopefully, but Bernard was determined to show both our hosts that he was the only man in my life. He kissed and tickled my sensitive nipples while he recovered for his second round, then he fucked me again.

I was still trying to catch my breath, with Bernard's arms around me, when I realized how badly I needed to pee. "I'll be back," I told him. I slid off the bed, found my clothes and put them on. Then I left the room. Some quiet jazz was playing from a sound system, and the crowd had thinned out. The remaining guests were either making out, dancing to their own beat, or arguing about something they probably wouldn't remember in the morning.

I found the washroom, used the toilet, washed myself and combed my messy hair. I liked the jasmine-scented hand soap enough to rewrap it in its paper, and keep it as a souvenir.

When I came out of the washroom, Bernard was dressed in his suit, waiting for me. "It took you long enough," he snickered as he kissed my neck and inhaled my clean scent. I wondered what sex in the shower would be like, and I decided to try it with him as soon as possible.

After Bernard rejoined me, we found Morris and Stacy in the main room of the suite, haphazardly dressed, with drinks in their hands. I thanked them for a lovely evening, Bernard and Morris smirked at each other, and we exchanged hugs all around.

As soon as Bernard and I were in a taxi, on our way to the train station, I asked him if he had collected any useful material.

"I'se the b'y that builds the boat," he sang. He reached into his pocket, and pulled out a crumpled note that read: "Stacy," followed by a telephone number and "XXX".

"Seriously?" I asked, not expecting an answer. "Jesus. When did she give you this?"

"When you were out of the room. She's a hot bitch."

I wasn't sure I liked this description of Stacy, since I couldn't be sure exactly what Bernard meant by "hot". "Are you planning to use it?" I hoped my sarcasm was painfully obvious.

"Sure will," replied my man. "I'll make a copy of this and show it to Morris. That should get a reaction."

I smiled in the dark.

At the train station, we snuggled on a bench while waiting for our train. "Too bad you didn't get any photos," I hinted.

"Show you later," he promised.

"Really? I didn't see you taking any."

"Bella, my dear, you were otherwise engaged." I knew this was true.

When we finally came home, we were exhausted. We stripped off our clothes, and fell into bed together like two puppies in a cosy basket, luxuriating in each other's presence.

Unfortunately, we both had work the next day. I took half a day off, since I knew that Bev, the manager of Awesome Accessories, wouldn't fire me just for that. Bernard had more of a work ethic, or maybe he just had a cast-iron constitution and restless legs. He set off on his rounds as though nothing could stop him.

During the week, my first orders for clothing came in, and I knew I couldn't fill them without help. Luckily, several of my co-workers at the shop were willing to work part-time for me, and Bev didn't seem to mind. I called all the women I knew who liked to sew, and some of them knew some drag queens who were more experienced at making their own ensembles than I was. I didn't care, as long as my little enterprise succeeded.

Bernard showed me the photos on his cell phone. At first, I was speechless. Everything was on display: Stacy's rolling breasts, Morris's cock, the reddish-brown bush between my spread thighs, and Stacy's head below my belly. "Oh my God, Bernard!" I said finally.

"Am I a photographer, or what?" he asked rhetorically. "I think these should be on the wall at the post office. Right under the Queen's Jubilee portrait."

I couldn't help laughing at the idea, even though I would be embarrassed to death. I didn't ask what he was really planning to do with them.

A few weeks after our adventure in Ottawa, I read a small article in the newspaper. Apparently Canada Post was planning to study the issue of home mail delivery for another year before making any definite decisions. The Minister had commissioned a report.

"Bernard," I said, shoving the newspaper in his face. "Did you see this?"

"I did, babe." He was grinning into my eyes. "Good news, eh?"

"You did that, didn't you?" I tickled his ribs, he grabbed my hands, and we play-wrestled until he held me down over his lap, as though he intended to give me a spanking.

"Me?" He faked a tone of surprise. "I just deliver the mail." He gave me a light slap before letting me up.

We laughed together until we were out of breath.